the
RACE

Also by Nina Allan and available from Titan Books

t h e R I F T (July 2017)

the
RACE

NINA ALLAN

TITAN BOOKS

for Chris

The Race
Print edition ISBN: 9781785650369
E-book edition ISBN: 9781785650383

Published by Titan Books
A division of Titan Publishing Group Ltd
144 Southwark Street, London SE1 0UP

First edition: July 2016
3 5 7 9 10 8 6 4 2

A CIP catalogue record for this title is available from the British Library.

Printed and bound by CPI Group (UK) Ltd, Croydon, CR0 4YY

the

RACE

one

JENNA

There have been Hoolmans living in Sapphire for hundreds of years. Like so many of the town's old families, we are broken and divided, our instincts as selfish and our minds as hard-bitten as the sick land we live on. We have long memories though, and fierce allegiances. We cannot seem to be free of one another, no matter if we wish to be or not.

My mother, Anne Allerton, walked out on the town and on our family when I was fifteen. After she left, my brother Del, whose nickname is Yellow, went a little bit crazy. He was crazy before, most likely – it was just that our mother leaving made his madness more obvious. I was scared of Del then, for a while, not because of anything he did especially but because of the thoughts he had. I could sense those thoughts in him, burrowing away beneath the surface of his mind like venomous worms. I swear Del sometimes thought of killing me, not because he wanted me dead but because he was desperate to find out what killing felt like.

I think the only reason he never went through with it was that he knew deep down that if he killed me, there would be no one left on the planet who really gave a shit about him.

Del and I are still close, in spite of everything.

It's easy to blame Mum for the way Del turned out, but then it's always easier to pin the blame on someone else when things go mental. If I'm honest, I'd say that Del was troubled because he was a Hoolman, simple as that. The legends say the Hools have always been wanderers and that restlessness is in their blood. When the Hools first sought refuge in England, they were persecuted for being curse-givers, though of course that was centuries ago. I was sometimes teased at school because of my surname but most kids soon got bored of it and moved on to something more interesting. It wasn't even as if I looked Hoolish, not like Del with his gorsefire hair and beanpole legs, but no one in class was going to risk kidding him about it, not if they wanted their head and body to remain part of the same organism.

If it hadn't been for the dogs, I seriously think Del would have ended up in jail. Del cared about his smartdog Limlasker more than he cared about anyone, including his wife Claudia, including me.

The one exception was his daughter, Luz Maree, who everyone called Lumey. Del loved Lumey as if a fever was raging inside him, and he didn't care who knew it.

When Lumey went missing, Del became even crazier. He swore he'd find his girl and bring her home, no matter the cost.

I think he'll go on looking for Lumey till the day he dies.

* * *

8

I've seen photos of Sapphire from when it was a holiday resort, before they drained the marshes, before the fracking. The colours look brighter in those old photographs, which is the opposite of what you'd normally expect.

Sapphire in the old days was a kind of island, cut off from London and the rest of the country by the Romney Marshes. If you look at the old maps you'll see that most of the land between Folkestone and Tonbridge was more or less empty, just a scattering of fenland villages and the network of inland waterways called the Settles. People who lived in the Settles got about mainly by canal boat: massive steel-bellied barges known as sleds that lumbered along at three miles an hour maximum if you were lucky. Whole families lived on them, passing down the barge through the generations the same way ordinary land-lubbers pass down their bricks and mortar. When the marshes were drained the parliament set up a rehoming plan for the sledders, which basically meant they were forced to abandon their barges and go into social housing.

The sledders fought back at first. There was even a rogue parliament for a while, based at Lydd, which was always the unofficial capital of the Settles. There was a huge demonstration, with people flooding in from all over the southern counties just to show their solidarity. The protest ended in street riots, and sometime during the night the hundreds of barges that had gathered to support the demonstrators were set on fire from the air.

More than five hundred people died, including children.

If you take the tramway up to London you can still see

dozens of sleds, marooned in the bone-dry runnels that were once canals, their huge, stove-like bodies coated in rust, some of them split right open like the carcasses of the marsh cows that once roamed freely over Romney but are now long gone.

Most of the sledders ended up in Sapphire, buried away in crap housing estates like Mallon Way and Hawthorne. There are those who say there are still people living on board some of the abandoned barges, the decayed descendants of those original families who refused to leave and who now scratch out a basic living in what's left of the marshes. There's a part of me that would like to believe those stories, because it would mean the sledders who fought so hard at the Lydd demo didn't die in vain, but really I think they're just fairy tales, the kind that get passed around after sundown to scare little children. Because I don't see how anyone could survive out there now. Most of the marshland is still toxic. Del says that in some places even the air is toxic, that it's not safe to breathe.

More than a hundred years have passed since the marshes were drained, which means there's no one left who remembers the Settles the way they were before. I get sad when I think about that. I've read about how in the days before the fracking, Romney plovers used to descend upon the waterways in their hundreds of thousands. How in the spring and early autumn the reed beds were white with them, as if a freak snowstorm had passed over.

It's hard to imagine that now. The only birds that can survive out in the marshes are crows and magpies. A magpie can eat just about anything and not get sick. Mum always used to say they were cursed.

* * *

When Sapphire first became a gas town there was a rash of new building – high-rise apartment blocks to the north of the town for the thousands of mineworkers, smart hotels and casinos along the seafront for the bosses and investors. The glory days didn't last long, but even after the drilling works were all shut down people kept coming. First there were the government scientists who were brought in to sort the problem with the leaking chemicals – Del says they were paid vast sums of danger money just to live here. Then once the government realised the marshes were ruined, a toxic swamp basically, they turned Sapphire into a dumping ground for illegal immigrants.

Later on, though, people came because of the dogs. It's what you might call an open secret that the entire economy of Sapphire as it is now is founded upon smartdog racing.

Officially the sport is still illegal, but that's never stopped it from being huge.

Mum was born in London. It's strange to think now that she lived here at all, that she exchanged her parents' lovely red-brick house in Queen's Park for a rickety pile of breeze blocks and clapboard on the westward edge of Sapphire, a town so worked-out and polluted that many Londoners are frightened to come here, even for a day. Mum first came to Sapphire on a jaunt while she was in college. Some of her mates had discovered the dog scene and later on Mum and a couple of the others got casual work and ended up staying for most of a summer. Mum met Dad at the track of course, where else? He was massively good-looking when he was young.

"He was so different from the other men I knew then," Mum said. "So full of life, somehow."

It was a vacation fling that should never have lasted, they had nothing in common. But Mum got pregnant with Del and decided to stay.

I travelled to the London house once, on the tramway with Mum and Del to visit my grandparents. I was only two years old though, so I don't remember a thing about it, not even the journey. Del was four. He says he remembers every detail, but I don't believe him. I'm sure that what Del thinks of as memories aren't real memories at all, they're just things he's been told. Other people's memories, in other words, stories he's heard so many times they feel like his own. Either that or they're memories he's cobbled together from old photographs.

There are photos of me in the London house, a sturdy-looking dark-haired toddler standing on an ironwork veranda between two strangers. The strangers are my grandparents, Adam and Cynthia Allerton. Cynthia has her face turned slightly away, glancing down at me as if she's afraid I might piss on her shoes or something. Adam stares grimly ahead, meeting the gaze of the camera as if it were the gaze of his sworn enemy.

You won't find my mother in any of the photos because she was behind the camera, but you can see her anyway, in Cynthia, that same eagle's beak nose, with the little bump in the middle, the same narrow ankles and flat chest. The same nervously fidgeting hands, laden with rings.

Our visit to London lasted two weeks. Mum told me years later that she and my granddad rowed the whole time we were there, almost from the moment we arrived. Granddad kept on at her to leave my dad and bring me and Del back to London to live.

"I want you out of that dump of his," he said. "It's no place to bring up children."

But Mum was having none of it. At that point she was still trying to fool herself as well as the world that she was happy.

Don't go thinking we were poor, because we weren't. We weren't rich either, but we did okay. My granddad – Granddad Hoolman, not my London granddad – ran a waste reclaim business, shifting the fracking effluent from the leaking well shafts to safe enclosures. My dad went into the business when he left school, eventually taking it over when Old Man Hoolman died.

The money was good, but it was good for a reason. Granddad Hoolman died of non-specific invasive cancers and so did my dad. Dad wasn't much over fifty when he copped it, but already he looked and moved and sounded like an old man. His insides were riddled with cancer, like mould in blue cheese, but it was really my mother leaving that finally did for him. All the fight went out of him, just like that. As if someone had reached inside and pulled the plug on his willpower.

He and Del were like poison for each other, and one of the first major bust-ups they had after Mum left was about the business.

"If you think I'm following you into shit-shovelling you know where to stick it," Del said. "If I wanted to commit suicide I'd get hold of a shotgun and blow my brains out. At least it would be quicker that way."

"You might as well blow them out anyway. Fat lot of good they've done you. Or me, for that matter."

He sat very still in his armchair, staring at Del with his look of I-told-you-so, as if it were Del's fault he was dying of cancer, that Del could stop it from happening if he'd only set his mind to it and stop being an arse. Del clenched and unclenched his fists and stormed out of the room. He left an atmosphere so thick it was like sulphur fumes, like a gas that might go off boom if you struck a match. I tried to find him but he'd charged out of the house somewhere. When I went back to the living room to check on Dad I found he'd fallen asleep in his armchair. The skin of his face lay slack and loose, like an old plastic bag.

The summer Mum left, the town felt airless, and hotter than a blast furnace. Dad was at work mostly, taking on extra shifts at the waste plant just so he could get out of the house. It wasn't only because of Del, I'm sure of that, it was because of me, too. We reminded him constantly of Mum's absence and he couldn't face us. Del and I lived mostly out of tins: canned ravioli and baked beans and those nasty little frankfurter sausages swimming in brine. They always stank of fish, those sausages. I only have to see a tin of them on a supermarket shelf for it to come rushing back – that fishy smell and the slippery texture, sour and salty and not quite natural. Those frankfurters seemed to sum up my life, really. It was not a good time.

I think the worst part was the feeling of helplessness. Dad's passive acceptance of everything – Mum leaving, Del's vileness, carrying on with a job he knew was killing him – made me seize up inside with anger and frustration. Del's moods were even worse. The way he yelled and swore at Dad made me feel like screaming.

I ended up resenting them both. I was desperate to escape, but I couldn't see how.

Dad used to take us to the dogs every weekend when we were kids. It was the one thing he always did with us, without fail, our family time. Del and I used to look forward to it all week. Dad was always after Mum to come with us, but she invariably refused. She claimed it was because she was opposed to genetic engineering but I'm sure that was just an excuse. She knew all about Romney Heights when she was in college, but that didn't stop her from becoming a race nut and drinking schnapps up at the Ryelands with the dog crowd until all hours. I think her refusal had far more to do with not wanting to be reminded of those times, when she was young and having fun and felt she still had choices.

The dog scene used to be her thing and now it wasn't – that's why she hated it. She would have poisoned it for Dad too, if she could have, but for Dad the dogs were sacrosanct, his one remaining pleasure. He wasn't going to give them up, not even for her.

"It's not like I even spend much," he said. "Just the odd

couple of shillings now and then. That's hardly going to bankrupt us, is it?" My father was the kind of man who would rather give way on something than get into an argument, but my mother's nagging about the track really got on his nerves.

"How can you stand those people?" she would say. "All those tin-pot godfathers and mining millionaires throwing their weight about. You do know that every shilling you spend there goes to line their pockets? The whole thing stinks, if you ask me. I don't know how you can bear to associate with them."

"I don't get within farting distance of those wankers, and you know it. I just want to spend some time with my mates, show the kids a bit of fun for a change. What's wrong with that?"

"You see enough of your mates down the pub. And I don't like the children being exposed to gambling."

"Exposed to gambling? I've never heard such bollocks in my life."

The row would rumble on until my mother became bored with it and slammed out of the room. Dad would take us to the dog track on Saturday, same as usual.

My early memories of going to the dogs all blend into one. Kids younger than ten aren't supposed to be admitted to the stadium but in practice no one cares, so long as they behave and don't get in the way. There's one photo I still have from back then, of me queuing up for treacle toffee at one of the refreshment stands. It's summer. My bare shoulders are streaked with sunblock and my hair is in plaits. Not the two identical rope-braids I wore for school, but twenty or so little scraggy ones that stuck out from around my head like twists of raffia. I was about seven, and I remember wanting to look like Ruby Challence, who was one of the best new runners that season and only nineteen.

Ruby Challence wore her hair in proper corn rows. Also, she had her nose pierced. I'd never seen anyone cooler in my life.

Sapphire dog track lies out on the coast road, about a mile from the centre of town, three stops on the tramway. It stands on a flat, scrubby outcrop of land that was once, many decades ago, the municipal coach park. The stadium is built from wooden slats, like a giant soup barrel. Everyone goes in the same way – ordinary locals and upmarket corporates and out-of-towners, all of us filing in together through the turnstiles. The out-of-towners especially fascinated me, and I always made a point of watching what they did. Both the men and the women had an odd way of speaking. I don't mean their London accents, I mean the way they laughed, too often and too loudly, like they were nervous of having their pockets picked. I used to search their faces, wondering what they thought was going to happen to them.

It's as if they thought the town might be contagious or something. Sad, really.

The out-of-towners mostly stayed at the Ryelands, a large hotel also on the coast road and more or less opposite the dog track. The place was enormous, with over a hundred bedrooms and a swish rooftop restaurant. Del said it used to be an insane asylum. I never knew if he was joking or not, but with its needle-eye windows and red brick towers I had to admit it was kind of spooky-looking, even at the height of the season with people laughing out on the roof and all the lights burning.

Most of the ground floor of the Ryelands was taken up by a casino – black-and-white marble floors, and a crystal chandelier so large that when I was a kid I used to worry about it coming loose from its support bracket and crashing down on the upturned faces of the crowd below. When I was older I had a summer job at the Ryelands for a while, serving behind the bar and waiting tables. It was hard work, but a laugh. Most guests came for the racing, so the casino only really got going once the stadium had closed for the night. I liked working at the Ryelands. It meant I had some money of my own, plus I enjoyed the gossip, the sense of belonging, the hot purple nights. I would have stayed longer, but the management found out I wasn't eighteen and asked me to leave.

You can go to the dogs every night of the week during the season if you want to, but the big races, the ones that attract all the smartest money and the fastest smartdogs, take place at the weekend. Friday nights are the biggest usually, unless it's a cup race, which are always held on Saturdays. The stadium's packed then. I know some people get nervous in crowds, but right from my first visit I found it thrilling, not just the racing itself but the whole atmosphere of the stadium – the shouting and swearing, the smell of frying onions and chargrilled meat, the row of kiosks by the turnstiles that sold souvenir programmes and plastic key rings and novelty pens. I was always on at my dad to buy me something or other from the souvenir stands, and usually he would. I still have some of those trinkets, stashed away in boxes with other rubbish, the kind of stuff you no longer need but can't bear to get rid of.

Things like that are not so much objects as language, a secret language of memory that everyone speaks. You pay a couple of shillings for a crappy tin key ring you know you're never going to use, and as soon as you get home you chuck it away in a drawer and forget all about it. But months, perhaps years later you find it again, and all at once you catch the aroma of roasting pigeon and cracked lentils, you remember the steadily rising heat of that afternoon, the row you had with your girlfriend because of the money you lost on a rank outsider, the great fuck you had later to make up.

It's as if for those moments while you're holding the key ring you have that day back again, and it makes you think. It makes you think about the past too, when the town was just a tiny fishing village and there were no smartdogs. It makes you wonder if the future was something we could have changed if we'd tried harder, or if everything that was going to happen would still have happened, whatever. Perhaps even before the universe existed it was already there – the fuel dumps, the tower blocks, the marble casino at the Ryelands, the dog track, all of it.

Perhaps the past and the future are really the same. Del says it doesn't matter because sooner or later the sun is going to explode and the Earth will die.

"The sun's getting bigger all the time, did you know that?" he told me once. "Bigger and hotter, and when it can't grow any more the whole thing will go up like an ammo dump. The biggest ammo dump explosion in the whole of history. Anyone who's still around then will be toast."

He tore a bite off his gammon sandwich and began to chew, staring at me all the while, daring me to contradict him.

I didn't though. I didn't want to give him the satisfaction. I know he's right in what he says, but I like to hope it won't be the end, that creatures who were smart enough to put a man on the moon will one day be smart enough to invent a way of getting us out of here before it's too late.

To find a new home for us to fly to, where we can start again.

I have to believe that, even though I'll be millions of years dead by then, and so will Del and so will Claudia. Lumey will be dead too, wherever she is. I have to believe that it matters, or what's the point? If you have nothing to believe in, you stop being yourself, and when that happens you might as well be dead anyway.

Del had no time for fancies like that, and as for the secret language of memory, I don't think Del bought a single race track souvenir in the whole of his life.

"Why do you want to waste your dough on that shit?" he would say. "That's half a race ticket you've just splashed away."

Del was there for the dogs, and that was it. Right from the beginning the dogs were his life.

If Mum had had her way, Del would have studied hard and gone to college. He would have graduated with honours, then left this town on the tramway, never to return.

He could have done it, too, if he had wanted to. Del was every bit as clever as our mother believed he was; cleverer, probably. But the only thing Del ever wanted was to be a runner.

He was a nightmare at school. He held the teachers and everything they told him in contempt.

"If those wankers have all the answers, how come the world's such a fuck-up?"

There was no answer to that, or at least none that would satisfy Del. By his early teens he was bunking off most of the time anyway.

The teachers made the usual fuss and sent letters to my mum imploring her to take control of her son but I reckon most of them were glad to be shot of him.

It drove Mum wild.

"Do you want to end up like your father?" That was the worst insult she could think of to fire at him, the heavy artillery, but he took less notice of her than he did of the teachers. Instead of going to school, Del would sneak off to the Hawthorne estate to hang with the gang kids, or go fishing for giant crayfish in Filsham reedbeds. Those fuckers were huge. Some of the kids insisted they were mutants, genetic deviations caused by pollution in the water table, but that was all crap I reckon, they were just big crayfish.

When it was too cold to go to the reservoir, they'd go to Charlotte House. Charlotte House was on Cliff Road, not far from the dog track. In Sapphire's glory days as a resort it was a seaside hotel, like the Ryelands only not so large. When the hotel business collapsed it became a sanatorium for traumatized war veterans, and when that closed it was boarded up and left to go derelict. A spooky place, but fascinating. There was still furniture in some of the rooms, including a wardrobe full of moth-eaten evening dresses, and a huge black desk with what seemed like hundreds of tiny compartments that wouldn't open. Del used to take his girlfriend there, Monica Danby. It was no secret that Monica hated the place. She said it was dirty and dangerous and that druggies went there, all of which was true but missed the point.

I remember Del once made Monica walk across the exposed floor joist on the fourth floor landing. Some of the boards had rotted away up there, so you had to be careful. We used to take it in turns walking across. It made your guts heave if you were stupid enough to look down, but the joist was quite wide and you couldn't have fallen through; not easily anyway, the gap was too narrow.

Monica was useless at stuff like that, though. She didn't fall, thank goodness, but she was in floods of tears.

I thought Monica would chuck Del after the beam-walk incident, but she didn't.

Del started going to school again after Mum left. At first I thought it was just his way of getting back at her, but of course Del wasn't the type to waste his own time on someone else's account and as it turned out his reason for returning to class was Emerson Rayner.

Emerson Rayner was what you'd call a classic nerd – a fat kid with bad acne, a near-genius at maths and just about the last person you'd have thought Del would hang out with. In fact it wasn't Em so much as his dad that my brother was courting. Em's dad Graeme was in the racing business – the manager of a medium-sized yard who also owned and trained dogs of his own. He was so unlike his son it was almost funny – a heavyset, barrel-chested guy with powerful shoulders and his long hair tied back with a bootlace like a motorcycle jockey's. He always wore the same pair of red leather Kuprow runner's gloves: engraved silver knuckle caps and styled short to the wrist. They were off the peg and not really old enough to class as retro but I loved them anyway because they had style. Only real pros can wear gloves like that and get away with it, and Graeme Rayner was a pro, no doubt about it.

Of course, Del started out seeing Em as nothing more than his entrance pass to the Rayner yard. But one of the oddest things in this whole story is that the two of them ended up becoming actual friends.

Gra Rayner's best dog was Swift Elin. She was a silver tip, so tall and light and skinny she could rest her front paws on your shoulders and you would hardly feel them. She was a multiple cup winner, and placed fourth in the league championships three years running. Swift Elin was very gentle off the track, but when she was racing she'd get her head down and give everything. She was so fast it was uncanny. It was as if her soul was charged by lightning.

Her runner, Roddy Haskin, was a dry old stick. I say old because that's how he seemed – burned out and way off beam and mostly silent. In fact he was probably around forty-five at the time I knew him. That's old for a runner, yes, but by no means extreme. He was as skinny as Swift Elin herself, but instead of looking like a silver ghost he had the appearance of a string of dried bacon rind. He spent most of the time he wasn't actually training roaming around the marshes with Swift Elin.

"Have you seen them?" Del said to me once. "Like fucking Siamese twins, the pair of them. I swear if you kicked one of them in the mouth the other would bite you."

They say a dog and its runner are like one tank of water that happens to get divided between two separate containers. It's unsettling to see at first but you soon get used to it, the same way you do with identical twins who are always together.

Swift Elin had strange eyes: pale blue, not like dogs' eyes at all. That's fairly common in smartdogs because of the gene splicing, but in the case of Swift Elin the crossover was especially pronounced.

When I first met Em's sister Sybil I saw at once that her eyes were the same colour blue as Swift Elin's and with the same eerie dreaminess. It made me feel strange at first, to know that Gra Rayner had obviously used his own genetic material in the creation of Swift Elin, but then I thought why not? If you're going to do it with anyone's, why not your own?

It was still kind of freaky though. I used to wonder what Em and Sybil's mother Margrit thought about it, but of course I never asked.

Margrit didn't go near the dogs much, I did notice that.

Del told me Gra used to get pretty frantic over Roddy's marsh-gallivanting. Smartdogs are worth a lot of money.

The best ones – cup winners and series champions like Swift Elin – are worth many thousands of shillings, especially if they're still of breeding age. No wonder there are people – greedy, desperate people – who see dog-napping as an easy way of making a quick pile.

"I mean, Rod's not exactly built like a barn, is he?" Del said. "Gra wants to give him a minder, but Rod won't hear of it. He says it interferes with their concentration." He laughed. "Totally mental. And that's just the dog."

Gra Rayner was right to be worried, though. If he were attacked in an isolated spot – one of the dirt roads up by Pett Level, for example – Roddy Haskin, who was built more like a wicker lobster pot than a barn, wouldn't stand a chance. Swift Elin would be easy prey. The thieves wouldn't bother with Rod – except perhaps to kill him if he got in the way.

Runners, even gifted ones like Roddy, are always expendable.

I became properly friendly with Em when I was sixteen. In a sense I couldn't avoid him because he was always around, but as time passed and I came to know him better I found I liked him. He read books for a start, and he was never afraid to talk about things seriously. He was eighteen months older than the morons in my own year, and at that age eighteen months can spell the difference between an outright plonker and an actual human being. Also I didn't fancy him, which I counted as a good thing. The guys I fancied always turned out to be dorks, and the fact that I could waste so much time thinking about them drove me crazy. With Em it was different because I could be with him without constantly wondering if he wanted to fuck me. It must have worked the same way for Em, too, because we soon got into the habit of hanging out together whenever Del was up at the lunges with Em's dad.

I thought of Em as a brother, I suppose, only more so. The trouble with Del was that you never knew when he was going to pull a mental on you. Em was always just Em, no added bullshit. I trusted him and I guess I loved him, and I guess I still do.

Em and I first ended up having sex because he was being an idiot over another girl. I didn't know Lily Zhang all that well because she was in the year above me, but when I found out it was her Em was hooked on, my mood did a nose dive. I don't mean I was jealous or anything – I just knew he was doomed. We were sitting out on the pier when he told me. It was a late afternoon in July. Em and I were right out at the end of the boardwalk behind the amusement arcade. We had to sit really close together in order to hear each other over the constant racket from the slot machines, and I think that's what made it easier for me to finally ask him what was going on.

He'd been weird for a couple of weeks and I was getting sick of it.

"Lily Zhang?" I said when he told me. "You have got to be joking."

"You think I'm fat and ugly," Em said. He took off his glasses and rubbed at them with the silly piece of yellow cloth he always carried in his pocket. The lenses were covered in smears, a combination of sea salt and sweat. He looked shrunken into himself and lost, a tubby little pier-end manikin trying unsuccessfully to pose as a star-crossed lover.

It was pathetic and sad, and it made me angry to see my friend reduced to this state, especially when his predicament was so obviously hopeless.

Lily Zhang was training to be a dancer. She had a scholarship to some London academy. She spoke in a quavery little girl's voice, and refused to eat anything unless it had been calorie-counted.

Her face, framed by shiny black hair, was a perfect oval.

It was impossible not to stare at her, but so what? You'd stare at a three-headed cat, but that doesn't mean you'd want to go out with one.

"Fuck, Em, no," I said. "I'm just wondering what on earth you'd find to talk to her about." I tried not to imagine them actually doing it. That was too revolting and ridiculous to contemplate.

"She smiled at me the other day." He looked as doleful and dejected as a rained-on badger.

"You're worth ten of her," I said. That raised a smile at least. He peered at me with his beautiful tea-coloured eyes and then replaced his glasses.

"Do you think anyone will ever want to do it with me?" he said.

"Don't be a nutter, of course they will." I placed my hand over his. It was the first time we'd ever touched except by accident, but it felt natural and it felt nice. We went back to my place. I knew Del was up at the lunges and probably wouldn't be home before it got dark. Dad was still at work – he never normally got in till well after seven on weekdays.

I'd never had sex before, but I'd sneaked plenty of looks at Del's secret webcam footage of him doing it with Monica, so I had a pretty good idea of what went on. I closed the curtains and we took our clothes off under the bedcovers. We took a while to get the hang of things but in the end we managed. What with the curtains and the bedcovers we couldn't really see each other's faces and that helped a lot, plus we were giggling the whole time and that helped, too. Em's stomach was big under his blazer and his dick was a funny upright thing, an indignant little schoolmaster of a dick, jabbing his finger at me, over and over, like he had a point to prove and was determined to prove it. But Em had lovely smooth shoulders and his hands, with his grandfather's onyx signet ring on his left index finger, were the hands of a genius who spends his whole life dreaming of unreachable lands.

It wasn't amazing, it was just a relief. Suddenly all the fear and half-truth, that sense of the world being one up on me – all that lifted away and it was as if I could finally get on with things. I reckon Em felt that way, too. Afterwards we lay there chatting, the same as always only more manic. Everything was exciting suddenly, or funny. I couldn't stop grinning.

"What do you want to do, when you leave school, I mean?" I asked him at one point. It was Em's final year and everyone knew the teachers at our school were banking on him. He was their prize cow, their best hope of exam glory.

Being under that kind of pressure would have driven me crazy, but Em didn't seem to mind and I reckon there was even a part of him that enjoyed it, that liked being liked for something. I suppose that's fair enough.

"I want to go to Imperial College and study aeronautical mathematics," Em said at once. Imperial College was in London, I knew that, which meant Em would be leaving town, for good, probably. What did you expect, you idiot? I thought to myself. That he'd stay here for you? Get real.

"Eventually I'd like to work on the space programme," Em said. "How about you?"

"I haven't a clue. I haven't really thought about it." It was true and I hadn't. The end of school seemed like a myth to me, a gateway you constantly walk towards but never reach. I had no idea what lay beyond that and I didn't want to know. What I wanted was to get away from Del and Dad and their constant fighting, the house with its grubby curtains and septic kitchen, the sense that everything was breaking down and falling apart. We'd become used to the day-to-day reality of my mother's absence but that didn't mean we were any closer to understanding what we should make of our lives now that she wasn't there to provide a context.

When Em asked me what I wanted to do my mind went blank. It was just like Em, to have a proper future planned out for himself already. Compared with him I felt incompetent and juvenile. Seeing myself through his eyes made me feel scared suddenly and I shifted slightly away from him under the covers.

Em reached for my hand.

"I like all that stuff you collect," he said. "You should do something with that."

"Stuff? What stuff?"

"You know. The stuff. Over there." He pointed with his free hand towards the corner of my bedroom where my desk was, with my crummy old laptop and my collection of shoeboxes. Some of the boxes still had their lids, some didn't. I used the boxes as containers for the junk I collected, flotsam and jetsam I came across in the street or on the beach: girls' hair slides, stray buttons, empty matchboxes. Odd things and shiny things. Magpie treasure. There was a piece of gold ribbon I found near the dog track, a wax doll's head with blue china eyes. None of it was worth anything – I suppose you'd call it rubbish, really. But I liked these things because I thought they were beautiful, and I wanted them to have a home somewhere.

It never occurred to me that the stuff might have a use.

"I like the colours, that's all," I said to Em. "I like lost things."

"Was I a lost thing?"

"A lost idiot, more like." I snatched the pillow from beneath his head and began beating him with it. He grabbed both my wrists and rolled on top of me and a moment later we were making love again. This time we were both more confident and it was better.

"Seriously though, Jen," he said later. "You're artistic – really talented, I reckon. You should give that some thought."

It's strange. If a teacher had told me that I'd have run a mile, not because I didn't like what they'd said but because it would have scared me. The idea of someone thinking I had a gift for something then looking on while I cocked things up, I suppose. That. But having Em say it was different. I knew he meant what he said, that he was serious, but I also knew he didn't expect me to perform for him, that we'd stay friends whether I turned out to be good at anything or not.

If it hadn't been for Em, I might have sailed on and on doing nothing. Doing nothing until the sun exploded and we were all toast.

I owe Em everything, I reckon. He woke me up.

Em and I became an item after that. We didn't make a big thing of it – we were spending so much time together anyway that apart from us having sex our lives carried on pretty much as usual. Only instead of going off to college and becoming a rocket scientist like he wanted to, Em stayed in Sapphire and did accountancy training. He set himself up as a freelance, and was soon making a lot of money. Most people would have said he'd done very well for himself, but I knew it was not the life he had once dreamed of.

He stayed for me, after all. And I could never bring myself to tell him to go.

We lived together for a while, but it didn't work out. I don't know why, not fully, only that it was my fault, not his. I was afraid to risk my feelings, I guess – afraid to love someone so much that it would hurt me, hurt me badly, if it ended. I think now that one of the main reasons I started my affair with Ali Kuzman was so Em would feel he had to move out – it was the only way I could think of to tell him to go. I know that sounds ridiculous, but I think it's so, even though I was in love with Ali, for a time anyway, far more than I wanted to be. Enough to think I was going to lose it when he went back to Pia.

I don't need to tell you who picked up the pieces from that shitty episode.

When Em packed up his apartment and left town it was a total sideswipe. I thought it was me, that he'd finally got sick of being pissed about, but when I asked him what was going on, all he would say was that he'd had a disagreement with Del.

"But you're always rowing with Del, Em, what's the big deal?"

"There's no deal. I need a change from this place, that's all."

I sensed there was more to it, but Em wouldn't spill and after a while I stopped pestering him. I knew he must have his reasons, but I didn't like it. Em and I had never had secrets before, not even during the Ali episode, and all I could think was that Del was up to something, something dodgy that Em wanted out of. I wouldn't have put anything past my brother.

I still feel guilty sometimes. I tell myself that if only I'd tried harder to find out what was going on I could have talked to Del, persuaded him, opened his eyes to the risks. That's all bollocks though, isn't it? Apart from anything else, since when has my brother Yellow ever listened to anyone?

He wouldn't have heard a word I said. He'd have told me to fuck off and mind my own business.

Knowing that should make me feel better, but it doesn't.

JENNA

* * *

To understand how Sapphire works, you have to understand the smartdogs, and to understand the smartdogs you have to understand the panic that was first caused by them.

The engineered greyhounds now known as smartdogs were the product of illegal experiments in stem cell research. The experiments originally took place at what was then a large governmental agricultural centre called Romney Heights. The nearest town of any real size was of course Sapphire, which was why most of the support workers – the lab staff and cleaning staff and technicians – came from here. The security was pretty tight – anyone found to be in breach of the lab's confidentiality agreement was fired on the spot – but the pay was good, and once you have a job like that you do your best to hang on to it. For the most part people were more than happy to stick to the rules.

There's a lot of hard science stuff I don't understand fully, but what it comes down to is that the government boffins at Romney Heights took eggs from a canine ovary and replaced some of the canine genetic material with human DNA. They fertilized those doctored eggs with dog sperm, and let them go on to become living dog embryos. Those embryos were then implanted back into the wombs of female greyhounds.

The scientists used greyhounds for their experiments because they are docile and easy to train. They are also naturally hardy and highly intelligent.

The process took a lot longer than I'm making out here, but the puppies born to those greyhound mothers were actually part human. I don't mean they were deformed, or monsters or anything – they looked no different from any normal puppies. But they were part human nonetheless, and their intelligence – what the scientists call their cognitive ability – was more highly advanced and adaptable than in ordinary dogs.

And of course those scientists were very excited, because nothing remotely like this had been achieved before. They hailed it as a radical breakthrough in biotechnical engineering.

It was Del who told me what the Romney Heights project was really about.

"They wanted to create a new kind of weapon," he said. "An animal primed with explosives that could be trained to penetrate a military or industrial stronghold and blow it up."

"But wouldn't the dogs be blown up as well?" I said. The idea horrified me.

"Of course they would, numbskull, sky high. Blown to bloody smithereens and fragments of gut. But dogs aren't the same as people, are they? Even dogs with human DNA aren't the same as people. You can always breed more, blow those up too if you want to. None of your conscientious objections about blowing up dogs. That was the entire point."

I could see more or less at once what he was getting at. By using smartdogs you could get into places and take risks you couldn't consider with a human strike force. And the smartdogs, like all dogs, would be happy to do exactly what they were told.

They did more experiments, experiments that involved both a smartdog and a human trainer having a bio-computer chip implanted into their brain. The chip was programmed with code from the dog's DNA, and facilitated a mental or empathic link between the dog and the human. Del says it's impossible to describe in layman's terms what it does, exactly, but basically it's as if the smartdog and its human trainer can hear each other's thoughts.

The scientists believed that the implants would change everything, which they did, only not in the way the scientists were expecting. The more the implant technology developed, the stronger the symbiosis between the dog and its runner. In symbiosis they formed a kind of mutual self-dependency – the dogs cared about their runners, sometimes enough to die for them, and vice versa. That wasn't what the Romney Heights scientists had been looking for at all.

Some of the scientists refused to continue with the use of smartdogs in the weapons programme. They insisted that the dogs' enhanced intelligence made it immoral for humans to exploit them in any manner that would bring them to harm. One of the scientists, Klara Hoogstraaten, even argued that all smartdogs should be granted rights under the Hague Convention.

When the lab management tried to have Klara Hoogstraaten sacked, she leaked the entire story to the tabloid press.

There was a public outcry. Some people were just concerned about the dogs being mistreated, others went one stage further and claimed that this was science run riot, that the smartdogs were the first step in a master plan to replace human manual workers with a slave race of engineered animals.

Most didn't give a damn either way. But the general shit-stirring made a lot of stink and in the end Romney Heights was forced to close down.

After that, implant surgery for smartdog runners became a legal grey area. Officially it was banned, in practice it just went underground. They closed down Romney Heights because they had to – after the Hoogstraaten business kicked off they had to be seen to do something. But it wasn't long before bootleg clinics started springing up, and when they did the politicos just sat back and pretended not to notice. The government were desperate to have the gene-splicing research continue, and here was a way of doing that, but with no risk to themselves – foolproof. They didn't have to commit any money to the project, because the clinics were *making* money, and if anything went wrong they could always scapegoat the greedy doctors.

They still had to be careful, though. Any adverse publicity surrounding one of the clinics and their whole cosy little system might implode, which is why a surgery that is theoretically outlawed is now probably the most rigidly controlled procedure in the country.

They can't afford to have anyone die on them, and that's why they turned down Del for his operation.

There was something wrong with his brain, some congenital defect. A tiny flaw the doctors felt certain would make no difference to his normal lifespan but that could make his brain go phut if he had the implant.

The doctors said that even then it would be unlikely, but as the surgery wasn't essential they were unwilling to take the risk.

Non-essential to whom, though? It's true I'm no medic, but I understood my brother well enough to know that the doctors might have killed him anyway, through disappointment.

All his initial check-ups were fine. The MRI was the final hurdle, just a formality really. No one expected to find anything. Del came back from that appointment in a black rage, not swearing and yelling the way he did when he was drunk or had got into a fight with someone, but clenched with anger, rigid with it, as if he were carrying the force of a bomb blast locked inside him.

He couldn't talk, or wouldn't. It was scary. Not even Limlasker would go near him, and I think that was what finally brought him out of it, having Lim avoid him like that. In the end the anger seeped away like floodwater down a storm drain and there was just this kid, lying face down on the bed with his dog beside him.

The next morning he seemed more together.

"Stupid cut-price morons," he said. "There are other places."

I didn't see what good it would do. I didn't dare say anything, but I was worried that if he went to another clinic the results would come back the same. As it turned out he didn't even get as far as being tested. The clinics all share their records via a central database, so the new docs knew what the old docs had found the second they punched Del's name into their computer.

* * *

Del set his heart on becoming a runner from the age of eight. It was the only thing he ever wanted, the one ideal he found to be beautiful and set his store by. When the doctors turned him down, he felt as if his life was over. He was a half-thing, a cripple, a drone.

There was also the question of Limlasker. Limlasker was an expensive dog. You could argue that he wasn't a dog at all, but a financial investment. Gra Rayner only let Del pick out a puppy in the first place because everyone took it for granted that Del and Lim would go on to compete in major races. For Gra Rayner, not running Lim would be like chucking thousands of shillings straight in the bin. If Del couldn't run Limlasker, he'd have to find someone who could, and the sooner the better.

Gra came good, though. I suppose in many respects Del was just as much a son in his eyes as Em was. He offered Del a job straight away as his trainee business manager, and said that Del could keep Limlasker, that he should consider the dog as a down-payment on his starting salary, and that he wouldn't be looking for anyone to take him over.

"I know you'll do me proud, you always have. And you and Lim, you're a team. That's not up for grabs."

I think it saved Del's sanity, that reassurance that Limlasker would not be taken away from him. He accepted Gra's job offer, and a year later he moved out of the house and into the leaky old barn that came with the building lot Gra had sold him just down the road from the yard.

The more time passed, the more Del gradually came to

accept the life he had. The job at the yard helped. He liked the power, definitely. He liked moving money around and organizing schedules and bossing the runners. He was good at what he did, and he enjoyed that, too. When Del cared about something he liked to be best at it, and I reckon Gra knew that. I think that's what he was counting on.

The biggest shock was Del's decision to give up Limlasker. It happened about a year after he started managing the yard for real, and shortly after he got together with Claudia.

"He should run," Del said to Gra. "The dog's in his prime. It's what he was born for."

Limlasker was almost four years old then. Smartdogs tend to have a longer racing life than most ordinary greyhounds, because the psychological component of their ability runs at a higher percentage than in non-engineered dogs. Gra was unsure at first. He was concerned that the natural bond between Del and Lim might interfere with the dog's ability to form a connection with an implanted runner, but Del brushed his objections aside.

"It's what he wants," Del said. "He'll win for you, big time. Trust me."

Del was right, as he usually was when it came to the dogs. He even found a runner for Lim himself, an unsmiling, rather taciturn girl he found at the track called Tash Oni. Tash was Nigerian, as tall as Del and just as skinny. For a while I felt convinced that Del was involved with Tash, that he was shagging her on the quiet or at least thinking about it, but it turned out that Tash was already living with someone, a news journalist called Brit Engstrom.

When Tash went in to have her operation, Del was there to collect her five hours later. He saw her home, and when after two weeks the doctors pronounced her fit, he took Limlasker to her himself, to live with her permanently.

Not many people could have done that. My brother has many faults but nobody could complain that he lacks courage.

When Del told me he was going to be a father I could barely believe it. What surprised me even more was that he seemed to be pleased. Del's always been a loner at heart. I never thought he'd settle down with anyone, least of all Claudia Day, with her soft voice and shy smile and fragile nerves. She wasn't even interested in the dogs, not particularly. I didn't think their relationship would last five minutes, to be honest. When Del insisted I go down the pub with him and then announced that Claudia was pregnant I almost choked on my beer.

He turned out to be good at it, too – being a dad, I mean. He didn't just care *about* Lumey, he cared *for* her too, changing her nappies and bathing her, schlepping her off to the yard as if he couldn't bear to be parted from her. Having a child seemed to reveal those aspects of Del's nature that had been kept secret from the world until then, buried beneath his anger like grass under snow.

It sounds corny to say this, but for me Del's love for Lumey was proof that such a thing as love truly existed and was not just some fable.

Del even chose her name – Luz, which means light. Claudia chose her middle name, Maree.

When Lumey was first born she seemed perfectly normal. It's true that she was slightly underweight, but the hospital said she would soon catch up and was fine otherwise.

They put Claudia in a side room for a couple of hours so they could monitor her blood pressure and then sent her home.

"They're afraid someone might steal my baby," Claudia whispered when I went in to visit. "That's why they're sending me home early. They think it's safer."

"Don't be ridiculous, Cee," Del said. "They want the bed, that's all."

He looked at me like: should I be worried? and I shook my head. New mums get all kinds of weird ideas, or at least that's what I'd heard, and Claudia was hardly the most logical person at the best of times. She seemed much better once she was out of the hospital, calmer than when she was pregnant actually, at least for a while. Then, just after Lumey turned one, she started coming out with a lot of stuff about how there was something not right, that her daughter was not developing as she should.

"She never speaks," she said. "I know it's too early for her to be using actual words yet – I'm not stupid. But you must have noticed how silent she is – she hardly ever cries, even. You can't tell me that's supposed to be normal for a one-year-old child."

"She seems perfectly all right to me," I said. "I'm sure she's fine. All children are different, aren't they?" I told her Del hadn't spoken a word until he was three, which was true, actually; I knew because Mum told me. Del was born surly,

I reckon. Anyway, Claudia seemed reassured, then a week later she was off again. I hadn't a clue what Del thought, until he turned up at my place one evening and started interrogating me about Claudia.

"Has Cee been saying anything to you about Lumey?"

"Just that she's a bit quiet," I said. "I told her it was nothing to worry about."

"She's driving me crazy with this shit. Cee, I mean, not Lumey." He sat down on the floor, leaning back against the wall and closing his eyes. He looked so young, doing that, so much like Del the way he was before our mother left.

"Tell me the truth, Jen," he said. "Do you honestly think that Lumey is okay?"

"Yes," I said. I looked him in the eye as I said it, which was my way of telling him I was saying what I really believed, straight up and no bullshit. When the chips are down he's still my brother. "She's different from other kids, that's all. Lumey's special."

"Special? That's what doctors say when they're trying to tell you your kid's a retard." His hands tensed themselves into fists. I could see he was trying not to lose his temper, but I could also see it was not me he was angry with but himself – for asking me in the first place, for making him voice the fears that were in his mind.

"There's nothing wrong with Lumey, Del." I kept my voice as calm and level as I could. "You can see that just by looking at her. She's happy as shit. She's just Lumey." I wasn't sure what I meant by that exactly, just that it seemed obvious to me that Lumey knew who she was and what was going on around her. Even at fourteen months she was sharp as a knife. So she didn't want to talk about it, so what? There'd be time enough for words when she was older.

There's enough talk in this world already and plenty to spare.

"Just let her work it out in her own time," I said. "When she feels like speaking, she'll speak."

Del didn't say anything at all at first and for a moment I thought he really was going to go off on one. Then I saw his hands unclench, and he let out his breath in a whooping sound, as if he didn't realise he'd been holding it until that second.

"That's what I reckoned," he said. "Lumey's bright as anything. It's just that Cee's got me scared to pick the kid up in case I drop her."

"It's not fair to blame Claudia, Del. You know what she's like. If anything happened to Lumey I think she'd lose her mind."

"You think I don't know that? I'm the one that has to live with it. If she carries on like this she'll drive us both nuts."

"Help her, then. Tell her you believe Lumey's fine and that she should stop worrying."

"I'll do that."

It wasn't like Del to say thank you for anything, but I could tell our talk had made him feel better. I fetched him a beer from the fridge and he flicked it open with his thumbnail, a trick he'd had off pat since forever.

The cap rolled away across the floor and under my workbench. Del took a swig from the bottle and then asked me a question.

"Who d'you think she looks like? Cee or me?"

His asking took me by surprise, because the answer seemed obvious. Claudia's like a big pink rose, no one in our family looks remotely like her. Del is angular and kind of scrawny-looking. His narrow chest and long arms have always made him look taller than he is. Then there's that sticking-up crest of yellow curls that first gave him his nickname, those lightning-green eyes.

"She looks like you, of course," I said. "Who do you think?"

He tipped his beer to me and gave me a rare smile.

"I reckoned that, too," he said. "Poor little monster."

Lumey was wonderful, actually. I've never been into kids particularly, but I was into Lumey right from the start. She wasn't just cute, she was smart, too. It was true that she didn't say much, but it was obvious she understood what words meant, you could tell that just from the way she started paying attention when you spoke her name. Then sometimes when she heard a new word, she'd grab towards the mouth of the person who had spoken it – as if she saw words as solid objects: living, darting sound-fish that she could catch between her fingers if she were only quick enough.

She was easy to take care of, too, because she never got bored. I could sit her in the corner of my work room with a couple of empty cotton reels and some scraps of patterned lining fabric and she'd be happy for hours just arranging and then rearranging those few things, playing some secret game of her own, all in silence and yet so attentive, as if she were listening to special music that only she could hear.

It was weird and a bit unnerving but beautiful, too. I knew Lumey was different, but I couldn't see how her being different mattered a damn. There are all kinds of words now for kids who refuse to accept the world as it's been laid down for them, but I thought that trying to make sense of Lumey was pointless, and might even damage her.

I will never forget the day she finally spoke. She was three and we were up at the yard. I can't remember even why I was there – most likely I was just hanging out with Del the way I sometimes still did.

I should explain that the first time I saw a smartdog up close I was totally freaked. I was five or six or thereabouts – at any rate, it was my first time at the track. Dad had already explained to us that smartdogs were different from ordinary street dogs, but I wasn't expecting to notice the difference as much as I did. Up till then I'd only seen them on TV, and apart from the mangy curs that hung around the municipal rubbish dump the only dogs I'd had any real contact with were my dad's mate Merle's brindle Staffie and the overweight spaniel Boris who belonged to Mrs Roberson who ran the fish shop.

The engineered hounds were different because they seemed more aware of you. They gazed at me with open curiosity, as if they were my equal. I wasn't used to that then, not in a dog, and I suppose it threw me off balance. I expected the dogs in the trackside pens to be pacing about and making a fuss, the way any animal will do if it's shut up for too long. The smartdogs weren't doing that, though, they weren't even barking. They were standing still and staring calmly ahead, as if they were listening for a signal that would tell them what to do and where to go.

As I say, it gave me the willies. That's just the way the dogs are, of course, and I soon got used to it. But Lumey seemed to get on with the dogs from the moment she was able to toddle across the yard. I know Claudia wasn't too keen on Del taking Lumey to work – she was afraid Lumey would catch something, most likely – but she was never going to put a stop to it, not just because Del liked having her with him but because Lumey herself was crazy about the dogs. She loved being around them, Limlasker especially; it was amazing to see.

On the day it happened, Carson Stringer was just about to head off to the lunges with his dog, Scallion. Scallion was huge, a great red horse-hound of a dog, gentle as piss like all smartdogs but still pretty impressive. When I saw Lumey rushing up to him I felt scared for a moment, just because Scallion was so big and Lumey so small.

I think Del must have felt the same, because he took a quick step towards her, as if to drag her away, but then at the last minute he backed off. He decided it was better just to let things take their course I reckon, but I could see why he was nervous.

Lumey gazed up at Scallion, stared at him with her eyes wide open as if she couldn't believe what she was seeing. Then she raised her arms high above her head, and said 'run'.

We all heard it, clear as anything. Lumey's first ever word.

The dog bent his great head towards her, swishing his tail.

"Holy fuck," said Carson Stringer. "She's going to be a champ, boss. You'd better cover your arse and get her signed up."

Everyone laughed, Del especially. Del was elated. "I knew she could talk," he kept saying to me afterwards. "The brainy kids always take longer. Don't they always say that?"

I told him I'd heard something of the kind, then I made a joke about like father, like daughter, and the way Del's face lit up at that, it hurt my heart. And I was happy, too. Happy for Del and happy for Claudia, who was going to float right up to the ceiling when she heard the news.

I knew it wasn't that simple, though. Lumey hadn't just spoken, she had *heard* as well. Not a sound that I could hear, but something. You could tell just from the way she stood, still as a sentry, *listening*. Something had passed from Scallion and into Lumey and then back again.

Like a silken cord, like a signal along a telegraph wire, like light.

I had no idea what I had seen, only that it had been extraordinary.

If Del noticed it too I didn't know, and I didn't ask.

* * *

47

I always liked the way the runners dressed, even as a kid. Not just the way they stood out from the crowd, but the way the clothes they wore seemed to strengthen their idea of themselves, to help them be what they were, and to be it better.

I'm not saying that a runner can't be a runner without runner's gants. It's not the gloves themselves that are special, it's the runners thinking they are. I've heard it said that strong thoughts can make magic, and a fine pair of gants – like a charm or a curse – is just something that helps strong thoughts take on a definite shape.

This was something that seemed clear to me from the first. I remember one Saturday when I was down at the track as usual with Dad and Del, waiting in line at the kiosks to get a kebab. From where I was standing I could see the dogs that were in the next race being led past on their way to the traps, their runners standing back from the trackside as the gates were closed. The video screen at the far end of the stadium stopped displaying an advert for 7-Up and started to show live footage of the smartdogs instead. The favourite for that race was a three-year-old particoloured male called Space Cadet. His runner was Kayleigh dos Santos, and when she went up to receive her start card I had my first clear sight of her.

Her hair was cropped close to her skull in a style I envied but that Mum had already said it was pointless for me even to think about. Dos Santos wore zip-up silver gants with a cerise leather cuff. Instead of the traditional knee-high boots, she wore a tatty pair of hi-top sneakers bought from Ku-dam or Primark. The contrast of the cheap chain-store shoes with the designer gants did something peculiar and thrilling to my insides. There was such daring in it, something so unexpected and so *rude* it made my heart flip up in my chest like a bush cricket.

What I didn't know at the time was that Kayleigh dos Santos had done time in prison for dealing glass. Runners are pretty evasive on the subject of glass. Most who have tried the drug won't admit to it, those who do talk about their experience often say there are no words to describe it anyway, so why bother trying? The compound makes the implant work better, apparently. It can't enhance the performance of the hardware – that would be impossible – but what it does do is put your brain into a state where it can engage more fully with the software processes and at a higher level.

The drug glass, like the implant clinics, is something that is supposed not to exist. It was developed by the police and the military as a coercive, to be injected into the brains of prisoners who were about to take a lie detector test. The cops claim a prisoner under the influence of glass is physically unable to lie, that the truth gets hardwired into every brain cell like a piece of computer code. The drug became known as glass because it supposedly enables you to see the world more clearly. Habitual users say that when you're high on glass the insides of things and even invisible things become revealed to you, clearly in focus, as through the lens of a microscope.

The downside of glass is that it soon begins to erode brain function rather than enhance it. Use glass long enough and hard enough and your mind gets cut to pieces from the inside. People have died raving in police cells through being overdosed on glass. Not that the cops would admit culpability in a hundred years.

Del always said that glass was shit in capsule form, that he'd known good runners ruined forever with just a single hit. Any of his runners caught in possession were sacked on the spot.

Like all the Class A Classifieds, glass has a high street value. For those of a criminal persuasion, dealing glass can generate a lucrative income.

"The dopeheads say glass takes them to the magic mountain," Del said to me once. "Too bad when they can't come down again. More fool them."

All runners are funny about their gloves, but in different ways. For some it's a trophy thing, a way of showing off how much money they've won. Jocks like that get a kick out of being photographed in a new pair of gants every week of the year – they collect them the same way they collect winning tickets. Others are just the opposite: they get fixated on one pair of gloves and won't race without them. I heard of one guy who had his gloves stolen or lost them or something and went completely berserk. He began losing races after that, one duff run after another, and ended up shooting himself. His case was extreme but not unique. All runners are natural obsessives, it's part of the temperament. What some people call the allure.

I was drawn to that, right from the beginning, the queasy excitement of it all, but it was Em who helped me find my vocation. Until he told me he liked it, the old junk I collected was just that – junk. Stuff I hung on to because I found it interesting but nothing more. But when Em said what he said about artistic talent it set me thinking. Perhaps other people might find the junk interesting, too. Perhaps seeing the specialness inside a thing, that secret store of memories contained inside even the cheapest and most commonplace of objects, was as much a gift as being good at maths, or having the natural empathy to be a smartdog runner.

Something clicked inside my head, it was as simple as that. As if the different parts of my brain were like a jigsaw puzzle: for ages they'd been all mixed up, now everything started falling into place.

I taught myself to sew from books I turned up in dumpsters, from printed patterns I found in old colour supplements or on the Internet, many of them so out of date that by the time I got my hands on them they were in fashion again. At some point I learned that the making of bespoke racing gauntlets was a specialist art I could earn a good living from, so long as I worked hard and learned to be choosy about my clients.

There are other glove makers in Sapphire, but I've never had any problem getting work.

For standard-model racing gauntlets I normally use buck hide. For Angela Kiwit's I used kid leather. Kid is expensive but it's softer and more pliable, plus the molecular strengthening treatments used at the tanning stage make kid almost as strong as buck these days in any case.

Angela Kiwit's specifications regarding the colour were pretty exact.

"You know those blue snake things on that TV ad?" Kiwit said when she came for her fitting. "That's the colour I want."

Oddly enough I had seen the advert she was referring to. I forget what the ad was for now, but it featured a massive shoal of electric eels, all rippling and waving in unison like an underwater flag. I didn't know if the eels were real or CGI, but I remembered the colour exactly: a strident neon blue, intense and translucent at the same time. Angela Kiwit had brought along a strip of cardboard torn from a cereal packet that approximated the colour pretty well but I didn't need it. I knew what she wanted – now it was simply a matter of tracking it down.

Angela Kiwit was on the up, one of those clients I knew could be important for me, not only because she was so talented but also because she had a great look, coupled with a natural knack for understanding what suited her. She was tall – about six feet, and that was without the four-inch stiletto knee boots. She wore decorative gaiters over the boots, silver lycra in imitation of the gang kids down on the Stade. Kit like that usually looks ridiculous on anyone past the age of twenty but on Kiwit it looked magnificent and the electric blue gauntlets she wanted me to make for her would be the final masterstroke.

I could see at once what she was getting at – she wanted the gloves to be a cheeky rip-off of the ultramarine elbow-length gants made famous by Leesa Muttola in the early nineties. The imitation was pretty brazen – you needed chutzpah as well as style to carry it off. Luckily for her, Kiwit had both. The gloves would be worth the outlay in TV exposure alone.

"I need them in a fortnight," Kiwit said. "Will that be okay?" She leaned back against the door frame, digging her right heel into the parquet and twisting her boot slowly in a half circle, hard enough to leave a substantial dent.

I made a scoffing noise, like *ha*. I couldn't help it. "You are kidding me?" I said. If it had been anyone else I'd have laughed in her face but I knew this contract could really take me places and I didn't want to lose it – Kiwit wasn't the only one who would get the exposure, after all. Kiwit kept digging her stiletto heel into my floor and saying nothing. I faced her down for about a minute then named a price that was twenty percent in excess of the usual. It was a fair price, too. Including beading and brocade work, an average pair of runner's gants takes about three weeks to sew by hand from start to finish. I could do the job in two, probably, but it would call for some serious overtime. Overtime's part of the business, but both of us were perfectly well aware of Kiwit's current standing in the league championships.

If she wanted the gloves that badly she could afford to pay me properly for my time.

She made a face, pursing her lips, which were painted the dense, contaminated scarlet of black cherries, or blood blisters. Then she folded her arms across her non-existent breasts and straightened up.

"If you can really get them done in two weeks I'll go for

it. I totally dig those gants you did for Benny Heppler."

Benny Heppler was a good friend of Del's. The gloves I made for him were quite plain, just black calf's leather, but sometimes plain gloves show your skill better because there's nowhere to hide. Also, Benny's gloves had some great stitching on the backs, really intricate stuff. That stitching alone had taken me a week to complete, but I wasn't about to reveal that to Angela Kiwit. I just smiled, told her I was glad she liked Benny's gloves, that they'd been great to work on. After I'd taken all the preliminary measurements, Kiwit paid her deposit and we said our goodbyes. I told her I would call at the end of the week so we could arrange a time for her to come in and check the fitting. Half an hour later I was on the tramway, on my way out to Romer's. I was eager to begin work on Kiwit's gloves straight away, and there were things I needed.

Romer's is the biggest track supply store in Sapphire and it's nationally famous. Not as famous as Gallant's, maybe, but then Gallant's is mostly for the tourists. They sell souvenirs, mainly, and the kind of standard issue kit you can buy off the peg from any decent factory outlet.

But if you want custom runner's gants or boots, or gantiers' haberdashery or uncut leather, then you go to Romer's.

There's been a Romer's in Sapphire for more than a century, since before the war. The current management have photos of the original Romer's Boot Store hanging on the wall behind the counter, a metal shack on a piece of waste ground with a rusty barbed wire fence marking the perimeter. That piece of waste ground is now the Sapphire Industrial Estate, and the rusty tin shack has morphed into a retail outlet covering more square footage than the Sapphire tramway depot.

To get to the fabrics and leather department you go right to the back of the store then down a flight of concrete steps into the basement. The smell down there is amazing – not just the leather but all the other stuff: wax polish and clean jersey fabric, enamelled buttons and silk lining fabric and polished chrome zippers. I love that smell. For me the smell of Romer's basement sums up everything in life that's most thrilling: the heat inside the stadium on a summer's night, crazy evenings in the casino bar at the Ryelands, passionate friendships and secret plans, most of all the scent of dreams in embryo, floating in the mind, not yet fully formed.

The first time I came to Romer's, all I could afford to buy were some small offcuts of purple kid leather from the remnants bin, and I was so afraid of looking a fool in front of the sales clerk that I didn't count my change, just stuffed it into my pocket without looking. It wasn't until I got home that I discovered I'd left a five-shilling note behind on the counter. I still kick myself for losing that money. What an idiot.

I used the purple leather to make a pair of wrist guards, using a pattern I'd come across inside an old racing magazine. It took me ages to complete them because I was scared of making a mistake and wasting the leather. When they were finally finished I thought they were a bit plain, not quite how I'd imagined them, anyway, and so I embroidered a dragon across one of them, using some bright green metallic thread I happened to find in a skip outside a building works on Braybrooke Road. I thought the dragon made the guards look better, more edgy. They were definitely more eye-catching, anyway. I gave them as a present to Sharon Young, who was a friend of Del's and one of his runners. She had always been very nice to me when I turned up at the yard or at races.

"No shit, these are awesome," she said. She insisted on giving me twenty shillings for them, which more than recouped the cost of the leather and made me blush so hard I thought I was going to faint from lack of blood.

I wondered at the time if she was just being kind. When I saw her wearing the guards at the track two weeks later it felt like flying.

As I was coming away from Romer's, I saw a magpie. Magpies are common in Sapphire, especially on the edges of town close to the marshes. I always tend to notice magpies if they're about, not just because of their striking plumage but because of my mother. Mum was terrified of magpies. Not terrified of the birds as such, but terrified of seeing them. She was convinced they brought bad luck. If she happened to see one she'd always pretend not to have noticed it, or else she'd whisper a rhyme under her breath to charm it away.

She wasn't a superstitious person normally, and so I found her nervousness around magpies rather endearing. I thought of her that day though, outside Romer's, and just for a moment I too felt afraid.

* * *

I was about halfway home when Claudia's call came through. The tramway carriage was pretty full by then – it was the middle of the rush hour – and I found it difficult to make out what she was saying. It didn't help that she was obviously on the verge of tears.

She kept repeating the same three words: Lumey is gone.

At first I thought she meant Lumey had had an accident, that she'd been injured in some way. All kinds of awful images rushed through my head – Lumey being crushed by a block of falling masonry, or caught between the thrusting pistons of a tramway car. Claudia began to cry. The general racket inside the compartment meant I had to shout to make myself heard and people were beginning to stare in my direction.

"Claudia," I said. "Take it easy. Tell me again."

"She's been taken," Claudia wailed. "Del says I'm not to tell anyone but I had to call."

"Taken? What are you talking about? Where's Del now?"

"Lumey disappeared from the backyard. About an hour ago, or perhaps it's more now. She was playing with her building blocks. When I went out to fetch her in for her nap she was gone. Del's out looking for her. He says we're not to call the police, that it could be dangerous for Lumey. He made me swear."

She choked on the final word and her weeping intensified. As I listened to her sobbing I found I could picture her exactly: pink cheeks shiny with tears, amber hair coming slowly adrift from its army of pins. The idea was exhausting. I couldn't decide if what she was telling me was real or a false alarm. It didn't take much to send Claudia into panic mode.

Then out of nowhere I remembered the magpie and went cold inside. I know it sounds ridiculous, but that's how it was.

"It's all right, Claudia, I'm coming," I said. "Just try to keep calm."

Claudia made a noise, a tear-filled gulping. It was difficult to tell if it meant gratitude or terror. I disconnected the call before she could clarify. I didn't mean to be cruel – it was just that there was no way I could help her from where I was, and having to listen to her crying down the phone was slowing me down.

Del's place was on the opposite side of town from Romer's, half an hour away by tramway at the very least. It would be quicker by taxi, but that would cost me a fortune, and there was no guarantee that I would find one at this time of day. All things considered, it seemed more sensible to stay on the tramway. The immediate shock of Claudia's phone call had worn off by then, and as we started grinding up West Hill I began to feel the first prickles of genuine anxiety. What if something really had happened to Lumey? It was unthinkable. I tried Del's mobile several times but it went straight to voicemail. Either he had it switched off or he was busy on another call. My mind was spinning with anxiety and frustration. I didn't care to imagine the state Del was in. If Lumey was missing he would be frantic, and when my brother was frantic he did stupid things.

It didn't bear thinking about. By the time I got off the tram I was in panic mode, too. Not as bad as Claudia, but getting there.

Del's tramway stop was Tackleway, a dusty unmade road that instantly became a mud chute whenever it rained. Tackleway is over two miles long in its entirety. If you follow it right to its end you'll come to the marshes. Luckily, Del's place was much closer, about five minutes' walk from the tramway stop and just below the West Wickham water tower. I half walked, half ran along the road, almost tripping several times on the uneven surface. When I finally arrived at the Cowshed, Del was standing by the gate waiting for me. He looked more angry than devastated, and for those moments before reaching his side I allowed myself to hope that Claudia had got it wrong after all, that the whole thing was a misunderstanding and Lumey was safe in the living room watching TV.

Del walked slowly forward to meet me. His yard boots scrunched on the gravel. There was a rip in his sleeve.

"There was no need for you to come," he said. "I was going to call you."

"Where's Lumey, Del?" I said. "Claudia seems to think she's gone missing. She sounded beside herself on the phone. How could I not come?"

I glared at him, waiting for answers. The breeze, drifting up from the shoreline, smelled of bladder wrack and sump oil. It tugged at Del's hair, tugging it back from his forehead like twists of frayed rope. I realised I was holding something in my hands, the parcel of trimmings and the blue leather

I had bought at Romer's. Romer's seemed an age ago, something that had happened in another life.

"Not out here," Del said. He sighed with what sounded like irritation. "Come inside."

Del rebuilt the Cowshed more or less from scratch. At the time Gra sold him the place, it was a half-derelict barn on an overgrown patch of wasteland backing on to the yard. The barn itself was barely habitable – the windows were boarded over, and there was a birch sapling pushing up through the floorboards in the downstairs hallway. Also the roof leaked. Gra offered to have the barn torn down free of charge so Del could put up one of the new prefabs, but Del said no, he'd prefer to do up the barn; he'd work on it evenings and off shifts, get the old shack watertight.

It took him a year and a half, but he did a good job. Once it was finished, the Cowshed made a lovely home, filled with the smells of new wood and old stone, the greenish, liquid light of the surrounding trees. Claudia once told me she found the place creepy, especially at night, and I had the feeling she would have preferred a nice new prefab but Del was crazy about the Cowshed and I could understand why.

When I arrived there in the late pink-tinged light of that dreadful afternoon I expected the place to be buzzing, but the lot seemed deserted. Del strode ahead of me up the path. As he put the key in the lock the front door was snatched open from the inside and Claudia appeared, her face all puffy from crying and pale as goat's cheese. Her right cheek bore dark streaks of what looked like mascara.

"Get back in the house, Cee," Del said. "It's only Jen."

Claudia stepped backwards and away from the door. Her arms hung limply by her sides. She looked from Del to me and then back to Del again. Clearly she was trying to work out if anything new had happened, if there was something we weren't telling her. She knew how close Del and I were. There are plenty of women who would have resented that but not Claudia. Or at least she never seemed to.

"There's no news, Cee," Del said quietly. "You'd be the first to know if there were." He touched her shoulder briefly but I could tell from the way his eyes slid off her that he was feeling impatient with her. For the moment at least she was an encumbrance. "Could you fix us some drinks, do you reckon?" he added. "I want to talk to Jen in the office, just for a bit."

Claudia bowed her head and walked away, to the kitchen presumably. I felt a bright flash of anger, not just for her but at her. How could she let Del talk to her like that? She should have refused, she should have said *whatever it is you're telling that bitch I have a right to hear it.* She let him treat her like a servant. I felt angry with myself too, for not insisting that Claudia be included in our conversation. But the truth was I didn't want her there. I still thought of her as a child, a habit I'd picked up from Del, I suppose. I know that doesn't excuse it. I guess we thought we were protecting her.

Del led me towards the narrow, L-shaped room that wrapped itself around the most northerly corner of the house, an offshoot of the main living room that served Del as his office and general dossing area. It was the place he went to watch the racing results and the late-night cop shows he liked; porn too probably, I never enquired. The living room itself was huge, taking up more than half the ground floor and with a long covered veranda overlooking the garden. Claudia normally kept the place super-neat but on that day it looked vaguely dishevelled, as if the house had been slapped in the face and was still recovering from the shock.

Some of Lumey's toys lay scattered on the floor – a wind-up mechanical rooster Del had picked up in some junk shop or other, and a selection of the ceramic tiles with pictures of farmyard animals and household utensils on one side and letters of the alphabet on the other. Lumey loved those tiles. Until she was about two it was always the picture side she liked best, but more recently I'd noticed letters cropping up more and more often in her little arrangements, and as we crossed the room to get to Del's den I saw that some of the tiles had been placed together to spell out whole words.

There was 'lumey' and 'dog', the kind of short and simple words that even younger kids would easily learn to recognise. But there was also 'race day' and 'champion' and 'dear prudence', words and phrases Lumey might well have heard spoken but was unlikely to have seen written down. Even with my limited knowledge of kids, the spelling seemed advanced for a four-year-old. Dear Prudence was the name of a puppy sired by Limlasker just the year before. Del said she was a talented dog but highly strung, and they were still looking for the right runner for her.

It was weird, to see her name spelled out on the floor like that. It was even weirder knowing that Lumey had been sitting right there, in her favourite place over by the window, playing with her tiles, making the peculiarly sweet little humming noises she used to make, most likely. Just a couple of hours earlier everything had been normal. Thinking about it made my guts ache.

We went into the den and Del shut the door, pushing hard to make sure it was closed properly. As soon as we were sitting down I asked him what the hell was going on.

"Why aren't the cops here?" I said.

"We can't call the cops," Del said. He made the same irritated sighing noise he'd made outside. "If we call the cops the people who've taken Lumey will most likely kill her."

"What planet are you on, Derrick? You tell me Lumey's missing. Claudia's going off her trolley out there and you're stuck on your arse doing nothing." I looked around the room. There were empty DVD cases and stacks of paper everywhere. The place was a mess.

I never called him Derrick unless I was really pissed off with him and both of us knew it.

"Listen," he said, in that calm, calculating voice he always used when he was playing for time. "There's stuff you should know."

"From where I'm sitting that would seem to be the understatement of the century."

"Hold your rag, Jen, this isn't helping. You've got to calm down." He leaned forward in his chair, his scrawny arse balanced on the edge of the seat, arms folded across his knees. "For a start, I know that Lumey's okay."

"What do you mean, you know?" I was listening now. I

knew we were getting to the heart of things. Everything I'd said until then was just a warm-up, my way of telling my brother I was frightened and upset. The thing is, I knew Del, and I knew from the moment I came up the drive and there were no cop cars that there was more to this business than first appeared. I understood that Del had sent Claudia away because he wanted to tell me stuff he didn't want her finding out, either because it was dangerous or because he knew he was in the wrong. Knowing my brother it was probably both.

"I had a phone call about an hour ago. I know who's done this and I know what they want. I can give them what they want, so there's nothing to worry about. What I need you to do is convince Cee of that. Everything will be all right, so long as we sit tight and play ball. No one knows, no one gets hurt – simple as that."

"You can't be serious," I said, but it was a token protest, my own play for time. I looked Del straight in the face and it was only then that I saw how scared he was really, how scared for his daughter. He was hiding it well and I believed he was telling me the truth about the phone call but he was still scared. Because he knew he was not in control, because he knew as well as I did that he was in the kind of situation where things can go wrong in less than a second.

Because he knew that Lumey was alone and probably terrified.

His eyes were like pinpricks: hard green water. He looked as if he wanted to kill the world.

"What have you done, Del?" I said. "I'm saying nothing to Claudia until you tell me the truth." I spoke more gently this time, but I felt certain he would know from my tone that I meant business.

"Okay, okay." He shifted around on the edge of his seat. He really did look awful, worse than Claudia in a way because Claudia was just frightened, whereas Del also knew he was responsible for what was happening. I wanted to go to him, hug him, tell him we'd sort this shit out together the way we always had. I couldn't do that, though. I knew that if I let him see I felt sorry for him there was a danger he would spin me a line, that he would tell me the story that suited him, rather than the story that was true.

I made myself hold back. It sounds cruel, but I had to, for Lumey's sake.

"I lost something that belongs to someone else," Del said. "Something that's worth a lot of money. They want their money back, that's all."

Del had been running glass. It wasn't just a one-off, either, it had been going on for years. He'd been using yard winnings to purchase large consignments of the drug through a gang who had a contact in one of the facilities where the medical-grade stuff was produced. He'd then sold it on to another group in London for a considerable mark-up. The glass was transported in canisters of fertilizer via the tramway. It was a foolproof system, so Del said – or at least it had been.

"Last week's consignment was intercepted," he said. "Either the cops got wind of it somehow, or they've known for ages and this is just their way of letting us know they want a piece of the action. Fuck knows. Only I was intending to pay off the supply guys with the proceeds from this lot and now that plan's scuppered. Which leaves the supply guys in the red with someone else. I don't give a shit about their problem, frankly, except that they've pulled this stunt with Lumey to twist my arm."

My heart sank. I knew at once that Del was right, that there was no way we could get the police involved. Not because of the glass – that was the least of it – but because of the supply people. If they found out we'd shopped them to the cops they'd come after Del and kill him. They'd kill Lumey too, of course, dump her body out in the marshes without a second thought.

The police were a lost cause anyway. Everyone knew the glass trade in Sapphire was out of control.

"Can't you borrow the money from Gra? I'm sure he'd tide you over."

Del laughed, a hard, bitter sound without a trace of humour. "Have you any idea how much I owe? Clearly not. You might as well suggest we go digging for treasure." He leaned back in his seat. "Anyway, stuff that, I don't want Gra involved. I can sort this thing myself – I've got it all worked out. You know it's the Delawarr Triple in just over a fortnight? I know this guy who'll bet big for a share of the proceeds, and by big I mean big enough to pay him off and the suppliers too. We finalize our account with the supply guys, they return Lumey by close of business. Job done."

He was grinning now, just a little, with the look of a wolf circling a sheep pen. He was pleased with his plan, I could see that, happy as a cow in clover.

So far as I was concerned it sounded insane.

"Haven't you forgotten something?" I said. "You have to win the race first."

"We'll win," he said. He sounded abstracted, as if the race result were a minor technicality and his mind had already moved on to more important matters. "I'm going to run Limlasker."

I gaped at him – I think my mouth really did fall open. I honestly considered the possibility that he might have gone crazy.

"You're living in cloud cuckoo land, Del."

"No," he said. "Trust me. I know what I'm doing."

What it came down to was this: Del was proposing to bet his daughter's life on a sodding dog race.

The Delawarr Triple is the biggest event in the racing calendar. It takes place on the third Saturday in June, just before the really hot weather starts to kick in. The stadium is always packed. It's a 1,100-metre race over hurdles, with the preliminary heats and the quarter- and semi-finals taking place throughout the course of the day. Victory in the Delawarr earns the winner ten full championship points, as well as a mighty winner's purse of 10,000 shillings. There's a lot of excitement surrounding the race, a lot of intrigue and rumour during the build-up, and of course a lot of money changes hands. I can't remember a single year when there wasn't some betting or doping scandal.

Occasionally dogs are stolen or killed. I remember one year there was a suicide, an out-of-towner who blew his brains out with a shotgun down on the seafront.

He lost his house in a bet, apparently. It happens.

Del had always been nervous around the Delawarr. He usually had a dog or two running and he usually made the semis at least but he had never run Limlasker. He said it was because Lim did better over flat but that was just a get-out. Lim had won his best races over flat, that was true, but he was a good hurdler. He'd won races all the way up to 900 metres.

The truth was that Del had never forgotten the business with Marley Struts. Struts had been a very young, very talented runner and Del's special protégé. There was a lot of buzz around him and by the evening before the race he was the odds-on favourite. But half an hour before he ran his first heat, Struts was taken outside the ground by some jocks on speed and beaten senseless. He suffered a hairline fracture of the skull and ended up having to have his implant removed. A year later Struts tracked down the people who did it and killed one of them with a crowbar. He's in prison now, serving life for murder. None of this was Del's fault, but he took it hard.

The real reason Del had never run Limlasker in the Delawarr Triple was because he was afraid something might happen to him. He tended to run younger dogs, dogs that would benefit from the exposure but without attracting too much attention. Marley Struts had attracted attention, and look what happened.

Limlasker was seven years old now and about to turn

eight. He was an old dog, by any standards. He and Tash were still winning races, but Del already had another dog – a nine-month-old bitch named Clearview Princess, Limlasker's granddaughter – picked out for Tash for when Lim retired. Limlasker would run one more season at the most.

It would be unusual for any dog of his age to run the Delawarr. It's true that some of the great champions have been five years old or more but they've always been dogs with a track record in that particular race. Red Kestrel was six when she won, but she'd been competing in the Delawarr for three previous seasons and placing higher each time. It was a race she wanted to win, anyone could see that.

Limlasker though – so far as the Delawarr was concerned, he was both a veteran and a novice, not a good combination. When Del told me he was planning to run him I thought he'd gone nuts.

But after my comment about cloud cuckoo land I kept my mouth shut. What else could I do? Del obviously meant to do this, and nothing I or anyone else could say would make any difference.

We sat Claudia down and talked to her. I did most of the talking, actually – I guess Del thought she'd be more likely to swallow our story if it came from me. We told her Lumey was safe, that she was being held as collateral against a business loan, that it was all a bit of a mix-up and Lumey would be returned to us in a couple of weeks.

If anyone asked she was to say Lumey was in Folkestone,

visiting her grandma. On no account was she to speak to the police.

"There's nothing to worry about, honestly," I said. Claudia blinked at me. Her eyes were shiny and kind of glazed over. It was like she'd been drugged. I felt lower than a louse, but what choice did I have? What I had said was not a lie exactly, and even if I went against my brother and told her everything, what good would it do? The facts of the situation wouldn't change, and knowing the truth would only make Claudia feel worse.

We all had our jobs to do. Del's was to juggle hand grenades, mine was to convince him he could perform a miracle. Claudia's was to shut up and keep out of the way.

The sooner we all got on with them, the better.

"Why not do something special for Lumey, for when she comes home?" I said to Claudia. "You could redecorate her bedroom. I'll help you choose the colours if you like."

I felt like a right idiot, suggesting that, but I thought it might help Claudia to have something concrete to focus on, and it did.

"I've been wanting to do that for a while, actually," she said. She was looking a little brighter, a bit less like a zombie on Valium, and I really started to believe that if we could only create a safe space for Claudia to live inside for the next week or so we might just come through this. I guess Del's madness was catching.

I agreed to stay for supper, and to come over to the Cowshed the following afternoon to help Claudia decide on a theme for Lumey's new decor.

Del was looking at me like I was some kind of genius. I wanted to thump him.

I didn't get home until after eleven. I felt exhausted, wiped out, but the idea of sleep seemed impossible. I paced around my apartment, pulling down blinds and checking doors, and all the time there was this horrible little voice inside my head, whispering to me all the terrible things that could be happening to Lumey at that very moment.

If she was even still alive, that was.

I did the only thing I knew that would help. I unwrapped the package of blue leather I'd bought at Romer's and spread it flesh side up on my workroom table. I stroked it gently, stretching it just a little with the tips of my fingers to test its strength. I flattened my palm against the downy underside, its texture so soft and so pliable I already knew how the needle would feel going in. Smooth and sweet as a silver spoon through a jar of honey. I opened the computer file with Kiwit's measurements, the photographs I had taken of her hands and arms, both front view and back. Not all gantiers bother with photos, but I have always found them essential because they help me imagine.

Angela Kiwit had very strong forearms. In isolation from the rest of her body, you might easily mistake them for a man's. The long hands with the tapering fingers did not quite match them.

For me, all hands are beautiful, the most complex and fascinating part of the human body. I spent some time studying those photographs, and at some point all thoughts of Claudia and Del and Lumey leaked silently away. I made a cup of tea and drank it. I thought about making a start on drawing the pattern but suddenly realised how tired I was – tired enough, finally, to sleep.

It was one o'clock in the morning and not quite dark. I love the long summer evenings. In winter it's the thought of those long light evenings that keeps me going.

The phone woke me just after seven. The caller was Del.

"I've just spoken to them," he said. "We've agreed a date for the exchange." He named a day, the Monday immediately following the Delawarr Triple. "They'll let me know the location nearer the time." He sounded okay, buoyed up even, back in control. "See you this afternoon," he said. For a moment I couldn't think what he was talking about, then I remembered I'd promised to go over and see Claudia. It wasn't a prospect I relished, but I knew there was no way I could get out of it.

"Fine," I said. "See you." I ended the call, then spent the rest of the morning measuring and cutting out the paper pattern I would use to make the gloves for Angela Kiwit. Pattern-making sounds simple but it's not. It's exacting work, and can't be rushed. It occupied my mind entirely, and the deeper I sank into my work-trance the less I was aware of anything except the sound of my own breathing, steady and deep and reviving and entirely calm.

It was as if my life had split into two separate halves: one mad, one sane.

* * *

Limlasker was Swift Elin's grandson. Swift Elin was tall, but Lim was taller, a hand's breadth at least. He had the same light blue eyes and silver coat, but whereas Swift Elin was silver all over, Lim had a black patch, like an inky handprint, on his left hindquarter. Del always used to say it looked as if he'd had his arse slapped.

When Tash first took over Limlasker, Del stayed away from them as much as he could, at first, anyway. He said it was so Tash could get to know the dog without feeling scrutinized, but really it was for Limlasker and himself. Del wanted Lim to understand that their relationship was to change. Later on though, Del began to supervise Tash and Lim's training sessions. Gra was worried that it wouldn't work, that the dog would become confused and his performance would be affected, but his fears proved groundless.

It was as if Del had told Lim he was giving him to Tash willingly, for a reason, and Lim understood and accepted that.

Greyhounds are different from other dogs, anyway. They hardly ever bark or wag their tails, but in their own quiet way they seem naturally empathic. Most dogs understand the world around them through their sense of smell, but greyhounds are sight hounds – they use their eyes for communication as well as for hunting prey. In other words, they're more like people – one of the main reasons greyhounds were chosen to be smartdogs in the first place.

It's weird, watching them train. The younger, less experienced runners tend to talk out loud to their dogs a lot, praising them and encouraging them or urging them on. Either the implant hasn't been fully assimilated, or they don't

73

yet trust their ability. All that changes as they become more experienced, and the most naturally gifted runners – runners like Tash, or Roddy Haskin – hardly ever speak to their dogs at all in the normal sense. Everything happens on another level, an invisible, sub-audible level of communication that turns their training sessions into a kind of silent ballet. If you keep quiet and concentrate hard you can sense that communication taking place. It's hard to explain but you can definitely feel it: a tension in the air, like electricity, the same sensation you get with lightning just before it strikes.

Watching Tash run Limlasker always gave me goosebumps. The two of them were special together – two faces of the same coin.

I ate a quick lunch then headed over to the Cowshed. I was worried that Claudia would either be in the depths of a catatonic depression or hyped up to the ceiling but she appeared perfectly calm. Thoughtfully, determinedly calm in a way that seemed just about as far from her usual vagaries as it was possible to get.

"I've been jotting down some ideas," she said, more or less the moment I arrived. "I should have done this ages ago. Lumey's a grown-up little girl now, she isn't a baby."

She made us some tea, and showed me her diagrams and notes, plans to turn Lumey's pink-and-white nursery into what Claudia kept calling 'a proper little girl's room'. The metal cot she slept in was to be replaced with a full-sized bed, the plush cerise carpet to be taken up and new wooden floorboards fitted. There was a nautical feel to everything. Clean, bright, cheerful. A room from a magazine feature.

"Do you think she'll like it?" Claudia said.

I said yes at once, without thinking, then realised I meant it; that Lumey, should she ever return to the room, really would be delighted by the blues and whites, the neat little bookcase Claudia had ordered, the wooden dressing table with its circular mirror and secret drawer. Any child would be. We went online and I helped Claudia to pick out a wind chime to hang in the window, an assortment of dangling glass prisms and brightly painted fish made out of tin.

I became quite caught up in it all, actually, giggling over trifles, searching out new things to waste our money on, and at some point I realised the fiction had taken me over, that on some level at least I'd conned myself into believing my own evasions. The realisation brought it all back to me: Lumey's gone-ness, the danger, our lies. It was as if a vast hole had opened beneath me, sprawling me backwards into nothingness. I thought of the old mine workings to the north of the town, the way the ground still caved in there sometimes.

People died in those collapses, several dozen every year.

I pictured myself struggling for a handhold in the falling earth, and supposed Claudia had felt like that a dozen times already today, a hundred, more. I excused myself then went to the bathroom and splashed cold water on my face. The water from the Cowshed's taps had a metallic smell, like old coins kept in a shoebox at the bottom of a wardrobe.

The smell always made the water seem colder than it really was.

* * *

I drank a final cup of tea with Claudia and then walked up to the lunges. The lunges was where Del put the dogs through their time trials, a high stretch of what was once parkland but that had been left to run wild, a wide stretch of couch grass and thistle with panoramic views of the coastline and out to sea. If you look east from the lunges you can see the whole of Sapphire spread out beneath you like a toy town. If you look west you'll see the marshes, stretching all the way to the horizon and beyond.

To the south lies France, just a short distance away across the Channel. Mum once told me that on a clear day you can see France from the top of the lunges but I've never been able to. Perhaps it's never been clear enough. Mum went to France once, just for a day when she was a student.

"What was it like?" I asked her.

She shrugged her shoulders. "We ate sugar buns. In a coffee house. There was a boy there," she said. I urged her to go on with the story but she wouldn't. She seemed cross with me for a while after that, but I knew her crossness usually meant she was feeling sad.

Tash was running Limlasker over hurdles. She was wearing a tatty white vest and a pair of old khaki combats. Her hands lay still at her sides, the nails varnished an opalescent pink and perfectly manicured.

The vest had patches of yellow under the arm holes.

Lim was a large dog but when he was running he seemed barely there, an outline of a dog filled with air, a space in the stuff of the world where a dog should be. You could hear him when he passed right by you – a swift pat-pattering where his feet struck the turf – but otherwise he ran more or less silently, a sleek ghost.

Limlasker means 'salmon' in old Hoolish. There are no salmon in England now, or only in the very far north. The rivers and briny lakes to the south of London are home only to roach and gudgeon and oil pike and a few hardy carp. But whenever I saw Lim in full flight I found no problem imagining what a salmon looked like: a magnificent silver superfish charging upstream.

I knew Tash wouldn't talk to me or to anyone while she was running. I could see Del in the distance, way off up the slope, marking timings. I sat down in the grass to watch. I didn't have a stopwatch, of course, so I couldn't check, but it seemed to me that Lim was running well, better than ever. Del had been easing off on him in recent months, entering him in fewer races, preparing him for retirement. But from where I was sitting he looked to be in peak condition.

It had already been agreed that when Tash started training with Clearview Princess, Limlasker would go back to the Cowshed to live. If he stayed healthy he'd live another ten years, and have a fine time, but of course Lim was lucky. Retired smartdogs remain valuable because of the implant technology, but they are also a problem. Many people, including some of the scientists who helped create them, don't like having smartdogs living with them in their homes. The decent yards sell on their dogs where they can, to cognitive research units, or to rich businessmen in London as pets for their kids. But every year there is a surplus – too many too-old smartdogs. Some are turned loose on the streets, or taken out to the marshes and abandoned.

Most are just shot.

I often wonder if the out-of-towners who come down to Sapphire for a weekend's racing know what happens to smartdogs when their careers are over. I don't suppose they think about it much, any more than they wonder about where the kids who sell them fried dough-balls or racetrack souvenirs go when they clock off for the night. The out-of-towners have never been to Hawthorne or Mallon Way, and they never will.

Thinking about it makes me angry, but I also know that without the out-of-towners and their money the situation in Sapphire would be much worse. Without the dog track and the boardwalk and the string of posh hotels along the Bulvard, the estate kids would have no jobs and no prospect of jobs. Hawthorne was bad enough anyway because of the chemo seepage, but after the tunnels under London Road subsided things became even worse. The road is so unstable now that only the army can navigate it, using those big caterpillar trucks of theirs, and you can guess how high up Hawthorne comes in their list of priorities. In summer you can smell the rubbish tips all the way from the Bulvard, if the wind happens to be blowing in the right direction.

Hawthorne is where you live if you have nowhere else. Del once told me that Tash lived up there for a while with her grandmother when she was a kid. I've never dared ask her about it, though there are abandoned smartdogs up on the estate, I do know that. Skinny as reeds and left to run wild.

When Del saw I was there he pocketed his stopwatch and came over.

"How's she doing?" he said. I knew he meant Claudia. He sat down beside me on the grass, his long legs bunched up, his green eyes watchful, a rangy yellow dog with scrawny limbs.

"She seems okay," I said. "Better."

"Thanks for helping out, Jen." He gazed out across the lunges, to where Lim was still running the hurdles. Tash stood immobile, lean and supple as a young tree, her eyes half closed against the sun, which was sinking over the marshes in a fissile incandescence of soap-coloured light. "Lim took two seconds off his PB today. I mean, two whole seconds."

"That's not possible, Del. Not at his age. It must be a fluke."

"It's not, though. Lim knows what's at stake and he's going all out. He's going to win for us, Jen. He knows he has to win, because of Lumey."

"What's Tash told him?" I knew that for all practical purposes the question was meaningless. What Tash knew, Lim would know too, automatically – that's just a natural part of being a runner. What I was asking, I suppose, was what Del had told Tash.

"Everything," Del said. "It's the safest way."

I thought he was taking a risk but it was too late to worry about that now. I sat side by side with my brother, watching the great silver dog course across the wide green sward and thinking for no reason at all about the old days, before Mum ran out on us and when Del and I were still kids. We had been close then, in a way that quickly receded after our mother left. That would probably have happened anyway, of course. Kids grow up, go their separate ways. Back then though it was just Del and me against the world, and we were fearless with it. We'd slink off and kick around the old waste dumps where our father worked, or else bunk off to Hawthorne to hang out with this kid Del knew who lived up there. Rico, his name was, Rico Chavez. Rico had this dog, Saltash. We used to nick stuff out of the abandoned flats.

I still have something from there, a brass button with a crown on it. From an old army uniform, it looked like. I found it on the floor, under a table. There were a fair few war vets living on the estates then. Most of those old coves are dead now. Sometimes when we were up there gallivanting one of them would come out on to his balcony and yell at us.

We'd run away laughing but some of them were scary as fuck.

Del was such a bright kid, but something nagged at him, deep down. A constant anger at the world that made him restless and wouldn't heal.

Em reckons it was that restless anger that got Del into dealing glass.

Tash let Lim complete one final circuit and then called him to her, silently and without a gesture. They came unhurriedly down the field to where we were sitting.

"Timings are great," Del said.

Tash nodded. She looked down at Limlasker, who

immediately drew closer to her, leaning his silky body against her legs. Tash rested her hand lightly on the top of his head. "He's in good shape," she said. "He'll do okay." I could smell her sweat, a bitter scent, rough as tree bark. Runners tend to perspire a lot during a training session, even though they barely move a muscle.

"Stay for supper, Tash?" Del said.

Tash shook her head. "We should get back." I thought of the house she shared with Brit Engstrom, a shack built from breeze blocks and corrugated iron, about three miles out on the Fairlight Road, at the edge of the marshes. Brit used a bicycle to get to and from town, but Tash liked to use the pitted lane as a running track, Limlasker trotting along by her side with his tongue hanging out.

Brit Engstrom's hair was very blonde and cut very short. She had a sharp, beaky face, and a scattering of powder-fine freckles across the bridge of her nose. She liked to cook using wild roots and herbs she gathered in the marshes. Claudia thought she was mad, that the plants she used in her recipes would be toxic from seepage, but Brit insisted that so long as you knew where to forage there was no real danger.

Brit was a freelance photographer. She took pictures of ruined buildings mainly, and abandoned industrial workings – the burned-out music hall, the rubble-strewn interior of the old Sapphire department store, the rusting gasometers and mining machinery at the town's northern perimeter. She sold a lot of her stuff for good money to advertising and commercial agencies in London. Brit also had a zany sense of humour. I could never quite figure her relationship with

Tash – the two were so different – but I liked her a lot.

Del invited me to stay for supper also, but I said no. I'd had enough of people, and I needed to work. I left Del and Tash to walk down the lunges to the marsh road, while I hiked up to the top of the sward where there was a cut-through to the main road and the Wickham Hill tramway stop. I was home within the hour. There wasn't much in the fridge, just some leftover potato. What with all the ongoing drama there'd been no time to go shopping. I heated a can of oxtail soup and mixed the potato pieces in with that. I watched the six o'clock news as I ate. I kept expecting them to start talking about a four-year-old girl, found murdered, but in the event there was nothing of that kind. When the news had finished I washed the dishes, and then went back to working on Kiwit's gloves.

I placed the completed paper patterns against the flesh side of the leather, pinning them in place as close together as I could without the danger of stretching. Kid leather is expensive, there's no point wasting any if you can help it. Once I'd cut out the pattern pieces I pinned them together using new pins bought especially for the purpose. While I worked I listened to music, an album by the Argentinean singer Paula Komedia that I'd first heard over at Brit and Tash's place. Brit told me the songs were based around the great poetical ballads of Saffron Valparaiso's *A Patagonian Odyssey*. The CD case contained an insert, with the lyrics in the original Spanish on one side and the English translation on the other. Paula Komedia's voice was high and sinuous. On some tracks she sang without accompaniment, on others she performed with a backing group – electric and steel guitars, accordion and flute. Listening to her made me forget where I was. When the phone rang towards the end of the last song I jumped a mile.

I thought it would be Del, calling to check up on me, but it was Em. We hadn't spoken in weeks, not since he left town, really. He'd left messages on my voicemail once or twice but I hadn't responded. This was partly because I was still angry with him for leaving. I knew I had no right to feel that way, but I couldn't help it. I felt abandoned and I was determined to let him know it.

Mainly though it was because I was afraid. Afraid in case Em's feelings for me had changed.

I missed him a lot. I missed his voice and his dry sense of humour, his habit of turning up to cook me meals. Also I missed sex with him. The thought of starting again from the beginning with someone new was both exhausting and depressing.

I was so pleased to hear his voice, though stupidly I did my best not to show it.

"Hey," I said. "How's it going?"

"Is it true, Jen?" Em said. "Derrick's plan for getting hold of the ransom money, I mean?"

For a second I couldn't think what he was talking about. I had no idea that Em and Del were still in touch even.

"It's all right," Em said. "Derrick's told me everything. But you have to talk to him, Jen, he won't listen to me. You have to tell him not to go through with this lunacy of his, that it's too much of a risk. Tell him I'll lend him the money, that I can have it in his bank account tomorrow. Can you do that?"

"I can try," I said.

"Good. That's all I'm asking."

There was a short silence. I was still finding it hard to take in that this was Em on the phone, that we were actually talking. But the longer he stayed on the line the more it began to feel like the old times, before I met Ali and made such a mess of everything.

"Is this what you and Del rowed about, Em?" I said at last. "Del dealing glass, I mean? You found out and told him to stop and he refused?" It was an idea that hadn't occurred to me until that moment but it made perfect sense.

"It was one of the things, yes. But don't worry about that now, it's not important."

"I still don't get it. I mean, Del hates glass. He's always ranting on about how much he hates the street dealers. None of this makes any sense."

I could hear Em's breathing, so close it was as if he were there in the room with me. I felt like crying.

Em sighed. "I think he saw it as a game," he said. "In the beginning he did, anyway. You know how much Derrick loathes the police. He liked the idea of making fools of them. It was only later on that he began to understand how much money he could make. I think the whole business was a prank that spiralled out of control."

I thought there was probably a lot of truth in what Em said. Del had to have something to kick against: first our mother and then the teachers and now the cops. And Del did hate the cops. He thought they were all either thugs or yes men.

"None of that matters now, anyway," Em insisted. "The only thing that matters is getting Lumey back."

"I miss you, Em," I said.

"I miss you too. Let's talk properly when all this is over. Can I call you then?"

"I'd like that."

I pressed the receiver hard against my ear and then ended the call. I went to bed soon after. I put the Paula Komedia album on again, letting the music unfurl itself around me in the dark as I brought myself off; light, barely-touching strokes at first, then right in deep, clenching myself around my fingers as I thought of Em with his schoolmaster's cock, of Paula Komedia as she appeared on the CD cover, her untidy waist-length hair, of the vast South American plains that I had never seen but only read about, heavy with horses, bright with pampas grass, clean and dry and yellow to the horizon.

I woke early, around five. I waited till seven and then called Del. I came straight to the point.

"I spoke to Em last night," I said. "He told me to tell you he'd lend you the money. He says staking everything on the race is too much of a risk."

Del said nothing at first. For a moment I thought he'd put the phone down.

"Are you still there, Del?" I said.

"Yes, I'm still here. I just wish that little prick would mind his own business."

"Don't call him that."

"I'll call him whatever I like. What the fuck's he doing, calling you anyway?"

"I think you should listen to him – he's trying to help you."

"The fuck he is. He doesn't have a clue what's at stake here. Not a clue."

"It didn't sound like that to me."

"Listen, Jen, just drop this, will you? I'm not having Emerson sodding Rayner calling the tune on me and I'm certainly not going to land myself in debt to him. I've told him that already. If you want to do me a favour you can call him back and tell him to piss off."

He sounded furious by then, ready to blow. I had no idea what could have provoked such a reaction, but I knew that anything I tried to say in Em's favour would only make things worse.

"Okay," I said. "Steady on."

"I mean it, Jen."

"I hear you."

He calmed down after that. He told me Claudia had asked if I'd come over at the weekend. "She's having a painting party or something. God knows what that's supposed to be."

I said I'd be round at some point but ended the call without being more specific. I felt furious with Del, not just for calling Em names but because I thought he was behaving irresponsibly. There was nothing new in that, but now was not the time for him to start throwing his weight about.

I was beginning to see that for Del, winning the Delawarr and showing the supply cartel who was boss was in danger of becoming an end in itself. He didn't want to be beaten. Neither did he want to go cap in hand to Em to get himself off the hook.

It was all so stupid, the same kind of impulse that landed him in this mess in the first place, but there was no point worrying about that now. The only question that counted at this stage was whether Del's plan had any chance of succeeding.

Partly this would depend on chance – weather conditions, the quality of the field – but what it finally came down to was Limlasker. Del seemed to believe Limlasker could do it, that he would give everything.

I hoped he was right.

Time went a bit strange after that. I phoned Claudia every day, but as the race drew closer our conversations seemed to become more and more strained. I came to dread them, to be honest. Claudia chattered away about Lumey's homecoming as if it were an established fact, instead of just one of a number of possibilities. I did my best to keep the pretence going but it began to feel wrong, not just putting a brave face on the situation but an actual lie. More and more often there came moments when I found myself wanting to drop the act and tell her the truth the way it was and damn the consequences.

In the end I kept with the programme but it wasn't easy. The idea that Lumey had been gone now for almost a fortnight, with no word or news or reassurance that she was okay – that was something we were all ignoring, even Del.

Del was never in when I called, so I didn't have to talk to him. That at least was a relief.

I worked on Kiwit's gloves, mainly. At the end of a week she came for her fitting. Some gantiers don't bother with a preliminary fitting – they trust to their original measurements and make alterations at the end as and when they are needed. I find the prelim essential though, an important part of every commission. It's not so much to make sure the gloves fit – if you've done your prep work properly that shouldn't be in question – as to get a proper feel for how they will look. I like to see how the colour of the leather suits the client's skin tone, the way the gauntlet hugs the contours of the wearer's arm. These sound like small things, perhaps, but they are crucial, the kind of subtle details that demonstrate the difference between a good craftsperson and a fine artist.

I always look forward to the prelim because it's then that I get to find out how well I've understood the wishes of my client. I never get tired of that moment, and it never stops scaring me. I knew Angela Kiwit was pleased the moment she saw the colour of the leather. She hadn't expected me to understand so exactly what she wanted. Either that or she thought that getting such a perfect colour match would prove impossible. But for me that had been the easy part. I had the colour right – I knew that already.

"Don't worry if they feel a bit loose," I said. "Most of this stitching is just temporary. I won't put the actual seams in until we've checked the fitting." I unrolled the right-hand gant from its muslin and slid it gently on to Angela Kiwit's outstretched arm. For the lining I'd picked out a silk in eau de Nil. Not the most obvious choice, perhaps – my first thought with that neon blue had been flame red – but after thinking it over for a few days the idea had begun to grow on me. Red would form a stronger counterpoint, but eau de Nil would be more subtle, not so much thrusting the blue into the spotlight as giving it depth by lighting it from within. I had the silk I wanted already, an offcut I'd picked up on spec from Romer's remnants bin months before. It was expensive but I liked it so much I couldn't resist it and I knew I'd find a use for it eventually. The silk's base colour – the softest and most subtle of greyish greens – was stippled all over with many dozens of tiny markings in a variety of other colours: violets and greys and mauves, colours that were similar to the green in tone yet formed a stunning contrast with the overall background. Some of the colour flecks looked random, like tiny ink blots or paint spots. Others, when you examined them closely, were formed to look like flowers or snowflakes. The overall effect was like a collage, or an artist's doodle. The silk was utterly gorgeous, a real one-off.

With some types of racing gant the design allows for the top part of the gauntlet to be folded back, forming a deep cuff that serves as a showcase for the lining fabric. I'll sometimes use a different fabric for that part of the lining, as a deliberate contrast, but in the case of Kiwit's gloves I had decided against this. With her strong, very muscular forearms I thought a plainer style would suit her better. Instead of cuffs I inserted a six-inch zip into the outer seam of each glove. The zips, made from solid silver, were of a striking and unusual design. Not only were they decorative in themselves, but if you wore them part way open the tops of the gauntlets could be folded back to reveal the lining.

It might seem like a waste, to spend so much time and effort on a glove's lining when mostly only the wearer would know it was there. But so far as I was concerned that was the beauty of it. The lining of Kiwit's gloves was like a secret weapon. Anyone of a more fanciful turn of mind might see it as a symbol for the innate talent of the runner herself. For me it was the hidden lining, as much as anything, that made the gloves special, and I hoped that Angela Kiwit would feel the same.

"Oh my God," Kiwit said. "They're amazing." She twisted her arm gingerly from side to side, as if she was afraid that any sudden movement might interfere with or destroy what she was seeing. I knew this nervousness would soon disappear, that within a day or two of taking the gloves home her caution would evaporate and she would inhabit them as their owner and not their slave. But just for the moment that look of shyness gave me a feeling of intense pleasure. It was proof that I was doing my job. Not that I needed proof, but it was nice to have.

"They fit well," I said. I lifted her arm towards me, checking first the line of the seam and then the overall flow. The long and narrow sheath lent the glove a heightened elegance, whilst the plain design seemed to emphasize the power and strength of Kiwit's physique.

This was what I had intended, and I felt satisfied with the result. "We can take it off now," I said. I undid the zip, then slipped the glove free of her arm and wrapped it carefully once again in its muslin sleeve. Angela Kiwit watched me in silence. She seemed reluctant to lose sight of the glove and that made me smile. People condemn the desire to own things as simple greed, but sometimes it is more than that, less base. Sometimes it's the only way we can convince ourselves we might live forever.

"They're amazing," Kiwit repeated. I found her hard to make out, to be honest. If you saw her on the street without her gloves on you'd most likely mistake her for an out-of-towner – she had that strut about her, that sense that not only was she used to having money but that she expected to have even more of it in the future. But in those moments when she forgot herself she had what all runners have: not just the pent-up energy, coiled like a snake at the heart of her, but that peculiar absence of being, the sense that what you were seeing was just a foil, that the essential Angela Kiwit resided elsewhere.

On the day she came for her fitting, Kiwit was wearing black jeans and red sneakers and an old grey vest top. Her dyed blonde hair was twisted into a loose knot at the nape of her neck and her roots were showing.

She still looked incredible. Radiant, somehow.

"They'll be ready on Friday," I said. "I'll give you a call."

She laughed, as if I'd said something funny, then leaned forward and kissed me on the cheek.

"Thanks," she said. "I knew you could do it. Perhaps you're my luck."

I smiled, waving the compliment modestly aside the

way you learn to do. It was only later that I realised what she had meant by it: Angela Kiwit was planning on wearing my gloves to run the Delawarr.

Why this had never occurred to me before I had no idea. Why else would she have needed them so urgently? The whole thing was obvious, once you thought about it.

Kiwit's dog, a brindled bitch named Tou-le-Mar, had run the Delawarr Triple the year before. She'd placed fifth, I thought, and when I checked the stats online I found I was right. Tou-le-Mar was a touch on the small side for running hurdles, but she was clever and very agile and extremely fast. She was in with a chance, no doubt about it, and having made it to the final before, Kiwit had to fancy herself – anyone would.

All I knew was, Del was going to go mental when he found out. I briefly considered withdrawing the gloves from sale, returning Kiwit's deposit and preparing myself for an industrial-sized delivery of shit.

I discounted the idea almost at once. What would anyone gain by it, least of all me?

Claudia called to invite me for supper.

"Please come," she said. "I can't wait to show you the room. It's almost finished."

I couldn't see a way to refuse. Lumey's new bedroom gleamed with wood polish and new bedlinen. In a strange way it already looked too young for her, the bedroom of a child who no longer existed. The room sang with cleanliness and colour and good intentions but all the time I was admiring it I could not put away the fear that Lumey would never sleep in that bed or take a book from that bookcase, and that even if she did, whatever had happened to her in the past two weeks would have made it impossible for her to ever be happy in a room like this.

She would never again be the same child, even if on the surface she appeared unharmed.

I told myself not to be an idiot, but it didn't work.

"We're having a little party for her on Monday," Claudia said. "Just Del and me and Hellin. We'd love you to come."

Hellin Tresow was a friend of Claudia's. Del couldn't stand her, for some reason.

"She looks like a backstreet abortionist," he said to me once. He was very drunk. "She gives me the fucking willies."

Apparently, Hellin Tresow was some sort of writer. I thanked Claudia for her invitation and said I'd be there. I figured it didn't matter either way. If Lumey was back then I really would be. If she wasn't then the stupid party wouldn't be happening.

I left straight after supper. I felt queasy with nerves, as if the whole oil-slicked, phosphorescent sea were sloshing around inside my stomach.

The slate of heats for the Delawarr Triple isn't drawn up until the morning of the race itself, although the list of competitors is made public a month before, with any additions appearing online as and when they register. Limlasker went in as a late entry, with Celia Lilac, one of Del's younger dogs, also added to the line-up as a blind. Celia Lilac was just twelve months old and still technically a puppy. Her runner, Tommy Hamid, was eighteen and something of a prodigy. The pair were too young and inexperienced to be anything but rank outsiders, but they looked good together and entering them for the race made perfect sense. In a year or two they might be in with a genuine chance, and to any interested spectators it would look like Del was playing canny. Preparing them for the big time, giving them a taste of the action, whatever. No one would expect them to progress beyond the heats, but they'd be watched. More importantly they would help to divert attention from Tash and Limlasker.

Limlasker was a famous champion and well respected. His late entry into the Delawarr would raise a few eyebrows, but with Tommy and Celia also in the running, most would assume that Del had chosen the Delawarr Triple to be Lim's farewell race, his final lap of honour, if you will. It was a fair enough assumption. No one would be expecting him to place.

I had to admit it was a strong plan. On the night before the race, Del phoned to tell me that Lim had run down the previous year's winning time three times that week in practice sessions.

"And he'll go faster during the race, he always does," Del said. He sounded high as a kite.

"I hope you haven't been overdoing things. You don't want him to peak too soon."

"That dog loves to race, you know that. He thrives on it. Why don't you trust me?"

An edge of irritation had crept into his voice, that tone, so familiar from when we were younger, that said I was a moron and what the hell was the use in him trying to explain anything to me anyway.

I knew he'd get next to no sleep that night, an hour or two around sunrise at the most.

"I do trust you," I said. "I'm just nervous, I suppose."

"Well don't be, and shut the frig up. This thing's a done deal."

"Get some sleep," I said. I wished I could say something more helpful, something that might break through his bravado, not to damage his confidence but to comfort him. I could barely imagine how lonely he must be feeling. He couldn't even talk to Limlasker, because Lim was with Tash.

The heats for the Delawarr used to be seeded, but there was always some controversy raging about how the rankings were arrived at, and so the system was dropped in favour of random computer selection. That seemed to work okay for a while, then someone accused someone else of hacking the program and loading the draw. Whichever system was used, the only certainty was that somebody somewhere would object to it. That's why the race board finally brought in the Rooster.

The Rooster is basically the same as the machine that's used for selecting the National Lottery, with the added attraction of it letting out a deafening klaxon blast at the end of each cycle – hence the name.

The name of each competitor is printed on to a plastic

ball, and to avoid any accusations of ball-tampering, each ball is weighed in public on an electronic scale. Once they've been weighed, the balls are loaded into the Rooster. The machine is operated by pulling a lever – the name of the person who gets to do that is decided by a prize draw. The balls speed round and round inside a transparent plastic drum. At the end of sixty seconds, balls are released into a drawer at the bottom in batches of six. The drawer is opened and the names read out. The prelim heats go up on the board in the order they are called.

The whole process takes about two hours, which sounds a lot but it's become part of the ritual now, people look forward to it. The dogs themselves stay out of sight in their pens until their heat is called.

As the race day dawned, there were one hundred and eighty registered participants for the Delawarr Triple. That made thirty preliminary heats, ten hurdles each over eight hundred metres. The first two from each heat would go through to the quarters – ten heats of six, again over eight hundred metres. The winner of each quarter, plus the two fastest losers overall, would then progress to the semis. The final field would be made up of the first-, second- and third-placers from each semi.

Every year you get someone calling for the system to be changed, because it's inevitable that one semi is slower than the other. But the public prefer a straight race over clocked times any day, not just because it avoids any allegations of clock-fixing but because it's more exciting.

The first prelim heats normally kick off around eleven. The quarters run from three till five, with the two semis lining up at six and six-thirty. The Delawarr Triple runs off at seven-thirty on the dot.

It's a huge day. As a kid I used to love it, the atmosphere most of all, that sense of being a part of something big. The end of June is often claggy and sulphurous, but not always. I remember race days during my childhood when the sky was a high pale blue and more or less cloudless. Dad was still a fit and healthy man back then. He'd give Del and me money for cracknels and race-day souvenirs and when we were a little older he'd let us place a bet on the race itself. Normally we weren't allowed to gamble but the Delawarr was an exception, a special occasion. Mum never came to the race, but she didn't harp on about the dogs the way she did most Saturdays, and she'd always have a late supper waiting for us when we got back.

She'd even tell us stories about her own first race day, before she met my dad and got pregnant with Del.

"I was crazy about one of the runners," she said. "Melton Craigh was his name." It was the same story every year but I still loved to hear it. I found a photo of Melton Craigh in one of the old racing magazines. He ran the Delawarr two years running but didn't place. He died aged thirty, from a degenerative condition of the spine. I wondered if my mother knew this – I never asked her. Melton Craigh in the photo had sticking-out elbows and very straight, very pale blond hair, as pale as Brit Engstrom's. He looked exactly the kind of person who would die young.

Years later and long after she left us, Del told me that Mum's famous crush on Melton Craigh had all been a lie.

"Craigh's career was over before she even arrived here,"

he said. "The first time she was ever at the track, Craigh was already bent double in a hospital bed."

"Why would she lie, though?" I asked him. Del just shrugged. I checked up on what he'd said and found he was right. Melton Craigh died before we were born.

After my telephone conversation with Del I thought I'd have trouble getting to sleep but I didn't. I remember putting the radio on. The next thing I knew it was morning and I was awake. I went to the window and looked out at the dawn sky, blooming with pale-bellied clouds, blotched silver-white and slightly glistening, like the skins of fishes.

It would be a fine day.

I arrived at the track just after eight. There was already a queue at the turnstiles. I stood in line and waited. The early clouds had mostly vanished and the heat was rising. Eventually I reached the head of the line. I could tell from the cheers inside the stadium that they'd already started weighing the balls for the Rooster. I wondered if Lim's name had been loaded yet. I knew Del would have been at the track since before seven, getting the dogs booked in and settled in their pens.

Behind me in the queue a small group of out-of-towners were exchanging animated remarks about the breakfast they'd eaten in one of the expensive cafes along the Bulvard.

"Delicious," said one of the women, a shiny blonde with a diamond nose stud and elaborate eye makeup. "It's perfectly safe here. Clive clearly didn't have a clue what he was talking about."

I wondered. For a moment I tried to imagine what it might feel like to change places with her, to run away like my mother in nothing but the clothes I stood up in.

A whole new life on the toss of a coin. I wondered what Clive would have to say about that.

Limlasker was slated to run in the third heat, Celia Lilac in the eighth, both good draws in that they were early. The thing with unseeded heats is that they're totally random, and obviously this can go either way. As it turned out, Lim was drawn against five novices – three pups in their first year of competition, and two three-year-olds, a dog and a bitch, both owned by out-of-town syndicates and running in the Delawarr Triple for the first time.

Lim galloped home, more than two full seconds ahead of the second-placer, the particoloured three-year-old bitch Trudi-Delaney.

"He was confused, I reckon," Tash said when I went down to the kennels to see them after their heat. "He wondered where the hell the rest of them had got to." She smiled, her long, slightly crooked teeth flashing in her dark face. The gear she was wearing could have been her training togs – black leather shorts and Adidas plimsolls, an ancient pair of gants in deep burgundy that Del told me had been a gift from her grandmother – but she looked powerful as a raincloud and taut with energy. Her hair was pulled back from her face in a gold bandeau. She was spectacular. I began to feel excited, to relax even. There was still a long way to go but the omens seemed good.

Of the two, Celia Lilac's heat turned out to be the tough one. Only two complete novices, and of the other three in the heat the dog, Melrose, was a former silver medallist. He was a stunning beast, pure black, still very leggy, and two hands taller at least than Celia Lilac. Even I could tell that Tommy was bricking it. It was a fast heat, one of the fastest of the morning, a three-way race between Melrose, Celia Lilac and a four-year-old bitch named Rachel Slim-Rachel. Melrose won the heat, but Celia Lilac finished second, just half a nose in front of Rachel Slim-Rachel.

Tommy was ecstatic and showing it. Del was not pleased.

"Cool it, will you, Tommy? You're going to wear the dog out. Calm down."

Celia Lilac was back in her pen by then, but Tommy was so high on adrenalin even I could feel it, all that loose energy pouring off him like sweat off a racehorse. Celia would be feeling that tenfold, perhaps more. Tommy might as well inject her with raw amphetamine.

Watching the heat made my heart race, but afterwards I felt more subdued. I wasn't thinking about Celia or Tommy but about Melrose, the one-time silver-medallist with the coat like black satin. He'd taken his heat with the same ease as Limlasker and with half a second in hand. I knew it was pointless to compare times between heats – a good dog will always come out faster in a fast heat, it stands to reason – but it was still a worry. Melrose's runner, the veteran Kris Kruger, looked cool as November. Melrose hadn't won big for a while but he was looking superb.

* * *

The remaining heats seemed to flash by. I'd more or less forgotten about Angela Kiwit until I saw her, coming out of the tunnel and taking her place at the trackside with the other runners from her heat, the twenty-sixth, which would have been a tough call for anyone.

Lowell Baker was the favourite in that one, with Lamborghini, but Kiwit seemed relaxed and I could tell by the way Baker kept glancing at her that he considered her his main rival.

As I'd predicted, she was wearing my gloves. Teamed with patent black knee-high lace-up Doctor Martens and a skin-tight black body stocking they looked incredible, and as Kiwit raised her right hand to the crowd I felt a shiver of pure pride slide down between my shoulder blades like melting ice cubes. As they released the dogs from the traps I suddenly knew that Tou-le-Mar was going to win the heat, that she would beat Baker's Lamborghini by a mile, and that's what happened. The crowd went insane. Lamborghini came in second, so he was through to the quarters, but it wasn't Lamborghini people were cheering for. He was an old dog now, after all, and there were already rumours that Lowell Baker was planning to retire at the end of the season.

Angela Kiwit, on the other hand, was a rising star. She loved her public and her public loved her.

She had what you might call watchability. A regular little People's Princess.

* * *

It wasn't until after lunch that things started getting tense. The running order of the prelim heats decides the line-up for the quarters. The field is divided equally in three, with the first- and second-placers from the first heat being matched with the firsts and seconds from heats eleven and twenty-one, and so on down the line. This meant that Celia Lilac would be running against Melrose again and this time she would almost certainly go out. Del wasn't bothered about that so much, but I could see he was worried about Melrose, the same as I was.

"That's a good dog," he said. The heat winners were being paraded around the track by their runners ahead of the official announcement of the quarter line-ups, as was the custom, and I saw the way Del was watching not just Melrose, but Kris Kruger too. The man was over fifty. He was wearing a pair of distinctly ordinary charcoal-grey gants, bought off-the-peg from Gallant's most likely, and with his shaven head and untidy stubble he looked like one of the drunks you'll see sometimes on the quayside at Folkestone, repatriated POWs straight off the boat from Argentina. They have a haunted look about them, those guys. It's as if they don't believe the war is really over, even though the rest of the world insists upon it.

Kruger was a bit like that – scary.

The running order for the quarters is reversed, to make things fairer, which meant that Limlasker, who'd run in the third prelim, would now be running in the eighth quarter-final. Celia Lilac and Melrose would run in the sixth. Lim's heat didn't look too bad on paper. There was Trudi-Delaney, who he'd already beaten by a mile in the prelims, and of the other four dogs he would be running against only one looked dangerous, a bitch named Phoolan Devi who had beaten Lim once before, three years or so back in the Keel Sweepstake. Phoolan Devi was very tall for a bitch, almost half a hand taller than Lim in fact. She was fawn in colour, with liquid brown gold-flecked eyes, the same eyes as her runner, Adriana Welitsch.

I'd wanted to make gloves for Adi Welitsch since forever. I kept hoping someone would recommend her but for some weird reason of her own she preferred to wear off-the-peg, like Kris Kruger only not so appalling. For the Delawarr, Welitsch was wearing elbow-length Plascars in vermilion red, which were okay really for readymades, but I couldn't help thinking about what I could do for her if only she'd let me.

I should have been worried about Phoolan Devi but I wasn't. I had another of those hunches I sometimes get, the same as with Lamborghini only stronger, a piercing certainty that came out of nowhere and struck like lightning. Some might say this is my Hoolishness coming out in me, but I don't know about that, I prefer not to analyse it. All I know is that these are feelings I never ignore. I sensed it in my gut, that Phoolan Devi would run like the devil but Lim would run faster. He would beat her easily, as easily as he'd beaten Trudi-Delaney in the prelim, and the stands would go wild.

It was as clear to me as if someone had walked up and handed me the next day's newspaper.

But that was all still to come. Before that was Celia's heat, Tommy Hamid lined up against Melrose and Kris Kruger. Celia seemed nervous going into the race, very jumpy, which was Tommy's fault mainly, and Celia was behind from the start. The race turned out to be mostly between Melrose and Saint Aquila, a dirt-coloured, rail-thin dog out of prelim fifteen. Melrose won, putting in a time not quite as fast as in his prelim but still a quarter-second faster than Limlasker's.

"What d'you reckon?" Del said to me as the placings went up on the electronic scoreboard. I knew what he meant without having to ask – was Kris Kruger on glass?

I shook my head. "Not him," I said. "He's clean." Glass users give off loose energy like static. Kruger seemed cold as iron, battle-hardened but not hyped, not at all. He was good at what he did, simple as that. Barring some freak accident, Melrose was going to end up in the final. All we could hope was that Lim wouldn't be drawn to run against him in the semis as well.

Tash seemed a bit on edge before her quarter, but no more than you'd expect, given the circumstances. Limlasker himself seemed perfectly calm. There was a slight delay in raising the gates – someone forgot to reset the clock, apparently – but once they were away the result was more or less decided in the first hundred metres. Phoolan Devi seemed slow and heavy beside Lim, who beat her by a full second and exceeded his own time for the prelim.

The crowd, as I had predicted, went berserk.

Angela Kiwit won her heat also, beating Gray's Inn from Lamborghini by a quarter-second.

* * *

The semis are time-selected, the fastest dog running in the first semi, the second-fastest running in the second, and so on. Melrose and Kruger had the fastest time overall, just one-tenth of a second faster than Limlasker and Tash. This worked to our advantage of course, because it meant that Melrose and Lim would be in different semi finals. Angela Kiwit, who had the third-fastest time in the quarters, would run against Kruger.

Melrose was the bookie's favourite but the odds against Tou-le-Mar had shortened considerably. The second semi was less easy to call. Limlasker had clocked the fastest time overall, but the other five dogs were so evenly matched it was difficult to draw a marker between them. One of the bitches, Empress of Ice Cream, was a previous Delawarr winner. She'd missed out on the early part of the season because of a hamstring injury but she'd been back at the track the last three weekends for warm-up races and won everything in sight.

Tash had fallen into a deep silence. That was normal before a race, but there was always something unnerving about seeing her in that state, so sheathed against the outside world it was almost as if she'd gone into a trance. It was just her and Lim now. Even after the dog was placed in the trap and the gate closed the two of them would remain a single entity, their thoughts shifting between them like spirals of drifting gas.

The idea of victory in the abstract is foreign to dogs. They understand about winning food, about winning love, but winning just for itself has no meaning for them. When dogs run for themselves they run together. They do not keep an account of which runs fastest. Much of the runner's skill lies in filling their dog with the human lust for being best.

The task for Tash was to fill Limlasker's heart and mind with the thought of Lumey.

The first semi turned out to be a record breaker, Melrose and Tou-le-Mar in a photo finish, followed by Chacqu'un a son Gout just a tenth of a second behind. The crowd was on its feet. I saw Kiwit, down by the finish line, turning cartwheels.

Lim came third in his semi. The first place was taken by Empress of Ice Cream, with Betty Talbot following in second. It was a slower race than the first semi, with the Empress's time half a second down on Melrose and Kruger's.

Del's hands were clenched into fists.

"Don't worry," I said. "It's okay. They're going to make it." I put my hand on his arm. I could feel the tension in his body, the taut hum of it, like electricity inside a wire. We never touch each other much, Del and I, and I thought he might shrug me off, but he didn't. It was as if he had finally gained a true awareness of what was at stake.

I should have been afraid too, but I felt calm inside, calm as still water. I knew with certainty that Lim had not been outrun, that he'd been holding back, saving himself for the final. I knew this like I knew my own name. Restraint of this kind would not come naturally to an ordinary dog, but Lim was a smartdog and he had Tash to guide him. I had the feeling Tash knew pretty much all there was to know about restraint, that there had been times in her life when her survival had depended on it.

"They're going to make it," I said again. I spoke softly, so that only Del could hear me, and little by little I felt him begin to relax.

I had become the strong one, the fierce one. I think at that moment Del felt convinced that I could save Lumey simply by the power of my own belief.

When I look back on it now, the thing I remember most clearly is that woman in the baseball cap, shrieking as if she'd been shot. The sound of her screams, muffled and heavy, floating up towards me like weed through water.

What was done took less than a second and by the time we realised what had happened it was already over. There was a token effort to find the criminal, to search the ground, but of course it proved fruitless. Whoever committed the crime had the advantage of foreknowledge. They also knew how to blend into the crowd, to cancel their existence in that place, to emerge again through the turnstiles as somebody else.

Just another innocent bystander going about their business, melting away into the blurry purple light of a summer evening.

The gates went up. Melrose and Tou-le-Mar were first away, both running flat out. They stayed pretty much level at first, but after two hundred metres or so Melrose began to flag. It was possible that he'd suffered a tendon strain – greyhounds are susceptible to leg injuries – but most likely he was just tired. He'd run four top-flight races in under four hours and he was not a young dog. He'd given all he had to give. He was worn out.

Tou-le-Mar by contrast still looked fresh as paint. More than that, she looked confident and it was easy to see she had power in reserve. Lim was hanging back just a little, loping along in the fourth lane and keeping in line with Betty Talbot, pace for pace. Betty had won a couple of high-profile races both this season and last; she was what you might call a promising newcomer, although I don't think anyone would have predicted her making it into the final of the Delawarr, not this year, anyway. She was a pretty dog, too, a bright, almost yellowish fawn with a dappling of lighter spots across her hindquarters. I bet Rudy Shlos is pleased as piss, I thought. Rudy was Betty's yardmaster, a drinking buddy of Del's and, as Del himself once put it, a moody bugger, but bloody talented. He'd been a runner himself in his youth, which probably accounted for his unpredictable temperament.

The Empress of Ice Cream and Chaqu'un a son Gout were running fifth and sixth. As they took the third set of hurdles I saw that the Empress had overreached herself. As she steadied herself on the farther side of the jump she was already half a length behind Chaqu'un and still losing ground.

Melrose too was weakening, the liquid, weightless glide-flight of his earlier heats steadily giving way to an effortful gallop. The strain on Kris Kruger was clear just from looking at him – the sheen of sweat on his brow, the rigid set of his shoulders, the way he kept chewing at his lower lip. I guessed this was probably his last race and I almost felt sorry for him.

As they reached the six hundred mark, Tou-le-Mar had begun to nose ahead, imperceptibly at first, then by a couple of inches. By the time they took the next set of hurdles, Melrose was running third behind Betty Talbot. That was when Limlasker made his move, diving past Melrose and snaking in alongside Betty. Then suddenly he was past her, chasing down Tou-le-Mar, the younger dog skittish and wild, feasting on Kiwit's energy like a brumby on sweetcorn. For the breadth of a heartbeat it seemed as if she might hold her lead, then Limlasker, brave Limlasker, soared up out of second place and drew level.

As they reached the last set of hurdles it was a two-dog race, Tou-le-Mar and Limlasker, the dancing girl and the ghost dog, heading for the final straight with less than an inch between them.

The final hurdles are at one thousand metres. After that it's a hundred-and-fifty-metre flat race to the finish. I gazed at Lim, the three-seasons champion flat racer, and realised he'd saved it all for this moment, for the moment he knew he'd be in his element, when he could chase down anything still in his sights and not even feel winded. As Lim took the final hurdle I glanced at Tash. Her arms were bunched at her sides as if she were running, but there was no stiffness in her stance, only alertness, and her expression, which before the race had been like stone, now seemed exalted. There was no smile on her lips, but the certainty of victory, the sheer joyous knowing, lay so clearly upon her face it was as if it had been painted there.

As his front feet touched the ground, Lim went down. The sight was so crazily unexpected my mind refused at first to acknowledge that it was real. I started forward, trying to see what had happened, and only then did I realise that Limlasker had fallen, that he was lying sprawled across the track in a tangle of his own limbs.

He was lying so still.

Still as an eiderdown, still as twigs.

Somewhere off to my left a woman screamed. I turned towards her instinctively. She was wearing jeans that were too tight for her and a red baseball cap and too much makeup. Whoever told her she looked good as a bike bunny had been sadly mistaken.

Then I saw Tash. She was lying on her side in the grass, her long feet in their tatty hi-tops pointed uselessly towards the track. Someone was kneeling beside her, one of the track jerries.

Somewhere in another world Tou-le-Mar was crossing the finish line. Angela Kiwit glanced up at the time clock then fell to her knees. Melrose put on a late spurt to snatch a surprise second from Betty Talbot. Chaqu'un and the Empress brought up the rear.

"He's been shot," Del cried, and he really was crying, though I don't think he knew it, hard little splinter-tears, forcing themselves out of his eyes like slivers of light. His face was ghastly, pale with an emotion I could not identify, fury and terror crumpled together like shredded paper.

"They've killed him, Jen, those bastards."

Then he was shoving past the barrier and on to the track and so was I. I was horrified by the thought of what I might see, but I knew I couldn't let my brother face it alone.

The track was in chaos. There were track jerries everywhere, some standing in a line with their arms linked trying to keep back the gawkers, others huddled together in a group around the fallen Limlasker. Off to one side I could see two medics lifting Tash on to a stretcher. From what I could make out she was awake, beginning to regain consciousness anyway. I wondered where Brit was, if anyone had called her. She didn't usually come to races, it wasn't her thing.

The overhead TV screens had all gone dark.

Del dashed across the track to where Lim was lying. One of the jerries stepped forward to try and restrain him but Del just pushed him aside without a word. The man staggered and almost went flying. Hot colour was rising in his cheeks and I saw him reach for his tazer. I shot out a hand and grabbed his arm.

"Don't," I said. "He's the dog's owner." My head was swimming. Inside my mind my words seemed unreal, lines from a soap script. They must have made sense to the jerry though, because he let us go past. I hurried to where Del was – on his knees in the dirt beside Limlasker. There was someone else there too, one of the blue-coated veterinarians who normally spend most of a race day hanging out in the drinks tent. He had a stethoscope pressed to Lim's chest.

As I came to a standstill beside Del, the vet shook his head.

"The dog's dead, I'm afraid," he said. "A great pity." He was stroking Lim's sides and back, patting his fur with neat, swift touches, and I wondered if I'd misunderstood somehow, if Lim was alive after all and the vet was trying to bring him round. But then the vet suddenly stopped what he was doing and straightened up.

"There," he said. He was holding something between his fingers, something that glimmered. "It went in at the belly. Whoever managed a shot like that was no amateur, I can tell you." He held the thing up to the light, a tiny shard of plastic, or perhaps glass, it was hard to tell just by looking. Whatever it was, the vet was saying it had killed Limlasker. I was still finding it all but impossible to grasp what had happened.

My throat filled up with tears.

"We'll initiate an investigation, of course," the vet was saying. He opened his bag and took out a small plastic screw-top container, the kind of thing normally used for storing medicines. He undid the lid and dropped the plastic dart inside. "I really am very sorry," he said. He started to walk away then, but Del grabbed his arm.

"Hold it right there," he bellowed. "I don't even know your name."

The man started backwards in Del's grip. He looked wary, but not scared, and I guessed he'd had to deal with situations like this before.

"Ezra Forrest," he said. He took what looked like a business card from the top pocket of his blue overall and handed it to Del. "We should have the results for you by

Monday. If you've not heard from us by three o'clock, please feel free to call."

Monday, I thought. I had the feeling I was supposed to be doing something on Monday, but I couldn't for the life of me think what it was. Then I remembered that Monday was the day of the party Claudia was meant to be throwing for Lumey's homecoming.

Del stood holding the veterinarian's business card and saying nothing. There was a bewildered look on his face, as if he was struggling to remember where he was, and there was something in the sight of him that broke me in two.

I knew a part of my brother had died with Limlasker, that the person I had known was gone for good.

The shard of high-density Perspex the vet removed from Limlasker's dead body was soon identified as a dart from a Wiskop gun. Lightweight and easily concealed, the Wiskop had long been the weapon of choice for many mercenaries, insurgents and contract killers, and whoever fired the fatal shot, as the vet had suggested, was most likely a professional – Lim had been travelling at close to seventy miles an hour when the dart went in.

The Wiskop fires on compressed air, which makes it virtually soundless. The poison contained in the dart – a nerve agent – acts more or less instantaneously.

Tash was okay. At the time the attack happened she was so wired into Lim's thoughts, so much a part of him that the suddenness of his death gave her a kind of mental whiplash.

There was no lasting injury though, and three months after the Delawarr she started regular training with Clearview Princess. She never talked about what happened to Limlasker but then she never talked that much anyway. She told Del she didn't want to compete in any races for a year.

"I need some time and so does Princess," she said. Del agreed on the spot.

We never discovered who fired the shot or who had hired them. Kris Kruger sent Tash flowers when she was in the hospital. Some months later – after Brit left, that is – they started dating.

The track jerries removed Lim's body from the track and took it away. One of them gave me a number I could call to reclaim it after the post-mortem. The cops took a note of our names and addresses and then buggered off. Del kept asking me where Tash was, and I kept telling him she'd been taken to the meds tent. He was clearly in shock, which made me feel panicky, because losing it was not an option. We had things to do.

"Listen, Del," I said. "I think we'd better ring Em."

"What the hell for?" Del said. He sounded as if he'd been drugged.

"The money, Del, remember? We have to get the money by Monday." I spoke as gently as I could, but I felt like shaking him. My brother was in deep trouble, the deepest.

Fortunately we still had an escape route. Or so I thought at the time.

Del's face seemed to darken. His expression changed from baffled to enraged. "I'm not taking coin from that bastard."

"If you have any other suggestions to make then now would be a good time to share them."

He stared at me speechlessly for several seconds and then waved his hand in front of his face as if batting away a fly. *Stuff it*, he was saying. *Do what you want, see if I care. Go to the devil.*

It took us ages to get away from the ground. The cops were everywhere by then, pulling people over, asking their questions, conducting random searches for weapons. Every time we got through one lot we seemed to come face to face with another. Fat lot of good they did, any of them. It was almost as bad outside the stadium – great crowds of people scurrying around like headless chickens, tweeting and snapping photos, speculating noisily about the identity and current whereabouts of the gunman. The bookies were besieged – no bets could be paid out until the track stewards were able to confirm that the race result would be allowed to stand, and that didn't look like happening any time soon. There were journos everywhere too, suddenly. It was total chaos.

Del and I ended up at a cafe just around the corner from the Ryelands, a place I remembered from when I worked there and where some of us liked to go for a late evening snack when we finished our shift. I sat Del down at a corner table and fetched him a coffee, then went back outside to call Em. The signal was better outside. Also I didn't fancy anyone eavesdropping.

Em answered on the second ring.

"Jen," he said. I could tell from the tone of his voice that he already knew – most likely he'd seen the whole thing on TV.

"Hi, Em," I said, just that, and then I started to cry, in great gutsy sobs too, like my heart was breaking. I hadn't cried like that since Ali Kuzman told me it was over between us. All I can remember thinking was that I hoped my tears wouldn't leak into the phone and fuck with the workings. It's funny, the things that come into your head at a time like that. Em didn't say a word – just let me cry until I was out of tears. We were able to talk after that. I was feeling a lot better, the way you always do after a good howling fit. I started telling Em he would need to get the money to Del the moment he could because the people who were holding Lumey would more than likely insist on being paid in cash. Del would have to draw it out of the bank in several chunks or it would look suspicious.

Em brought me up short.

"Everything's in hand, Jen," he said. "The money, I mean. Can you get Del to call me?"

"He'll call you," I said. I promised I'd ring him back later. I ended the call and went back into the cafe. Del was on the phone. As I approached the table he flung down his handset. It collided with his coffee cup with a dense little thud. A dark dribble of coffee began to trickle down from the rim towards the surface of the table.

"Who was that?" I said.

Del glared at me as if I'd said something obscene.

"Crace," he said.

"Who's Crace?"

"He's the guy who's arranging the handover, who do you think?"

"Did you tell him we've got the money?"

"Yes, Jen, I told him we've got the money. But it's no fucking good."

"I don't know what you mean."

"What I mean is they've reneged on the deal. Lumey's gone."

He stood up from the table, shoving it forward and scraping his chair loudly against the tiles. The coffee cup tipped over. Brown liquid coursed across the Formica and cascaded on to the floor in a frothy stream. Del looked at me as if I were vermin then pushed past me and headed for the door. The coffee cup rolled in a slow arc then fell off the table and smashed. I stood still where I was, only dimly aware that people were staring at me. I saw Del walk past along the pavement outside and then out of sight.

As I turned to go after him I noticed he'd left his mobile behind on the table. I picked it up, and after a moment's consideration I pressed the redial key. There was the familiar hum and click as it tried to connect, then an automated voice told me that the number I was calling was no longer available.

It was difficult to know what to do. I stood outside on the street, trying to make sense of what had happened. People swept by in their dozens, finally leaving the area of the race ground in search of food, or friends, or the quickest way home. Del's words rang in my head, that Lumey was gone. I still didn't understand what he meant, and now he was gone, too. In the end I did the only thing I could think of, and rang Em again. He picked up at once. It was almost as if he'd been waiting for my call.

I told him what I knew, which wasn't much.

"Go home, Jen," he said, when I'd finished. "Leave Del to me. I'll call him right now."

I suddenly felt as if I might start crying again. "But I can't just leave him," I said. "I should do something."

"We can't do anything until we know what's going on. I'll call him and try to find out. I'll ring you back as soon as I know what the situation is."

"You can't call him, though. He left his phone behind. I've got it here."

"Then I'll try his work mobile, or the house number. I'll find him, Jen, don't worry."

"Do you promise?"

"Yes, I promise. Please go home. I'll feel easier in my mind if I know where you are."

In the end I agreed, not because I thought it was the right thing to do necessarily, but because I was exhausted and upset and at the end of my rope. I kept going over everything in my mind, wondering how many other details Del had neglected to tell me, how much of his original story had even been true. Nothing felt real any more. All I knew was that I'd been a fool to go along with my crazy brother's so-called plan.

If I'd said no at the start, perhaps we wouldn't be in this mess now. I couldn't help thinking that it – whatever it was – was somehow my fault.

Finally I was home. I made myself some supper and slumped in front of the television, watching an idiotic sitcom and waiting for something to happen. I was pleased to be inside my own apartment, relieved and comforted by the sight of familiar objects, the smell of food, the locked front door. My relief made me feel guilty but I could not let go of it.

Del's mobile wouldn't stop ringing. Each time it went off I jumped, thinking it might be a call from the mysterious Crace, but the display screen told me the various callers were all people I knew. Gra Rayner must have phoned a dozen times at least. There were also calls from Del's deputy, Lars Andersen, Lars's wife Leah, Hellin Tresow. I didn't pick up. It was Del's job to talk to them, not mine. What was I supposed to tell them, anyway? I had no idea.

At around eleven o'clock Em called me on the landline. He told me he'd been trying to get hold of Del all evening but with no success.

I went to bed soon after that. I stayed fully clothed, partly because I couldn't be bothered to undress but also because I kept expecting Del to turn up, or the police, and I didn't want to be caught half naked when they did. Nobody came, though. I dozed on and off for a couple of hours then showered and changed. It was beginning to get light again. I thought of calling Em, but I didn't want to wake him, and the idea of ringing Del made me feel afraid. It sounds stupid now I know, but I kept having this terrible fear that they were both dead, Del and Claudia I mean, that Del had murdered Claudia and then killed himself.

In the end the only choice left to me was to get myself over to Del's place and find out. I was in a right state by then, and I reckoned that whatever I found when I got there, nothing could be as bad as the things I was imagining.

Claudia answered the bell.

"Jennafer," she said. "Derrick's not here." She peered out at me through the gap, warily, as if she couldn't quite believe it was really me standing there. She was wearing a light-blue smock dress, freshly ironed, and blue rattan sandals. There was a large, fresh bruise on one cheek. I knew immediately that she was different, that she'd changed somehow. She'd never called me Jennafer before in her life.

"You'd better come in, I suppose," she said eventually. She stepped away from the door and I went inside. I went to hug her and then drew back. She didn't want me near her, I could tell. It was weird. It was like she'd become someone else, someone who didn't like me all that much.

"Derrick's out looking for Lumey," she said. "That's what he says, anyway." We were in the kitchen by then. I glanced about me, searching I suppose for signs of disorder in the house and not finding any. Claudia paced brusquely back and forth, fixing coffee. Every now and then she raised a hand to touch the bruise on her cheek. She didn't look at me once the entire time.

"Has there been any news yet?" I asked. "Do you know where she is?"

My questions sounded stupid and tactless, even to me. Claudia appeared to ignore them and I didn't blame her.

"I had a phone call last night," she said eventually. She handed me a mug of coffee. "It was a woman. She advised me not to try looking for my daughter, because she was already far away and I would never find her. She said she was being well looked after and wouldn't be harmed. As a mother herself, she thought I at least had the right to know that my child was alive and would remain alive. She said she was sorry for what I was going through, but it couldn't be helped. Then she put the phone down. I keep hoping she'll call back, but I know she won't."

She looked at me then, bang in the eye. I stared down at the floor.

"Derrick tried to snatch the phone off me," Claudia said. "That's how I got this." She fingered her bruised cheek again. "I told him to go fuck himself. I know you'll find that hard to believe – your brother's mousy little wife using the 'f' word on him, but it's true. I told him he could go fuck himself. The phone didn't matter by then, anyway. The line was dead."

"Claudia, I am so sorry." It was all I could think of to say and once again she ignored me.

"I'm not going to ask you any questions, because I know you don't know anything other than what your brother told you in the first place, and a fat lot of good that's turned out to be. Neither of you even know why Lumey was taken."

"It was the glass suppliers," I said. "They were keeping her until Del paid them."

"The glass bust was a put-up job," Claudia said. "Derrick

found that out a week ago. The criminals who sold him the drug bribed the police to bust him because it gave them a perfect cover. They knew he'd never dare get the police involved when Lumey was taken – he was in too deep with the glass people. They also knew it would take time to raise the ransom money. All the time they needed to get Lumey away."

"I don't get it," I said. I felt stunned. Not just by what she was telling me but that she knew – that she knew, in fact, a hell of a lot more than I did. I realised that my hands were shaking.

"Lumey can communicate with the dogs without an implant," Claudia said. "Something like that, anyway. I've seen her doing it. I'm assuming that makes her valuable and that's why she was stolen."

I gaped at her.

"You think I'm so stupid," she said. "You and Derrick, so busy trying to nursemaid me you didn't even see what was under your noses. I've known for a long time what Lumey can do. You only have to watch her for five minutes. I know it's real. I think that's why it took her so long to start speaking normally. She thinks the way she speaks with the dogs *is* normal, that it's us who can't talk. You and Del were so wrapped up in your own lives you never noticed. Someone else did, though. Too bad. Still, at least they did me the courtesy of letting me know my daughter hasn't been raped and murdered."

"Scallion." The word burst from me, like a curse.

"What?"

"Scallion – Carson Stringer's dog. Lumey said her first ever word to Scallion. I know because I was there." It seemed important, somehow, to stress that. It was all coming back to me, that day at the yard, Lumey lifting up her arms to that massive red dog and saying 'run'. Something had passed between them, something extraordinary – I felt it happen, but I chose to ignore it. Most likely Del had felt it too, and done the same. Only Claudia had come anywhere close to guessing the truth.

I was beginning to see myself as she must see me – the person who had pretended to be her friend but who instead had patronized and betrayed her.

She was right – I had thought she was stupid, or if not stupid then weak. I had misjudged her, because she was different from me, mainly – because she had a gentler and more accepting way of being.

I longed to apologise, to say sorry, but I had the feeling it was already too late. Claudia had closed her mind to me forever.

"I want you to go now, Jenna," she was saying. "I don't mean forever, and I'm not blaming you for what's happened, not really. I know you only did what you thought was right. Just leave us alone for a bit, okay? I'm sick of being lied to."

I nodded and put down my cup. "What are you going to do?" I said.

"I don't know. Right now I can't even think without it hurting." She paused. "You and Del, you're bad for each other. I know it was tough on you growing up, with your mum leaving and everything, but that's all in the past now. You should let it go."

Just for a moment I felt the purest, brightest anger flare

up inside me. What could she know of the two of us, how dare she presume? Then I did what she said and let it go.

"You're probably right," I said. I went soon after that. I walked away up the drive then took the tramway down to the Bulvard and had breakfast in one of the cafes there. It was Sunday, and hot. The entire place seemed to be swarming with out-of-towners.

The Romney Marshes are not all the same. To the north of Sapphire they're pretty much what you might expect – stony scrublands now rather than actual marshes, bleak, grey wastelands punctuated by the rusting, pylon-like structures that are all that remain of the shale gas industry. Once you get as far as Tonbridge it's not so bad. The land is less polluted, and when you travel through on the tramway you see things – stone-built cottages and cart tracks, a bicycle leaning against a gate, a tiny granite church with a square tower – that make you realise there really are still people living out there, still living their lives as normal, in spite of what the newspapers try to tell you.

Still, I wasn't used to seeing empty space in such large quantities.

Tonbridge itself is a dump, a quarry town with only one main shopping street and made up mostly of those gigantic ten-storey apartment blocks that were built to house the gas workers – gas workers who, in the case of Tonbridge, never materialised. The quarry workers live in them now. The quarry pays well, which is why a large number of Sapphire's illegal immigrants migrate to Tonbridge. That's where most of the passengers left the tramway.

After Tonbridge the landscape changed again. As we drew closer to London, the wide, wild expanse of open marsh began to give way once more to stony scrub and then to a semi-industrial wasteland of derelict office blocks and overgrown factory yards that appeared similar to the polluted barrens that formed the immediate hinterland of Sapphire. I was shocked to see that the southern outskirts of the city still showed signs of bomb damage – vast craters full of oil-scummed water, acres of burned-out warehouses. Off to one side I spotted one of the old furnace chimneys. It stood alone amidst the ruins of several others, their broken uprights jutting out between the rusting girders and twisted stanchions like pointing fingers.

Look what you did, they seemed to say. *This is your fault.*

An old tramway carriage, ripped almost in half, lay on its back in a field of nettles. It looked about as insubstantial as a cardboard food carton, torn open by monster hands and then rudely discarded.

This made the war seem horribly close still. The things that happened then, the stuff you read about in books and see in films, seem so awful you can hardly believe any of it was ever real. The broken tramway carriage and the burned-out factories forced me to accept that these events happened, that people had died.

Over a million of them, that's what Del said. It made me feel sick.

At Croydon the edgelands started to be replaced by the

suburbs proper. Large tenement houses stood to either side of the tramway tracks, their rear verandas flapping with drying laundry, their overgrown back gardens choked with weeds and broken refrigerators and breeze-block barbecues. Here and there on patches of waste ground I spotted shack-like temporary dwellings constructed from plasterboard and corrugated iron, the kind of miniature shanty towns that spring up one week and are torn down the next. It was only then that I began to see how vast London was, and how chaotic. A great whale of a city that could gulp you down without noticing and swallow you whole. I felt lost inside it already. I hoped that Em would be there to meet me at the station, as he had promised.

Em lived to the north of Croydon, in Gypsy Hill. The name sounded serene and romantic, but as a concrete physical place I could barely imagine it. The Gypsy Hill tramway station turned out to be a smooth, box-like structure made of glass and granite, straddling the tracks like a giant aquarium. As the train came to a standstill I caught sight of Em, standing waiting for me on the platform just beneath the exit sign. As we hugged each other in greeting I felt my nervousness about being there slip its hooks out from under my ribs and sneak away. I pressed my face against Em's shoulder, smelled his smell – Daz washing powder mixed with the summer-ripe, slightly musky odour of his underarm sweat. He'd lost some weight, and had a new pair of glasses.

I knew the moment I saw him that we would fuck. Knowing that made me want him all the more.

"You didn't bring much," Em said. I had my old canvas rucksack, the same one I used during my final year of school and that I still carry everywhere. It contained my wash bag and two changes of underwear, a clean T-shirt. That was all.

"Why?" I said. "Should I have?"

I linked my arm through his as we left the station. We were okay, always would be okay most likely, but we had stuff to talk about.

Em lived in Cadence Road, a long, scruffy cul-de-sac not far from the station, lined with dusty plane trees and multiple fast food outlets. Em's flat turned out to be in one of the tenement buildings I'd glimpsed from the tramway, a five-storey mansion block with flaking pinkish-grey render and wide steps leading up to the entrance. It looked old, pre-war most likely. The front door opened on to a large square hallway with scuffed woodblock flooring and a carved black umbrella stand. I'm not sure what I'd been expecting – the shiny, chrome-and-glass land of rich bankers and corrupt gas officials Del was always on about, I suppose – but this wasn't it.

"It's not very grand, I'm afraid," Em said. "I like it here, though. And it's useful being close to the station."

"It's fine," I said. "It's nice." The building seemed even bigger from the inside, vast, in fact. Each landing had several apartments leading off it. I heard snatches of music coming from behind the closed doors, people talking, once even laughter. Our footsteps clattered noisily on the uncarpeted stairs.

Em's apartment was on the fourth floor. The rooms of the flat were not large – a compact sitting room with a kitchen alcove, plus a bedroom with a tiny bathroom leading off it – but everything was clean and neat, and there was even a small balcony. From the balcony you could look out over the rooftops towards the avenues and grand houses of Blackheath and Greenwich. A silvery flash at the horizon was the river Thames.

The room was stiflingly hot, even with the balcony doors open.

"There's some beer in the fridge," Em said. "Are you hungry? We could have a bite to eat here at the flat, then go into town for dinner later on?"

"That sounds great," I said. "I'm starving." I put down my rucksack and went to hug him. "It's good to see you, Em, it really is."

We drank beer and ate saveloy sandwiches and we talked. It was almost a month since the Delawarr, more than six weeks since Lumey's disappearance. I'd been in touch with Em by phone pretty much every day, though I'd seen nothing of Del or Claudia. Del did call once. He said that if anyone were to ask I was to say that Lumey was enjoying an extended holiday with her grandparents.

"Which grandparents?" I asked him.

"Who cares. It doesn't matter. Honestly, Jen." Our conversation was awkward, to put it mildly. The strain in Del's voice was plain, though it was harder to tell if it arose out of grief or from the weight of the many promises made to Claudia. Promises to keep away from me, most likely.

I didn't enquire. We go back a long way, Del and I. Either we'll patch things up eventually or we won't. Even if we don't, my brother knows I will always care for him and that's all that matters.

There had been no further news of Lumey. Little by little she was slipping away from us, the real child replaced by memories, the memories less and less grounded in reality as the days went by.

"Claudia thinks Lumey can talk with the dogs," I said to Em. "Without an implant, I mean. She thinks that's why Lumey was taken." I'd put off saying anything to him about my conversation with Claudia, not because I wanted to hide anything, quite the opposite. I wanted to see his face when I told him. That way I'd know what he really thought.

Em was silent for a moment. I took another bite of my sandwich. Em had layered some kind of spicy chutney with the saveloy. It tasted delicious.

"She's probably right," Em said finally. "I've heard of something like it before." He took out a handkerchief and wiped his mouth, then began telling me about a conversation he'd had with a work colleague a few months back. "We were talking about the war, and Thierry was arguing that most war crimes don't arise out of hatred, they arise out of fear, which in many cases is just a more refined form of ignorance. It's ignorance of an enemy's true motivation that leads us to fear them. Thierry said that any future wars would be won by the side that was most advanced in its development of empathic intelligence. He seemed to think that empathic intelligence was the future."

"You're talking about mind reading?"

"Not mind reading, exactly. I think true telepathy – the

kind you see in films – is probably a myth. But something approaching it, definitely. A kind of empathic sixth sense. The work that's been done with the smartdogs is just the start. All runners are natural empaths to an extent, we've known that for a long time. The implant is just a facilitator for their inborn talent. Children like Lumey though – children who don't need an implant at all to communicate – they're the next stage. A new race, almost. And yes, as Claudia said, that would make her very valuable indeed." He paused. "What does Derrick think?"

"He says he doesn't need the cops, that he'll find her himself. He says he won't stop looking until he does."

"How is he, Jen?"

"He's all right. He's taking care of Claudia." I wiped my greasy fingers on a paper napkin. "I know he misses you."

"I miss him, too." He took a sip of his beer. Em always drank his beer from a glass, a habit I found rather endearing. "I can't help thinking that this has all been my fault, you know. That there was something I should have done, or done better."

"We all think that, Em, and we're all wrong. If I said that to you, you'd tell me the same. Anyway," I said. "Lumey's still alive." I told him about Claudia's phone call from the mysterious woman and what she had said. "They have that, at least. Del thinks they're lucky, luckier than some, at any rate. He said that to me himself."

"He's a strange bastard."

"Don't say bastard," I said, and we both smiled, remembering how Em's mother Margrit always used to tell Del off for his foul language. Margrit hated swearing. She loved Del though, she and Gra both, and he loved them back.

* * *

We ate dinner just off Borough High Street, at a small Anatolian restaurant not far from the London Bridge tramway. Em had taken me on a tour of the city's main sights – the Houses of Parliament, Buckingham Palace, the London Eye – and afterwards we walked back across the bridge into Southwark, browsing the second-hand bookstalls along the Embankment and the antiques market, where Em insisted on buying a gift for me, a glass-crystal pendant with an old-style London shilling embedded inside.

"It means you'll return," he said. He hung the pendant around my neck. The river's surface shimmered with coloured lights. At the restaurant we ate chargrilled lamb with couscous and talked about the old days. I told him about the time Del made Monica Dalby walk across the exposed floor joist on the fourth-floor landing of Charlotte House.

"What an arsehole," Em said earnestly, and I laughed. "I found a twenty-shilling note up at Charlotte House once. Someone had rolled it up and pushed it into a crack in the wall of one of the upstairs toilets. The toilet stank like a cesspit, but the note was brand new. I remember I spent it on back copies of *Astronomer Royal*."

We collapsed into giggles. Then we finished our wine and went back to Em's place and fucked. Afterwards we lay side by side, close but not touching because of the heat. I felt sweat pooling and then drying in the hollow of my collarbone.

"Would you come and live with me in London, Jen?" Em

said to me at last. "If I found us somewhere bigger to live, I mean?"

"I don't know, Em," I said. "I'd have to think about it."

I took his hand in mine and squeezed, and he squeezed back.

For Adi Welitsch's gloves I chose grey doeskin, with a pale pink lining. The pink silk – the colour of mallow – was watermarked all over with tiny roses.

When she first saw the colour of the lining, Welitsch seemed a little unsure. Then she laughed her brisk, no-nonsense laugh and said okay.

"I'd never have chosen that pink in a million years," she said. "I'm amazed you thought of it."

"I know you'll like it," I said. "When the gloves are finished you'll see what I mean." I was still in awe of her, just a bit. When I asked her who recommended me she just smiled. Then she said she'd been noticing my work for some time and fancied treating herself, though I suspect it was Angela Kiwit who encouraged her to come and see me. The press like to play up the rivalry between Kiwit and Welitsch, but I've seen them in town together more than once, having coffee at Goldfrapps, on the Bulvard, or just walking their dogs along the front and shooting the breeze.

Welitsch is half Hoolish, and proud of it.

It's August now and very hot, even at night. When I open the windows the sea breeze creeps in, bringing with it the reek of seaweed and the song of crickets. On summer evenings the crickets never stop shrieking. Some people say it gets on their nerves but I like it.

For the backs of Welitsch's gloves I've chosen a hornet motif – two life-sized hornets, one for each hand and embroidered in silk. The black silk is shiny as onyx, the yellow like fire. The colours sum up Welitsch perfectly, somehow. I haven't told her about the hornets though – I want them to be a surprise.

I draw the needle carefully through the leather, making sure not to snag it. The aim with this kind of embroidery is to create a smooth surface, and so the stitches must be very fine, one-twentieth of an inch at most. With stitching this intricate I work more by instinct than by sight.

I like to listen to music as I work, and this evening I'm playing a CD by Paula Komedia, the same CD I first heard at Brit and Tash's place out on the marsh road. The long, meandering songs about the war, the tangled guitar riffs and driving rhythms she wrote to accompany the words of Valparaiso's *Patagonian Odyssey*.

Brit and Tash split up not long after the Delawarr. Del said they'd been having problems for some time.

Argentina is two thousand miles away across the Atlantic. I have never been there and most likely never will. I have heard there are wild horses there, great cities on a grassy plain that have never been bombed. I close my eyes for a moment, trying to imagine them, the way you screw your eyes shut at the end of a dream.

You're trying to recapture its magic, but you never can.

two

CHRISTY

Sapphire revealed itself to me only gradually, a town within a town, nestled in the shadows of my birthplace as the truth of a thing lies concealed within its outward appearance. You'll imagine that I created Sapphire as an escape – from the ordinariness of my own life, from the difficulties I found in making friends, from the isolation I felt after our mother left. I've learned not to waste time denying this – some of it is probably true after all, at least partly – but my main reason for writing about Sapphire was because the place felt so real to me, and I wanted to imagine it in greater detail.

Whenever I wrote about Sapphire, it was like being transported there. The best way of making magic happen is to describe it.

I first began writing when I was still in my teens. I had no intention of showing my scribblings to anyone else. I wrote for myself, as a kind of journal, or like those letters you write to a lover after a break-up and never send. If it hadn't been for my friend Robyn, things might have stayed that way. Robyn kept on at me to send one of what she called my stories to a magazine.

"The way you write is special," she said. "You have a unique voice." That's the way Robyn spoke – she had a gift for making even mundane things sound exciting and magnificent – and in the end I did as she suggested, more to shut her up than anything else. I never dreamed that anyone might actually want to publish something I'd written, but that's what happened.

"I told you," Robyn crowed. She seemed to take it for granted that I would be successful, that people would want to enter the worlds I created. I did not share her confidence, but either way, it was out of my hands now. There was no going back.

Writing stories felt necessary to me but it could also be frightening. There were times when I found myself afraid of what I might discover – about my brother Derek, about myself. But even the worst secrets cannot stay buried forever. I believe that secrets are alive, like worms in subsoil. When the weather is dry the worms dig deep in search of water.

But when it rains you'll find them burrowing to the surface.

Our mother left for good when I was fifteen. The last words she spoke to me were to tell me to tidy the yard. There was nothing unusual in that. When Mum was upset or angry or just needed time to think she always got rid of me by telling me to clean something. I never minded. It was always better to be out of her way when she was feeling unhappy.

Our backyard was often filthy, ankle-deep in dead leaves and plastic carrier bags and other rubbish. It was my job to clear it up, to sweep everything together and stuff it inside the heavy green refuse sacks that Mum kept in the cupboard under the sink. My brother Derek called the yard Christy's Domain. He rolled his eyes as he said this, leaning on the word 'domain' as if he meant to frighten me with it. He'd stolen the word off the cover of a James Herbert horror novel he'd pinched from a house clearance in Manor Road. The book lay around in his bedroom for ages, a scuffed paperback with a purplish-black jacket and a picture of a giant rat on the front. The story was meant to describe what might happen to London after a nuclear bomb strike, but mostly it was about people getting killed and eaten by mutant rats.

The book frightened me, but it interested me, too. I remember a wet Sunday afternoon in November when I barricaded myself inside the one of our three sheds whose roof didn't leak and pretended that nuclear war was going on outside. I didn't need to imagine the rats, they were there already. I was always catching sight of them, especially last thing at night, dashing back to the place where they lived under the shed. They were normally sized though, which disappointed me, not much bigger than the school gerbil.

Our house was on Laton Road, a large Victorian semi my father was able to buy cheap because of the state it was in. Dad did it up himself mainly, but there were some things that never got finished and so there was a makeshift feel to it, the sense that all his efforts might begin to unravel at any moment.

The garden was enormous, a hundred feet long at least

and half as wide. The end closest to the house was concreted over – that was the yard. The rest of the garden was grass and a few soggy rose bushes. At the far end was a single apple tree that sprouted dirty white blossom in spring but never produced a single apple as far as I know. There were three large sheds, two up near the house and another halfway down towards the apple tree. The sheds had been there since forever and seemed permanently on the point of falling down. My father used them as storage space for the business. What didn't fit into the sheds ended up under tarpaulins in the garden or in the yard.

The neighbours were always complaining about the state of our garden, but that didn't stop them using it as a dumping ground for their own rubbish. We had all kinds of things chucked over: broken bicycles and half-empty paint tins, dustbin bags full of soiled nappies. Once we even had an old mattress. I suppose the neighbours thought we had so much of our own rubbish that we wouldn't notice theirs. Every fortnight or so my father would hire an open-bed truck, skim off the worst of the detritus and drive it to the municipal dump over near Bexhill. It cost quite a lot to dump stuff. You could dump ordinary household refuse for free, but the security guys there knew Dad was in house clearance, so he had to pay trade rate. It all added up.

From October to late March the sheds sagged with mildew and trapped condensation. They became a refuge for thousands of woodlice, also leggy grey spiders that dashed towards you at a ragged canter the second you opened the door. In summer the sheds filled up with sunlight and the smell of creosote. There was another smell too, like dust mixed with grass clippings, that rose up from the boxes of old newspapers that were everywhere about the place, inside the house as well as in the sheds. Dad was always saving up newspaper to use as packing, so it tended to accumulate. If you dug to the bottom of some of the boxes you could often find papers dating back ten years or more.

Those old newspapers fascinated me. The stories about out-of-date murders and people I'd never heard of who used to be prime minister gave me an odd feeling. I couldn't stop thinking how weird it was that at the time the paper came out the stories I was reading now had still been happening. It was as if just by opening the paper I could travel back to that time, actually live in it for a moment. I especially loved the photographs, the grainy black-and-white images of people stepping into cars or on to jet planes, moments of passion or anger frozen forever.

I spent a lot of time reading those papers, not knowing if the emotion I felt was excitement or sadness. I thought of the newspaper stories as history, like we learned at school only not as dead.

On the night before my mother left it rained. The weather had been dry and hot for weeks, but that night it came down like a waterfall. I lay in bed, listening to the thunder rumbling in the hills around Battle, wondering if the summer was over and hoping it wasn't. I could hear Mum's voice in the next room, talking on the phone to one of her friends. I couldn't hear what she was saying, but I could tell she was complaining about my dad by the way she spoke, her voice rising and falling in agitation, whining and sighing like the wind in the telegraph wires. The familiarity of that sound was almost comforting, seeming to suggest that nothing would change.

Dad was downstairs, watching TV, the same as most nights. He seemed not to care what was showing, so long as it went on until late. By the time I fell asleep he still hadn't come up.

When I went downstairs the next morning, Mum was already in the kitchen drinking coffee. She was still in her dressing gown, a red velour wraparound my father had bought her for Christmas the year before. Her hair was a mess, which was a bad sign. My mother's hair seemed tied in to her moods the way dried seaweed is supposed to be tied in to the weather. When she was feeling okay about stuff it lay smooth and flat between her shoulder blades like polished brass. The morning she left it was sticking out from around her face in all directions, motionless and stiff as thorn twigs, bulked up about her shoulders like wads of foam packing.

"Go and tidy the yard, Christy, would you?" she said. She glanced at me briefly with reddened eyes, then turned away and stared down deep inside her coffee cup. Something about her voice unnerved me. It was as if she was pretending to be angry just to keep me away from her.

The radio was playing *The Archers*. I went outside. The rain had stopped just before it got light, but the sky was still overcast and there were puddles everywhere. The air felt damp and cold. I hugged myself and shivered as I realised I'd forgotten to put on my coat. I thought about going back inside to fetch it then decided against it.

The yard was covered in leaves. I unlatched the door to the small shed, the one nearest the house. The smell inside had altered overnight, the warm reek of creosote replaced by the stench of musty newspapers and damp earth. I pulled the door to behind me and stood in the half dark, still shivering. Rain-coloured light trickled in between the boards, outlining the shape of the door in streaks of grey.

I had the feeling that something bad was about to happen. I had these feelings sometimes, these *hunches*, and I knew that once they started it was hard to stop them. The yard broom stood in the corner of the shed. Its bristles jabbed upwards like torture spikes, like the hair of the *Struwwelpeter* in the weird German cartoon that had so terrified me when I was six. I snatched at the broom, almost knocking it over, then took it outside and began to sweep the leaves into a pile. As well as sweeping the leaves I cleared the gutter run-offs and drain overflows, where more leaves and pieces of rubbish lay clumped together in sodden stinking masses.

I hated cleaning the drains, because you never knew what might turn up there. Mostly it was just stray sheets of newspaper and the odd supermarket carrier bag, bloated to three times its usual size with mud and water. When Derek was younger and Mum was still able to make him help me with the yard cleaning he would pull the bags out of the drains and hurl them at me. I used to pretend I thought it was funny, because if I yelled at him to stop that would only make him do it all the more. The bags mostly landed on the concrete anyway, bursting and releasing their watery, shit-coloured contents back into the yard.

I began shovelling the pile of rubbish into one of the bin sacks. There were snails on some of the leaves, glistening and conker-coloured. I picked off every one I could find, placing them carefully into the space between the back of the shed and the garden wall, a mossy crevasse, snail paradise. I watched one as it gained purchase on the brick, its feelers nudging the air as it inched upward.

I hoped it would be safe there. It bothered me that there were so many and that every time it rained there were always more. I knew I couldn't be expected to save them all but I still got upset when I thought of them trapped in the rubbish sacks; the idea was horrible. I slid backwards out of the gap, my foot sliding on a soft, slippery object at the base of the wall. I bent down to pick it up, expecting to find another of the rain-filled carrier bags, a waterlogged bread bag maybe. It slipped wetly between my fingers as whatever was inside slithered slowly towards one end like pieces of rotten meat inside an out-of-date freezer bag. It was heavier than it looked, and the stink was sickening. I realised it was something awful, something dead. I dropped it at once. It slumped to the ground with a nasty little squelch that made me think of dog turds, although I knew this wasn't a dog turd because the smell was different.

I stooped closer to examine it: a flesh-coloured sac, pinkish-grey, with a bloody ragged opening in one end. I snapped off a twig and poked at it, turning it over. It was only then that I saw what it was – a dead rat, rotted away inside and partially eaten. It had been there for weeks, most likely. I prodded it again with the stick, trying to force it back behind the shed. A cat had probably got it. There were many cats in our vicinity, massive, half-feral tabbies that slipped in and out of the shadows like the ghosts of the pampered housecats they once had been.

In the summer you could hear them all night, fucking and fighting and killing rats until the first light of dawn.

The cats fascinated Derek for some reason, and over the long, scorching weeks of that last summer before Mum went we developed a craze for cat-watching. We used a stepladder to climb up on to the roof of one of the sheds, from where we enjoyed a bird's-eye view over all the straggling back gardens of Laton Road. The night air lay soft and heavy on us, like a blanket, and through the shallow, purplish half-darkness of mid-July and early August we would spy on the cats as they prowled the overgrown back alleyways on the lookout for rats or escaped hamsters or whatever was going.

"Look at them, they're like bent coppers," Derek said. It was too hot to sleep. We hauled rugs and cushions up on to the shed roof and made a kind of den there. We called it moon camping. It was often only as it began to get light that we finally fell asleep for an hour or two.

The hours between four and six are the hours of enchantment. The world emerges from its dark time and begins to feel okay again. It's easy to believe then. In gods or alien races, in fairy folk or monsters. In anything.

I tied the bin bags closed and hauled them over into the corner by the outside tap. The yard looked grey and empty now, stripped of colour. As I carried the first two sacks down the side passageway to where the dustbins were kept I heard the rumbling of an engine out the front. It was the weekend, so there were fewer cars about and the sound seemed louder than normal in the Sunday stillness. I stopped what I was doing, letting the rubbish sacks slide down to rest on the ground either side of my feet. I pressed my face up against the side gate, which had a broken slat in the centre that you could peer through.

What I saw was my mother, climbing into the back seat of a waiting taxi. She had her winter coat on, for some reason, burgundy red like her dressing gown but with a black velvet collar. Her yellow hair had been combed back into a ponytail.

She was carrying a green leather holdall, something she'd picked up for a fiver on Kemptown market and that I knew she loved.

Just before she closed the taxi door she looked back at the house. At the time I believed it was me she was looking at, that she knew somehow that I was there, watching her from behind the gate. Later I began to think I had imagined it. Then she slammed the taxi door shut and the cab drove away.

I finished loading the bin bags into the dustbins and then went back inside. I ran straight upstairs to my room. I was shivering again, even harder than before, even though the central heating had been switched on since I'd been outside and the house was now warm. My brother's door was closed, vibrating gently to the sound of some CD or other. There was no sign of my father, but on Sundays it was rare for him to appear before midday.

I sat down on my bed, hugging my knees and staring at the books in the bookcase as if the words on their spines contained a coded message I had to decipher. The room felt like it was in abeyance, holding its breath.

I held my breath with it. I don't know how, but I knew my mother wasn't coming back. My room looked the same as before, but the world beyond it had changed for good.

With Mum gone the place went downhill pretty quickly. We lived on frozen fish fingers and tins of ravioli, stuff my father brought home in bulk from the cash-and-carry. Dirty dishes piled up in the sink until one or other of us got sick of it and did a mass washing-up. None of us mentioned Mum leaving or where she might be. It was as if we were trying to pretend to one another that it hadn't happened. I kept hoping that there might be a sign from her, and jumped every time the phone rang or the doorbell went, but it was never her and as the weeks of her absence began to mount up even the idea of her began to seem less real.

The not-knowing made a sound inside my head like the wind gusting at speed along an empty alleyway, and opened a queasy emptiness inside me, the fear that I was about to lose my balance, the same way I had when I was ten and suffered an infection of the inner ear. I was off school for weeks. In the end a lot of black stuff came out of my ear and after that I started to feel better. Mum grumbled all the time I was ill. She bought me magazines to read, with film stars in them and recipes for chicken fricassee. Her hair stuck out like tumbleweed. She used wide-toothed tortoiseshell hair slides to hold it back.

I kept dreaming about her, even when she was actually

there in the room with me. I dreamed she was still a woman but not my mother. When I woke up I stared at her closely, trying to work out if the dream had been real or not, but I could never decide. My mother grew up in Croydon, in a chaotic, rambling house full of rescue greyhounds and sheet music. Her mother taught violin at one of the private schools in the near vicinity. Her father was a lawyer of some kind. He hired my father to clear some furniture, a kitchen dresser and a mahogany wardrobe they'd recently inherited but didn't have room for.

Mum was seventeen. She once told me the only reason she agreed to go on a date with my dad when he asked her was because she knew her father would go berserk when he found out.

"I'm not angry with you," she said to me during that period of my illness. She held my hair back with both hands, as if she was trying to see my face better, trying to secure a clearer memory of what I looked like. "It's just the whole bloody thing, you know?"

Her name was Marcia, said like Marsha, which I thought was pretty. It was as if she was always trying to remind me she wasn't mine to keep.

Without Marcia inside it the house felt like a shell, the shell of one of the large, glistening candy-striped snails in the yard, for instance, the animal inside consumed by some malevolent parasite. It scared me sometimes, just to be there. My mother never liked the Laton Road house. Now that she was gone the dust and broken camcorders and boxes of old newspapers were free to take over.

Once something is broken it changes its nature. There was an old radio in the living room that Dad was always saying he'd fix but never did. I don't know if he even knew how. It was square and heavy, and looked like the radios you sometimes see in old war films, with everyone gathered round listening to one of those noisy speeches by Hitler or Churchill. It was made of Bakelite, which I knew was a kind of plastic. I liked the smell of it, the way you could open up the back with a small brass catch and see the wires inside.

It didn't work though. Just sat there on the sideboard, gathering dust. Soon there was enough dust to write your name in, and then more dust over that. The dust seemed to me to be a sign that the thing was dead.

I hated those dusty dead things that were suddenly everywhere. I wanted to be free of them, but the act of simply dusting them seemed too small to make a difference. I kept my own room tidy and clean, but on the landing and in the rooms downstairs the broken rubbish multiplied and grew dustier by the day.

If you look at a broken camcorder for long enough, its original purpose begins to seem obscure. Run your fingers over the moulded black plastic, the exposed lens, clouded now with dust, like a wide, dead eye. There's a maker's name on the handle but you've never heard of them, and it's hard to believe that an object with so little life in it ever did anything. It's an exhausted artefact, a proof of something maybe, but you don't know what of. You wonder if what you're holding in your hand has floated up from the past, or arrived here from the future or from somewhere else.

When you look at it lying on a rubbish dump with other broken things you feel a deep sadness. Almost as if the world that ever thought to produce such a thing – your own world – has outlived its usefulness.

School was the only thing that stayed the same. This felt strange to me at first, because everyone there kept talking about things that no longer mattered to me. It was as if my life had slipped and fallen through a crack in time or something, or else the school had, I wasn't sure which. Whole days would go by and I was unable to remember a single thing that happened in them. Gradually this changed. I started to feel safer at school than I did at home, because it was easier to predict what might happen there. I liked the identical shape of each day, the way people and objects fitted neatly into patterns. Like the cobalt-blue exercise books, stacked one on top of the other on the teacher's desk at the front of the class. The pink lines of feint, the particular smell those books had, like new chalk.

I even liked the headmistress, Miss Wisbech. She dressed plainly and sensibly like most of the other teachers, except for her glasses, which were by Dolce & Gabbana. The glasses suited her, actually. In some odd way they *were* her. It was impossible to imagine her without them.

In the November after Mum left, Miss Wisbech stopped me in the corridor and asked me to go with her to her office.

"Is it true what I've heard?" she said. "That your mother is no longer living with you at home?"

Her office was steeped in files. There was a large photograph on her desk, a kid of about five with curly hair and clutching a model steam engine, one of the posh metal kind, Hornby probably. I knew about Hornby railway sets from Derek.

"She died," I said. The words were out before I could stop them. They waved themselves jauntily in my face, like little red flags.

"Oh," said Miss Wisbech. There was a long silence. I looked down at my feet, not daring to catch her eye in case it made me come out with something even more messed up. I could feel myself blushing with shame, but even so I didn't regret the lie I'd told. I knew it was the only thing I could have said that would stop Miss Wisbech or anyone else from asking questions.

The carpet in Miss Wisbech's office was dark green. It was speckled with bits of white, the tiny discs of paper you find packed inside the chest cavity of a hole punch. I drew mental lines between them, forming a random pattern of join-the-dots.

"Do you need any help, Christy?" she said at last. "Any help at all?"

I shook my head silently. I wondered what would happen if I told her about the broken radio, the way the dust kept covering up the other dust on the fogged-over dial.

She let me go. I was late for maths, but only by five minutes.

Derek started going out on the van with Dad when he was eight. By the time he was fifteen, he was working in the house clearance business full time.

Mum wanted Derek to go to university. The rows about Derek's future went on for hours – usually they finished with Mum in tears. In the end – just before she left, this was – the school sent her a letter saying that Derek had been classified as 'ungovernable' and they had 'regretfully come to a decision' to exclude him permanently.

Derek Blu-Tacked the letter to his bedroom wall. When eventually it fell down he threw it away.

Derek took to the business straight away. Partly it was the sense of freedom – driving around in the van all day, with no two days ever the same and always that feeling of something new happening. But he also had a genuine liking for old things. He handled objects carefully and with precision, and sometimes if you went out on the van with him he'd tell you about them. He was fascinated by the interiors of old houses and by what you could find there. He ended up knowing more about antiques than Dad, and Dad had been in the business practically from when he was in kindergarten.

There was a picture Derek kept in his room for a while, an old oil painting of a woman leaning on a veranda rail. The woman in the painting looked just like Derek's girlfriend Monica. The day after Monica dumped him, Derek took the picture outside into the yard and kicked it to pieces with his Doc Martens. For ages afterwards there were tiny shining patches all over the concrete, flecks of gold colour from the smashed picture frame.

Sometimes, if he felt like it, Derek would take me with him when he went to price up a job. I enjoyed those drives. It was good to get out of the house, to see other places. In the week after the Christmas of the first year – no Christmas card from Mum, no nothing – Dad and Derek were booked to do a house clearance on West Hill Road in St Leonards. Derek had been given the keys in advance, because the property was empty and there would be no one there to let them in on the morning of the job. It was a massive job, Derek said, seventeen rooms in total. When he asked me if I wanted to go and have a look at the house with him I said all right.

We drove there along the seafront. The tide was in, and even though the temperatures were close to freezing there were still windsurfers out.

"Morons," Derek said. "In this weather? I hope they drown themselves."

The sea was clear green, softly ruffled with mother-of-pearl, like antique jade. The surfers were ploughing through it, whipping the surface into whiteness, like the froth you see on top of a glass of champagne. I had tasted champagne only once, at a party for my mother's aunt who had just died. I found it strange that any family would hold a party for a dead person, but Mum explained that her Aunt Louise had been an actress on the London stage.

"She was quite famous, in her day," Mum said. "This is what she would have wanted."

Mum was wearing a dress made from pale blue silk. There were tiny beads of glitter all over it, like pinpricks of light. Later, once she'd had a glass or two of the champagne, Mum told me that the blue dress was one of Aunt Louise's.

"I snuck upstairs and pinched it," she said. The alcohol on her breath had the same sour smell as stinging nettles.

"Right after the funeral. Aren't I a riot?"

She raised her glass to me and giggled. She looked like she was made of glass herself, tall and bright and gleaming, exquisitely fragile. I never saw her like it, before or since.

West Hill Road is on the Bexhill side of St Leonards. It runs along the top of the cliff, behind the large, ship-shaped apartment block called Marine Court and above the road that runs along the seafront called the Marina. The house we were going to see was called Charlotte House. It stood on the south side of West Hill Road, close to the cliff edge and with nothing between it and the English Channel but empty air. There was a car park at the back, half overgrown with brambles and with notices that said KEEP OUT and UNAUTHORISED VEHICLES ARE LIABLE TO CLAMPING. The building itself was massive, with steep red gables and a long veranda, the kind of oversized Victorian villa my father always referred to as a white elephant. Charlotte House used to be a hotel in the old days, then a nursing home. Eventually it became too expensive to run and so the owners closed it down and boarded it up.

"It's just the top floor we're doing," Derek said. "The rest is empty already, apparently."

He parked the van in the car park. He didn't seem nervous about being clamped, so I supposed we were authorized. The sight of the house gave me goosebumps, because it was so large, probably.

"Are you sure it's okay to go in?" I said.

"Of course. It's a job, isn't it?" He took the keys out of the ignition. "Let's go."

The entrance to the fourth-floor flat was through a side door.

"Belonged to the caretaker," Derek said. "Gone gaga, probably. Either that or he can't manage the stairs anymore."

The stairs were very steep, and uncarpeted. I wondered about the old man and where he was now. It made me sad to think of him being taken away. The stairwell was a dark and dingy green, lit by a single overhead bulb that somehow had to do for the entire hallway.

Dangerous for an old man, I thought. Perhaps if they'd put in better lighting he could have stayed here longer. Derek unlocked the door to the flat and we went inside. There was a strange smell, a musky, sweetish odour that Derek said was mothballs.

The flat was stuffed with things. Some of them were in boxes already, but most of what remained still had to be packed. A job this size would take most of a day but it would pay good money. The main room was at the front. It was filled with light, the sea-green, liquid light of the water below. The floorboards were bare and dusty. There was a big cloth-covered sofa, an enormous glass-fronted cabinet crammed full of ornaments, so many of them that the cabinet doors wouldn't close properly. The things inside were pretty: porcelain egg cups shaped like baskets, blue Wedgwood beakers and china horses, stuff like that.

"See that?" Derek said. He opened the doors of the cabinet, easing them gently apart so that nothing fell out. "That's Capo di Monte." He reached inside and drew out a porcelain ballerina, one leg flung delicately outwards and raised at the knee. Her skin was a bluish, translucent white. Her costume, her tutu, was a soft violet colour.

Her hair was yellow like Mum's, and like Derek's.

Derek rested the ornament on the palm of his hand. His fingers gripped the base, very lightly, just to steady it.

"That's worth a good couple of quid, that is," he said. He tapped the porcelain with his thumbnail, making it ring. "There's other stuff here, too. Good stuff." He put the ballet dancer down on the sofa. "If you see something you like, let me know."

He wanted to give me something. We hadn't exchanged presents at all that Christmas, none of us had. I thought this was probably Derek's way of trying to make up for that.

I liked the little dancer's purple tutu. I thought Derek would probably give her to me if I asked him to, even though she was valuable. Derek was like that sometimes. I left him taking more ornaments out of the cupboard and walked away to explore the rest of the flat.

Beyond the main room there were many smaller rooms, a labyrinth of corridors and storage closets and oddly shaped lobby areas. The place gave me the creeps, just a little bit, and I could see why Derek hadn't been too keen on coming here alone. Some of the rooms were empty, others were piled high with old furniture. I realised this was what happened when a world got dismantled: the actual space remained the same, but its meaning became altered. Whole lives were erased.

Most of my mother's things were still at Laton Road. We edged cautiously around them, pretending they were invisible, or that if we left them alone for long enough our mother's possessions would go away by themselves.

I ended up in a room that had once been a bedroom. As well as the bed there was a desk and a wardrobe, a heavy-looking oval mirror in a dark wood frame. The single window was narrow and pointed, too high up the wall to see out of unless you stood on a stool. On the floor underneath the desk was a box of books. I bent down to examine them, old novels by John Wyndham and C. S. Lewis and E. Nesbit, all writers I had heard of but not yet read. The books were in hardback, all with their original dust jackets. There was something about them I liked – the smell probably, musty and time-soaked, like old library books – and I thought I might perhaps ask Derek if I could have them. They were more interesting than the china ballerina, at any rate. I stood up, and as I turned around to face the door I caught sight of myself in the mirror. Looking into it was like staring into a pool of murky water. I saw my own neat figure, my own dark, rather wispy hair and wire-framed glasses. I knew the girl in the glass was me, yet at the same time she seemed not to be me. Indeed I knew she was not, that although she looked just like me she was someone else.

She gazed back at me from out of the glass, and in the moment when our eyes met I understood that she knew it, too.

I felt cold all over, then hot. I stretched my hand out towards the glass, reaching for the other girl's fingers. It seemed suddenly very important that we should touch. If we touch, I thought, then we will swap places. I will be where she is, and she will be here.

The idea was scary but it was also exciting. There's a

whole other world out there, I thought. Let's do it. I stepped forward to touch the glass, but in the instant before I could do so I heard Derek's voice.

"What are you doing in here?" he said. He'd crept up on me without my hearing him, and as I span around to face him the other girl slipped away. I felt her go, disappearing silently into the deeper, greyer spaces of the huge apartment that I now knew lay somewhere on the other side of the mirror glass.

I understood at once that our moment had passed. A chance had been offered to me and I had missed it. I still don't know if I regretted the girl's departure, or if I was relieved.

"Just looking," I said to Derek. "Can I have these?" I gestured towards the box of books under the desk.

"Okay," Derek said. "Are you sure that's all you want?" He spoke absently, his attention already elsewhere. The books he barely glanced at. "Christ," he said. It was the desk he was looking at, one of those dinky little slant-topped bureaux with candy-twist legs. "I think that's a Sheraton."

"It's nice," I said, not caring. "Is it worth anything?"

He gave me a look. "Only twenty thousand quid," he said. "If I'm right, that is." He ran his fingers reverently over the surface of the polished wood then turned sharply away, making it look as if he'd lost interest, although I knew he had not. I picked up the box of books with their musty scent, like the newspapers we had at home only stronger.

I could feel the girl in the mirror watching me leave. I knew if I turned around right then I would catch sight of her, but I did not dare.

I thought about the incident afterwards, from time to

time, but mostly I just accepted it as something peculiar that had happened but that was over now.

I did sometimes wonder though, how it would have been if I'd had a sister instead of a brother.

It was Derek's girlfriend Monica who helped me fill in my application form for college.

Derek had girlfriends before Monica, but Monica was the first one he really cared about. She had slightly slanted eyes and very fair hair. Not yellow hair like Derek's – Monica's hair was the colour of hay at the height of summer. She lived in a tiny two-room flat on the top floor of one of the crummier-looking terraces on Braybrooke Road. The ground- and basement-floor maisonette was the home of a retired policeman. When he sold up and moved to somewhere smaller he hired Derek and Dad to clear away all the stuff he no longer had room for. Derek met Monica when she came home on her lunch break. He asked if she'd go for a drink with him when she finished work and she said yes.

Monica worked in a flower shop down in the Old Town, and not long after she started going out with Derek she fixed me up with a Saturday job there. I liked the job because it meant I had some money to spend. Also I enjoyed the work. I liked fixing up the window displays, and helping customers choose the right flowers. The shop's owner, Diane, did all the more complicated stuff, the wedding floristry and so on, but she taught me how to create simple bouquets and sometimes she let me cash up the till.

Diane was seriously obese and often found trouble breathing when she went upstairs. She was always carefully dressed, though. She liked soft colours – rose pinks and primrose yellows, the same colours as her flowers. She had a thing about gloves. She owned dozens of pairs of them, maybe hundreds – I don't think I ever saw her wear the same pair twice, although I suppose she must have done, it was just that I only ever saw her once or twice a week. She wore gloves winter and summer, and when she came into work in the morning the first thing she'd do would be to take them off and lay them down on the counter, one neatly across the other in an 'x' shape. It was like a ritual with her, a way of settling herself for the day ahead. Diane's gloves fascinated me, not just because they were beautiful – many of them were hand-made – but because of the way they made you stop thinking about Diane's large body and concentrate instead on her dainty hands. It was almost like a magic trick, an act of vanishment, something I suppose she'd learned to do long ago and that was now so much a part of her she no longer thought about it.

In spite of her fatness, Diane was graceful and pretty. And unlike my mother Marcia she was naturally kind.

"You have a real gift for floristry, Christy," she said to me not long after I started working for her. "I'd take you on full time if I could afford to."

"That's really nice of you but I want to go to college," I said. Diane was the first person I dared to tell about this ambition. I was seventeen then, my brother Derek was almost twenty. I'd been hoping Diane might help me fill in the forms, but when I asked her she shook her head and said she couldn't possibly.

"I'm useless at forms," she said. She didn't want to get involved for some reason, that was obvious. "Can't you ask one of your teachers?"

"I suppose," I said. The problem with asking a teacher was that there was always the risk they would start pestering me with questions about my mother. Also I was afraid of looking an idiot. I still wasn't certain which courses I should apply for. I liked History best but I was afraid I wasn't clever enough to make a success of it. Derek always insisted that all that stuff about kings and queens was boring, but I was mad for it. I used to take books out of the library – books about Queen Matilda of England and Queen Elizabeth and Anne Boleyn – because I was addicted to the stories they told, stories that reminded me of fairy tales, only with more danger in them, more blood and revolution, more death by fire. I knew all the dates and battles by heart, but when it came to writing anything down I would lose my nerve. When I was asked a question in class my mind went blank.

"Perhaps I'm just stupid or something," I said to Monica. Monica was round at our house two or three evenings a week by then. Sometimes she'd go to the pub with Derek, but mostly she'd stay behind with me and we'd sit in watching the game shows on the kitchen portable. Monica knew about Mum leaving but we never talked about it. We bitched about the flower shop customers instead, or chat show hosts, or other things we'd seen or liked to make fun of. Having Monica around made life easier generally, because Derek made more of an effort not to be an arsehole. More than that though, I just liked being with her. She was fun and she stuck up for me. No one had ever done that before, or bothered much about what I did, one way or the other.

"Of course you're not stupid," Monica said. "Don't talk like that. You're so bright it's scary. Anyway, it'll do you good to get out of this place, spread your wings a bit."

"I suppose," I said again. I still wasn't sure, about anything. I found it hard to recognise the person she was describing. "Why didn't you go to college?"

"I wasn't ready. Not like you." Monica shrugged. "I'll get around to it later, probably."

She helped me fill in the forms, then showed me how to prepare a Personal Statement. I got my father to sign the consent form when Derek was out. When I finally received my offer from South Bank University, Monica insisted on taking me out for a drink to celebrate.

"I haven't got in yet," I said. The offer still depended on me passing my A levels.

"I know. But you will." She hugged me and kissed my hair as she sometimes did. Both of Monica's parents were dead – they'd been killed in an air crash.

When Monica's birthday came around, Derek gave her an antique pendant made from silver and Venetian glass that was called Murano.

In the summer of the year after our mother left, my brother raped me. It was a boiling hot day in August. I was sixteen.

I'd spent most of the day by myself up in Castle Meadow, reading a book called *Memoirs of a Survivor* by Doris Lessing.

It had been lent to me by Miss Wisbech, who'd come up to me in the corridor just before the summer holidays started and put the book right into my hands.

"I hope you'll find time to read this, Christy," she said. "I think it's the kind of story you might enjoy."

I had no idea what I'd done that would make her think that – I wondered if she'd been secretly spying on me in the library. I said thank you and then walked away before she found the chance to add anything else. I expect my behaviour must have seemed rude to her, but I was surprised and a bit embarrassed. I'd never heard of Doris Lessing, and I was afraid the book might be boring, or that I might not even understand what it was about. But when I actually started reading it I found it was okay, quite exciting really, and no more difficult to follow than the John Wyndham stories that had been in the box of books Derek had given me from Charlotte House. *Memoirs of a Survivor* was set in an unnamed city that was probably London, only as in *The Day of the Triffids* everything had descended into chaos. There were gangs of kids in the streets who kept setting fire to things. A lot of the ordinary people were trying to escape from the city into places like Wales.

In spite of the terrible things that were happening, the woman telling the story set down her thoughts in a calm, almost cold way. She was supposed to be taking care of a girl called Emily, but really it seemed to be Emily who was in charge.

Emily had been abandoned by her mother.

I liked the way Doris Lessing just wrote what happened

and didn't much add to it. Most of all I liked the way she had managed to transform London into an imaginary city. It was an idea that had never occurred to me, that you could write about a real place, a place you knew well, and that just by changing or adding small details you could turn it into somewhere quite different. A place where good things happened, or bad things did.

A place of your own that you could escape to whenever you wanted. It made me wonder whether it might be possible to change Hastings into a place where weird things happened, the same as Doris Lessing had done with London only even stranger.

At around four o'clock I left the meadow and began walking home. My books were in my gym bag, and I was carrying my sandals. In summer I often went barefoot, even in town. The pavements were hot. If I stood still for too long in one place I could feel the soles of my feet burning.

When I was halfway down St Mary's Terrace there was a cloudburst. It happened suddenly and without warning, a clap of thunder so huge and so terrifying that for a moment I thought a bomb must have gone off. Then the sky seemed to split open. Rain poured down, so heavily and so fast it was like a single sheet of water.

I flung my arms above my head and screamed. I waved my sandals in the air, then flung them down like flatfish on the streaming pavement. I felt a massive energy coursing through me, as if my blood had been replaced by lightning, and for one endless, joyous moment it felt as if the world I knew really had ended, and another, more surprising world had taken its place. A world like the one Doris Lessing had written about perhaps, in *Memoirs of a Survivor*.

I ran through the streets, slipping and sliding on the jet-black asphalt, my arms flung out to either side to keep me from falling. I remember I couldn't stop laughing, that my laughter seemed to come from somewhere outside of me, a laughter-demon. The gutters coursed with thick brown water, like angry rivers. People cowered wetly in doorways or hurried indoors.

I burst into the hallway of Laton Road and stood there, dripping. I was expecting to find the house empty – Dad and Derek had a big job on, something in Tonbridge or Tunbridge Wells. Dad had said they wouldn't be back until six at least, which was part of the reason I'd decided to come home early.

As it turned out, they finished sooner than they'd expected. It's strange, how many of the things that help decide how your life goes seem to happen by chance.

Derek appeared at the top of the stairs. The happy madness that had been filling me up, that feeling of being energized, disappeared as soon as I saw him, just like that. It was as if I'd been unplugged from the mains or something.

"You look like a drowned rat," Derek said. He was wearing jeans but his top half was naked. I could tell from the way his hair was spiking out that he'd just had a shower.

"It's raining," I said. "You're home early?"

"Jake was free after all, wasn't he?" Jake Hom was a half-Chinese kid who Dad sometimes hired to help with the loading. He was skinny, like Derek, but very strong. "Dad's down the pub. Get that wet shit off – you'll catch pneumonia."

I looked down at myself and saw that my T-shirt had become transparent. The flesh of my arms and belly gleamed pinkly through the soaked cloth. My nipples, a darker pink, like the hearts of roses, were clearly visible.

A small pool of water was beginning to gather about my feet.

Derek came slowly down the stairs to where I was standing. He hoisted me up, seizing me with both arms the way he used to do when we were younger, pressing me against his chest then slinging me over one shoulder in a clumsy fireman's lift.

"You're soaked to the skin," he said. "Slippy as a newt, you are."

"You beast," I cried, kicking out at him. "Put me down, Del." I didn't know yet if I was joking or if I really meant it. I was afraid of Derek. I hated to admit it, even to myself, because admitting I was afraid of anything was a source of shame to me. But I had reason to be scared of Derek, because I knew he was dangerous, or at least that he could be, the kind of person that didn't give a damn for the feelings of others and so might do anything. He might hurt someone just because he wanted to, or because he wanted to find out what it felt like to harm them.

It was almost as if he was mad. As if he'd been made with something missing, I don't know.

The worst thing about it was that you never knew when he was going to do something awful. A lot of the time he acted pretty much the same as everyone else.

I knew he knew I was scared, but he never let on. It was a game we played, a game of dare, like when he threw the plastic bags of stinking water at me and I'd pretend it was funny.

"You're the beast," he said. "A filthy little swamp otter."

He rushed me up the stairs and into my room. Both of us were screaming with laughter. He dumped me down on the bed, winding me slightly but not hurting me. I could feel rainwater soaking out of my hair and into the pillows.

Derek grabbed me around the waist and began tugging my shorts off.

"Fuck off, Derek," I said. I was still giggling like a moron. I kicked out at him, but he caught my ankle, gripping it hard and forcing my leg back down on the bed. His eyes had narrowed into slits and he was breathing hard.

I think I knew then what was going to happen, half-knew anyway, but any idea of fighting it never really had a chance to get started. He was stronger than me, bigger, and besides if I fought him it would mean admitting that I was afraid. The game between us – our pretend-game, our *charade* – would be burst wide open, and Derek's power over me would then be absolute.

"Have you done it with anyone yet?" Derek said.

I shook my head. "Course not." I knew he was talking about fucking, though the idea that he should ask me felt all wrong. I twisted my body to try and free myself but his hands had locked themselves even more tightly around my shins.

"Good," he said. He swung my ankles apart and raised them, making a 'v'. "Got a boyfriend, some guy you're into?"

I shook my head again, this time more fiercely. There

was a chance Derek knew about Tim – Derek had a way of finding things out, especially those things you least wanted him to know – but there was no way I was going to tell him, not unless he dragged it out of me by force.

"You will soon, though," he said. "Some randy little nerd who can't wait to stick his cock in your cunt. I reckon it's time I showed you what's what."

He had my knickers in his hand by now. He dropped them to the carpet with a wet little thump. Then he unzipped his jeans and shrugged them off. He had a particular way of doing that, graceful, like a dancer, that I always admired. He was down to his underpants. His bare legs were long and slightly knock-kneed, just like our mother's.

His ribs stuck out like the bars of a cage. Derek was always skinny as a yard-dog.

"It's better if I'm the first," he said. "It won't be so painful then, later."

He was kneeling on the side of the bed. I could see the bulge in his pants, the fat coil of his swelling penis. "Touch it," he said, and when I did the iron-bar hardness seemed not to be a part of him at all. His features became stiff, strained, as if I'd hurt him in some way. His breath was quick and shallow and I could almost make myself believe I could hear his heart beating, battering up and down like a tack hammer in his narrow chest.

"Keep still," he said. I was shaking with cold, though the room was still stiflingly warm from the heat of the day. He leaned across me and pulled me under him, and then lay straight as a rod with his chest against mine. His movements felt clumsy, almost nervous. When he went inside me it hurt a bit, though not nearly as much as I'd been expecting. The most horrible thing was not the pain at all, but the wrongness, his noisy breath in my ear, him growing out from between my legs like a root, me wanting to kill him and knowing that I couldn't, that I'd have to lark around with him afterwards as if nothing had happened.

He humped up and down a couple of times then tugged his penis out of me and rolled away. My stomach hitched with nausea. I curled on my side.

Get out of here, you shit, I thought. Just get the fuck out.

"Don't tell Dad, or I'll kill you," he said. Just that.

He buggered off after that, and when I heard the front door slam downstairs I knew he'd gone out and most likely wouldn't be back for some time. I lay where I was for a while, listening to the sounds of the house and thinking about just shoving some spare clothes in my gym bag and running away. Where would I go, though? I felt disorientated and not quite real. It was as if my mind had become separated from my body somehow. I knew I had to coax it back, hold out my hand to it as if it were a scared animal. I knew I had to pull myself back together or he would have won.

In the end I got myself into the bathroom and under the shower. I turned it on full blast, remembering the rain, the maddening cloudburst, the steaming pavements. The water was hot, hotter than I normally liked it, but that was okay. As the feeling began to edge back into my toes and breasts and fingertips I took the soap from the side of the bath and began to wash myself, scrubbing and working up a lather, making sure I soaped each and every part of my body, touching it with my own fingers, even the parts that hurt.

Especially the parts that hurt.

My body was mine and I wanted it back. I would not let him take it.

I watched the streams of white soap bubbles run down my legs, sudsing over my feet then disappearing into the plughole.

You have a new skin, I told myself. What happened in there just now is already over.

I towelled myself dry, then put on clean jeans and a T-shirt. I gathered up the wet clothes from my bedroom floor, stuffed them inside a supermarket carrier bag and chucked them in the dustbin. After that I went back upstairs to my room.

When I happened to catch sight of myself in the mirror above the wash hand basin I was surprised by how normal I looked.

The town of Hastings is set on two hills, the East Hill and the West Hill. Between the East Hill and the West Hill lies the Old Town. Eastwards from East Hill lies the village of Fairlight, then the Romney Marshes. There are no other towns of any size along the coast until you get to Folkestone.

To the west of West Hill you have the new town, the sprawl of Victorian terraces that were built when Hastings became popular as a holiday resort in the nineteenth century. Many of these houses are large, with attractive square bay windows and long back gardens. Some of them have been renovated in their original style, but others are in a bad state of dilapidation. Many of the gardens are not well tended, and so the town is blessed with a larger than normal abundance of wildflowers. In the spring there are bluebells everywhere. In the autumn there are Michaelmas daisies. Their colour – a soft mauve – is unique among flowers.

In the centre of town there is a pedestrian precinct, characterised by smaller, badly stocked branches of the newer chain stores. Along Queen Street and the roads adjoining it there are more local businesses. Some of them have stood their ground for many years, others struggle on for a while and then fizzle out. There are half a dozen hairdressers, a tattoo parlour and tanning salon, an electrical repair store that also sells vacuum cleaners, three used furniture stores, two bakeries and a large number of charity shops and fast food outlets.

Along the seafront there are three competing amusement arcades, two doughnut stands, two fudge shops and five fish-and-chip restaurants. One of the fish-and-chip places, The Blue Dolphin, has an entry in the Good Food Guide. These local businesses cling to life like limpets to rocks, threatening to die each time the tide goes out yet never quite doing it.

Aleister Crowley spent his last years here. The serial killer George Chapman bought his arsenic here. There are plenty of people in Hastings who still believe in witches.

From time to time you might hear of a murder, but not so often that you would call it commonplace.

Walking in the town can be strenuous because of the hills.

* * *

My best friend at primary school was a girl named Cindy Rogers. We were kind of like sisters, or how I imagined sisters might be anyway, and always together. Then I was off sick with the ear infection and everything changed.

I was nervous about returning to school in any case, because I'd been away so long. It wasn't like I'd just missed a day, it had been several weeks. I might as well have been a new kid, which was a fate worse than any trip to the headmaster's study. I was especially nervous about seeing Cindy, because I knew even before I'd set one foot inside our form room that something was different.

At the beginning of my illness, Cindy sent me jokey little notes in pale pink envelopes, some of them delivered by hand but others sent through the post with actual stamps on, the new stamps with the garden birds, which Cindy knew I liked. Her letters came every other day at first, then less frequently, then finally not at all. I told myself that was all right, because Cindy knew I'd be back at school soon, so what was the point?

I knew I was lying to myself. Within five minutes of stepping into the classroom, I knew that Cindy had a new best friend, Samantha Ridgway, and that I was history. To do her credit, Cindy didn't just dump me like some of the more ruthless girls would have – she made a big show of pretending to include me in everything they did. Even so, the situation was irreparable, and I was heartbroken. I didn't want just to be included. I wanted my friend the way she had been before Samantha Ridgway, with her raspberry-scented lip balm and crystal monkey pencil sharpener.

I hated Samantha, or not Samantha exactly, but the space she occupied. I also hated myself for hating, for admitting to myself that I was upset. I was nice to Sam and Cindy – I even sat with them sometimes at break time, the way they wanted. Then finally I had a huge crying fit, right in the middle of the playground at the end of lunch hour. No one knew what was wrong and I refused to say. Eventually I rubbed the tears away with my fists and went in for double English as if nothing had happened. I arranged my books across my desk like a crash barrier, which I suppose they were.

Four years later, Cindy Rogers was one of what I thought of as the eye-makeup girls, girls with boyfriends off the Hawthorne estate and who wore tights in American Tan instead of socks, girls so different from me they might as well have been beamed in from another planet.

I think Cindy might even have had sex with Derek at some point. I never asked her.

After Cindy, I made a pact with myself not to be taken in again. I made new friends, or pretended to anyway, girls I hung around with at break time or sat next to in class. I came to know the scent of their skin, the precise conformation of pencils and broken jewellery and makeup items they liked to carry in their pencil cases. I knew the number and timbre of the silver bangles that drooped from their wrists, the bizarre particularities of their most common spelling mistakes. I never let these things matter to me though – not the way they had mattered with Cindy Rogers.

After Cindy it felt less of a risk not to have friends at all.

* * *

Tim Leverson was in the year above me. He was tall, and very thin, with wavy dark hair. We both wore the same kind of glasses. Tim was a library monitor. I was spending more and more time in the school library, over lunchtimes especially, and as Tim was usually there as well I suppose it wasn't surprising that I began to notice him. I liked the careful way he handled the books. He moved cautiously and spoke quietly, the opposite of Derek.

It was ages before we actually spoke, months probably. In the end I had to dare myself to go up to him and say something – it didn't matter what, just so long as I addressed him. It was the only way I knew of defeating my shyness. In the end I went up to the library counter and asked him if the library held any books by Doris Lessing. I knew the answer to my question already, but that wasn't the point.

"I think we do," he said. He took me over to the 'L' section, where there were two Lessing books on the shelf, *The Golden Notebook* and *Briefing for a Descent into Hell*. I decided on *Briefing for a Descent into Hell* because I liked the title better. I took the book over to the counter, and Tim stamped it out. When I returned it a week later he asked me if I wanted to go for a walk with him after school in Castle Meadow.

"Come for supper too, if you like," he said. "My mum won't mind."

I said I couldn't go for supper because my dad would be expecting me back but I could go for a walk. The thing was, I was scared to go inside Tim's house. It seemed a long time since I'd been anywhere that wasn't Laton Road, and I was afraid I might have forgotten what the rules were. I felt safer in Castle Meadow, or out on the cliff path. It was on the cliff path that Tim and I first kissed. We'd been sharing a packet of crisps, and so Tim's mouth was dry and salt-tasting. I liked that taste, and also the feel of his teeth, pressing down very softly on my upper lip. I felt giddy inside and had to step back. It was the end of June by then, and butterflies were rising and falling on the thistles.

The thistles were a deep purple colour, like amethyst crystals. Some of them had already started to go to seed.

Briefing for a Descent into Hell was about a man with amnesia. The doctors thought he was mad and tried to treat him with drugs, but inside the mind of Charles Watkins, something completely different was going on. First he was at sea in a rowing boat. Then he made landfall in an empty country with an alien city. I loved the world inside Charles Watkins's head, and felt angry with the doctors for trying to take it away from him. Once again I found myself captivated by the idea that the landscape of a place might be altered just by imagining that it was. Or that a make-believe place could become more real inside someone's mind than the outside world. I tried to imagine myself as a traveller like Charles Watkins, coming to the town of Hastings for the first time. The new Hastings was almost the same as the old one, but not quite. The best comparison I could think of was the way things looked when you took two photographs of the same street, a few seconds apart. At first glance the two would seem identical, but once you examined them more closely you'd see that they weren't the same at all, that there were dozens of tiny differences that when you added them together made two completely different versions of the same reality. In the first photo the street is empty. In the second a woman appears suddenly – you couldn't see her before because she was outside the frame. You probably moved your hand or changed position between photos, so the second image shows more of the houses to the right of the post office. The sun's behind a cloud in the first picture, not so much in the second. Stuff like that.

What you're actually looking at is two different worlds, a moment apart. Sometimes, when I walked across town to meet Tim or to visit the library I secretly pretended that I was going out into the streets of my imagined Hastings instead of the real one, and the more I imagined it, the more I was able to lose myself in this unreality. I talked to Tim about books whenever we met, but I never told him about my private version of the town and the people who lived there. I was afraid he might think I was as mad as Charles Watkins.

I began to keep a diary instead, a journal of my secret town and what I did there. I found I enjoyed writing things down and making things up. Both seemed much easier when there was no teacher looking over my shoulder.

I never thought of myself as a writer, though, not then. The idea seemed crazy.

* * *

Tim had name down for the Oxford entrance. I wasn't completely sure what that involved, only that at the end of it, Tim would be going. He was a year ahead of me, in any case. Whether he got into Oxford or not, he would still be leaving.

"It won't make any difference to us," he said. "I'll write to you every week, and you can come and visit."

"You'll forget all about me once you're actually there," I said.

"Of course I won't. Don't say that."

It was the closest we ever came to having a row and it made me feel stupid and ashamed and empty. I wondered if things would be different if we'd had sex already. There were times when I almost wanted to, but whenever I thought about actual fucking I felt myself freeze. I remembered the rain coming down in a torrent, and of soaping myself between my legs until I was sore.

I thought of Derek threatening to kill me if I ever told anyone.

I'd never paid that much attention to my body before, but now I hated to take my clothes off, in the school showers especially and even in my bedroom at night. I found I could never stop thinking about how Derek was only downstairs watching TV, or in his own room just a couple of steps away along the hall. I would step quickly out of my jeans, then slip my bra off under my T-shirt and slide into bed.

So long as Dad was in the house I felt safe, only never quite.

I learned to touch myself, but it was never Tim Leverson I thought of as I did it. The idea of him looking at or handling my body made me shrink up inside.

I think I was afraid that as soon as anyone touched me they would turn into Derek.

I thought of the girls from my favourite novels instead, Marian from *The Unicorn* by Iris Murdoch, or Sophie Wender from *The Chrysalids* by John Wyndham, her body grown hard and strong from her life in the Fringes. I imagined Sophie's knee thrust between my legs, her grubby fingers pressing down firmly in the centre of the pink wet swollen flower-bud of my clitoris. I thought of her pushing her fingers inside me and then I came, in a rush, like falling downstairs in the dark. This fantasy of Sophie was a secret, joyous thing that had nothing to do with Tim or Derek or anyone but me and Sophie. It felt so different from any of the crap about sex that got shown on TV.

Afterwards I liked to read, on and on into the small hours. I liked to think of Sophie asleep in the bed beside me, turned on her side with her back to me, the tangled strips of her long brown hair falling between the jutting angles of her shoulder blades.

The stars above the house, like antique earrings on a velvet backcloth.

Tim won a place to read English and Philosophy at Jesus College. In the final month before he left, I considered telling him what had happened with Derek, but when it actually came to it I found I couldn't. Telling him would have meant explaining so many other things. Why I'd never invited him to our house, for instance, or that my mother wasn't really dead, but only missing. Why I'd left it a whole year before telling him anything in the first place.

Derek was the kind of person Tim instinctively avoided – a sullen, silent youth with yellow hair, on the surface not so different from the wasters who hung around in the Gateway supermarket car park, swigging cans of Foster's lager and overturning the shopping trolleys. Those guys were losers, anyone could see that, but they didn't look like most people's idea of a rapist and neither did Derek.

I thought that if Tim didn't believe my story I might die. Or just stop, like the old Mickey Mouse alarm clock I'd had since I was six and that suddenly and inexplicably gave up working.

Mickey now stood permanently lopsided at twenty past five.

I knew I should throw the clock away but I couldn't bear to.

I put on my red sweatshirt and brushed down my hair and went to have supper with Tim and his parents to celebrate Tim getting into Oxford. Tim's parents were both teachers. They spoke to Tim as if he were their equal, a person who lived in their house with them and who they liked very much. The place was full of books, books everywhere.

"Will you be going to college next year too, Christy?" said Bella Leverson. She was a nice woman, with curling reddish hair and protuberant eyes.

"Of course she will," Tim said. "She's going to read History."

Tim sounded different when he was with his parents, more confident and just a tiny bit full of himself. After supper we went up to his large room in the attic and Tim put on a new record he had, an album by The Smiths that he kept calling radical. We lay on his bed and kissed, then Tim slid his hand down the front of my jeans. I lay very still and held my breath. I suppose I was waiting for him to start turning into Derek. Luckily it didn't happen. I let myself drift. There was a spider on the ceiling, just a small one, over in one corner. I fixed my eyes on it, its eight tiny limbs spread out like the points of a star, and tried to imagine the room from its perspective.

A kingdom of wonders and monsters. A raucous unstoppable din of electric light.

Tim wrote to me from Jesus just as he'd promised and then he stopped. I imagined he had met someone else, someone brilliant, or at least less of a psychological disaster area. I kept on writing to him for a while as if nothing had happened, then I stopped too. It was winter by then, early December. I kept remembering how much my mother had hated the long dark evenings, the curtains already drawn at four o'clock, the town's steep pavements slippery with rain. She used to say that winter was like being in prison. For the first time in ages I found myself wondering where she was now and if she was happy. It felt like trying to push open the door to another country.

You are too stupid, I thought. Too stupid to get into

Oxford. That's why he's stopped writing. What else did you expect?

I ached inside, but I couldn't cry. It was as if my chest and throat were choked with stones.

Then a couple of days before Christmas, Monica told me she was going to break up with Derek.

"He's so possessive, Chris," she said. "He thinks he owns me. It's not normal. I don't know how to deal with it any more."

Her revelation made me unhappy. Having Monica around had brought a sense of rhythm and normality back into our lives – if she left us there was always the chance that Derek would go off the rails again. Plus I knew I would miss her. I didn't want her to go.

"Do you have to?" I said.

"I'm sorry, Chris. It might make a difference if he really loved me but he doesn't. I don't think Derek could love anyone, not properly, he isn't capable of it. It needn't make any difference to us though, we can still keep in touch. I'll want to know how those exams go, for a start."

"Aren't you going to wait till after Christmas?"

She shook her head. "I can't do that, it wouldn't be fair. Now that I've made my decision I have to tell him."

Dad was ill by then – he had cancer. Jake Hom the Saturday boy had agreed to go full time, but even so Derek was working flat out, doing twelve-hour shifts sometimes. He was pretty knackered. He needed more help really, but he was trying to keep going until the New Year before hiring someone. Taking on new staff over Christmas would cost a packet, he said. He had five days off over the holiday period and I knew he was looking forward to having a break.

He'd booked a table, for the four of us including Monica, at the Royal Victoria. When Monica dropped her bombshell I remember thinking: that's it now, we won't be going, bang goes Christmas. I didn't care about Christmas, not really, but it was one more thing. I stomped down hard on my toes to keep myself from crying. It felt like Cindy Rogers all over again.

"When are you going to tell him?" I asked Monica.

"Tonight," she said. "As soon as he gets in."

We stopped talking about it after that. Monica fixed us some cheese and pickle sandwiches and we took them up to my room to watch TV. I tried to pretend everything was normal, even though I knew it wasn't. I tried not to think this might be the last time, but I couldn't help it. It was as if Monica had become less solid, less really there. In the end I was just wishing it would soon be over.

Derek came in around seven. Monica glanced at me knowingly and then went downstairs. Nothing happened at first. I could hear her moving around the kitchen, making him supper, sausage and bacon probably, and the sound of them chatting. Every now and then one of them laughed.

I turned up the volume on the TV and began to eat my way through the rest of the box of chocolates Monica had bought for us, Thornton's Continental, which she knew were my favourite. There was a celebrity quiz show on the BBC, and after that an Agatha Christie film, set in a grand hotel somewhere in Devon. About half way through I realised I'd seen the film before with Derek, or some of it anyway. I couldn't remember how the film ended though, and I supposed that Derek had done his usual and switched it off the moment he got bored.

Derek thought Agatha Christie murder movies were pointless and tame.

"All those posh gits walled up together," he said. "The only mystery that wants solving is who I'd shoot first."

I didn't say so but I thought he was wrong. There was always something comforting about Agatha Christie. Even though someone had to get murdered there was something Christmassy about it.

When the film finished I turned off the television and went downstairs. Since his illness Dad lived down there, mainly – he'd taken over the side room, so he could be closer to the kitchen and have his own bathroom. There was a light showing under his door, and I could hear the faint murmuring of the chat show that had come on after the Agatha Christie. Aside from that the house was quiet. The kitchen lay in darkness. I was expecting to find the room in chaos but when I switched on the light I found the washing up had all been done and everything cleared away. There was a broken plate in the waste bin but that was all.

There was no sign of Monica, or Derek. When I checked out the front for Derek's van I found it was gone.

Perhaps they made up, I thought. Or perhaps she never told him, after all.

Derek came in around six the following morning then

left again almost immediately to go to a job. He brought home Chinese takeaway that evening as he sometimes would. He didn't mention Monica at all.

On Christmas day Derek and our father and I all dressed up the best we could manage and drove over to have our lunch at the Royal Victoria. Derek was in a good mood. He drank a bottle and a half of Cava and for a while I was afraid he might turn nasty but apart from throwing up in Dad's bathroom when we got back he was mostly okay.

Dad didn't eat much but he had a few drinks. None of us wanted to admit how ill he looked.

I gave up my job at the flower shop straight after Christmas. I wrote a letter to Diane, telling her I needed to concentrate on my exams, but really it was because I didn't want to risk running into Monica. I was embarrassed, I suppose. I somehow knew she wouldn't keep her promise to stay in touch with me and she didn't. It was as if she'd vanished from the Earth altogether. I missed her a lot at first but in the end I got used to it. When I wasn't in school I mostly stayed in my room, reading and doing my school work and writing my journal. The idea of going to college had started to scare me shitless but I clung to it anyway, I suppose because I knew there was no alternative.

For my History exam I wrote an essay about Lady Jane Grey. I wrote that Jane was disliked by the men at court because she was well educated and held strong opinions. They thought she was dangerous, so they had her beheaded.

She was only sixteen when she died, younger than I was. I found the thought very upsetting. I put that down, too.

I became so involved in writing the essay that by the time the three hours were up I'd almost forgotten I was sitting an exam. When I arrived home, Dad was asleep in his room and Derek was out on a job. Neither of them remembered it was an exam day. When my results came through in August I wrote Monica a note, sealed it inside an envelope and posted it through the letterbox of the house that Monica lived in on Braybrooke Road. I never received a reply though, and a week before I was due to enrol at college a For Sale sign went up outside.

Monica was now as gone as my mother. I made myself forget her after that.

Derek seemed to avoid me after Monica left, which was okay by me. A couple of days before I left for London, he asked me if I needed any help moving my stuff.

"We can go in the van, if you want," he said.

I told him there was no need.

"It's only one suitcase," I said. "I'll be fine on the train."

He seemed relieved, and it was as if he wanted me to be gone every bit as much as I wanted to go. On the morning of my departure he presented me with a new laptop computer in an expensive carrying case.

"You're bound to need one," he said. "I chose this model because it has an extra-long battery life."

I'd never owned a computer before and I was chuffed to have it. I embraced Derek awkwardly, the first time we'd physically touched in several months. I tried to remember how long it had been since we'd sat out on the shed roof together, watching the cats and smoking Dad's Marlboros and talking nonsense in the purple twilight. I wondered if he was sorry for what he'd done to me, if he ever thought about it even. He was my brother and I felt I should have known these things, but they were questions I found impossible to answer, or to ask.

I felt sick and sad and desperate to get away.

Most of the rooms in halls were reserved for overseas students, so I had to find digs elsewhere. A woman I'd spoken to in the student accommodation office sent me a list of flats and bedsits within a reasonable distance of the college, and I chose the one that looked most affordable, a room in a family home between New Cross and Peckham. The room was in an extension that led off the kitchen, which made it separate from the family's main living space and so a bit more private. There was a toilet and a tiny shower cubicle, also a two-ring hob for cooking on, although Lana Sobel said I was welcome to use the main kitchen whenever I wanted to. Lana Sobel was a physiotherapist at Guy's Hospital. Conrad Sobel worked at Heathrow Airport, though I never discovered exactly what he did there. Their two sons, Abel and Curtis, were twenty and twenty-one years old. With their broad shoulders and big grins they seemed to immediately fill any room they entered. They came and went at random intervals, usually accompanied by one or other of a succession of girlfriends.

All the Sobels laughed a lot. At the weekends Lana would cook up huge quantities of jambalaya and a Jamaican dish called jerk chicken and they would have friends over. Their parties often went on into the small hours. I envied the family's easy habit of being together, and wished I could find a way of being more like them, but their noisy openness unnerved me and I felt unable to emulate it. I thought of the Queen's Road house very much as their domain, and came and went from my tiny corner of it as quietly and unobtrusively as I could. None of them was ever unfriendly towards me, but I had the feeling they thought I was rather standoffish.

I liked being in London almost immediately. I liked the tall terraces and odd little shops, the dusty plane trees that flanked both sides of Lewisham Way. Also I felt safe there because nobody noticed me or cared who I was. I felt nervous about starting the course though. Getting to and from the South Bank campus was no problem, as buses ran up from New Cross Road to London Bridge every ten minutes. My worry was that I wouldn't be good enough, or that I would make a fool of myself in front of the other students, who like the Sobels seemed already noisily at ease with communal living. I was fascinated by their casual intimacy, their instant dismissal of any person or subject they considered as dull.

Things became easier after I met Robyn Duschamps. Robyn was studying Economics, but she was taking some of the History modules, which is how I met her. Robyn's parents were divorced, and she referred to them by their first names, Sara and Eugene. Eugene Duschamps was originally from Haiti. Sara, like Conrad Sobel, was from Jamaica. Robyn had dark brown skin and pitch-black kinky hair which she wore scraped back from her face in a red rubber band. The thing about Robyn was that she never seemed to give a damn what people thought of her. She was clever and never tried to hide it. When after a couple of weeks of knowing her I asked her if she'd read through an essay I was writing on Matilda of England she said it was excellent and that I should get serious about my writing.

"What do you mean, get serious?" I said.

"I mean you should stop being afraid of getting stuff wrong and put your arse on the line. Say it how it is, how you see it. You have an unusual way of looking at things, Christy. Hasn't anyone ever told you that before?"

I shook my head.

"Well, you have."

I wasn't sure whether to believe her or not, but Robyn seemed to have an opinion on everything and she wasn't shy of letting people know it. I remembered Miss Wisbech, the way she'd come up to me in the corridor that time and said she thought I might enjoy reading Doris Lessing. I could imagine Robyn and Miss Wisbech getting on like a house on fire.

I wondered what Robyn would think of my Sapphire journals, if I were to let her see them, of the stories I told myself about an imaginary town. They were an unusual way of looking at things, definitely. I wondered if Robyn would think they qualified as telling it like it is.

* * *

186

I would have preferred to stay on in London over Christmas, but Lana Sobel told me she had guests arriving for the holidays and that I had to be out of my room from December 19th until just after New Year.

"You can leave your stuff, that's fine," she said. "It's just my brother and his wife in your room, they won't hurt a thing."

I dreaded returning to Hastings. I hadn't been in contact with Derek all term, except to tell him I'd be home for Christmas. I had no idea how things would be there. The first surprise was Derek himself, who seemed so chatty and so cheerful I barely recognised him. The second was that he had a new girlfriend. You didn't have to be a mastermind to see the two were connected.

"Hey, Sis," Derek said. "This is Linda. We just got engaged."

They were sitting side by side at the kitchen table. They both had mugs of coffee in front of them, and I noticed they were looking at property details, those print-offs of houses for sale you get given by estate agents. Derek never called me Sis, for a start, but I didn't dwell on the weirdness of that just then, because most of my attention was focussed on Linda.

Linda had the same very fine, pale hair as Monica, but instead of wearing it short and cut close to her head she had it long, almost down to her waist. She had that white, kind of blotting paper skin you can see all the veins through. Her forehead bulged outwards slightly, fixing her with a look of almost permanent anxiety. She was very skinny, and there was something otherworldly about her. She was one of those women you absolutely cannot help staring at.

If Derek had told me she was a visiting member of an

alien race I might even have believed him.

Linda was a dancer. She taught modern dance and ballet at a private studio in St Leonards. I think she and Derek met in a bar, though I don't know for sure. I could see at once that Derek was smitten, and I mean seriously. The way he looked at her, it was as if he had an engine running inside him and I knew it meant trouble. When I first saw Linda sitting there next to Derek at our kitchen table the image that sprang to my mind was of the porcelain ballerina in the china cabinet at Charlotte House, the pretty glazed ornament that Derek had said was Capo di Monte.

I remembered the way Derek had cradled the figurine between his hands, the tense excitement in his eyes as he gazed at her.

When Derek said they were engaged I thought he was joking. Then I saw the ring on Linda's finger, a cluster of diamonds and pearls, intricate and delicate, like the sweet-scented alyssum flowers in our backyard that forced their way up through cracks in the concrete in early summer. It was a beautiful piece of jewellery, an antique – I knew Derek would never have bought anything from a high-street jeweller.

The ring suited Linda's hand perfectly.

"It's lovely to meet you," I said.

Linda smiled, and I realised she was nervous. More nervous than I was, probably.

"We're selling the house," Derek said. He drew the various sheets of property details towards him across the table and began sorting them into a pile. "We want to get somewhere together, somewhere decent. This place is fucked."

"What about Dad?" I said. It was the only question I could think of that felt safe to ask.

"Dad? He'll come with us, of course. There'll be plenty of room for you too, obviously."

He spoke impatiently, as if my questions were irrelevant, a minor annoyance. I was in college now anyway, and both of us knew Dad wouldn't live much longer. The news of the move should have pleased me but it didn't. I felt there was too much riding on it. I also didn't like the nervy, all-or-nothing way Derek was behaving.

"When's this supposed to be happening?" I looked directly at Linda as I spoke, hoping to get some kind of reaction out of her, but once again it was Derek who answered.

"We'll be putting the house on the market at the end of January. Dad's agreed."

The house was in our father's name still, but I knew he would agree to anything Derek wanted – he no longer had the energy to fight him. I didn't know much about the ins and outs of house-buying, but it wasn't difficult to put two and two together and realise that Derek most likely wanted to get things underway before Dad became too ill to deal with the paperwork. It was Dad who'd have to sign on the dotted line, after all. It was either that or get wound up in probate for months and months, and I knew Derek hated to be made to wait, for anything.

Linda was just sitting there, silently smiling. I realised she hadn't spoken a word the whole time I'd been there. A strange little shiver went through me as I wondered if she was dumb, a real-life version of Hans Christian Andersen's

Little Mermaid, who gave up her voice so she could get closer to the prince she loved.

I always hated that story, mainly because I could never get over how stupid and selfish the prince was, but in any case Linda turned out to be nothing of the sort. She could speak just fine. She was nice, too. Derek seemed keen for Linda and me to get to know one another, and in the days following my return to Laton Road we ended up spending a fair amount of time together. I was surprised to discover how well we got on. The day before Christmas Eve, Linda invited me over to her flat in St Leonards so she could show me the present she'd bought for Derek, a gorgeously expensive cashmere sweater she'd dithered over for hours in some London boutique.

It was ridiculously beautiful. When Derek finally tried it on, on Christmas morning, it seemed to transform him.

"What do you reckon?" Linda said. "Do you think he'll like it?"

"You're joking, aren't you?" I said. "He's going to love it."

Linda's flat was part of a large house at the top end of London Road. The flat had its own private entrance, which you reached by climbing a twisting wrought-iron staircase at the back of the house. The flat's two reception rooms were long and narrow, almost as if they'd been squeezed out of the main house and on to a ledge overlooking the garden. The bathroom, on the other hand, was enormous, with a claw-footed cast-iron bath and a porcelain sink so large you could have drowned a dog in it. There were pretty glass bottles of perfume and lotion everywhere, and all the floorboards in the flat were sanded and varnished. There was the waxy, clean scent of furniture polish. Everything shone.

The flat seemed to be Linda's perfect habitat, Linda personified. I found it hard to imagine her ever wanting to leave.

She made us celebratory cocktails in crystal glasses, champagne with something purple in it, and tiny gold hearts that slowly dissolved in a ball of pink fizz.

"Happy Christmas," Linda said. She put on a CD, a string quartet playing slightly off key, accompanied by the sound of children's voices. Normally I wouldn't have said much, but the drink made me talkative.

"Are you really engaged to Derek?" I said. It was the question I'd been dying to ask for days, even though I was slightly scared of learning the answer. We were sitting side by side on Linda's sofa, drinks in hand and shoes off, bosom buddies. The sofa was cream-coloured, draped with a sheet of woven fabric Linda told me she'd brought back from a trip to Morocco.

She turned to look at me. She was cradling her glass in both hands and gazing at me in a forthright, appraising way that made me think at first that she was angry. Then she said something strange.

"Nothing's been decided yet. Derek and I only met in October. It's early days."

"But the ring?" I said.

"That's just a private joke. Derek spotted it in an antique shop in Birmingham. He said he knew he had to buy it for me the moment he saw it. I put it on my wedding finger because that was the finger it fitted. When you came in the other day, Derek had only just given it to me. He said it was an early Christmas present. I had no idea he was going to tell you we were engaged." She held up her hand and twisted it from side to side, making the ring sparkle in the light from several floor lamps.

At least that explained her silence. She'd been totally flummoxed.

"You've discussed it since, though?" I insisted. "You have told him you thought he was joking?"

"It's not the kind of thing you need to explain, is it? Not when you're close to someone. Derek knows how I feel about marriage. We'll take things as they come, see what happens."

Linda smiled at me hopefully, as if that settled everything. I had the feeling she was looking to me for reassurance, that she wanted me to agree that yes, of course my brother would understand that the whole engagement thing was a joke, a private understanding between the two of them, that it could never have been for real or at least not yet. I felt numbness spreading through me, body and mind, worming its tendrils into my muscles like the dissolving golden hearts in the purple champagne.

It's the drink, I thought, knowing it wasn't.

"What was Derek doing in Birmingham, anyway?" I managed to say.

"Oh, I don't know. Something to do with a piano. He was back by eleven though. He hates having to stay in hotels."

She was right about that, at least. Derek never spent a night away from home if he could help it. I remember feeling surprised that Linda knew this about my brother, the kind of detail that was unimportant in itself but the fact that she'd picked up on it seemed to mean at the very least that she genuinely cared about him.

Perhaps she did love him, after all. Perhaps everything would turn out all right.

As I was leaving the flat to go back to Laton Road, Linda asked if she could have my address in London, and my phone number.

"It would be nice to keep in touch, don't you think?" she said. What I thought was that it was odd, because we hardly knew each other, but I gave them to her anyway. I didn't expect to actually hear from her. I thought it was just the kind of thing that people say on the spur of the moment.

I was wrong about that, though. I didn't hear anything for ages, from her or from Derek, but then just after the Easter vacation I had a phone call from Linda, asking if she could come up to town and take me to lunch one day. I was surprised, but said yes, partly because I wasn't quick enough to think of an excuse not to, but also because I was curious to hear how things were going. We arranged a suitable time, and then three days later there I was, meeting her at Charing Cross as if we were old friends. She arrived just after midday, dressed in a button-up black jumpsuit that would have looked ridiculously unflattering on most people but made Linda look like a *Vogue* cover model. The jumpsuit's buttons were silver, and shaped like thistles.

"You look amazing," I said. I kissed her cheek.

"It's vintage," Linda said. "A bit sixties, isn't it? Do you really like it?"

"On you I do," I said.

She laughed, and hugged me around the shoulders. "Where shall we go?"

We ended up in a small Italian cafe close to Leicester Square.

"So, how's college?" Linda asked. I snapped a breadstick in half and said things were fine.

"I got a 2:1 for my Queen Matilda essay," I said, but I could tell from the way she kept staring past me and out of the window that she wasn't really interested.

"Have you made any special friends yet?" she asked. She gave a nervous little laugh and shook back her hair. She was wearing purple eyeliner, and eyeshadow in a delicate mauve colour. I noticed belatedly how tired she was looking. I began telling her about Robyn, and the violent row she'd recently got into with a guy in her tutor group, but Linda cut me short almost at once.

"I don't mean that, I mean boyfriends."

"No boyfriends," I said. "Sorry." It wasn't true, actually, because earlier in the spring semester I had met Peter. Peter was a mathematician and Robyn's new housemate, a big guy with John Lennon glasses and beautiful hands. Robyn told me he'd once wanted to be a pianist, and it was true that every time I passed by his room I heard music coming out of it, CDs of elaborate-sounding keyboard works performed by musicians I'd never heard of, Glenn Gould and Sviatoslav

Richter and Maria Yudina. The music fascinated me. I started dropping in on Peter to find out what he was listening to, and we became friendly from there. His room was outlandishly neat, the tartan bed cover spread smoothly over twin pillows, the rows of complicated-looking textbooks all in order. He spoke slowly and in fits and starts, as if he were struggling to express ideas that had only just occurred to him. He never talked about the work he was doing, and when Robyn told me he'd won several high-profile mathematics contests in his early teens it came as a genuine surprise.

He always seemed pleased to see me, and I found him curiously restful to be with. The way the smile spread gradually across the curves of his gentle moon face was like the sun coming out. He and Robyn seemed to get on very well. They were as different in temperament as you could imagine, but they both enjoyed locking swords over points of politics or philosophy and once they got started they didn't hold back. Their discussions unnerved me at first because they seemed so hostile, but I soon learned that so far as they were concerned that was part of the fun. Once they were finished they'd make Irish coffee and put on a romcom and it was like all the shouting and point-scoring had never happened.

They were like opposite twins. I know that phrase makes no sense, but that's how it was. In a way, Peter and Robyn became my surrogate family. I was spending more and more time round at their place and one weekend in late March, when Robyn had gone home to Cambridge to visit her mother, I ended up staying over. Peter and I hunkered down on the sofa and watched all five *Planet of the Apes* videos, one after the other. By the time *Battle for the Planet of the Apes* had finished it was two o'clock in the morning and we were both very drunk. I was supposed to be sleeping in Robyn's room, but I ended up collapsing on Peter's bed and just not leaving. We wrestled for a bit, just pissing about, and then Peter suddenly asked me if I would sleep with him.

"Couldn't you just give me a handjob? I'm so desperate for a fuck I'm going crazy."

I was surprised how easy it was. I liked Peter so much I couldn't bear to say no. I knew how embarrassed he would be the next day, and the thought of how that might spoil our friendship made me decide it might be better if I just went through with it. We turned out the lights then got under the covers and slipped out of our clothes. Peter's body was large and broad and his flabby stomach was soft as a girl's but his hands were lovely, dextrous as a dancer's. They reminded me of Linda's hands. Peter groaned loudly when he came, like someone had just dropped a rock on his foot, and afterwards was so sweet and so seemingly grateful that I felt glad we'd done it. We talked on and on for hours, in whispers even though the flat was empty apart from the two of us.

From then on we were kind of an item and I suppose it showed. "Oh fuck," Robyn said when she returned from Cambridge and found us cuddling on the sofa. "Just don't go all lovey-dovey on me, that's all I'm asking."

I wasn't sure if Peter and I would stay together, but even then I found it difficult to imagine my life without him. Things were so different from the way they had been with Tim. With Tim there had been this *thing*, this high-octane yearning uncertainty, the sense that something was expected of us, ready or not. With Peter, sex just happened and it was no big deal. It was my friendship with Peter, more than anything else, that made me see that Derek and what Derek had done to me didn't have to define the way I thought and felt.

Being with Peter showed me that I could say no to Derek controlling my life, the same way I'd have said no to Derek raping me, if I'd known how. Slowly I began to realise that my brother's opinions and his violence and his cruelty could be relegated to a part of my mind where they no longer held any active influence over my future. I think that's why when Linda asked me if I had a boyfriend I said no. I didn't want the news getting back to Derek. I didn't want Derek to know anything about me or about my new life or what I was doing.

"There just isn't time, not with all the essay-writing and everything," I said to her. I tried to laugh it off, to make it seem unimportant, but Linda's question made me feel uncomfortable and embarrassed. I sensed it wasn't me we were talking about, that already we'd moved on to something else, the thing, whatever it was, that had prompted Linda to ask to see me in the first place.

"That's a shame," Linda said. "College should be fun, shouldn't it? It's no fun if it's all about work." She glanced quickly around the restaurant. "Listen, Christy, do you mind if I ask you something?"

"What's wrong?" I said. For a minute I thought she was going to tell me my father had died, but then I realised almost at once that didn't make sense. Dad being dead wouldn't have made her start acting antsy the way she was.

She wouldn't have bothered coming up to London to tell me, either. It was hardly big news that he was on the way out. Derek would have phoned me instead.

"It's Derek," Linda said. "He's all set on me selling my flat, but I don't want to do that. I think we should wait, you know, with your dad being so ill and everything. But every time I suggest putting it off he gets all in a state. I'm in a bit of a fix, actually. I was wondering if you'd mind having a word with him."

"He won't listen to me," I said hurriedly. "We're not all that close."

I realised that Derek and I hadn't had a proper conversation, just the two of us together, since his assault on me. Most likely we never could now, not ever. I couldn't tell Linda that, though. And what I knew for sure was that the idea of me advising him to back off from Linda was simply ridiculous. He would tell me to piss off out of his business and that would be that. I felt annoyed with Linda for not seeing that, for even suggesting it. The whole thing was her fault anyway, for letting Derek believe they were engaged. My stomach felt bound in a knot, like a woodlouse someone had prodded with a piece of twig. Linda clasped her hands together on the Formica tabletop then started fiddling with her rings, the diamond-and-pearl cluster Derek had given her and another one I hadn't seen before, a narrow gold band set with a tiny arrow of yellow quartz.

"I'm sorry," she said. "This is my problem. I know you tried to warn me. I've been so stupid."

"Is there anywhere you could go?" I said.

"Go? What do you mean?"

"Nothing," I replied. I felt stupid for even mentioning it. "I just thought that if you went away for a while he might calm down."

"That's just crazy though. I can't let him rule my life like that. Anyway, there's my job." She turned away from me and started fumbling in her handbag. I thought she was looking for cigarettes, but after a moment's searching she pulled out an envelope. It was grimy and slightly crumpled, bent at the corners. She glanced quickly at the front of it then handed it to me across the table.

"I found this in the glove compartment of Derek's van," she said. "It's addressed to you, and I thought that you should have it."

The envelope had an Oxford postmark and had been torn open along the top. I recognised Tim's handwriting immediately.

"I haven't read it, in case you're wondering," Linda said. "It was like that when I found it."

I wanted to ask her how come she'd been poking about in Derek's glove compartment in the first place, but I couldn't speak. I took the letter out of its envelope and unfolded it. *Dear Christy,* I read. *I keep hoping that I'm going to hear from you. I don't understand what's happened.* The letter was dated the April of the year before. I'd stopped writing to Tim in the December. I remembered how I'd felt, that aching emptiness. It was horrible to know that Tim had gone on writing and waiting and hoping, longer even than I had. That he'd believed in me even when, unbeknownst to him, the version of me he was writing to no longer existed.

My thoughts were racing. I wished that Linda would leave, so I could read the rest of Tim's letter in private. I wondered how many other letters there had been, if Derek had hidden these also or simply destroyed them. Over the next couple of days I tried to write to Tim, to explain what had been done to us and to say sorry. I must have started two-dozen letters in total, but I never finished any of them and in the end I gave up. It was all too late. Besides, there was Peter to think about.

"Are you okay, Christy?" Linda said.

I nodded.

"It's from a friend," I said. "I must have mislaid it somehow."

"I suppose," Linda said. She gave me a look. "It's funny how it ended up in Derek's van though, isn't it?"

We stared at one another for a moment in silence, then Linda told me she'd stopped being in love with my brother and probably never had been. There was someone else.

"His name's Alex Adeyemi," she said. "We were together for ages before I met Derek, but things went wrong for a bit and we weren't seeing each other, so when Derek asked me out I said okay. That wasn't fair on Derek, I see that now. Alex got back in contact just after Christmas and I agreed to meet him. He wants us to get back together permanently. Everything's such a mess."

"What are you going to do?" I said. I felt shaky inside, kind of sick. Some of it was Tim still, but mainly it was Linda and what she'd just told me. I couldn't believe what she'd done, her stupidity. I realised she didn't know my brother at all. She had no idea what he could be like when he got angry, what he was capable of.

When he found out about this Alex guy he was going to go berserk.

"I'll have to tell him, won't I?" Linda said. "Tell him it's over."

"Tell who? Alex?"

"No, of course not. I have to tell Derek. It would never have worked out, anyway. We're two totally different people." She sighed, and once again I saw how tired she looked. "There has to be a way to make him see that."

"What about Alex?" I said. "What does he think?"

She shifted in her seat, looking uncomfortable. "I haven't told him. About Derek, I mean. I didn't want to complicate things. I've been able to keep up the pretence until now because Alex doesn't want to pressure me – he still thinks of himself as the guilty party, I suppose. He must know something's not right though. I feel awful, making excuses all the time about why I can't see him. I can't keep on with it."

"Perhaps if you told Alex the truth he might be able to help you sort things out."

"Maybe," she said. She was silent for a moment. "But then he would know I carried on sleeping with Derek, even after I said I was still in love with him, and that would be terrible. Anyway," she said, glancing across at me as if to check I was still listening. "I know this sounds stupid, but I'm afraid that if Derek finds out about Alex he might do something. Something awful."

"You're scared of him." Our eyes met for a second and then we both looked away.

"You think I'm being ridiculous," Linda said.

"He's my brother." It was a strange way for me to answer, not an answer at all really, but at that moment it was the only way I knew to express what I felt. That Derek was my brother and I knew he was crazy. I knew it better than anyone.

"What should I do?" Linda said. She looked close to tears.

"I don't know yet," I replied. "I'll have to think about it."

"I'm so sorry. I should never have got you involved in this."

"We need time to work things out, that's all."

"I've been trying to work things out for months. It's driving me mad." She hauled a tissue out of her bag and blew her nose. Her beautiful face looked very pale and very still, the face of some antique maiden carved from alabaster. "I don't want you worrying," she said. "It's simple really. I just have to tell him."

I walked with her back to the station. It was mid-afternoon by then, and the sun had come out. The train was on time. I saw Linda on to the platform then caught the next train back down to New Cross. By the time I was halfway there I'd managed to push the business of Linda and Derek to the back of my mind. It seemed to me that she was right – this was her problem and she shouldn't have involved me.

I was as fed up with my brother as it was possible to be. I was sick of thinking about him.

Did I believe that Linda was actually in physical danger?

That's a question I can't answer honestly, because I still don't know.

The following morning I received a letter from her. She thanked me for a lovely afternoon, and told me I should forget everything she'd told me about Alex. *I've decided not to see him again,* she wrote. *If you break up with someone there's always a reason. I was stupid to think I could make it work. I'm going to tell him it's over.* She said that Derek had had an offer on the house, and that she was starting to get excited about the move.

I didn't believe a word of it, or not entirely. I guessed her reasons for writing the letter were much the same as my own reasons for not wanting to tell her about Peter and me: she didn't want the story getting back to Derek. I also took her words as a sign that she'd decided to sort things out in her own way and I hoped that would be the end of it. But then about two weeks later I had a telephone call from Derek.

"Dad's worse," he said. "If you want to see him alive you should come now." He paused. "I've had to put the house on hold and everything."

"How bad is he?" I said.

"He's still normal in his mind, if that's what you mean. But the doctors say he's only got days. A week at the most. They transferred him to the hospice yesterday, St Mary's, and you know what that means."

I said I'd come straight away, and I was on a train from London Bridge in less than an hour. Derek met me at

Hastings station and drove me over to the hospice in the van. We barely exchanged a word the entire journey. I remember I was scared, scared that Dad would no longer recognise me, but I was wrong about that.

The man in the bed was still Dad, but a less concrete version. It was like seeing an actor on TV, playing the role of Dad, sick.

It was as if somebody was trying to rub him out.

When he saw me he tried to sit up, but fell back immediately against the pillows.

"Dad," I said. "Don't do that. There's no need."

He smiled weakly. There was a needle taped to his hand.

"Chris," he said. "Derek told me you might be coming."

I sat down on the plastic chair beside the bed. I was pleased to find he had his own room, with a view of the hospice garden. There were crocuses in bloom. Under a tree in the furthest corner I could see two nurses, sitting side by side on a wooden bench and chatting, taking a break. I was normally terrified of hospitals but this place seemed different. Most people when you ask them say they'd prefer to die at home in their own beds, but I felt a deep relief that Dad was here, in this bright clean space, surrounded by people who knew how to help him, instead of alone in the cluttered and airless downstairs room at Laton Road.

I hugged him briefly around the shoulders then quickly withdrew. It had been years since we'd had physical contact of any kind. I was ashamed to find I did not want to touch him now. I felt distressed by what was happening to him, but I had no idea how I should talk to him, not because he was dying but because we'd never talked.

It came to me then that I knew nothing about this man who was my father. I knew he liked Jeffery Deaver novels and Guinness and motor racing on the TV, but aside from those small details he was a stranger to me. I wondered what he thought he knew of me in return? Did he remember that I was at college now? Other than the daily routine of the business, did he remember anything of his life with us at all?

As a family, we had fallen fatally out of touch with one another. It was easy to blame my mother for leaving, but was it not just as much my fault, or Derek's? I had never tried to get to know my father properly, to see inside his world. Derek and I had been close once – with one horrible, desperate error that had been ruined. Nobody was to blame and yet we all were. Instead of reaching out to one another we had dived inward, into worlds that lay in close orbit but never touched.

We had forgotten we were even related. It was too late now.

Looking at my father in the hospital bed I felt an immense sadness. I felt disgusted with myself, but also the desire to be rid of this situation as soon as possible. I could do nothing to change what was happening and I did not belong here. The smiling, soft-voiced nurses made me feel in the way.

"How are you getting on, Dad?" I said.

"I'm really all right," he said. "Since they've managed to sort out the pain I'm not bad at all." He patted my arm briefly, then laid both hands in his lap as if their job was now finished and he had no further use for them. I sat silently beside him, thinking of things I might say and then rejecting them, one after the other. After about ten minutes one of the nurses brought me a cup of tea.

"That's Kiran," said my father. "She has a little boy named Jonah. She showed me a picture of him."

"She seems nice," I said. I asked him to tell me about the other nurses and he seemed happy to do that. He seemed peaceful in himself, but I couldn't get away from the idea that he must be lonely, that he must be wondering what his life had been about and what he had come to. These thoughts made me want to cry. I stayed for about an hour, then caught the bus into town and went straight back to London.

My father died the following day. I returned to Hastings eight days later for the funeral. I went to the crematorium straight from the station. There were more people there than I would have expected – Dad's drinking pals from the Hughenden Arms and their wives, his brother Clive who lived in Bromley and Clive's stepson Mickey, some other people I didn't recognise but who Derek said were business contacts. After the short service we all stood around in the grounds of the crem for half an hour wondering what to say to each other then went our separate ways the minute we could.

It was a sad day. There was a sense of futility about it, the feeling that Dad's life had been a waste of time. I tried not to think about Mum but it was hard not to. When Derek asked if I wanted to go and have a pub lunch with him and Linda I agreed at once. I was desperate to put the funeral behind me, and besides that I was hungry. Linda looked better than when I'd seen her in town, fuller in the face and with a bloom to her cheeks that had not been there before.

"Have you guessed?" Derek said. "Linda's expecting. It's early days but she's definitely pregnant. We did the test yesterday."

I glanced at Linda but she immediately looked away. "Congratulations," I said to Derek. "What's happening about the house?"

"We'll have to stay put for a bit while the will goes through probate. The solicitor says it's fairly straightforward, so it shouldn't take long. You're in line for half the money, did you know that?"

"I hadn't thought about it," I said.

"We've been thinking it'd be best for you if you left it in the house. More secure, I mean. And there's always a home for you with us, you know that."

He seemed relaxed and in control, what you might call happy. The afternoon passed. When Linda went to the Ladies I followed her in. I thought she might want to talk, but she just made some breezy remark about the pub being crowded then darted back into the saloon before I had the chance to say a word. I was mystified by her change of heart, but then reminded myself that it was none of my business.

When I arrived back in London I asked Lana Sobel if I could keep my room on over the summer. She seemed surprised but then agreed it would be okay.

"We hardly know you're there," she said, and laughed. I trailed around New Cross and Deptford looking in shop windows until I found a cafe that was advertising for waiting staff. The manager didn't seem keen when she found out I was a student, but when I told her I'd be willing to carry on working during term time she hired me. We agreed I should work three days a week on a rota basis. The work was more tiring than my old job at the flower shop, but it bulked out my grant and meant I could set some money aside for emergencies. I knew that Derek would do everything he could to hang on to my half of the house money. It never occurred to me that I had a right to it, that I could bring a court case against him if he tried to deprive me of it.

That first summer in London was strange. Robyn was spending the vacation in Port au Prince. Her letters arrived at intervals, filled with the excitement of being in a new place and with the news that she was thinking about going out to work there permanently once she'd finished her degree.

They're really short of teachers here, she wrote. *But the children are just amazing. I don't want to leave.*

I'd never imagined Robyn as a teacher but I felt sure she'd be good at it.

Peter stayed on in London for a couple of weeks after term ended, but then he left to go on holiday with his family in west Wales. They hired a cottage there every year, apparently. He asked me to go with him, and I was tempted but in the end I said no. I knew I would lose the cafe job if I went. Plus I was actually quite looking forward to some time by myself.

"I'll still be here when you get back," I said to him.

"It's bound to rain the whole time anyway," Peter said. "It always pisses down in Wales."

We had a laugh about that, and I felt none of the anxiety

that had consumed me when Tim left for Oxford. I was never in love with Peter but I did love him. The trust between us was complete, and never in question.

I didn't hear from Linda again until the end of August, when Lana Sobel knocked on my door and told me I had a telephone call. I thought it might be Peter but it wasn't. I didn't recognise Linda's voice at first. She sounded very faint, very far away.

"Christy? Is that you?"

"Yes," I said. "It's me. Are you okay?"

There was an odd kind of breathy silence, and then I realised Linda was crying. What I was hearing down the line was the sound of her sobs.

"Are you all right, Linda?" I repeated. "Is it something to do with the baby?"

I wondered if she'd suffered a miscarriage or something – it was the only thing I could think of that was awful enough to account for such obvious grief. My heart lurched at the thought, and I remembered the hideous pink-white slipperiness of the dead rat behind the shed at Laton Road.

"There is no baby," she said. She gave a bitter little hiccoughing laugh. "I was pregnant for less than a month. He should never have said anything."

Had she lost the baby after all, or had she got rid of it? She didn't say and I couldn't decide which would be more upsetting. I only knew that if Linda had had an abortion and Derek found out, things would be bad.

"What is it, then?" I wished she hadn't called. I found Linda's apparent need of me, her mistaken belief that I held a kind of secret rapport with my brother, oppressive and troubling.

Did she not, I wanted to ask her, have friends of her own?

But at the same time I could not ignore her. Derek was my brother, after all, and I thought I might just be the only person on Earth who could truly imagine how trapped and alone Linda felt.

"It's Derek," she said. "He found out about Alex."

My heart missed a beat.

"When did this happen?" I said.

"Last night. He caught us coming out of The Tower, at the top of London Road. We'd been in there for about an hour, just having a drink, and when we went to leave Derek was just *there*. He went for Alex like he was – I don't know, possessed or something, just knocked him down in the street and started kicking him. If some people hadn't come out of the pub I don't know what might have happened. It was awful, Christy, it was just horrible."

She started crying again, in that way you do when you've finally got something terrible out in the open and there's nothing left to do but let it take you. I felt helpless and I felt scared. Ever since the rape there'd been this tiny corner of my mind where I'd let myself believe that it hadn't happened, that it had all been in my head and so there was never any need to think about it unless I chose to.

Hearing Linda crying like that, it brought everything back.

"Where's Derek now?" I said at last.

"I don't know. I honestly don't know. I daren't go near the house. Alex seems to think I'm overreacting but I'm really frightened. I keep thinking he's going to turn up here. Should I call the police?"

"No," I said at once. "Let me talk to him first. Just stay where you are and I'll be there as soon as I can."

I heard her sigh with relief, and I could tell that I'd said exactly what she wanted me to say, that she felt better just from hearing me say it, at least for the moment. She believed I was in control, that I would know what to do. She was wrong of course, and so was I. I should have told her to call the cops, to go right ahead and tell them everything, that my brother had had this coming to him for years.

Did I honestly think I could make him see reason? Was the thought of Derek in the back of a police car so hard to take?

I was a fool, I see that now. But I was scared, too. More scared than Linda was, probably, because I knew Derek better.

I was outside Linda's flat and ringing the doorbell less than three hours later. No one answered, so I rang the bell again then bent down and peered through the letterbox. There was a light on in the hallway, but no sign of movement. I sat down on the steps to wait. It occurred to me that Linda might have gone to Alex's place, wherever that was, and I cursed myself for not thinking to ask for his phone number.

I waited for at least half an hour, all the time getting more and more agitated. In the end I left Linda's and headed over to Laton Road. It was all I could think of to do. I took the shortcut through the park, trying not to think too much about how Derek was going to react when I turned up out of the blue like this. If he guessed I'd been talking to Linda behind his back he would go mad.

The van was gone from out the front but I thought that might be a good sign. If Derek was out on a job then things must be getting back to normal. Or perhaps he and Linda were out together somewhere, talking things through in a civilized manner like rational human beings. I knocked on the glass then rang the bell and waited, not wanting to burst in unannounced. When no one answered I let myself in with my own key.

I could tell as soon as I stepped inside that the house was empty. I called Linda's name anyway, then Derek's, my voice rattling around in the silent hallway like a penny inside a broken slot machine. There was no answering call.

I went through to the kitchen. Clean dishes were stacked neatly on the draining board, and there were fresh soap suds clinging in gleaming clumps to the upturned washing-up bowl. There was a smell of onions and cooked fat. It was clear that someone had been there in the kitchen only minutes before.

I wasn't sure what to do next. It seemed logical just to wait, to make myself a sandwich and a cup of coffee and see what happened. But I was beginning to feel a bit freaked out. The house was too silent, too empty, and it was giving me the creeps. I realised I was afraid to go upstairs, even though I felt certain there was no one up there.

I checked the answerphone for messages. I didn't expect to find anything useful – the people who called the house were mostly Derek's clients – but when I pressed the button for playback the voice I heard was Linda's, after all.

Derek, pick up the phone, she said. *I know you're in there.*

She sounded upset, on the verge of tears. Her voice was muffled by the sound of passing traffic. Which suggested she'd been calling from a phone box and not from the flat. Also I thought it was strange, the way she'd said 'I know you're in there' instead of just 'I know you're there'. It was almost as if she'd been looking directly at the house when she made her call, as if she'd been ringing from across the road, which perhaps she had. The message had been left just an hour before. I was trying to decide if I should stay where I was or return to Linda's flat when the phone rang. I was so startled I almost cried out. Hesitantly I reached out and picked up the receiver.

"Christy?" It was Linda. God knows how she knew I would be there. She sounded totally panic-stricken. "Please come. I can't talk for long, because I know he's around here somewhere, hunting for me. He said he just wanted to talk, but he's not making sense. I'm terrified, Chris. I think he wants to kill me."

"Don't be silly," I said. I asked her where she was, and she said The Dolphin, one of the pubs on Rock-a-Nore Road. "Just wait there, will you? You're in a crowded pub – nothing can happen. I'll be there in fifteen minutes. Just hang on."

I left the house at once, cutting up through Elphinstone Road and then across the railway bridge towards West

Hill. About halfway there I started wondering if I'd left the kitchen light on, or whether it had been on already when I arrived. I wasn't sure either way. It was too late to worry about that now.

It was a warm night, and the restaurants and bars along the seafront all had their doors open. Music and drinkers were spilling out into the road. The Dolphin was packed. I pushed inside, working my way through the main bar then through the pool room and out into the small walled beer garden at the rear. No sign of Linda anywhere. I even went into the Ladies just to check but she wasn't there either. I made my way back out on to the street. I was starving hungry – apart from a pasty at London Bridge station I'd had nothing since breakfast. I was beginning to feel deeply annoyed as well as frustrated. It was as if they were playing with me, sending me out on a wild goose chase then watching from somewhere nearby and laughing like drains.

Why would they do that, though? What would be the point? And there was no doubting that Linda really had sounded petrified. I walked to the next pub along, which I knew had a phone box outside, and dialled the number of Linda's flat. No reply, not even an answerphone message – either Linda didn't have one or it wasn't switched on. I thought about calling Laton Road but didn't. What was I going to say if Derek picked up?

I hung around a bit longer, walking up and down the stretch of road between the two pubs, but there was still no sign of Linda, no sign of Derek either, and it was beginning to get dark. I decided I'd return to Laton Road. If Derek was there I'd tell him some story then catch the train back to London first thing in the morning.

I was really pissed off by this time, and for no reason I could pin down I was also frightened. I had started to get the idea that I was not in Hastings at all but in some fake version of it, a decoy town. Even though the streets and cafes and houses were all perfectly familiar to me, I kept thinking I was going to turn the next corner and find myself lost.

Eventually that's what happened. The Old Town is a warren anyway, a labyrinth of criss-crossing twittens and narrow courtyards, and on the night I went looking for Linda it seemed to expand. Strange houses loomed up out of the twilight. Streets I was expecting to find were no longer there. I walked for what seemed like miles along one alleyway, and when I came out I found I was in the kitchen yard of what looked like The Swan, a pub I knew had been destroyed by a bomb during World War Two. I recognised it from the old photos.

I could see lights inside, hear voices. Uncanny. I felt all the tiny hairs along my forearms standing on end.

It was as if I were living inside a story, or inside the journal I'd written about Sapphire, about Jenna and Del.

A sense of wonder overcame me then, in spite of my fear. I wandered around for what seemed like hours, no longer trying to find the pathways I knew but concentrating instead on inventing new ones, streets that would eventually take me where I wanted to go.

The shop windows were all lit up. I saw ships in bottles and ceramic greyhounds, silver earrings shaped like fishes or magpies, everything glimmering softly under coloured lights. I saw a woman, leading a child by the hand. The woman seemed to be in a hurry, but the child kept dawdling. Her hair was a nest of yellow curls, just like Derek's. She pointed at something in one of the windows. The woman spoke some words to her and they moved on.

In the end I stumbled upon a path that I knew would lead me out on to Castle Meadow. The Old Town lay beneath me, a twinkling of tiny lights caught between two hills. From this distance the place was unknowable, the real shifting into the imagined, like smoke into the base ground of the coal-coloured sky.

I gazed up at the moon, as if to check it was still there, that it was still our moon I was looking at and not some other alien satellite in a distant galaxy. I was still sweating from the exertion of my upward climb.

When I arrived back at the house Derek's van was parked in the drive and I could see lights on upstairs and in the hall. I let myself in with my key. After a minute or so Derek appeared, looking down the stairs towards me from the upstairs landing.

I felt terror for an instant, realising we were alone in the house together, remembering. Then the feeling evaporated. I knew he'd never hurt me again, that he wouldn't dare. Don't ask me how I knew that, but I did.

"Chris?" he said. His face looked drained of all colour. He looks like his own ghost, I thought. Then I realised that's what we all are, when it comes down to it. "What are you doing here?" he said. I didn't answer. He came down the stairs towards me, one step at a time. When he reached the bottom step he stopped and then sat down.

"I'm fucked," he said. He rested his forehead briefly against his hands and then looked up at me. "I mean, what a total balls-up this day has been. Christ." He looked burned out, almost pitiable. He was wearing the cashmere sweater that Linda had bought him for Christmas, and when he moved his right arm I saw the delicately pattered cream wool was marked with a stain the colour of rust from wrist to elbow. The wool had puckered up slightly around its edges.

Otherwise, the jumper looked clean.

"Have you had anything to eat?" I said to him. He looked at me as if I'd gone mad.

"Why, are you hungry?" he said.

"Like the wolf." It was an old joke, an ancient pop lyric. Both of us smiled.

"There's some bacon in the fridge if you want it. There's bread on the side. It might be a bit stale, though."

"I don't care."

I went through to the kitchen, took the bacon out of the fridge and fried up six rashers. The white sliced bread in its plastic packet was a day past its best, as Derek had said, but still perfectly edible. I spread on some Flora and made up two sandwiches. I ate mine immediately, standing up, leaning against the kitchen counter, the bacon still so hot it burned the roof of my mouth. Derek stayed where he was at the foot of the stairs. When I took him his sandwich he ate it, though more slowly.

"Are you staying?" he asked me.

"Just for tonight. I need to get back."

"Tomorrow's Sunday."

"I have things to do."

"Do you want me to get you a duvet and stuff?"

"Don't worry about that. It's late. I'll sleep in Dad's room."

I bedded down on the sofa in the side room, covering myself with one of Dad's old car blankets. The room seemed unnaturally silent, empty finally, as if it had given up its ghost when my father died.

This house, I thought. It's so over.

I fell asleep soon after that. I felt exhausted.

Peter was back in London a week later and so was Robyn. By the time we all graduated, I had entered and won the Cavendish Essay Competition, an annual contest run by the college. A short while afterwards I published my first short story in *London* magazine. When Robyn went off to do an MBA at Princeton, Peter and I moved in together, to a garden flat in a building towards the Peckham end of Queen's Road. I carried on working in the cafe for a while; later I got a job at the library in Forest Hill. I wrote in the evenings and at the weekends. My first collection of stories appeared five years later.

I more or less fell out of contact with Derek. I thought of him sometimes though, thought of him the way he used to be, when we sat out on the shed roof through those endless August evenings, giving unsuitable nicknames to the neighbourhood cats and feeling like we were kings of the world, a race apart.

"I can do anything I want," Derek said. "Anything I fucking well feel like." He blew smoke from a Marlboro. I rolled over on to my back and gazed up at the sky. The sky was mauve, translucent amethyst. The tarred felt roof of the shed was still blissfully warm.

I went over and over the night of my fruitless search for Linda, trying to make sense of it, trying to work out what must have happened and trying to convince myself I was mistaken. I confided my fears to no one, not even Peter.

If you fear your brother might be a murderer, how do you come to terms with that?

I told myself that if Linda was really dead I would have heard something.

Nothing ever added up, not quite. I suppose I could have tried calling Linda's number, but I never did.

three

ALEX

Alex hadn't been back to his home town in twenty years, not since his parents moved to Scotland and he split up with Linda. Not that these two events were connected but they had become linked in his mind, simply because they had happened so close together. Alex had wanted to move too, not as far as Inverness but definitely out of Hastings and preferably back to London. Linda had been happy where she was. She liked her job at the dance school and didn't want to leave, even though she knew there were likely to be better opportunities for her in the capital.

It was the only thing they really rowed about, the biggest stumbling block to their relationship and the main reason they'd split up in the first place. Alex carried on where he was, working at the Gateway supermarket in Queen's Road and trying to amass enough money to get away on. He found he couldn't forget Linda though. He kept waiting for her to get back in touch but she didn't. At the end of three months he finally caved in and phoned her.

He remembered how just hearing the sound of her voice

had brought tears to his eyes. Linda sounded pleased to hear him, too. They were on the phone for two whole hours. She wouldn't let him see her at first.

"I think it's safer if we just talk for now, don't you?" she said. Alex had gone along with it at the time because he would have done anything to get back with her and it was better than nothing. There was even something exciting about it, at first anyway, something romantic. It made him feel like a horny teenager again, complete with the endless jerking off and falling asleep in the afternoon from lack of sleep.

Later he found out that the whole not-seeing-each-other business was because of Derek Peller, was because Linda didn't want Peller to find out about him. Next came the appalling scene outside The Tower and he had lost her again. Alex hated men like Peller, thugs who got their way through bullying and violence, and Derek Peller he hated especially because he'd shagged Linda. He remembered the feeling of rolling in the gutter outside the pub, the taste of blood on his lips from where he'd bitten his tongue, the ringing in his ears, the unspeakable urge to get up and hit Peller, to slam him in the face hard enough to break his nose, to send the blood flying, to render him silent.

At that moment, Alex had wanted to hit him hard enough to kill. If he could have killed him, in that instant and without thinking twice, he would have done so. At the time, Alex's flight to Sierra Leone had seemed like the ultimate fuck-you gesture, but Alex realised in hindsight that it had more to do with not wanting to be in the same physical space as Derek Peller. Even a whole country was not big enough for the two of them. The knowledge that Linda had fucked Derek Peller, that she had enjoyed fucking him, sucked his dick too probably, had worked its way inside him like a thorn.

Looking back on things now, Alex saw that his buggering off to Freetown was all about his own bruised ego. After Freetown came the job on the *Standard*, and later, Janet. Linda, and Derek Peller, became his past.

But now Derek Peller had resurfaced in the guise of his sister, Christy. He had forgotten Peller even had a sister, although Linda had mentioned her once or twice towards the end. Christy Peller had seen his byline on the Dale Farm piece. She had sent him an email, inviting him to come for lunch at her home in Hastings.

I think you once knew Linda Warren, who was a friend of mine, she had written. *I would like to talk to you about her, if that's possible.*

Alex wondered why she hadn't asked her questions there and then. He was tempted to write back and say he was too busy to travel to Hastings at the moment, and that if there was anything he could help her with they might just as well talk about it by email. But the more he thought about it the more curious he became. It would be interesting to meet Christy Peller, who was a writer now apparently. There might even be a story in it.

Also he needed a break from London and all the Janet stuff. Hastings was less than two hours away by train.

He sat down at his computer and looked up Christy Peller online. She hadn't published much – a collection of stories and two novels – but she definitely existed. He wondered what she wanted to know about Linda. While he was searching for more information about Christy's writing career, he noticed that his daughter Leonie was online. They messaged back and forth a couple of times. Leonie had scored eighty percent for her school science project, which had involved identifying wildflowers on three different bits of waste ground in Dalston and Hackney. Leonie had found and correctly named thirty different flowering plants in all. Alex stared at the list she sent him, which he thought read like a poem. Unborn tears constricted his throat and for a moment or two he was unable to begin typing a reply. Leonie was saying she was glad the flower project was over now because she was bored with it.

I want to write about our trip to Granny Adeyemi's. That was really real.

Alex sometimes wondered what the hell had got into him, dragging Leonie up to Inverness like that, letting his mother fill his daughter's head with stories about her childhood in Lagos and how different everything was now from when she had lived there, especially for girls, how interesting and exciting life in Nigeria could be these days.

Alex wondered how long it would be before Leonie started clamouring to be taken to Lagos to see her relatives there. She was already making noises about it, asking questions. Alex didn't know why the idea disturbed him so much.

I can help you with the essay, if you like, he typed.

That's OK – I'm fine by myself. But you can be the first to read it when it's finished.

She was growing up so quickly. Perhaps that was all he was worried about, after all – losing her, becoming less important to her with each day that went by.

Leonie Baxter Adeyemi was ten years old. Two weeks ago when it was Alex's weekend to have her, she'd found a stash of his old photographs in the bedroom cupboard, the ones from his Freetown escapade. Now all she could talk about was how she wanted to be a war correspondent when she grew up.

Because war would be really real, Alex supposed. He could only hope she would grow out of it. He was beginning to learn that he would have little choice or influence either way.

He was scared, but he was proud, ecstatically proud. So proud of his ten-year-old daughter he could punch the air.

He messaged Leonie goodnight (*get to bed now, chicken, it's late*) and then emailed Christy Peller and told her he'd be happy to accept her invitation. He didn't mention Linda, or anything else, just asked her which dates would be most convenient for him to come. He sent the email, then went on to Amazon and ordered copies of Christy's story collection and one of her novels.

He received a reply to his email the following morning. Christy said that any day that suited him would be fine by her, so long as he let her know two days in advance. Her email included her address in Hastings, and a link to a map. Alex emailed her back immediately. *I'll come next Wednesday if that's all right*, he wrote. He signed himself Alex, then deleted it in case it came across as too familiar. A. Adeyemi made him sound like someone's solicitor. He settled on Alex Adeyemi and then clicked Send.

* * *

He booked two nights in a B&B on Harold Road, which was on the edge of the Old Town and not too far from Christy Peller's place on Rotherfield Avenue. He wasn't entirely sure why he had done this. He could have been there and back in a day, easily. But the idea of seeing Hastings again appealed to him suddenly.

He wondered if this was still about Janet, and decided not. It was a year since they'd agreed to part. He didn't miss her very often and suspected the feeling was mutual. He missed Leonie of course, but he had her staying with him every other weekend and Janet let him see her whenever he wanted in between. Janet was good like that, great in fact, but then she had never been a vindictive person. She was reasonable about most things, thank God.

Leonie seemed okay with the arrangement, which was all that mattered.

Alex knew he was a good dad; he'd been a good enough husband also, he reckoned. The trouble, as it turned out, was that he was no good at being both things at once. He and Janet had been better than fine until Leonie. Leonie had got down between them somehow, like a steel tent peg. There was no doubt in Alex's mind that he would die for Leonie. He also loved being with her, had loved being with her from the first, when all she could do was eat and shit and cry. His feeling for her, perhaps because it had arrived in his life so unexpectedly, continued to overwhelm him on a daily basis.

The downside was the effect that this had inflicted on his

feelings for Janet. It was not that he had stopped loving her, rather that there was no space left over inside him for that love to exist. The thought of intimacy with Janet tired him. The laughs and chats they used to have, the good sex – these things seemed as much a part of his past now as Derek Peller.

He could no longer see the point of his marriage or of the effort that would be required to sustain it. There was his work, and there was Leonie – that was enough.

Anything else, including Janet, seemed a waste of time.

He supposed that made him an arsehole but he didn't care. Janet thought he was having an affair and he let her believe it. It seemed simpler, somehow. Less painful than the thought of trying to tell her the truth.

He spent the journey down to Hastings reading some of the stories in Christy Peller's collection. The longest story was called 'Allegra', and was about a ballet dancer who left her home on the Kent coast to become a soloist with a modern dance company somewhere in Scotland. The world of the story was familiar in some ways, but it was also strange. Electricity was rationed. Most people had gone back to writing letters or talking on the telephone because the Internet was restricted or unreliable. The dancer, who was called Allegra, became obsessed with a man who kept turning up at the theatre to see her dance. The man's name was Caton. He sat in the same seat each night and left flowers for her at the stage door but could never pluck up the courage to actually speak to her. Competition within the dance company was fierce, and Allegra developed an eating disorder, something like anorexia, Alex supposed, but it wasn't named. One night after leaving the theatre Allegra fainted in the street. Caton called an ambulance and waited with her until it arrived, then disappeared forever into the night.

Was Caton meant to be Allegra's guardian angel? Alex thought that could be one explanation, although the story worked well enough just as a story. Christy Peller described the events of the story in some detail but didn't explain them. For Alex, the story had the pent-up solemnity of a black-and-white photograph. He thought it was good, but he also felt frustrated because he wanted to understand more about what had happened.

Allegra was supposed to be Linda, that was obvious. The thing that impressed Alex most about the story was the way Christy seemed able to write convincingly about the ordinary everyday life of a dancer in a modern ballet company. On the whole, people tended to believe that because dancers' bodies were slender they were also frail. Christy Peller wrote of Allegra's Achilles tendons stretched taut as steel wires, her toes concussed from the impact of a difficult landing.

She spoke of the blood seeping out from beneath her toenails, darkening the pale pink of her pointe shoes, unfurling slowly along the threads of silk like the curlicued, perfumed petals of night-scented stock.

Alex liked especially Christy's use of the word 'concussed'.

He could have taken a taxi to the B&B but decided to walk. He took the long way round, along the seafront. It was windy but the temperature of the air was pleasantly mild. Monster gulls swooped and cried and mocked him from the rooftops. The gulls in Hastings were huge, vicious as dive bombers, he remembered that. Give them the chance and they'd steal the fish and chips right out of your hands.

The B&B was called Church View. The woman who opened the door to him seemed diffident and vaguely nervous, as if she had forgotten what exactly she was supposed to be doing there. Alex noticed there were two buttons missing from her cardigan.

The room she showed him to, though, was spotlessly clean.

"Mr Abeyemi, isn't it?" she said. "Are you here on holiday?"

"Sort of," Alex said, replying to both questions simultaneously. He felt the surprise he always still felt when someone made a reasonable attempt at getting his name right. He was pleased to find that his room was at the top of the building, away from the noise of the road and overlooking the back garden. The garden was crammed with pink hydrangeas and an enormous concrete bird bath in the shape of a clam shell.

"I'm Trudi," the woman said. "I'm just downstairs if you need anything." She backed away from him and out of the room, smiling her nervous smile before edging away along the landing. Alex found himself liking her; she seemed to share his own bewilderment at the way life was progressing. Once she'd gone he closed the door and crossed the room again to the window. At this distance the grassy flank of the East Hill was as smooth and unblemished as the green baize covering a card table. The sea sparkled at its eastern edge, brilliant as rhinestones. The view across the East Hill and towards the shoreline was, Alex supposed, what the temporary residents of Church View mostly paid their money for, that comforting closeness to their pasts as they were embodied in all those things relating to the English seaside – the fish-and-chip shops, the postcards on spin racks, the amusement arcades and pony rides, that whole amiable rambunctiousness that was not quite innocence and yet posed as such. Such cheeky, dirty-kneed non-culpability you would be churlish if you didn't believe it was at least harmless.

Even as a child, Alex had never been able to understand what made the tourists come here. He remembered the coaches pulling up, the newly released grandmothers, the pale-skinned fathers-to-be shuffling about in chilly confusion on the tarmac before sidling off towards the fast food outlets and the souvenir shops. He remembered most of all the constant, overcast loneliness of the feeling that he did not belong here.

He had left the town behind long ago, and he wasn't altogether surprised when his parents left, too. It was as if the two decades they'd spent here were an aberration, a mistake that took a long time correcting but a mistake nonetheless.

It was strange, he thought. He'd never spoken about the town to anyone, not even to Janet.

He had lunch at a pub in the Old Town, then decided he would go and have a look at Christy Peller's house on Rotherfield Avenue. Hidden away at the top of West Hill, the street was tricky to find unless you knew where to look. At the top of Croft Road a right turn led him into Bembrook Road. Tracy Chadwick, Alex remembered, had lived on Bembrook Road; Tracy Chadwick, who had been persecuted for having what his tormentors falsely believed was exclusively a girl's name, and who as a result had seemed determined to make Alex Adeyemi suffer even harder. Alex liked books, wore glasses, and was no good at football, so he was an easy target. Being the only black kid in the class was the icing on the cake. Some of the parents at least seemed embarrassed by that particular brand of name-calling. They made moves to rein it in, even if they couldn't be bothered to stamp it out entirely.

For some of the name-callers this only gave the forbidden words and phrases a greater allure.

Nigger

Nignog

Monkeynuts

Ape features

Black bastard

Idi Amin

Alex remembered one kid had called him a black-arsed eunuch. He had to look eunuch up in the dictionary and when he found out what it meant he felt confused and ashamed. He recognised the power of the insult, which seemed greater than the ordinary kind because he did not understand how it might apply to him.

For the minority of kids who feared the thick ears and the bawlings-out that might result from the illicit use of such disgraced currency there were plenty of other, less contentious insults they could choose from: specky, four-eyes, spod, dork, geek, spaz, faggot, virgin. Alex kept his parents in the dark as much as he could about the bullying. Once though, when Wayne Baker called him nigger right there on the street in front of his father, he saw in David Adeyemi's eyes along with the anger some of the fear and shame that always twisted his own guts when he heard such things. A fierce heat rose in his cheeks and for the rest of the walk home he could not look at his father.

He wished he'd chosen some other road for them to walk down.

Alex's parents were both teachers. They met at the South Bank Polytechnic in the London borough of Southwark. His father David was a Londoner by birth, his mother Marielle came over from Lagos on a scholarship. After graduating they left London for Hastings, on the south coast, because housing was cheaper there and because teachers of maths and physics were in short supply. Alex remembered summers from his early childhood, long weeks spent visiting relatives in Lagos and further inland at Ibadan. He remembered unrelenting heat and the shrieking of bush crickets, a rattan linen chest that was big enough to hide inside, his agonising boyhood crush on his cousin Bella. Then there was a period of about six years when his father could only get supply work and money was tight. The summer trips to Nigeria were postponed indefinitely. When his mother got made up to head of department things became easier again but Alex now found himself reluctant to accompany his parents on their resumed summer pilgrimages. He was in the sixth form by then anyway, so it was easy to fall back on his studies as a reason for not going. But the fact was he was confused by his dual identity.

No one in college called him nigger but there were still dozens of little ways he felt he stood out, not because of the colour of his skin, but because of the insults he'd been subjected to because of it.

He no longer knew how to trust people. He expected trouble, even when there was none. He could never decide which race he properly belonged to.

In Nigeria he felt painfully shy, painfully English. Photographs of Bella sent to them by the Lagos Adeyemis revealed a young woman glowing with confidence and vigour, a trainee hotel manager in Abuja with a smile that could have brought that city's maelstrom of traffic to a screeching standstill. Alex remembered the adoring little notes he used to write to her with cheek-flaming chagrin. He wondered if Bella remembered his one and only, fumblingly tentative attempt to kiss her. He hoped she did not.

She probably hasn't thought of me in years, Alex thought. She most likely doesn't even remember my name. The red dust of Lagos, the cloying heat, dense with the scents of tamarind and mango, the woven rush matting, soft beneath his bare feet, of the long, white-painted rooms of his aunt's house, Aunt Clo herself, with her coarse, braying laugh and her wickedly ribald, devoutly ironic sense of humour. These things seemed out of his reach, forbidden to him just as true belonging to England was forbidden. He longed for a sense of home, for one of these places to claim him as its own. He supposed that a part of it at least was his fault, that he was secretly unwilling to surrender himself to either.

He honestly couldn't say why this was. The idea that his disjuncture had anything to do with his being black annoyed him intensely, as if some kid older than himself, the kind of smug bastard who did well in athletics as well as mathematics, had pushed ahead of him in the queue for alienation, claiming the credit for something Alex had worked hard to achieve with no help from anyone.

His encounters with racism made him feel sick. He wanted to deny that the world contained such aberrations. The fact that he could not made him feel ashamed, embarrassed for a world that could fall for such an obvious con.

He had no idea if the individuals who called him nignog or golliwog had ever heard of the slave trade or the Biafran War. He hoped in a way that they had not. If they knew about such things and still didn't give a shit he'd have to feel embarrassed for them too, as well as hating their guts, and these were feelings he didn't want to find space for.

By the time he went away to college he had accepted his emotional as well as his racial isolation as a part of himself, like his too-narrow shoulders and general uselessness at football, something he could do nothing about but that needn't screw up his life unless he let it.

It was only when Leonie was born that he began to worry. He could not help remembering, then, the way he'd been treated by his peers. The thought that Leonie might have to suffer a similar humiliation made him lose sleep at night, even though he knew Leonie would be growing up in London and at the beginning of a whole new century. Things had always been different in London, but the whole country was changing now in any case, not right in its mind yet exactly but at least not as insane as it had been.

He wasn't sure how Janet would react when he first began reading to Leonie from a book he'd found in Foyles bookshop, on the Charing Cross Road, a volume of Yoruba fairy tales in their original language. He knew no more of the Yoruba language than Leonie did, but that was the point of it: they could learn together, it would be fun.

"Are you okay with this?" he said to Janet. She looked at him as if he were crazy, which perhaps he was.

"Of course I'm okay with it," she said. "What did you think, that I would want to deny our daughter access to her cultural heritage? How can you even ask me that?"

Janet seemed more comfortable with the thought of Leonie's cultural heritage than he was. But what was that cultural heritage exactly? Leonie was different from him in so many ways. She had been different from the start, and if she was even vaguely bothered by the things that tormented him while he was growing up there was no outward sign of it.

Leonie had the disconcerting habit of tackling problems head on. If something interested or disturbed her she would ask a question. When they travelled to Inverness to visit her grandparents it had been all questions. It was after their trip to Scotland that Leonie first asked him if she was really Nigerian or really English.

Alex knew it would be wrong to do anything except

encourage her in her search for answers, but still he felt scared for her. Standing in Bembrook Road, thinking about Tracy Chadwick – where was he now? On remand, most likely, or else working behind the bar in some dive in St Leonards – he couldn't help asking himself, as he asked himself daily, if he was doing everything he could to keep his daughter safe.

Safe from what, exactly, he didn't know. Alex believed that knowledge was power – it was what he lived by – but he knew also that things could change around you in an instant, and that when they did it was always those who were different that were made to suffer.

The houses on Bembrook Road were a mixture of 1950s council semis and newer three-storey townhouses and blocks of low-rise flats. Rotherfield Avenue jutted out at right angles from the junction of Bembrook Road and Egremont Place, a single row of rather attractive 1920s terraces. The houses had small front gardens, variously decorated with terracotta planters and overgrown forsythia bushes. The pavement in front of the terrace was uneven and sloping, with miniature thickets of groundsel and dock leaves sprouting thickly between the cracks. There was also a back access, a strip of potholed tarmac where people could park their cars or stow their bicycles.

It was an odd little road; down at heel, Alex thought, yet saved from being depressing through the grand sweep of its vista over school playing fields and, beyond them, Castle Meadow. In spite of its proximity to Bembrook Road and its haul of bad memories, Alex found he could understand why Christy Peller had chosen to live there. He knew already which house was hers – the last in the terrace. He gazed down the hill towards it, wondering if she was in, wondering how she might react if he were to turn up unannounced. For the first time, he felt genuinely curious about her, Christy Peller as a person, and not just as a connection with her older brother.

He spent the rest of the afternoon walking the cliff path. As he made his way back to the B&B, he felt a momentary but genuine sadness that he had never brought Janet here. Janet, he felt certain, would have liked the town. Janet's innate and generous capacity for liking things had always been one of the characteristics that had most attracted him. He went upstairs to his room and made himself a cup of instant coffee in the plain white mug provided for that purpose. The house felt silent around him, and Alex wondered if he might be the only guest staying there.

He ate dinner in the same pub in the Old Town where he'd had lunch then returned to his room at the B&B and read the remaining stories in Christy Peller's collection. They were all similarly odd. 'At the Cedars Hotel' recounted the final days of an old piano teacher dying in Aberystwyth in the off-season. 'The Raincoat' was about a child who became lost at a funfair and saved the life of a pederast. 'Dogs' told the story of a woman who was taking part in a scientific experiment. 'Brock Island' appeared to be a continuation of that story, some years in the future. As with the electricity rationing in 'Allegra', there was something about each of the stories that seemed to place it beyond the reach of ordinary time. The old woman in 'At the Cedars Hotel' reminisced about Queen Victoria as if she were still on the throne, and yet the peculiar nephew who came to visit her used a laptop computer and a mobile phone. In 'Dogs', the viewpoint character had a computer chip implanted into her brain that helped her communicate with her deaf-blind daughter, yet the mayor of London was still Ken Livingstone, and the nurses at the hospital where the operation was performed talked about the 7/7 tube bombings as if they'd only just happened. Parts of the stories reminded Alex of the science fiction he had enjoyed as a teenager, novels by Samuel Delany and Philip K. Dick, but he'd more or less given up reading science fiction when he discovered George Orwell's essays, and the writings of Nadine Gordimer and Chinua Achebe.

By the time he finished reading the book it was after midnight. He washed in the tiny bathroom then went to bed. He fell asleep almost at once, only to wake suddenly less than an hour later, filled with the unsettling conviction that there was someone in the room with him. He could not get rid of the idea that the person was Derek Peller. He got up to take a piss, mostly as an excuse to switch on the light. There was no one in the room, or in the bathroom, nor was there anyone hiding in the wardrobe or in the cupboard-sized shower cubicle. He rinsed his hands under the cold tap and went back to bed.

He wondered if it was Christy Peller's book that had made him jumpy, though it was more logical to suppose his anxiety over Peller was natural, that it would be foolish to revisit old haunts without being prepared to encounter a ghost or two.

He remembered how Peller had come up to him in the street, stepping quickly like he meant business, then his fists, two fierce blows, one uppercut to the chin and one to the stomach. The pain had been sickening but the shock was worse, the realisation that something like this could happen to anyone, on any street, at any time.

Alex knew how it felt to be thumped, to be knocked down in the school playground, to have the contents of his duffel bag redistributed over a wide area. He had learned these things a long time ago, from the likes of Tracy Chadwick and his friends. Derek Peller though, that was different. Alex understood at once that it was *him* Peller hated, not his blackness or even his nerdiness. Peller was hateful but he had never been stupid, and for someone like Peller, simple bigotry was too general, too unthinking, too much like someone else's point of view. Peller would have despised slogans, Alex realised, almost as much as Alex despised them himself.

What Peller hated was the fact that Alex had *dared*. Dared to get in his way, to insist upon his desires, desires that ran counter to those of Derek Peller. That he had dared to think he mattered, to believe he had agency.

Freaks like Peller acted alone, they were loose cannons. Heroes, or mass murderers, sometimes both.

Alex remembered the taste of blood as his face slammed into the pavement, the terror that Peller was going to start kicking him, kicking him until he fell unconscious or his kidneys ruptured.

Linda screaming, then beginning to cry, to weep like a

child. The pain and then – once Peller was gone – that odd leap of excitement, the knowledge that today was no longer a day like any other.

Time had leached these events of their substance, of their bright immediacy. What remained was more elusive, grey as ash.

Alex lay awake for some time with his eyes open, the darkness soft against his limbs, like a coating of dust. He felt removed from his own world, the way he always tended to do when he was obliged to sleep in a bed that was not his own. The bed, a queen-size divan, made him think of a bunk on board a ship. The sea was rocking him back and forth, and he was returning to the harbour of his home port, a narrow, mean-minded place, rife with old rivalries and uneasy memories.

He could not call such a place home. But then where else could home be?

The following day was overcast but dry. Alex ate breakfast at the hotel. He was half hoping Trudi might be on duty, just so he could experience the pleasure of seeing a familiar face, but there was no sign of her. Instead he was served by a middle-aged man with a sizeable paunch who introduced himself as Rog. The breakfast – sausage, black pudding, fried egg – was surprisingly good, and Alex found himself curious as to whether Rog had cooked it himself.

He had expected to find the dining room empty, but five out of six of the tables were occupied, by mature couples for the most part, which Alex supposed explained the quietness of the hotel the previous day.

"You're busy at the moment, I see," Alex said to Rog.

"We're chocker from Easter onwards, that's always the way."

"Is Trudi working this morning?" Alex said.

Rog regarded him sharply. "No, she's not. She doesn't really work here anyway, she's just staying with us."

"As a guest, you mean?"

"She's the wife's sister. She hasn't been well." He began collecting Alex's breakfast plates together, clattering them noisily in a way that seemed to suggest that the subject was closed.

"I see," Alex said. There had been nothing funny about the exchange, yet he could feel laughter bubbling up inside him and threatening to burst free. He waited until Rog had disappeared into the kitchen then made his escape.

He was supposed to be at Christy Peller's at twelve, which gave him time to kill. He decided he would do what he'd resolved not to do – he would go and have a look at the house where he had grown up. He suspected this had been his intention all along. The house was at the top of West Hill on Emmanuel Road, a solid Victorian terrace with a weathered front door. His parents had first rented and later purchased their two-storey maisonette from the house's owner, a Mr Emmanuel whose surname was a strange coincidence and whose first name they never discovered. The Adeyemis had the ground floor and the first floor and the use of the garden. Mr Emmanuel lived upstairs.

"The colour of a person's skin makes no difference to

me, that's what I say." And indeed he did say it, so often, Alex thought, that the sentence seemed to add up to more than the sum of its parts. As a young child, Mr Emmanuel had scared him. His clothes ponged, and he had a habit of coming to the door at odd times – when he knew Marielle would be there by herself, mainly, or there with just Alex, which amounted to the same thing. Once the property was properly theirs, things were better.

Alex remembered his mother and father on the afternoon the contracts were finally exchanged, the two of them standing outside on the back lawn, clinking glasses, both their faces shining with a fierce kind of pleasure Alex had never seen there before. His mother had jumped in the air, whooping like a schoolgirl, pouring the remains of her supermarket-bought, sparkling white wine over her head as if she wanted to bathe in it.

I name this ship HMS Great Britain.

These strange sights and sounds made Alex's heart race. He realised that what he was seeing was the birth of freedom, a version of it anyway. No need to be scared now – if you owned your own home no one could kick you out, no one could tell you to get back where you came from, because you came from here and you had papers to prove it.

For Alex the house meant freedom too, but it was also a prison. His room was at the back, overlooking the garden, and from its book-crowded, paper-strewn space it was possible to believe that the outside world of the town – of Tracy Chadwick and his friends, of the pasty-faced youths outside the Grafton pub who sniggered at him and made monkey noises when he walked by – no longer existed. He built a haven for himself in that room, a space that was so much a reflection of his own inner world that in the end the world of his room and the world of the town became so out of synch he was almost afraid to venture outside.

These memories were still painful. He hated to think that they would always be a part of him.

He stood in the road outside the house, looking up. The exterior of the terrace had been recently painted, and the whole building looked brighter, newer. He supposed Mr Emmanuel must be dead by now, the contents of his poky upstairs rooms cleared out and tipped into landfill. The thought made him shiver. He remembered the tawdry little bedsit in Devonshire Place he'd rented straight after finishing college and during the six months he'd spent working at the supermarket and going out with Linda and wondering what the hell he was supposed to be doing with his life. The flat was his own first attempt at freedom and it had failed. No matter how thoroughly he cleaned the bathroom and the greasy kitchen tiles, no matter how he arranged and rearranged his books and few possessions on the Fablon-covered shelves in the murky living room, the place steadfastly refused to become a home. It reeked, persistently and damply, of impermanence.

He thought things would improve for him in London and for a while they did. Now that home had also failed him, or rather he had failed it.

Maybe it wasn't the place after all, so much as himself.

Alex turned his back on Emmanuel Road and began walking downhill towards Croft Road and Castle Meadow, alternately thinking about calling Janet and resolving not to. As he crossed the wide swathe of green grass on the other side of Bembrook Road he watched a man throwing a Frisbee for his dog, a brindled Staffie with a studded leather collar. The man, who was Alex's age or thereabouts, seemed vaguely familiar and Alex supposed they had probably been at school together.

He had twin tattoos on both forearms, charging bulls.

I suppose he thinks the dog makes him look tough, Alex thought. The Frisbee swept low to the ground and the dog charged after it, clapping its jaws shut on the yellow plastic like a steel trap snapping the neck of a scurrying mouse.

"Go, Charlie!" yelled the bull-man. "Go get 'em, Charlie-boy." He spread his arms wide, and the dog raced back towards him, letting the Frisbee fall to the ground in its final approach. It bowled wobblingly across the grass as the dog leapt, weighty and compact as a bouncing bomb, vertically upwards into the bull-man's outstretched arms.

The bull-man clasped the Staffie hard against his chest in a kind of rapture. The dog's tongue flapped and lolled, caressing his cheek.

Alex felt a lump in his throat, and suddenly he was remembering Linda as he'd last seen her, begging him to go home, telling him she'd sort it out, that she'd sort it, *just go*.

"But the guy's dangerous, Linda," Alex had said. "He's some kind of maniac. We should call the police."

"Oh for God's sake, don't be stupid," Linda said. "He's different when he's with me. Let me talk to him. I'll call you later and we can–"

She broke off to blow her nose, never finishing the

sentence, never telling him what it was they could do. The delicate skin beneath her eyes was swollen from crying.

Alex left in a huff, still seething. His jealousy of Peller, for the moment at least, still monumentally greater than his love for Linda.

Had he loved Linda really, anyway? It was all so long ago. It was hard to be sure now of anything he'd felt back then. He'd had a girlfriend at school, or rather a girl *friend*, a friend who was a girl. Her name was Marian. She had crooked teeth and was slightly gawky but she knew what a plebiscite was and she always came top in maths, beating even Kev Stringer, who ended up winning a scholarship to Cambridge. It was Marian who first told him that Chip Delany, author of *Nova*, was a black man. Alex still had no idea why nothing had happened between him and Marian, except that neither of them had the guts to make the first move. He ended up losing his virginity not to Marian but to Chloe, a girl he met in his first week at uni and before Chloe's snooty friends had taken their chance to put her off him. Their relationship had lasted only a month or so, but after those first few fumbling, magical encounters the business of sex was never again so embarrassing or so desperate.

In his final year he met Janet Baxter. They almost got engaged then. Instead they had a massive row about one of Janet's ex-boyfriends and split up three weeks before finals. Alex felt crushed by the break-up, which as it turned out wasn't the end. He and Janet met again, at someone's wedding, three years later. Six months after that they were married themselves.

He had met Linda on the rebound from that first cataclysmic break-up with Janet. Linda was beautiful and talented. Unlike many beautiful and talented people she was also kind. Alex had no idea what she saw in him. For a while he was as happy as a pig in shit, but then the trouble started. He wanted to leave town and she didn't, they split. Three months later they were back together again but if Alex were honest with himself he knew it was doomed, even then, because their problems hadn't changed or gone away. Also, he had no idea Linda had been involved with someone else in the interim, mainly because she never said a word to him about Derek Peller until it became impossible not to.

When Alex finally found out he was mad as fuck. Mainly because he hadn't suspected, not for a moment. It took him a couple of weeks to work out that Linda was scared of Derek Peller and even when he did realise he felt pretty smug about it. He hoped the fear might go some way towards making Linda realise what a gigantic wanker Peller was. He didn't take it that seriously though, not until Peller knocked him down in the street outside The Tower.

He remembered coming out of the pub with Linda. They'd been arguing a bit – about Peller, what else – then Linda started crying and Alex suddenly saw himself for the moron he was.

He was a coward and a bully. He was as bad as Derek Peller, if not worse.

"I don't give a shit about that arsehole," he said suddenly. "All I care about is you and me."

He put his arm around Linda's shoulders and she leaned

in close. They started walking back down the road towards Linda's flat. Alex felt a peculiar lightness overtaking him, the sense that so long as he and Linda stuck together everything would come out all right. Derek Peller seemed to hit him out of nowhere. Alex realised he still hadn't worked it out even to this day, the exact direction Peller had come from. He remembered thinking: he's going to kill me. He could hear Linda screaming – Derek, *Derek* – as if it were just the two of them in the street and he, Alexander Adeyemi, was nowhere at all.

The night smelled fresh and dark, like soil after rain.

He spent that night at Linda's place. He didn't remember much about it, just Linda cleaning the cuts on his face with Dettol and dosing him with paracetamol.

The following day he called in sick at Gateway. His whole body felt sore and aching, but it wasn't just that. He felt nervous of going outside, though he would never have admitted that to anybody and least of all to Linda.

Linda went to work as usual. She called him at lunchtime to check he was okay and then again at four o'clock to tell him her classes had overrun and she would be late. When she still wasn't home by six Alex tried calling the dance school but the switchboard was closed. As he listened to the voice of the answerphone inviting him to leave a message, the thought started circling in his head that Linda was with Peller, that she'd decided to get back with him after all, that the two of them were holed up together in The Tower having a good old laugh about him.

He felt sick of her, sick of them both. He gathered his things and left, slamming the door behind him on his way out. He headed for the Railway Arms, a dive of a place just up from Warrior Square. He normally avoided that kind of pub like the plague, but he told himself it was a free country, he would drink where he damn well chose. Two guys with tattoos glared at him ominously as he went in but the cuts on his face and the look in his eyes must have made them reconsider their options.

He sat in the darkest corner of the pub, angrily downing his beer and turning the pages of a *Daily Express* someone had left behind and wondering how the hell he had ended up there.

What are you doing with your life, Alex? His mother's voice.

He was damned if he was going to call Linda, but of course it was the first thing he did when he got in.

The phone in her flat just rang and rang. There was no reply.

He resigned the tenancy on the Devonshire Place bedsit then took all the remaining money out of his bank account and booked himself on a flight to Freetown, Sierra Leone, convinced he was going to be the next John Reed. Alex had recently seen Warren Beatty's film *Reds*, and Reed was his hero.

He didn't see Linda again for many years.

* * *

"You're Alex," Christy said.

She was small and dark, with the narrow wrists and skinny arms that reminded him, out of the blue, of a woman he had spoken to in Freetown whose husband had been mortally injured by the rebel forces. The woman had seemed both frightened and defiant, and Christy Peller seemed a little bit the same, Alex thought, her face familiar to him through its wary expression. It was the face of someone living under siege from their private fears.

Her hair hung loose to her shoulders. The ends curled up slightly and she was beginning to go grey. She was wearing blue jeans with a blue-and-grey plaid shirt tucked into the waistband.

"Come through and I'll make some coffee," she said. "Lunch will be ready in about an hour."

The house on the inside was box-shaped, the hallway surfaced with red-and-black quarry tiles. A panelled-in staircase led off it immediately to the right of the front door. There was a row of brass coat hooks, faded sage-coloured wallpaper stencilled with a William Morris pattern. The effect was subdued but calming. Christy showed him through to the room at the back, a cramped-looking sitting room dominated by a large green-tiled open fireplace. There were postcards on the mantelpiece, and a few framed photographs. To the right of the fireplace and immediately behind the door there stood a low, fat sofa upholstered in cocoa-coloured corduroy. Opposite the sofa was an armchair in the same fabric. Between the armchair and the sofa stood a wooden coffee table. Alex noted a large, gilt-framed mirror above the fireplace and a glass-fronted bookcase with one of its panes cracked. The walls of the room were painted cream, and a tall sash window looked out on to the garden. It was a pleasant room, Alex thought. There were just the books, the fire, the sofa, the things you need. There was no sign of a desk, or a computer, and Alex supposed that Christy Peller did her actual writing in another room.

"Please, sit down," Christy said. "Coffee won't be a moment. Do you take milk or sugar?"

"Neither, thank you," Alex said. He sat down in the armchair, but once Christy was out of the room he stood up again and crossed the floor to examine the bookcase. He was expecting it to contain copies of Christy's own books, for some reason. In fact it was filled with volumes by writers he'd heard of but never got around to reading: Alice Munro, Ingeborg Bachmann, Flannery O'Connor. John Cheever and Raymond Carver he had read, because he did them at school. He remembered reading Cheever's story 'The Swimmer', thinking he was going to hate it because the book's green-and-grey cover made Cheever seem dull. The story turned out to be riveting, magical almost, and Alex ended up reading every story in the volume. They were weird but he loved them.

"Do you like Cheever?" Christy said. She had returned to the room without him noticing. Alex turned round hurriedly, the Cheever volume still in his hands. Christy was carrying a tray with two mugs on it, faintly steaming, and a plate of custard creams.

"I haven't read him in ages," Alex said. "Not since school

really. But I liked him then." He replaced the book carefully on its shelf. Christy set the tray down on the coffee table.

"I think Cheever's very special," she said. "It's strange to think that most of his stories are more than fifty years old now. I don't think they've dated at all."

"A teacher of mine said she thought that what Cheever's stories most represented was the gradual decline and fall of the bourgeoisie," Alex said. The memory came back to him clearly: Miss Foregate, in her ancient Harris Tweed skirt and horn-rimmed glasses. She had seemed ancient to him, though Alex supposed she'd probably been in her early thirties. He hadn't thought of her in years.

"I suppose that's true," Christy said. "But I don't like to think of his stories that way, it makes them sound pompous. Cheever wrote about people, not politics. He was interested in how the lives of ordinary people can become unfastened from reality. That's how I read him, anyway."

"I think that's right," Alex said, remembering how he'd felt when he first read 'The Swimmer'. It was a terrifying story, even though nothing much happened in it apart from some guy deciding to set himself a bizarre swimming challenge. It felt odd, talking to Christy Peller about John Cheever. He didn't know Christy at all, she was a stranger to him, and yet because of the people they had in common – Linda, and Derek, and Cheever – his intimacy with her had become curiously accelerated.

He wondered what he was doing there really, why she had summoned him.

"Are you from Hastings originally?" Christy said. Her

question was innocent enough, Alex supposed, yet he knew how questions like this still made him bridle, his temper stretched thin and tight, like cling film over a jam jar. He had never become used to it, this insatiable curiosity people seemed to have about his origins. Even now, when he knew that the questions were not the same, perhaps, as they once had been, the tight-lipped, near-demands for proof of residency his parents used to have to endure on an almost daily basis.

Mostly, people were just interested. Where was the harm in it?

The shame of it was, he would have liked to speak of Lagos more often. He would have liked to tell this woman about the life of the port, about the unmade, red-dust roads of the interior. He would have liked to describe Aunt Clo to her and Uncle Midas and his cousin, Bella, to share his memories of the carefully tended garden behind their house, to describe its sounds.

He was able to talk about these things with his parents of course, but it was surprising, Alex reflected, how rarely he did so.

"Yes I am, I was born here," Alex said. "I'm based in London now though, I haven't lived in Hastings since my early twenties."

Something passed across Christy's face then, a faint shadow. His Aunt Clo would have said *she has an inkling*, but Alex had never believed in inklings, or astrology, or any of that stuff, even though Aunt Clo once told him he had a talent for it. When he told his mother what Clo had said, Marielle Adeyemi had scoffed.

"She's a little bit crazy, my sister," she'd said. "Take no notice."

And it was true that Clo had always put her trust in the spirit world even more than she had lately come to rely on the Internet. *With the spirits you don't get no power cut*, she insisted. *You ever heard of broken satellites in the after-world?*

Alex tried to ignore the feeling he had, that Christy Peller was about to reveal a secret to him, something important that would reshape the landscape of his life.

"I've been reading your articles online," Christy said. "I really liked the Dale Farm piece, and the piece about the football hooligans. You're a very good writer."

"Thank you," Alex said. "I'm glad you enjoyed them." Christy Peller was holding her coffee cup in both hands, clasping it by the base as if she were using it for support. She looked pale and nervous, almost as if she were afraid of him, or of something he was about to say to her, but how could that be? It was she who had invited him here, not the other way around.

He remembered what Linda had said about Christy, that she seemed scared of her own shadow.

"She barely said a word to me for ages," Linda said. "She's a bit strange."

"That's hardly surprising though, is it, when you think who her brother is," Alex had retorted. "She's scared stiff of him, I bet."

At the time he'd spoken out of pure contrariness – he wanted to see Derek Peller as the villain of the piece across all categories. Now he wondered if he'd been right after all. If he'd had an inkling. Linda in any case couldn't have had much in common with Christy, they were such different people.

Alex remembered a particular afternoon, when he clocked off early from the supermarket and walked across town to meet Linda at the dance studio. She was teaching a class of girls, visiting from Eastbourne or Bexhill or somewhere, not trained dancers, just ordinary schoolkids in their PE kits. He remembered Linda in her leotard and leggings, showing one of them how to position her foot beside the barre. The girl was overweight, and it was clear she felt exposed in her boxy green shorts and Aertex shirt but Linda spoke to her gently and with a smile, placing her own foot beside the girl's in its chubby-soled gym shoe. He remembered the way the fat girl smiled as she suddenly grasped the essence of what Linda was showing her, beautiful for a moment as she forgot how uncomfortable she was normally made to feel with the sight of her own body.

He sensed that Christy felt the same discomfort, but for different reasons.

"I wanted to ask you about Linda," Christy said suddenly. Her voice was unsteady, and Alex realised that this was it, that the mystery surrounding his visit was about to be solved. "You went out with her, didn't you? Linda told me about you."

"We were together for about six months, and then we split up," Alex said. "You do know that Linda was seeing your brother Derek?"

"Yes, of course." Christy set her coffee mug back down on the tray, and Alex noticed with a shock that her hands were shaking. "I thought of Linda every day, for years," she said. "I still think about her now. I wonder how her life would have been if she'd never met my brother, where she'd be living and what she'd be doing. Linda was so gifted. I liked her a lot."

Was? Alex thought. *Liked?* He felt an odd little shiver go through him, coursing up through his feet and into his fingertips like the shock waves from a minor earthquake. That's what it's like when the world rearranges itself, he thought. That's what it's like.

"I've done something very wrong," Christy said, and then stopped. She seemed to shrink inside her clothes, to diminish, and Alex knew she must be feeling what he was feeling, that sense of embarrassment that hits you when you've been assuming the person you're talking to understands you perfectly and then you suddenly realise you've been in different conversations all along.

"You think Linda's dead, don't you?" Alex said. Understanding flowered inside him, unfurling inside his head like the fragrant, curlicued petals of night-scented stock. Who wrote that? Alex thought, then realised that Christy herself had written it, or something like it, when she was describing the blood seeping from under the dancer's toenails in her story 'Allegra'. "You think Derek killed her."

"I should have warned her," Christy said. "She didn't know what he was like, not really. Nobody did. I let her down. I should have called the police but I didn't. It's all my fault." There were tears in her eyes now, diamond-bright, glistening globules. As Alex watched, one of them toppled over the rim of her lower eyelid and fell into her lap.

"It's not though," Alex said. He realised with wonderment that his presence here was required after all, that there was a point to all this. That he had been called, as Aunt Clo might have said, for a reason. "It's not right. Linda's not dead. What on Earth made you think she was dead?"

Christy looked up at him from where she sat on the corduroy sofa, her eyes still full of tears and a dawning bewilderment. "I saw Derek," she said. "The night Linda disappeared. I couldn't find Linda anywhere, and there was all this blood on Derek's sleeve, dried blood. Then later on I found Linda's engagement ring."

After they had eaten their lunch she showed it to him, a cluster of diamonds and pearls on a yellow–gold band. Alex had never seen the ring before, and he realised that Linda had most likely taken it off before each of their meetings. She must have given it back to Derek in the end, a final way of telling him that things really were over between them.

It would have hurt her to do that, Alex knew. Linda always loved pretty things, delighted in them like a magpie, like a child. It had been one of the most charming and innocent aspects of her character.

"I found it in the garage of our old house on Laton Road," Christy was saying. "It was in one of the drawers of the old tallboy Derek always used for storing his sales receipts. I came back to help Derek with the house, you see. To clear it out before he went to Australia. I suspected for years that Derek might have done something terrible to Linda but I kept telling myself I had to be wrong, that if anything had happened to her I would have heard something. Finding the ring brought everything back. But by then – I don't know, it just seemed too late for me to say anything. It would have looked like I'd been covering up for him. I couldn't bear the thought of it."

"Derek's in Australia?" The news had caught Alex so off guard he had barely taken in the rest of what she was telling him. There was something almost mythical about it, this conclusion to the Peller saga, the kind of thing that only normally happened in stories.

"Yes. He went out there to be with our mother. I think he likes it there, better than he liked it here, anyway. I just hope he stays there."

"But Derek having the ring didn't mean Linda was dead," Alex said later. "You must have realised that, surely?"

"I was frightened," Christy said. "I didn't want to know the truth, so I let things carry on the way they were."

Two days after Peller's attack on him, Alex tried calling Linda's flat again, but it was the same as before, the phone just ringing and ringing with no reply. By then he was feeling worried as well as angry. He had been over their final telephone conversation so many times he no longer knew how much of it was a genuine memory and how much was invention. Either way, there was nothing that offered a clue as to what had happened. She'd said she would be home late, that was all.

She had not been joking.

In the silence of the dingy flat on Devonshire Place the idea that Linda had gone back to Derek, after everything that had happened, began to seem less and less likely. That had been his own paranoia speaking. Linda was impulsive but she wasn't crazy. Alex telephoned the flat again the next day and the next, and when after three more days there was still no reply he called the dance school and asked if he could speak to Linda Warren. There was a long pause while he was put on hold, then the switchboard operator, Susan her name was, came back on the line and told him that Linda wasn't available.

"She's teaching at the moment," Susan said, and the smug knowingness in her voice was all that Alex needed to know that she was lying. Linda was there all right, she just didn't want to speak to him.

He slammed the receiver back into its cradle. Tears dug into his cheeks, like shards of hot glass.

In that moment Alex knew he'd had it with the town, and with Linda too. It was time to leave.

Looking back on it now, Alex knew that if it hadn't been for his fury at Linda he would probably not have had the courage to make a break for it.

In a way, he owed Linda his future. He owed her everything.

He saw her again, just the once, years later, coming out of a delicatessen on the Fulham Road. He recognised her immediately – her way of walking, that gossamer lightness, was unmistakable. She was wearing a pair of old tracksuit bottoms and plain black plimsolls. She was as lovely as she ever was, perhaps even lovelier.

It did the world good, Alex thought, just to have her in it. He no longer thought about or cared why she left him, so suddenly and without explanation. She was sick of them both most likely, him and Derek Peller. Probably she wanted her freedom as much as he did.

Whatever. It was a lifetime ago. So over.

As she stepped down from the pavement their eyes met. For a second Alex felt sure that Linda recognised him, that she was about to say something. Then she looked past him over his shoulder and walked away.

"Linda's not dead," Alex said to Christy. "She just moved on, that's all, the way we all do."

They went outside. A fresh breeze was blowing. They walked down along the edge of the playing fields towards Castle Meadow.

"What made you come back here?" Alex said. "To Hastings, I mean?"

"It was the money really," Christy said. "Half the money from Laton Road was mine. There was just enough for me to buy this house outright – I couldn't have afforded to do that in London." She pushed her small hands into the pockets of her jeans. "And after Peter died I felt I needed a change."

"Peter was your husband?"

"We were never married, but we lived together for almost twenty years. Peter died of cancer. I still miss him."

Alex fell silent, not wanting to crowd her memories with unnecessary speech. "Do you think you'll stay here?" he said at last.

"I'm not sure what I'll do in the long run. But it's fine for now." She shook her head, and Alex had the sense that she was still trying to get to grips with things, to sort out the facts as she now understood them from the fictions that had tormented her for so long. "Thank you for coming, Alex. I can't tell you how much today means to me. It's such a relief to finally know the truth."

"I'm glad I came." And it was true, he was glad. He knew his time with her had changed things. In some unaccountable way it had straightened him out. A part of him wanted to confide this to her, to explain, but his greater self resisted.

He knew it was not Christy Peller he should be talking to now. Their time together was done.

They sat down to rest on a bench at the edge of the playing fields. Alex watched the monster gulls, banking and swooping and diving in the gusty cross drafts. They're like spirits of themselves, he thought. The idea of gulls, become wild fantasies. Grey ghosts.

"Do you think I was a coward?" Christy asked suddenly.

"No more than anyone," Alex said. "No more than me, anyway." And then he was remembering what happened in Freetown, the euphoria of those first days, the sense that finally he was doing something, being someone, going where he ought to be going. Those first days it had not even felt particularly dangerous to be there. There was a lot of hanging out in cafes, a lot of talk of revolution and *the establishment of a free state*, a phrase that was used and reused until it finally disintegrated into a slogan. Then the woman journalist was shot in the face and everything changed. Alex had never spoken to her but he had seen her around. He knew her name was Stef and that she worked for Reuters.

He started to shake all over when he heard. He was unable to fit his image of the young woman in khaki Bermudas to the words, coarsened as they were by fear and grief, of the older, more experienced newspaperman who told him what happened to her.

"Her whole lower jaw's gone. Frigging mess her face is now, worse than an animal. If you ask me she'd be better off dead."

Alex felt that the man had shown him a tiny, perfect glimpse into hell. He had tried to forget, not to know, but the thought of the woman's shattered face would not leave him. He was too afraid to go and see her, but he wrote a report of the incident, including comment by witnesses, and then flew home to London. He sold the story almost the minute he stepped off the plane. The paper that bought it soon got back in touch and asked him if he was interested in doing a piece on factory closures in Sheffield.

We like your style, they said. *You have a freshness of approach that is most unusual.*

He accepted the commission at once. He knew that what had happened with the Reuters woman had forever put an end to his idea of himself as a war correspondent.

This had been the shape of his cowardice.

Whatever. It was an age ago. So over.

He said goodbye to Christy Peller and made his way back to the B&B. He dozed on the bed for a while, then washed and changed and had supper at the Jenny Lind. He treated himself to a cognac, then decided he would return to his room at Church View and watch some mindless TV.

When he was halfway up the Bourne he stopped. He took out his mobile phone and keyed Janet's number.

He was afraid that Leonie might answer, because it was Janet he wanted to speak to, and having Leonie there in the background would only distract him. He was in luck though, it was Jan who picked up. She sounded surprised to hear him, but in a good way, Alex thought, or at least he hoped so.

"Hey, you," Alex said. He hadn't said 'hey, you' to her in months. "How are things?"

"Things are fine," Janet said. "You sound odd though. Has something happened?"

"I want to come home," Alex said. "I made a mistake."

"Everyone makes mistakes," Janet said. "The trouble is they can't always be put right again."

"This one can," Alex said. When he realised he believed his own words, his heart seemed to turn in his chest and perform a somersault.

four

MAREE

Maud's hair is long, to her waist. In the winter months it goes dark, like the rain-dampened roofs of Asterwych, dark as peat. In summer it reveals flecks of amber, the same colour as the soft down on her calves and forearms. The hair between her legs is mossy, like pond weed.

Maud is hurting because she knows I am going away. She's afraid I will forget her.

"Don't be silly," I tell her. "We'll have letters. Letters are better than anything in the world."

I say this because I want to comfort her, but also because I feel that it's true. Words written down on paper are better than words spoken out loud, better even than mind-speech. Words written down on paper stay alive. They are the parts of ourselves we secretly bury and leave behind for those who come after us. Written words are like the ancient stone castles of Inverness-shire – they stand and stand and stand.

I tell Maud I won't have lovers in Kontessa, only friends. We are lying on a blanket on the rough grass that covers the hills that look down on the Croft. Our limbs are lengthening like the days, the air is filled with the scratch of ripe pollen and the rustle of grass seed, the mauve scent of heather. Maud and I paint each other's shoulder blades and wrists with henna tattoos and pretend that these days, like the summer before them, are not hurtling towards their end.

Their fleetness is terrible: blunt as a hammer blow, cunning as a rat. As the summer wears itself out I find that I am seeing things differently. It's as if I'm watching myself from the outside, through a spyglass. Everything I do seems interesting suddenly, and also final. I choose to spend more time with Maud than I really want to, because I know that for her these last few weeks feel like the end of her world.

When we have sex I feel as if we're doing it in front of a camera. I watch myself through the days, growing away from Maud, separating myself from her inside my mind and wondering if this is happening because I know we must part or if it would have happened – was already happening – anyway.

I know a chapter of my own life is ending, but I can't get away from the idea that this summer is more important for Maud than it is for me.

Perhaps I'm mistaken. Perhaps these days that I am throwing away will turn out to have been the best days of my life.

A week before I am due to leave I walk into Asterwych on my own and visit the tattoo parlour. When the tat guy asks me what I want, I tell him I want him to make a tattoo of the design that Maud hennaed on to my wrist the day before. The design, like three twisted grass stalks, is still crisp and clear.

"That'll be fifty shea. All right?"

It is more than I was expecting but I say yes anyway. The tat guy wipes disinfectant over my arm with a cotton wool pad then goes to work. I lie still in the upright leather chair, listening to the whining buzz of the tat gun and feeling the curious burn-prick-burn of the needle thudding in and out of my flesh on its chrome-steel ratchet. It hurts but not too much – I have established that I can bear the pain, and I know it won't get any worse. I can relax and almost enjoy the sensation, like the first time I had sex with Wolfe when I was fourteen.

When it is over I feel a brief flash of regret at what I have done, mostly because I know how pleased Maud will be when she sees the tattoo. She'll see it as a sign, that I am binding myself to her forever.

Still, it's too late now.

"All right?" says the tat guy. "Not feeling woozy?" He uses a clean white rag to wipe off the blood then turns my wrist first to one side and then to the other, checking his work the same way a metal welder might check a mended section of copper piping. He claps a gauze dressing to my wrist and secures it with sticking plaster.

"You should keep that on for twenty-four hours," he says. "It'll be fine after that."

I pay him the fifty shea and then leave, walking along the High Street towards the narrow brick pathway that leads up to the Croft. Will I come into Asterwych again before next week I wonder?

I doubt it. This feels like goodbye.

* * *

Maud and I shared a bedroom from the beginning. The first thing she said to me was to ask me when my birthday was.

I couldn't remember, so Maud said I could share hers and Kay said okay. The boys – Caine and Wolfe and Garland – were all older than me when they were chosen for the programme and they could remember their own birthdays. Sarah was born in Asterwych. Her birthday was the fourteenth of April. She was brought to the Croft to live when she was two weeks old.

For a while I believed that Kay was my mother as well as Maud's. I carried on thinking of her that way long after I was told the truth, but lately I've noticed that my feelings for her are beginning to drain away. Tomorrow, Kay will travel with me to Faslane. At Faslane I will go aboard the *Aurelia Claydon*, the steamship that will carry me across the Atlantic to Bonita, which is a port city in Thalia. The programme's main research unit is based at Kontessa, a city on the plain at about an hour's remove from Bonita. Sarah and Caine and Garland are already there. Wolfe would be travelling with me, if he were still alive.

If Kay could have got me on board a hopper flight she would have done, but there were no subsidized places available, so I must go by sea. A sea voyage is always dangerous, because of the whale convoys, but for the moment at least the danger seems remote to me and therefore not real. It is Kay who appears anxious, and I remember she was the one who taught us about the Atlantic whales in the first place, years ago in morning study. She made us copy a chart into our exercise books, showing how many ships had been lost to whale convoys in the last twenty years.

When I tell Maud I shall be travelling to Thalia by steamship instead of by hopper all the colour drains from her face, and I know she is thinking about the *Gisela Stuart*, the *Medway*, the *Faslane Princess*, the TV images of shattered wreckage and bloated bodies washing up on the beaches at Jonestown three weeks later.

"It'll be fine," I say. I brazen it out like I did with Kay only less sincerely.

Maud wants to travel to Faslane with us but Kay won't let her.

"It's a pointless waste of the train fare," she says. "You have to say goodbye at some point, you know that. Don't make things difficult."

Kay is tense and Maud is angry. Her eagle's-beak nose, so like Kay's, juts like a crag.

"It would be awful anyway," I say to her. "With Kay there, I mean."

We say goodbye on Wych Hill instead. Maud sets her alarm clock for four o'clock and places it under her pillow so it won't wake the rest of the house when it goes off. We pull on our windcheaters and sneak down the back stairs. There is thick dew on the ground, and by the time we reach the summit our trainers are soaked. We sit side by side on the damp grass and watch the sun rise over Asterwych. The light is greenly translucent, like sea-washed glass. I feel a hard pain inside my chest, as if a stone is lodged beneath my breastbone. The ends of Maud's hair trail in the grass. After a while she reaches out and takes hold of my hand. I know I'll cry if I look at her, so I don't.

When we arrive back at the Croft it is still only six-thirty. No one even knows we've been gone.

"When the car gets here, don't come down," I say to Maud. I don't want her making a scene. Now that the time is almost upon me I just want to go. "Start writing me a letter instead."

She is already crying a little. I put my arms around her and hug her, smelling her smell, the stringy green reek of her armpits, the cloaky scent of her hair where the wind has tangled it together into damp knots. I kiss her on both eyelids and then I let her go. I ache for Maud, even though she is standing right here in front of me, even though I know there is no point in aching for Maud now, ever, because I will probably never see her again after this next hour.

I am glad Kay wouldn't let her come on the train with us. I think of Maud's pond-weed pubes and freckled thighs, and I want to weep out loud.

Kay has ordered a car for us. The car will carry us to Inverness, for the through-train to Glenver. The car crunches on the gravel, creeping forward towards the gates like a large black beetle. Kay opens the hatch at the back to put in my suitcase and then we get in. The vehicle's interior smells of old leather and dogs. The car reverses in front of the house and then drives away. I see the shadow of the Croft, sliding off the bonnet like a loose grey blanket. I feel empty, as if

I am already gone from here and this is just a memory, as perhaps it is.

The journey lasts eight hours in all. The further south we travel the flatter the landscape becomes: sparse heath cover and scrub-edged reservoirs, strange, stony little villages whose granite cottages clamour eagerly around a steel-framed pump house. Here and there I glimpse factories, and once an old fracking station, rusting derricks rearing from the ground like the beached carcass of an Atlantic whale.

The northern lowlands are all potato plantations and chicken hatcheries, nothing to look at for miles and miles. As the evening draws close I find I can see the lights of Glenver on the horizon. I know I shall not see anything of the town, because a room has been prepared for me at one of the travellers' hotels along the harbour front. Kay will take me as far as the hotel then catch the return train. By the time she gets back to Asterwych it will be after midnight. I stare at her as the train draws alongside the station platform at Glenver, the long straight back and jutting nose; Maud's features, only more refined and less telling. In a little under an hour we will be parting forever.

All these years, and I feel nothing at all. What is wrong with me?

The hotel is square and grey as a barracks, and when Kay tells me it used to be a submarine base I am not surprised.

* * *

The solar panels that make up the roof cladding gleam silver as the last of the evening sunlight passes across them.

Kay accompanies me to the reception desk. She seems nervous, unsure of herself in these unfamiliar surroundings. I have never seen her like this before and I wish she would leave. She stands awkwardly in front of me and I can tell she is waiting for me to hug her, or to say something meaningful and earnest, but I do neither.

This is the only chance I have to punish her and I take it.

When I ask myself what I am punishing her for, I don't have a proper answer. There is just the sense that it feels necessary, and that Kay herself will know the reason better than I do.

Instead of hugging her, I shake her by the hand.

"Goodbye then," I say. I turn back towards the reception desk. The man on duty gives me a form to fill in. Once I have done that I will be free to go to my room.

"You will write to us?" Kay says. I pretend not to hear. I know it will be all right, that once she is on the train Kay will persuade herself that I behaved spitefully because of her refusal to let Maud travel with us.

Later, before it is dark, I take a walk along the quayside to one of the souvenir kiosks, where I buy some postcards. On the back of one of them I write a short message – *sorry, but I was upset – you are a saint*. I write in Gaelic, which is Kay's native language. The front of the card carries an image of the harbour front, together with a simplified map of the

Faslane estuary. If I post the card this evening, Kay will most likely receive it the day after tomorrow.

By then I shall be at sea, and this moment will already be ancient history.

There is a dog at the hotel, a mongrel with green-gold eyes and yellow hair. She's not a smartdog but she's still very bright. She has a collar around her neck, and a silver identity disc engraved with the name 'Rosie'.

She sits beside me on the front steps of the hotel. People think that what we do with the smartdogs is some kind of magic, but it's not at all. It's more like listening than actual speaking, catching the shape and drift of the dog's thoughts as you might listen to and make sense of a new piece of music. Dogs can understand some spoken language because we teach it to them, but they don't comprehend speech in the same way that people do. For us, words are objects as well as sounds, a physical arrangement of letters on a printed page. Dogs have no written language, and so for them a word is just a sound with learned associations attached. When a familiar word is spoken with a new intonation, a dog will hear it as a different word entirely.

Try to imagine a word as picture and sound only, cutting out all associations with the written alphabet. Let the image it conveys expand inside you, let the sound of it fill up your mind. If you can free yourself, however briefly, from the idea of letters, then you will have taken a step towards understanding what we do.

Rosie doesn't speak to me because she doesn't need to. She is happy just to sit and watch the road, her long jaw slack, her mind drifting in slow circles like sun-shot cloud. I caress her narrow head. She leans against my knees, panting a little. It is a warm evening, hazy with midges, stewed purple as plums. I find myself thinking of Lim, who wanted so very much to understand letters, who was always so sad when I told him that the way a word looked written down wasn't important. I have not thought of Lim in a while, but the memory – which is somehow both vague and distinct – fills me with confusion and a sense of longing as it always does. Rosie registers my shift of emotions almost at once. She lifts her head towards me and whines.

I laugh and give her a hug. "It's all right, my girl," I say. It is not my laugh that reassures her, but my touch and the feelings of rightness that come with it. Her tail beats gently back and forth on the concrete step, stirring up dust.

My room is on the third floor. There is an iron-framed bed against one wall, a small Formica-topped desk beneath the window. Both desk and bed are bolted to the floor. There is a spotlight screwed into the window frame, and the light can be twisted one way to light the bed, the other way to light the desk, an arrangement that seems as economical to me as everything else in the room. There is an open rail for hanging clothes. I cannot imagine that the room has changed much since it was the land quarters of a working submariner and that suits me fine. If I sit still on the bed I can hear other people, passing along the corridor outside or climbing the stairs to the next level or watching TV in their rooms. Their nearness is reassuring, and I realise suddenly that this is the first time I have been alone in a room knowing that no one will enter unless I invite them. I find I'm not sure what this means to me. My nerves simmer, feeling exposed, like earthworms twisting on streaming asphalt after a rainstorm. I don't want to unpack my suitcase because there's no point, I will be leaving here first thing in the morning.

I decide to undress instead. I take off my sneakers and jeans and vest and pull my nightshirt on over my head. One of the buttons catches briefly in my hair, which is yellow as rapeseed and coarse as an overgrown thornbush. I wear it cut short, because that's the only way of keeping it under control.

Sarah once told me that soon after my arrival at the Croft all my hair fell out.

"It was straight before, can you believe that?" she said. I'm not sure that I can.

I am slightly knock-kneed, flat-chested as a boy. My name is Maree. I am registered with the surname Forrest, the same as Kay's. When I asked Kay what I was called before she said she didn't know.

I am tired from the day. Not tired enough to sleep yet, but it feels good to lie down on the bed and close my eyes. I ask myself if I am afraid, and think probably not. People are only frightened when they have something to lose.

I don't know what is waiting, and that excites me.

* * *

Finally, I am on board. My cabin, with its built-in bunk and pull-down writing desk, is not so different from my room at the hotel. When I unpack my suitcase I find the clothes I have brought fit easily into the twin storage boxes under my bunk. There is a smell of varnish and clean bed linen. The shared toilet facilities are at the end of the companionway.

The *Aurelia Claydon* is mainly a cargo vessel. I don't know what she is carrying exactly, though I have heard it might be food or building materials, and one of the other foot passengers, a tall, strident-voiced woman named Dodie Taborow, insists it is horses. Most people on the ship are crew. The space for passengers is limited. Also there is not much call for civilian traffic between Crimond and Thalia, even now that the war has been over for fifty years.

She is not a graceful ship. She has the twin red funnels and tubby white sides of an overgrown bath toy. On her port side and just below the gangway her hull has been patched. This means the ship has recently been in collision with something or else has been fired on. Neither possibility is reassuring.

She sits snugly in the water, waiting to leave. We gather in the saloon, a long, low-ceilinged lounge where our meals will be served and that also doubles as a passenger meeting area and recreation room. The Chief Steward's name is Djibril. He explains to us the fire regulations and also the lifeboat drill. Afterwards he takes us on a tour of the ship, telling us which parts we are allowed to enter and which are off limits.

He seems very young to be so responsible, not much older than me. Like most of the male crew members he wears his hair long, secured at the nape of his neck with a piece of black cord. By contrast the three women working the engine room have their hair cut short. It is hot below decks. The Chief Engineer, Juuli Moyse, has her hair shaved so close to her skull that I can see globules of sweat glinting on her scalp like beads of glass. Juuli Moyse has a stern expression but I like her immediately. All her movements are sure and calm, as if the *Aurelia Claydon* is a nervous beast in need of gentle handling. I admire her confidence, the efficiency of her movements as her hands pass over the coils and ridges of the ship's inner workings. I would swear she knows if all is well with the ship or not simply by touch.

Juuli Moyse lives and breathes the ship and in some strange way she is as much a physical part of it as the steam shaft or the rudder control. I smile at her, and as my reward I see her mouth curve upwards slightly at one corner.

After the engine room, Djibril takes us to see the galley, the stewards' deck, the passenger sun deck, and the navigation room. The navigation room contains the charts database and the radio, which is fixed in a dura-cell housing to prevent electrical short-outs and also water damage. Off the navigation room is the switch room, with the control panel for the ship's four great searchlights. Once we are in the Atlantic, the lights will be left on all night. Djibril explains that the fore and aft searchlights can penetrate the water to a depth of fifty metres. Officially, the searchlights are a protection against collision with other shipping. We all know what they are really for, though it's seen as bad luck to mention it.

Apparently Atlantic whales, whose natural habitat is deep water, dislike bright sunlight. The searchlights are meant to discourage them. Whether this actually works is a matter of debate.

There are about a dozen foot passengers in all. My first instinct is to hold myself aloof from them. There seems little point in becoming close to anyone when I know that once the voyage is over I won't see them again. Some of them will be gone even sooner – Dodie Taborow has already informed everyone that she will be leaving the ship at Brock Island, and several of the other passengers will be disembarking early also.

And yet, I feel a huge curiosity about them. The Croft was like a family, but we were always discouraged from forming friendships outside the programme. Most of what I know about the world comes from books. The idea of getting to know some other people is exciting and strange. I am used to being in crowds because of our trips into Asterwych, but when it comes to starting a conversation with a stranger I still feel shy. I know so little about anything, other than my work in the programme. I'm afraid of seeming stupid or naive. When I remind myself that everyone on board the ship is a stranger to all of the rest of us I find this makes me feel more confident.

We have the *Aurelia Claydon* in common at least. It is a start.

Dodie Taborow is from Lis, a district known as Jeunefille. Even if you were to take no notice of the clothes she wears – the shiny brown boots, the teal-blue button-up jacket with the astrakhan collar – it is obvious from the way she speaks that she has money. I don't hold this against her as I know Maud would, perhaps because I find her fascinating to look at. With her hands covered in rings and her faded glamour she's like an aging film actress.

As we sit drinking our first cups of coffee in the saloon, Dodie Taborow informs me that she's been recently widowed.

"I'm sorry to hear that," I say. She tells me that her husband's name was Wilson, and that he worked as the shop manager of a large iron-smelting works in Corton. When Dodie Taborow asks me who I am and where I am going I tell her I am a teacher and that I'm on my way to take up a position as a languages assistant in the city of Kontessa. This is what I've been told I should say, and it seems to work. It is clear that Dodie Taborow is not interested in me so much as in my possible suitability as a confidante. She soon stops questioning me about my provenance and moves on to other, more interesting subjects.

"You've seen that poor girl," she says, once she's finished giving me the lowdown on Wilson's coronary. "I think somebody said she was in a fire."

I know the woman she is talking about. I noticed her earlier when Djibril was giving us our walkaround. The right side of her face looks normal, but the left side has been mostly destroyed. What is left resembles a battlefield – a jumble of pinkish ridges and corrugated scar tissue. Her left eye is gone, the distended flap of her eyelid has been sewn closed over the socket. It is hard to tell how old she is. She is wearing a blue boiler suit and her long dark hair is plaited in a single braid. When I first saw her I assumed she was part of the crew.

She is sitting by herself in a corner of the saloon, drinking coffee and reading a newspaper.

"What's her name, do you know?" I ask Dodie Taborow. I think it's the first time I have asked her a question, rather than the other way around. The sight of the girl's disfigured face fills me with horror, yet there is something else too, something behind the fear that is almost wonderment. The girl has clearly suffered terribly, yet still she is able to sit here, to read the paper and drink her coffee and get on with her life. What truths does she know? What thoughts is she having? I wonder if someone who has suffered as she has would hate people who have not suffered, or be indifferent to them.

Is her calmness here in the saloon an act of heroism, or is it simply that she has no other choice? I notice the way Dodie Taborow stares at her, like a greedy magpie, and yet I sense she feels no pity. The girl is a subject for gossip, nothing more. What has happened to her has not happened to Dodie Taborow, and therefore does not properly exist. For Dodie Taborow there is not even a girl, not really, just the remains of a face, a thing of such extraordinary ugliness and wrongness it no longer belongs to the girl, but to the world, to be looked at and gawped over, like any other monstrosity.

I feel I have to know the woman's name. If I know her name she will be someone, and not just something.

"I don't know. Lin something, I think," says Dodie Taborow.

Lin. I can see at once how the name would suit her. A firm upright, strongly supported, like a tough green branch.

I would like to talk to her but I have no idea how I might go about it. She seems so alone in her corner, but perhaps that's what she wants. How can I know?

There are other passengers still in the saloon: a bearded middle-aged man with horn-rimmed glasses, two elderly ladies who I think are sisters, their narrow limbs strangely attenuated, like the limbs of spiders. The sisters talk together quietly in what I presume must be the Thalian language and this by itself makes me curious about them. I have resolved to become fluent in Thalian, to use the two months of this sea voyage to master its basics. I have brought several books to help me in this purpose – a parallel text edition of Saffron Valparaiso's *A Thalian Odyssey* and a field guide to the wildlife and birds of the Indic Basin – even though Kay has told me there will be no need.

"You'll be living mainly inside the compound," she said. "Everyone connected with the programme speaks Crimondn."

She has assured me that the compound is enormous, almost the size of Asterwych and with as many citizens. The idea of living inside a compound disturbs me rather. Hearing the two sisters chatting companionably together, I realise I cannot think of anything I want less.

As well as the bearded man, there is another, younger man named Alec Maclane. He is stout, but good-looking. He is wearing a fine cashmere waistcoat and gold cufflinks. He looks the kind who could easily afford a hopper flight, if he wanted it, and I wonder what he's doing, going by sea.

Dodie Taborow leans close to whisper in my ear, confiding that Alec Maclane is rich but also unlucky.

Unlucky in love? I wonder. Unlucky at cards?

"He has a fatal disease," Dodie says, then changes the subject. When later on that day I happen to see Maclane on deck I observe him closely, looking for signs of illness, but I see none. He has a curiously rolling gait, as if arthritis or rheumatism is causing him to favour one leg over the other, but other than that he seems perfectly healthy and I wonder if Dodie Taborow has been misinformed. Alec Maclane seems courteous and gentle and I rather like him. The other man, the bearded man, I do not like so much. There is something secretive about him. I haven't found out his name yet and amazingly Dodie Taborow doesn't know it either.

"He looks like a government man, don't you think? A politico?" She purses her lips as she looks at him, but whether with distaste or in fascination it's hard to tell.

"Let's go on deck," she says suddenly, and I agree at once. Djibril has already been in to tell us that the ship will be departing from port in half an hour. As we get up to leave, I notice the bearded man looking at me. I try to look away but it is too late – he catches my eye and I am forced to return his gaze.

There is a flicker of something between us, and for a moment I wonder if he is using an implant. For some reason the idea repulses me. I tug my thoughts away, with some difficulty.

It was like that with Kay, just sometimes. Each time it

happened I found the experience similarly unpleasant, like catching her with her clothes off.

Is the bearded man some sort of spy?

I make up my mind to avoid him as much as possible.

We are on our way. I stand at the rail for a long time, gazing back at Faslane as it shrinks and dwindles, becoming first a green-grey smudge on the horizon and then disappearing altogether. We are still in the mouth of the loch, not in the open sea at all yet, but I feel cast adrift from my old life already. I can feel Dodie Taborow regarding me with curiosity. I wish she would stop.

"Is this your first sea voyage?" she asks me. I say that it is. I realise she has been watching the receding coastline just as I have, and I wonder if this is a journey she had been intending to take with her husband Wilson, or if he was to have remained behind in any case, alive or dead.

"I love the sea," she says. "I sometimes wish I could stay at sea forever. Life would be simpler that way."

Her voice has taken on a wistful quality. I ask her why she is travelling to Brock Island. I wonder if the bluntness of my question might offend her, but if anything she seems pleased that I have brought up the subject.

"I have a son who lives on Brock," she says. "Duncan." She is silent for some time, and I begin to think I must have upset her after all. Then she lets out a sigh. Pale sunlight envelops her hands, sparking her rings. "Duncan and Wilson had a terrible row. They haven't spoken for ten years.

Duncan doesn't even know his father's dead yet. I'm going to Brock to break the news. I know he'll be devastated."

"Will he return with you to Crimond, do you think?"

She laughs, a short, brittle sound, like a twig snapping.

"Duncan will never leave Brock, not now," she says. "He's as stubborn as his father." She turns her face into the wind. Her hair blows back from her forehead like a silver mane. Her profile is gaunt and somehow timeless and full of dignity, and to me at that moment she appears like a ship's figurehead, or like an aging queen: faded but still full of vigour, still fighting her battles.

"Fathers and sons, who needs them?" she says. "I wish I'd had a daughter. Like you." She touches my hand where it rests upon the rail. "You're very young to be travelling so far alone, Maree. What do your parents have to say about that?"

"My parents are dead," I reply. The words are out before I can examine them for flaws. It is surprising how thorny they sound when spoken aloud. "It's all right," I add quickly. "It happened ages ago. I was still a baby, really. I don't remember them at all." I can feel myself blushing. I feel embarrassed but I don't know what about – it isn't my fault that they are dead. Mostly I don't want Dodie Taborow to feel sorry for me, and by a miracle she seems to understand that. We stand together in silence for a while, and then she asks me if I have anyone who will be meeting me when I get to Bonita.

"One of the other teachers from the school is being sent to pick me up," I say to her. "There's no need to worry."

This at least is a truth of sorts. Kay has told me that someone from the programme will be waiting at the dockside to collect me. If by any chance this person is not there I am to go straight to the harbour office and they will put me in immediate contact with the compound's administrators. There is indeed, as I have said to Dodie, nothing to worry about. I stand beside her at the rail, feeling the throb and hum of the ship's engines passing into me through the soles of my feet. The sense of being in motion, of drawing away from one thing and heading towards another, is oddly restful. It occurs to me that even if my parents were still alive I might still be leaving them. It's strange to think of that, like being given a secret glimpse of another world, and reminds me of an odd idea of Maud's, about how the world we live in isn't the real world, that the real world lies elsewhere, in a parallel dimension where the New War never happened and there are no such creatures as smartdogs. Maud said she'd read a story like that in a book somewhere, although she could never remember the title or the author and I privately suspected she had made it up herself. I found it amusing when she first told me about it but afterwards a shadow seemed to fall across me and I felt afraid. What if it was all true, after all? What if the person I knew as myself didn't really exist? Suppose I was just a template, a mirror-image of another girl in another world who even at this moment was begging me for her life back so she could stop having nightmares?

A foolish idea perhaps, but still a powerful one. I do not like to dwell on it.

"What did you mean, when you said you wished you could stay at sea forever?" I ask Dodie.

"Oh, just that when you're at sea it's so much easier to

exist without the need for things. You exist and you observe, but that's the sum of it. Life tends to simplify itself rather beautifully." She spreads her arms out along the deck rail and gazes down into the water below. The sea is bluish-grey, the colour of steel. I notice that some of the other passengers have come out on deck, the two tall sisters and a man in a purple blazer and Alec Maclane. The sisters are wearing identical blue mackintoshes, though there is no sign of rain.

I tell Dodie I have letters to write, and we agree to meet again for supper, in the saloon.

I return to my cabin, where I try to write to Maud and find I cannot. Too much has happened already, too many new things that she will never see and never know about.

Already our lives are diverging, irrevocably.

Already she is like a figure in a dream.

The programme's main facility in Kontessa was originally set up by the military. Everyone assumed it was a centre for espionage, which it was, at least for a while, but once the war was over that all changed. The programme remained in Kontessa because it was easier to maintain privacy. The programme's ongoing series of experiments into human and alt-human language systems is the most complex and far-reaching work in applied linguistics ever undertaken. That's what Kay told us, anyway.

Kay always insisted that without people like us – Caine and Sarah and Garland and me – the programme would no longer exist. It would have been shut down in the aftermath of the war, along with all the other spy stations and radar communications centres and underground munitions facilities that were part of the machinery that kept the war running. Kay is one of those people who tend to talk about the war a great deal. Not that she is old enough to remember anything – it was over twenty years before she was born.

Peter Crumb, the Croft's programme administrator, has a Thalian mother. Kay used to have sex with Peter sometimes, up in his study on the second floor – I know because I heard them. As Peter Crumb's room was directly above our bedroom it was sometimes hard not to. The idea of dried-up Peter Crumb exercising his cock used to make me feel queasy, but I found it interesting to imagine Kay with her legs apart, gritting her teeth and seizing her pleasure like a dog tearing at a piece of gristle. It cut her down to size, somehow.

Maud used to listen to them quite openly, even placing a glass against the ceiling so she could hear better.

"Can you even bear to think of it?" she would say. "The two of them rutting away like pigs in a mud bath?" She would make this token protest then dissolve into giggles. I think Maud might have had a crush on Peter Crumb for a while, God knows why. He was attractive in a way I suppose, with his high cheekbones and silver hair, kind of haunted-looking, but for me there was always something a bit creepy about him.

Once, while we were doing it, I told Maud she should imagine that I was Peter. I thought she'd squeal with disgust or burst out laughing but she came instead, almost at once, just like that.

* * *

Everyone knows that the smartdogs were first developed in Crimond, but it was in Thalia, at the facility in Kontessa, that scientists began to do detailed research into how smartdogs think. The original experiments all involved Petronella del Toro. She was already in her twenties when they discovered her, a lab technician working at the facility and the first of what the scientists liked to refer to as a new race of natural empaths. Petronella was able to communicate with smartdogs without the aid of an implant. The scientists recognise the value of the work they did with Petronella but nowadays they generally prefer to work with children. They say a child's ability is the purest, because it's instinctive rather than learned. Also, a child is easier to nurture and to train in the ways of the programme.

I cannot remember a time *before* I spoke with smartdogs – that's why I was recruited into the programme. I've known about the programme since I was eight. Kay says we're working to improve the world and I've never found any reason not to believe her.

Wolfe thought that Kay and Peter Crumb and the rest of them were all lying to us, which I guess is why he ran away. None of us knew what he was planning, not even Caine, who loved Wolfe like a brother. After Wolfe left, Caine changed. I don't mean he changed towards the rest of us – he was always the kindest, least selfish person you can imagine – but he became more turned in on himself and less happy. He began asking questions about the programme, about the Kontessa facility and what it might really be for.

"It's not just about the smartdogs," he said once to me

and Garland and Sarah. "There has to be more to it, or why all this secrecy?"

This was the summer before he went, he and Sarah. The nights were very warm, and throughout June until the middle of August it never quite got dark. I would wait until Maud was asleep, then sneak outside and join Sarah and Caine and Garland on the roof of the coal store. We'd take blankets up there, and cushions. Sometimes Sarah and Garland would smoke cigarettes they'd bought secretly in Asterwych. They were careful always to gather up the butts and hide them until they could dispose of them in a waste bin on their next trip to town. They knew Kay would go crazy if she found out.

Caine didn't smoke. He talked to us about his ideas instead. We liked to listen to him because he was Caine, but I don't think any of the three of us took what he said all that seriously. Somehow, Caine had got hold of the idea that what the programme was really about was the analysis and decoding of alien language systems.

The first time Caine used the word alien Sarah burst out laughing. When she saw he wasn't joking, she turned the laugh into a cough, then quickly stubbed out her cigarette against the roof tiles.

"I'm not talking about little green men," Caine explained patiently. "I mean alien as in different from us. AI is an alien language, so is computer code, so is anything non-human or even alt-human. We have no idea what else is out there and neither have the scientists. We're all in the dark here – but we're even more in the dark than they are, because they're not telling us the whole story. They say we're a new race and that they have a duty to protect us, but that doesn't give them the right to treat us like children. Without us, there'd be no programme. Surely we have the right to know what all this is for?"

Caine was the eldest of our group. I'd also say he was the most gifted. He could speak three different languages fluently and knew the rudiments of half a dozen others. He never boasted about it though, or about anything. His parents were both killed in a house fire. I was stupidly in love with him for a while. I'm sure he knew, but he never said anything because he knew how terribly it would embarrass me. Caine would never hurt a soul. He was Caine.

"But even if what you say about the alien languages is true," Garland said. "What's so bad about that?"

"Nothing, necessarily," Caine said. "It's the secrecy that's bad. If there's nothing to hide, why not tell us the truth?"

"What's the point of them, anyway?" I said. "What are we expected to do with these alien languages once we've translated them?"

I listened to the sound of my words, rising up through the August twilight like coloured balloons. Caine once told me that sound goes on forever, even when we can't hear it any more. Every word that every person ever uttered is still out there somewhere, floating around in space, travelling onward forever. What if aliens really are out there somewhere, listening in to all our stupid conversations and wondering what in God's name we're on about?

"Language is power," Caine said. "If you know what someone's thinking, you're already one step ahead of them."

Two months later, at the end of September, Caine and Sarah were driven to Inverness, where they were put on a hopper flight to Thalia. I went off by myself, into the hills above the Croft, where I could cry without anyone knowing. When Maud asked me later where I'd been I tried to look blank.

"Just around," I said, trying to make out it didn't matter where I'd been, that it was just a day like any other. She looked at me strangely but left it at that, which was unusual for her – normally she'd go on and on until I was either forced to tell her or make something up. The one thing Maud hates most is feeling left out.

I know it's hard for her, being Kay's daughter and living at the Croft and being so close to us all but not really one of us. I would hate it, I think. I sometimes think that Maud is stronger than the lot of us put together.

Sarah promised she would write to me from Thalia but she never did. I never received a letter from her, anyway.

Kay said we shouldn't feel hurt, that they'd be busy with work, and that we'd all be together again soon enough.

I wonder about that. Now more than ever.

Am I anxious about what I'll discover?

Not really. Not yet.

When I told Dodie I didn't remember my parents, that was the truth. It's not the whole truth, though. I do remember some people who used to look after me, a woman especially. When I asked Kay about them she told me they were house-parents at the foster home where I was placed after my parents died. I came to live at the Croft when I was four. When I was six years old, Kay explained to me that my own mother and father were both killed in a massive tramway accident.

"There were fifty-six fatalities," she said. Fifty-six, she repeated, as if knowing how many people died somehow acts as proof that the crash really happened. I've searched many times for more information about the accident – in the library at Asterwych where there is free Internet, in the microfiche files Peter Crumb hoards in his study – but I've never been able to find anything that matches up with what Kay told me.

When I finally confide my doubts to Maud she just shrugs and says my parents were probably politicals.

"Or perhaps they just sold you," she adds. "Like with Sarah's mother." Her face goes slack and stolid, the way it always does when she knows someone is displeased with her.

She knows we never talk like that about Sarah. It's almost a rule.

I change the subject because it's easier than starting an argument. But I go on looking for information about the tramway crash and not finding it. And then, not long before her departure, Sarah tells me about my arrival at the Croft.

"You were so quiet," she says. "You wouldn't speak for ages, not to anyone. I remember you kept wetting the bed. Kay went mental."

Sarah giggles at that, and so do I. This was all so long ago and I remember none of it. It might as well have happened to another person. Sarah's mother runs a coffee shop in Asterwych. She set up the business with the money donated to her by the programme for giving up Sarah. Sarah used to go for supper with her, once a month. Sarah was an experiment, the only one of us who had an implant. Mostly we never thought about it. Caine was always trying to reassure her, telling her she'd have been the same as us anyway, which was something that felt true even if it wasn't.

No one knows who Sarah's father is, or was. I guess Sarah's mother needed money very badly. Caine used to say you should never judge people for what they do, because most of the time they can't help it. At least Sarah's mother knows where Sarah is, and that she's safe.

I do remember Limlasker, who was a smartdog, huge and white, with a black marking across his hindquarters, like a handprint.

Limlasker was taller than I was. He filled my world.

I used to hug his neck and listen to him thinking, his faraway, secret thoughts, like soft poems, like the special private words of a lost brother.

I never ask anyone about Limlasker, because when it comes to Lim I couldn't bear to be lied to. I don't want anyone to tell me he never existed.

* * *

At half-past six I make my way to the saloon. Dodie Taborow is already there, sitting at a corner table with Alec Maclane.

"Maree!" she calls. "Over here." She raises a hand and waves, flashing her rings. Alec Maclane's presence seems to have reinvigorated her. I notice also that she has changed for dinner. I wonder briefly if my own jeans and blouse are now out of place.

Alec Maclane regards me solemnly. His eyes are grey and rather beautiful. His formal way of dressing and general courtliness made me assume he was of an age, but now that I see him close to, I realise Maclane is quite a lot younger than Dodie, perhaps by as much as twenty years. This discovery disturbs me, though I would have thought Dodie more than able to take care of herself. Maclane has changed for dinner also – he's dressed elegantly in a flamboyant paisley shirt and velvet trousers. He looks a little tired around the eyes, but certainly not ill. This so-called fatal disease of his is still a mystery.

"We've been talking about getting together a four for Quest," Dodie says excitedly. "Alec is a county champion. Do you play cards at all, Maree? We'd love you to join us."

"*Was* a county champion," says Alec Maclane, gently correcting her. "That was ten years ago." He looks down at his hands, which are plump and white and beautifully cared for. I am reminded of the hands of a conjuror we were taken to see once, in Asterwych, and for a moment the image of the conjuror seems to cancel out the image of Alec Maclane, to replace him somehow. It's as if time has slipped backwards for an instant. It makes me feel dizzy.

In answer to Dodie's question, I shake my head. "Only whist, and gin rummy," I say. I do my best to smile. "I'm no good at those, either."

Dodie looks disappointed for a second but soon brightens up again. "I've heard the Carola sisters play," she says. "I shall have to look into it."

I presume the Carola sisters must be the two elderly Thalian women. We eat supper, which is snapper baked in sea salt. I quickly become accustomed Maclane's presence. He seems to exert a calming influence on everything around him. When the meal is over I excuse myself and go up on the passenger deck. I watch as the sky turns first to mauve and then to charcoal. The moon rises. I hear two crewmen talking quietly together on the deck above. I do not recognise their language – possibly it is Glasier. In a day's time we will reach the Channel, the narrow strip of sea that separates Crimond from Farris. After a brief stopover at Charlemagne, Farris's most westerly port, we will call at the Espinol port of Lilyat. After that we begin our journey across the Atlantic.

Between Lilyat and Thalia there is nothing but ocean. I lean upon the guard rail, looking down. When you stare at it for long enough, the ocean appears to become a unified body, greater even than itself, a massive single-celled organism with its own consciousness and will and desires. Perhaps it even has a language of its own, one of Caine's alien language systems, something we might ascertain but not comprehend.

The ocean is never just one colour. It is like a gigantic refractive prism, containing all colours. Large seabirds – I think they are called kittiwakes – follow the churning water in the wake of the ship. Sometimes they dive right into it, remaining beneath the surface for many seconds.

Further along the deck I catch sight of the two women Dodie Taborow referred to as the Carola sisters. They stand together at the rail, gaunt and grey as ash trees, feeding the kittiwakes with bread crusts, presumably left over from their supper. The gulls are in a lunacy of excitement, shearing through the air towards them, tearing the chunks of bread from the sisters' hands.

The women don't seem afraid though. Rather they seem thrilled by what is happening, gasping and exclaiming to one another in the rolling, curvaceous accents of the Thalian language.

As before, they are dressed plainly, in identical grey jersey dresses that appear to exaggerate their thinness. I wonder if they are pleased to be returning to Thalia, and what it was that brought them to Crimond in the first place.

There are many Thalians living in Crimond now, and vice versa, but these women are old enough to remember a time when it was still difficult to obtain a visa for travel between our two once-warring countries. There are still those who feel uneasy, both with those who used to be the enemy and with themselves.

Kay once told me her father still had to leave the room when anything about the war came on the TV. His own father had died in the bombardment of Lis, and he could never forget it.

"There was a boy at my school who was Thalian – his name was Ecco," Kay said. "Dad didn't like me to say hello to him, even. We had some terrible arguments about it."

I wonder if it's because of her father's prejudice that Kay feels she needs to talk about the war so much and so often. I stand still, gazing at the Carola sisters who have run out of bread for the kittiwakes and who are now staring out to sea instead, their hands clasped in front of them, craning their necks forward as if scanning the waves for a sight of something marvellous, wonder or horror. I would love to step forward and greet them in their language, but I feel too shy. I whisper to myself instead, trying out the few words of Thalian I have so far mastered and trying to pluck up the courage to approach them.

Do people in Bonita still say 'by the Goddess' or is that one of those quaint anachronisms only an ignorant tourist would come out with? I realise how little I know about their country, and feel embarrassed and ashamed at once.

"They were both whirligig pilots, how cool is that?"

The voice comes from directly behind me. I turn around quickly, startled. The voice that has spoken is unknown to me, but I recognise the face at once, how could I not? In reality it is just half a face, the ruined features of the woman called Lin who Dodie Taborow tells me has been in a fire.

Her single eye is the colour of mercury, and has the slanting appearance that normally marks a Chinoit or Korati ancestry. Her jaw is long and strong. Her mouth, which is mostly undamaged, is full-lipped and wide. She gazes at me steadfastly, without blinking. It's as if she's inviting me to look at her, challenging me to do so, and once I am over my embarrassment I find I cannot stop staring. It is impossible not to be fascinated by something so outside the set parameters of what a human face is supposed to look like.

I find myself wanting to touch her skin, to explore her face with my fingers, to learn what it means.

"My rig came down and there was a fire. My ejector seat fucked up – because of the heat, probably. I fainted briefly, and this side of my face became melted to the windshield. They had to cut most of it off to remove the plastic. That's the deal."

She speaks the words quickly and fluently, like part of a speech she's learned or a theatre audition. She raises her remaining eyebrow: did I do okay?

"I didn't –" I stammer inconclusively. I can feel myself blushing.

"I know you didn't. No one does – that's what pisses me off."

I like her forthrightness, her lack of apology. It's as if her words are cards in a high stakes game. She stands firmly upright, not turning aside. I like that, too.

"Is your name Lin?" I say to her. It's the only question I feel I can ask without looking a fool.

"Yes it is, Lin Hamada. Don't tell me people are bitching about me already?"

I can feel myself wanting to laugh and in the end I can't stop myself.

"Of course not. Someone happened to mention your name, that's all."

"The lady with the rings, I bet?"

"Yes. She said you'd been in a fire."

"And she's right. But that's very old news now, therefore boring. Do you feel like getting a coffee? I can't believe how good the coffee is on board this tub."

"I'd like that a lot," I say. It is very nearly dark now. I see that the Carola sisters have gone inside already, that I am standing alone on the deck with Lin Hamada. The kittiwakes have gone too, flown away into the darkness to who-knows-where. I hear the thump-thump-thump of the ship's engines, the endless rapid churning of the sea beneath.

"Was it true what you said?" I ask Lin Hamada. "About the sisters being helicopter pilots?" I know that 'whirligig' means helicopter – it is the word they use on TV and in the newspapers. It is the kind of word – like 'collateral' and 'incoming' – that people use when they want to make it sound like they understand militia-talk, even when many of them have never laid eyes on a helicopter or even on an aeroplane or an ordinary hopper. These flying machines are like mythical beasts – everyone knows what they look like but few people have ever seen them in the wild.

What Lin has told me about the Carola sisters seems impossible. I am already longing for it to be true.

"They haven't seen active service for a long time, but yes, they were both commissioned officers in the air corps. They gave a flying demo at my airbase once. They were pretty awesome."

Every now and then you might see a hopper passing over Asterwych, flying so high it's just a speck, a black dot in the side of a cloud, a distant murmur of engines. I know from books and from TV that airplanes, like roadcars, were once a common form of transport for ordinary people. Now they mostly mean big business, or war. I have never seen an aeroplane close to.

A smartdog is more intuitive than a human being. It takes its empathic abilities for granted, the same way we take it for granted that we can talk.

For a smartdog, there is no dividing line between thought and emotion. An emotion is a kind of thought, and a thought is just an inside picture of an emotion.

Most laypeople think that smartdogs don't know the difference between truth and lies, that for a smartdog the definition of truth is the word of its runner.

All of this is wrong. Nearly all smartdogs will know at once if their runner is lying to them. It is true that they don't have an abstract understanding of these concepts in the way that people do – for a smartdog the truth is 'as things are' and a lie is 'something else' – but a smartdog will obey a runner who is lying not because it can't tell the difference, but because it believes the runner must have a reason for lying.

A smartdog has no concept of death. It fears pain, incarceration, being attacked, separation from its runner. But there is no cipher for death itself within its lexicon, no image-word-emotion that can encompass it.

When a smartdog embarks on a mission it does not think about what has been strapped to it. It thinks about what its runner has asked it to do, which is to carry a certain burden from one place to another. It does not fear being blown up – it fears being unable to complete the mission and so displeasing its runner.

There have been many instances of runners refusing to comply with military objectives, refusing to lie to their dogs, refusing to send a dog on a mission that will ultimately result in its destruction.

Demonstrations of this kind of obstructive behaviour usually result in the runner being dismissed from the programme. In some cases, runners have had their implants forcibly removed.

So far there has been only one recorded case of a smartdog refusing a mission. The dog's name was Pathfinder; her mission was to carry a short-range thermonuclear device into an armaments facility on the outskirts of Condiaz. There were a thousand civilian employees working on site at the time.

Pathfinder did not have sufficient understanding of her situation to realise that the bomb she carried could be detonated anywhere and at any time. It became clear she believed that the weapon could only be triggered by her entering the armaments compound. She was within half a mile of her target when she veered off course and headed out into the desert. In spite of repeated interventions from her runner, she refused to return.

The mission's controllers eventually gave up on her. They detonated the bomb in the desert and repeated the mission a week later with a different smartdog. The dog, Moonrise Kingdom, carried the device right into the compound where it was successfully detonated. It was not discovered until afterwards that the earlier attempt had triggered the spycams, and the compound staff and most of their equipment had been relocated.

Garland, who will be leaving the Croft next summer, once said something strange. He said we were in danger because as far as the scientists who ran the programme were concerned we were unreliable.

"If they could do what they do without us, then they would," he said. "They would love it if they could replace us with machines."

Perhaps that's what they're trying to do anyway – perhaps Caine was right. A couple of days after Garland said what he said I had a nightmare, about a computer trying to smartread a smartdog, and getting everything wrong.

Lin is lying on her back on her bunk, her long body stretched full length, her hands behind her head. She is lying so that the bad side of her face is turned into the pillow. I don't know if this is the most comfortable position for her or if it is something she does automatically, without thinking. Her feet are bare. They are long-toed and hard-looking, like the roots of young trees.

"Fuck," she says. "That's amazing."

"You believe me?" I am astounded at myself and a little frightened. I have never spoken to any outsider about the Croft, or about the programme. It does not matter that up until now I had no one to tell – the feeling of crossing a line is still so strong I can almost feel that line snapping, like a piece of fishing twine, its broken ends wrapping themselves painfully around my ankles.

When we were small, Kay was always drumming it into

us that we should never tell anyone how we lived or what we did. She hinted but never stated outright that if we broke this rule, people would come from Asterwych and force us to go to ordinary schools with ordinary children. The fear of being separated from one another, of having our home broken up or interfered with had its effect. We kept ourselves neatly locked up in an invisible cage.

I didn't plan to tell Lin Hamada about any of this. It just happened.

Lin blinks her single eye then looks up at the ceiling.

"Of course I believe you," she says. "You're like one of those dogs, aren't you? You can't tell lies."

"I can do what I want." A small jolt of anger flashes through me and my heart is racing. Lin seems to be saying that I have no will of my own, that my will has been engineered out of me, and this makes me feel scornful. Is what I say true though? Can I do what I want?

"I don't mean that you can't – just that the act of telling a lie would make you uncomfortable. It's something you wouldn't do unless you really had to. That's true, isn't it? I'm right about that?"

I am sitting on Lin's floor, with my back pressed up against the wooden storage unit that opens out to make the writing desk. The cabins are almost too small to accommodate two people at once, but here we are anyway. Lin's cabin is as tidy as an ordnance cupboard and I find myself wondering if her life as a soldier – as a pilot – has boosted her awareness somehow, if it hasn't made her just a tiny bit empathic.

When I think about lying it makes me feel seasick, which

is odd, because I haven't been seasick once since coming on board.

Is Lin right in what she says, or is it just the thought of lying to *her*?

"Lying is pointless because it never leads anywhere," I say, evading her. "It's always a dead end."

"That depends on what you're trying to achieve," Lin says. Then she asks me if I had any choice about going to Thalia.

My throat feels tight. I'm not sure how to answer her, because the truth is I don't really know. I think of Wolfe, what happened to him. But surely Wolfe was different, too ill at the end to understand what he was doing?

Kay told us Wolfe was dead, that he couldn't have survived for much longer in any case, even if he'd stayed at the Croft.

Caine always said that was bollocks, and Caine never swore. We didn't discuss it though, it was all too awful. I try to imagine what might have happened if I'd said to Kay or to Peter Crumb that I didn't want to be a part of the programme any more. An image comes to my mind, of myself, clearing tables and washing cups in Sarah's mother's coffee shop in Asterwych.

Would that have been so terrible? The image has a strange fascination. I am surprised to discover that I do not find it entirely unpleasant.

"The programme is what I've been trained for," I say in the end. "It's – my job."

"Most people still get to choose their jobs, though. Up to a point, anyway."

"Did you choose to be a soldier?"

Lin laughs, an odd, harsh sound, like a crow cawing. "You're joking. I was crazy for it. It was the only way I could think of to be free."

"Free of what?" As I ask my question I realise a strange thing: that I am unable to picture Lin Hamada as a child. Does she have brothers, sisters, parents? I cannot tell.

"Free of the ground," Lin says. She laughs again. "I am an impatient person. Impatience is my defining characteristic. I don't like to wait – for anything. Being stuck in one place all the time – that would drive me insane."

I sense that she is saying what is true for her. I wonder what she will do, now that her injuries have made her unfit for life in the military. Once again she answers before I can ask.

"I'm going to Brock," she says. "I've landed a job flying their mail service. They don't call it that, though – they call it intra-island communications. They have three beat-up Landseers they bought off the CAF and I get to captain the whole fleet." She grins. "I'm even more beat to shit than the planes, so I guess we're made for each other."

I have seen Brock Island on the map. It is shoe-shaped, a large and mountainous island that was once a part of the Thalian mainland but split off after an earthquake thousands of years ago. Before the war, Brock used to be a Crimondn colony. It's governed by Thalia now, but its links to Crimond are still strong – half the population is Crimondn. I think it must be a strange place to live, neither one thing nor the other. I've heard also that it rains a lot.

"It'll be great," Lin is saying. "It'll make a nice change,

303

not having people trying to shoot me down all the time. Not at first anyway."

I grin back, but weakly. I know this sounds foolish, but already I am feeling her absence, the loss of her. Like the loss of Maud, only worse, because Lin is here with me now and Maud is gone.

"There's one of those deep space research centres in Kontessa, isn't there?" Lin says, changing the subject away from herself and back to me. "All those supercomputers or whatever. Government boffins staring through telescopes and drawing big salaries and never getting anywhere?"

I feel surprised and a little shocked by how much she knows. Kay always liked to make out that no one outside of the programme knew about the programme, but clearly either Kay knows as little about what goes on in the world as I do, or she was lying. It's hard to decide which. Caine knew about the research station, for a start. One of his ideas – one of the things he used to talk about when we were out on the roof – was that they'd been picking up transmissions from space they couldn't decode.

"That's where we come in," he said. "To them we're just another type of software. Expensive and temperamental software, too."

"So you think the compound could still be a spy station?" Sarah said.

"I don't think it's as much spying yet as monitoring," Caine replied. "All I know is that they need us, because we have different ways of understanding language. Different from their own, I mean. We're freaks, basically. If we weren't so useful to them they'd probably be hunting us down and shooting us."

When Sarah asked Caine who 'they' were exactly, he just shrugged as if that wasn't the point. "The people in control," he said. "There's always someone, and it doesn't matter whose side they're working for, they're always the same."

Could Lin be one of them? A secret spy?

If Lin is a spy I would know, and I know she is not.

"Do you believe what he said? Your Caine?" Lin says. "Do you believe that the compound has been receiving transmissions from alien beings?"

I shake my head slowly. I'm not saying no exactly, just that I don't know. And Caine was never 'my' Caine, ever, no matter what I might have liked to imagine.

At the Croft we were taught the art of focus, to concentrate hard on solving small and intricate problems. The larger, outside questions were for other people. I have always known that smartdogs were originally developed as weapons of war. But all that was a long time ago.

It's easier to accept that as the truth, because to believe anything different would be too awful.

If we are running the smartdogs, who's running us?

Again the vision comes to me, the sudden image of myself, cleaning tables in the cafe in Asterwych.

It means the freedom of knowing that no one is watching me, that no one cares who I am or what I can do.

"I don't know what to believe any more," I say to Lin. "That's the problem."

"Well, I guess you'll find out when you get there," Lin

says. She flips over on to her side and slides down from her bunk. Her face is turned away from me, and I wonder for a moment if she is angry, angry at my naiveté, impatient with my lack of curiosity. I wouldn't blame her if she were – I feel angry at myself. But then I see she is just searching for something in one of the under-bunk drawers.

"Do you know this record?" she says. "Have you heard it before?" She is holding something out to me, a compact disc. There is a picture on the front, a brightly coloured clockwork rooster made from tin. I like the picture but I don't know the album, which is by an artist called Paula Komedia. I shake my head. I have never cared all that much about music. Maud used to listen to bands on the radio but I could never get into them. I could never decode their significance. Caine used to go to Peter Crumb's room sometimes and listen to records with him, symphonies and concertos, choral works by composers I'd never heard of.

It occurs to me suddenly that Caine and Peter Crumb might have been lovers.

Is that how Caine came to know so much? Through his lover, Peter? Peter Crumb with his haunted expression and watchful eyes?

The thought pierces me like a piton. I don't know now if I will ever find the strength to tug it out of me.

"I first heard this on my base," Lin said. "Paula Komedia is massive in Thalia."

I watch her as she inserts the disc into the wall slot. All the cabins have CD/DVD players, though I have not used mine because I have nothing to play on it. First there is silence, then three descending notes on a guitar. The notes repeat themselves, whispering, echoing, hesitating on the brink then plunging downwards into what sounds like a storm-wind of other instruments. I can pick out the sound of a flute, an accordion, a bass viol, some kind of percussion instrument that might be a tambourine. It's cacophony, and yet it makes sense, because out of the maelstrom rises the firm and strident voice of Paula Komedia. Paula Komedia's voice is silvery and sinuous, curving up and around the other sounds, binding them fast. Now and then it cracks wide open on a high note, gusting fire. I cannot decide if the music is ugly or beautiful, only that I want to go on hearing it.

There is a liner sheet with the lyrics, strange songs about wild horses roaming the pampas, an abandoned *finca*, a woman who flies her aeroplane into the sun.

What Komedia's music reminds me most of is Limlasker, running.

"She wrote all the songs herself," Lin says. She is listening with her eyes closed, and now that she is at rest, sunk within herself and not noticing me, I find I am able to see the whole truth of her face and not just its destruction. The unhurt parts rise out of the ruins, like the wreckage of an aircraft, crashed in bleak moorland. I want to touch her cheek to say how sorry I am that this terrible thing has happened to her, but I can sense she wouldn't want this, not the saying sorry part anyway. She is who she is now – what is there to apologise for? "The lyrics are based on the Thalian Odyssey. Do you know it?"

"I have a copy, in my cabin. I haven't read it yet though."

I am glad, relieved to be able to say I have at least heard of it. I know that *A Thalian Odyssey* is supposed to be one of the greatest works of literature in the world. Its author, Saffron Valparaiso, was middle-aged by the time she finally completed it. She was a poet, then a soldier, then a teacher and then finally a poet again. She was killed, near the end of the war, by a terrorist bomb.

Valparaiso's work was banned in Crimond for many years.

We are docked at Lilyat and will remain here all day.

The sun pours down on the decks of the *Aurelia Claydon* like spilled yellow paint. After Lilyat we will be continuously at sea for almost two months, and so everyone is taking the opportunity to go ashore. Except, it seems, for Alec Maclane, who will remain on board.

Dodie Taborow explains that the sun doesn't agree with him.

"He can't walk all that far, in any case," Dodie adds. "Because of his illness, I mean."

I still don't know what's supposed to be wrong with Alec Maclane. What I do know is that Dodie has become very attached to him. She hurries to his cabin half a dozen times a day taking him small treats – a magazine, a packet of halva, beef tea in a special mug made from Chinoit porcelain – and when she's not with him in his cabin they're together in the saloon or walking on deck. In the evenings before supper they have cocktails served to their table, called Martinis.

Dodie always seems to be on a kind of high when Maclane is around, sparkling with nervous energy in a way that makes me feel uncomfortable without knowing why.

I keep wondering if it's true that Maclane is sick. I wonder if perhaps Dodie believes that he will die soon, and that perhaps if she is good to him he'll leave her his money. Dodie has money of her own, I know that, but Maclane is in another league. Maclane is what Maud would call a seriously fat cat.

If I could make myself believe that was all, I would feel less worried. The thing is, I can sense that Dodie really likes Maclane, that she hopes her life will be changed for the better because of him. I don't mean money. Dodie is different from when she first came on board, less sad and less careful. She has let down her guard and this makes me afraid for her. Afraid that she will be hurt, or else made to look a fool. I'm not sure which would be worse for her.

I have read that Lilyat is one of the biggest seaports on this side of the world. Also it is the last stop on the map of Evror. West of Lilyat there is nothing, just the Atlantic, until you wash up on the shores of Brock Island. The Atlantic seems to be everywhere in Lilyat – because the city sits on such a steep gradient, the ocean can be glimpsed between the buildings from most places. There is a strong reek of brine, which reminds me of my walks with Maud to the Offshore to buy winkles and crab cakes. There are many kiosks along the harbour front, selling sun hats and fish patties, iced lemonade. I stand on the quayside, alone for a moment while I wait for Dodie to finish arguing with one of the taxi drivers. They are solidly built, these drivers; men for the most part, smelling strongly of tobacco and garlic and their own sharp body odour.

The sun here is bright as a sword, dangerous and opulent as laudanum. The people seem bold and cheerful. They chatter together in excited voices. Many of the older women are brightly dressed. Their shawls, made from coloured cotton, remind me of the outspread wings of burnet moths, resting on heather.

The younger women wear vests and jeans like my own, only newer and more fashionable. Their black hair is plaited into thick braids that dangle between their shoulder blades like glossy silk ropes.

Dodie tells me she has visited Lilyat before, several times, with her husband Wilson. The price of a cab has clearly gone up since she was last here.

"He's charging me a fortune," she grumbles. "Let's take the tramway."

I am glad that Dodie knows which platform we should be waiting on, the local price of tokens and how many stops it takes before we get to the centre. It means I can float along without feeling anxious, watching this city as it unscrolls itself around me, the gleaming rails of the tramway clawing their way up the tilted streets like ladders, scrabbling to find a foothold on the dusty cobbles.

The only city I have visited before this is Inverness. It is hard to find any equation between the two.

"It's not too bad here if you don't mind the hills," Dodie says. She's wearing a smart linen suit with a lemon-coloured blouse, a wide-brimmed straw hat which she calls a boater. I realise how out of place she looks here, how foreign.

"I don't mind at all," I say to her. "I'm used to climbing." This is the truth. We get off the tramway at one end of a wide, smoothly paved shopping street that Dodie tells me is where everyone who visits Lilyat comes to shop for the leather goods and jewellery for which the city is famous. We move slowly along, gazing into the windows of the various boutiques, those facing the street itself and those on the smaller, narrower alleyways that surround it. This single commercial district of Lilyat seems to me bigger than the whole of Asterwych put together. The goods on display – leather handbags and wallets, pearl-handled penknives, silk scarves in a variety of colours – entrance me. I stand still, gawping foolishly at a silver brooch in the form of a bumblebee. The insect's body is carved from amber; its outspread wings are fashioned from the twisted-together strands of silver wires. The sight of it makes me ache inside. It's like the feeling of falling in love, or the first dim-witted awareness of a slow-acting poison.

I don't normally care a damn for owning things, but I care about this.

"Have it!" Dodie exclaims. She insists on paying for the brooch, seems almost as excited by the prospect of buying it as I am. We enter the shop. Dodie scrabbles in her handbag for coins, laughs with what seems like happy relief as I hand them over. The brooch's seller is a middle-aged woman. Her still-black hair is combed behind her ears so smoothly it has a sheen to it, like silk or fresh paint. She places the silver bee in a small cardboard carton, then wraps the whole thing quickly and expertly in a piece of red crêpe paper. She speaks some words to me, words I cannot understand because they are in Espinol. I find myself blushing hot red. Supposedly I am an expert in linguistics, yet in the everyday languages of Evror I am as good as dumb.

"She's saying the brooch will bring you luck," says Dodie, who I know speaks Espinol and Farrish very well. She smiles broadly at the woman, then turns back in my direction and raises an eyebrow. I do not like that raised eyebrow, which seems both to mock the woman and decline the good luck. I reach forward to take the wrapped box. My fingers brush the woman's skin, and for a moment our different warmths merge, becoming one.

"*Obri-gada,*" I offer hesitantly. The woman smiles. Dodie is already making her way back out on to the street.

We have lunch at midday, in a cobbled courtyard crowded with small round tables and ironwork chairs. A large yellow dog lies asleep in the shadowed angle of the wall. I order a dish made from potatoes and sliced sausage and a vegetable I've never tasted before called aubergine. The food is delicious, strongly flavoured, and I feel full very quickly. Dodie appears to eat very little, though she fills her wine glass again and again from the carafe on the table. She looks down at her uneaten meal, and I know suddenly and without any doubt that she is thinking of her son, Duncan. I wonder what makes it so hard for her to speak of him aloud. Is he injured, or in prison, or sick in his mind? I would like answers to these questions, but I don't wish to pry. I sense that Dodie's most valued possession is her pride.

"You and Alec have become very good friends," I say instead. "Do you think you'll keep in touch with him after the voyage?"

At the mention of Maclane's name, Dodie's eyes light up immediately. She blushes.

"Of course, you don't know," she says. "Alec will be disembarking with me at Brock. He has business interests there."

"That's good," I say, and then fall silent, not knowing what else to say. I feel more afraid for her than ever. I wonder if Dodie will finally be tempted to tell me about Maclane's mysterious illness, but she just smiles, and adds that Alec has not lived in Crimond for many years.

"Will he be staying on Brock for good, then?" I ask. Dodie clasps her hands together, and I notice that among the many items of jewellery weighing them down she still wears her wedding band. The backs of her hands are flecked with liver spots, the joints of her fingers swollen with what looks like arthritis but could just be the heat.

"We don't know yet. There are still things to be decided." She smiles again, but less forcefully. I realise I have grown fond of Dodie. When she leaves the ship at Brock I'm going to miss her.

By the time we leave the restaurant the heat has intensified, and many of the shops have brought down their shutters. We return to the ship. The *Aurelia Claydon* nestles against the harbourside like a plump white bird. Dodie seems very tired and we go straight to our cabins. I remove my clothes and wash myself all over. The water runs grey with dust. I put my jeans back on and a clean T-shirt and go up to the passenger deck. It is less crowded than usual – most of the other passengers are still ashore – and I am hoping that I might find Lin. There's no sign of her though. I decide to go and look for her in her cabin.

I turn around to go below again, and almost collide with the bearded man, coming up.

I can see the comb-marks in his damp hair, and his very clean white shirt looks freshly ironed. He smells faintly of some kind of aftershave or cologne.

The idea occurs to me that he's been following me. I know it's stupid but it won't go away.

"Excuse me," I say. I move to one side, trying to edge my way around him, but he stands still in the middle of the doorway, refusing to budge. I will either have to go back out on deck or force my way past him. Doing that will mean making physical contact, which I don't want to do.

"Did you enjoy seeing some of Lilyat?" he says. Again, that thought that I'm being spied on, but there's no sense to it. Almost everyone has been ashore. The question is perfectly ordinary, a commonplace.

Commonplace or not, I still don't trust him.

"It's a beautiful city," I say. I try to keep my tone neutral. I can feel his eyes on me. It's as if he's trying to catch me out in something. But again, the thought doesn't make sense.

"It is, a fine city," he agrees. "I'm glad you think so." There are tiny beads of sweat on the sides of his nose where his glasses are pressing. I see also that he has something in

314

his hands; a book, with a red cloth binding. I cannot see the title. I wish I could. I am always curious about what people are reading.

"Yes," I say. Like Peter Crumb, the man has a talent for reducing me to words of one syllable.

"Watch the step." He stands aside at last to let me pass. My first instinct is to rush away, but now that my way is clear I feel less threatened. I find myself asking him if he's from Lilyat himself. He speaks like an Espinol, and has the same skin coloration as the stocky taxi drivers on the quayside.

He is a dark shadow in the doorway now. The bright sunlight, streaming past him, hides his face from me.

"Not at all," he says, and laughs. "I barely know the place. I lived in Madrid for a while, and liked it there. But my real home is Kontessa del Arios, where I was born."

So he's from Kontessa!

The coincidence seems bizarre, but I cannot help admitting that I feel excited by it. There are so many questions I would like to ask him!

It's strange, but I don't think I fully believed in this faraway city until I heard this peculiar man speak its name aloud.

"It means princess on the plain," he says.

"Is it nice there?" I ask, rather lamely.

"Yes it is, very nice. Very *temperate*." He looms above me in the doorway like a giant. "I don't think I introduced myself. My name is Nestor Felipe. Nestor, as you may already know, means traveller." He puts out his hand to me and I have no choice but to take it. His handshake is firm. The skin of his palm, in spite of the heat, is almost dry.

"Maree Forrest."

Felipe nods, as if I'm confirming something he knows already. "It's very good to meet you, Maree. Now, enjoy the rest of your afternoon." He inclines his head, then walks away from me up to the deck.

The sense that he means me harm is beginning to fade. It is a small thing perhaps, but shaking his hand has made me feel differently about him. Also I like it that Nestor means traveller – there is a mystery surrounding that, and an elegance which I find rather suits him.

He does want something from me, though. I feel sure of it.

It is all very strange.

Caine told me that the Hoolish people revere the whales as much as they fear them. To be taken by a whale is to die a hero's death.

There is a film, made many years ago by the famous anthropologist Leander Duvall, that follows a clan of seafaring Hools of the old orthodoxy as they prepare one of their number as a human sacrifice to one of the vast baer-whales that lead the whale convoys across the ocean. They named the beast Mir-Fasen, which means 'map of the world' in old Hoolish.

Caine says that no one really knows how long Atlantic whales live for.

"Some people reckon it could be a century or more," he said. If this is true then there is every chance that the whale Mir-Fasen is still alive.

The Hools, whose native homelands are a loose scattering of islands to the north-east of Galgut, are traditionally a seafaring people. There was a time when all the Hoolish people revered the whales, worshipped them as gods. Things are different now. The Hools have expanded their trade routes all over the world. Nearly all of the two million Hools who live permanently in Crimond were born there, to parents or even grandparents who were born there also. The majority of Hools are completely secular. Most have never seen an Atlantic whale, any more than I have.

Hools of the old orthodoxy are what Caine calls a dying breed, but they do exist. The true orthodox live permanently at sea, aboard steam-barques the size of small villages. Their life's task is to follow the whale convoys as they pursue their decades-long migrations across the Atlantic.

To make his film, Leander Duvall lived on board one of the barques for more than six months. He worked as a full member of the crew, and became close friends with many of the men and women whose lives he was studying. They allowed him to film those aspects of their lives and beliefs that few from outside the community had ever witnessed before, including the sacrifice.

Orthodox Hools believe that their islands and people have a secret and ancient link with the Atlantic whales and their cycle of migrations. If the whales stay safe, then so do the Hoolish people and vice versa. By offering periodic sacrifices of themselves to the great baer-whales, they hope to keep that mystic relationship in balance.

Atlantic whales are not carnivores. They feed on

microscopic plankton, which they filter from the water through great sieve-like organs that form a part of their jaw structure. Atlantic whales are dangerous to humans because of their size, which is colossal, and because some of the baer-whales seem actively hostile towards any kind of shipping activity in their home waters.

Though the Atlantic whales are our planet's largest mammals, little is known about their habits and lifestyle and behaviours. In spite of their vast size, the whales remain elusive, a mystery. A lot of what is known about them would not be known, if not for Leander Duvall's film.

The film's climax shows the sacrificial victim, whose name is Kollen Jonniter, being bound head to foot with ropes and then flung into the water close to where the whales are swimming. Shortly before this happens, Duvall interviews Jonniter in front of the camera. The young man appears calm, yet frightened in a way that seems to have robbed him of his personality. He does not look to be the same man who played deck quoits with his shipmates the evening before.

Jonniter and his wife, a strongly muscled woman named Celia, have already said goodbye to one another, an hour before. Celia's head has been shaved, according to tradition, and she has been settled below decks in the company of some of her friends. She will not be forced to watch the ceremony itself. Celia is half Glasier, which makes her unusual in this community. Most orthodox Hools still prefer to partner amongst their own people.

Celia tells Duvall she is already pregnant with Jonniter's child.

"I know already that my child will be a strong child, because of its father," she says.

If the baby is a boy she will call him Mir-Fasen, in honour of the whale. If it is a girl, she will be Mir-Fasna.

"My God, it's huge," Maud says. "How did it fit?"

She is staring at Jonniter's dick, which stands exposed. It's the first time we've seen the film, and we're watching it in secret. We are thirteen. Maud giggles, then covers her mouth with both her hands.

After Jonniter is thrown into the sea, Mir-Fasen rears up in the water. Duvall uses a telephoto lens to move in close. The whale's movement causes a miniature tidal wave, and all at once it's possible to see Kollen Jonniter, suspended in the wall of water like an insect in amber. His head is thrown right back, as if he's trying to snatch one last lungful of breath from the sea-filled air. His arms are still bound tightly to his sides. He's like a man-shaped parcel, a hero-sized packet of rubbish that's been thrown overboard.

The largest of the Atlantics, the baer-whales are so enormous that from a distance you might mistake them for small islands. It ought not to be possible for such a beast to oust its weight out of the water like this, but Mir-Fasen is doing it anyway. The whale's great striated belly looks as big as the side of a building, pinkish-grey and blotched with algae, streaming with run-off from the disrupted ocean.

"This all happened years ago, didn't it though?" Maud says. "There's no way this could happen now. No one believes in stuff like that any more."

She is staring, wide-eyed, at the tiny dark speck that is still Kollen Jonniter. I know that she is wondering, as I am, if the man is dead yet, or if he is still alive and aware of what is happening.

Two seconds later and the question no longer matters. It's impossible now for Mir-Fasen to lever himself any further out of the water – one more inch and he'll topple backwards and be drowned. Uncannily, he seems to know this. He pitches forward with an unearthly roar, belly-flopping down on the ocean like a gigantic flat iron.

He lands right on top of Jonniter. There is nowhere else for him to fall – Jonniter is directly beneath him now – but something in the whale's behaviour – a kind of savage gleefulness? – convinces me that the beast knows what it has done and that it meant to do it.

One of the things Duvall's film highlights is how keenly intelligent the Atlantic whales are; as intelligent as human beings, maybe more so.

"They were orthodox Hools," I say to Maud. "I don't think there are any of them left now." This is a lie, but I speak it anyway. I want Maud to believe that the horrible thing she's just seen couldn't happen again. I want her to be reassured, because I care for her. Even if I can't feel the same reassurance myself, making Maud feel better is important to me.

Caine tells me that secular Hools condemn the orthodox

practices as superstitious nonsense, but that doesn't mean they don't still go on.

The second time I see Duvall's film I am with Sarah. It is late at night, and we're watching TV together in the downstairs kitchen. We stare at Jonniter, gasping for air in the side of the wave like a crawfish in glass. As the film ends, a printed caption informs us that Celia Jonniter left the barque six months later, when it anchored near to Brock Island to take on supplies. She did not return. When her baby was born she named her Grace.

A second caption states that the day after Jonniter's death, his ancestral island of Mis-Lan, which had been suffering a freak drought and water rationing, enjoyed its first substantial rainfall in nearly a year.

The programme closes with images of Kollen Jonniter on the night before he died, leaning against the deck rail of the barque and staring out across the water.

When evening comes, the *Aurelia Claydon* weighs anchor and steams out of the harbour. With the lights of Lilyat still in sight, she begins to head due west into the Atlantic.

I am expecting the fore and aft searchlights to be switched on immediately, but Lin says they won't be activated for another three days.

"The whales never swim this close to the coast," Lin says. "The water's too shallow for them. There's no point switching the beams on too early. It's a waste of power."

We stay on deck until darkness falls. For the first time today the air is cool enough to feel refreshing.

"Are you scared?" Lin asks me at some point.

"Not really. I don't think so." I want to say that having her there makes me feel safe, that as long as she's somewhere nearby I feel that nothing bad can happen, but that would sound crazy. Instead I ask her if she's seen Leander Duvall's film about the Atlantic whales. Amazingly, she smiles.

"God, yes. My brothers had a tape of it. We were always watching it. The guy who gets thrown in had an enormous cock."

So Lin has brothers, and they had fun together. I imagine them all bunched up together in front of the TV screen, pointing at Jonniter's penis and nudging each other and sniggering, just as Maud did. The idea that Duvall's film might be something to laugh over is still distressing to me. The thought of finding amusement in someone else's pain and terror – even if it is long over – makes me deeply uncomfortable.

The concept is alien to me, I suppose.

The word alien makes me think of Caine.

I wonder if we're the aliens, after all. An alien race, forced to live inside a compound not because we're valuable but because if people knew what we were we'd be driven out.

Lin is watching me out of her single eye. She looks concerned.

"I don't think it's funny, really," she said. "But we were just kids. Kids can be cruel."

"You have brothers?"

"Yes. Three of the buggers. You can imagine what our household was like."

She tells me their names are Ken and Miki and Akio and that they're all in the military. "We're all a bit mad," she says. "Especially when we get together. But I do love them."

I wish I had a brother of my own. I can't imagine what it feels like, to know that someone is bound to you by blood, by genes, that you're together in the world almost as part of the same organism.

"Some of the old orthodox philosophers believe the Atlantic whales are gateways, did you know that?" Lin says. "Tunnels in space and time, junction boxes between one part of the universe and another. According to these philosophers, the people who are sacrificed don't die, but are spewed out into a new world, as heroes. Completely wacko, but I kind of like it."

I have never heard of this belief before, and I like it too, even though I know it cannot be true. It comforts me to think of Kollen Jonniter sliding feet first into a new morning, his fight for air forgotten, his skin gleaming in the light of a different sun.

The most northerly of the Hoolish islands is called Sar-Dat. It lies at the very edge of the Atlantic whales' summer breeding ground, the vast, semi-saline lake-ocean that in Crimond is known as the Arctic Race but that the Hools call the Hellen-Say, the Sea of Helen.

"I flew over it once," Lin tells me. "It was so cold up there I thought my gears were going to freeze."

* * *

The days on board seem very long. The further into the voyage, the further they seem to stretch out, like the white wings of kittiwakes, like the slatted foot-worn boards of sun-bleached jetties. The decks and companionways of the *Aurelia Claydon* have become our whole world.

The days are long because there is nothing to look at. The Atlantic stretches away on all sides, endless-seeming, making a nonsense of distance as well as time. Occasionally we catch sight of other ships, but this happens so rarely it would be easy to believe that we have lost our way somehow, that we've come unstuck from the real world and are sailing unknowingly towards a destination that will never appear.

The passengers are like a second crew now. We have developed between ourselves a version of that same camaraderie, that same mutual antagonism. Small wars break out. New alliances form and reform. Everyone is always hungry for the next piece of gossip.

Dodie Taborow is still spending all of her time with Alec Maclane. In spite of her expensive clothes and dominating laugh there is something brittle about Dodie, something fragile and faded and easily hurt. She makes me think of the women on the sewing patterns Maud and I found once, packed away in the attic of the Croft. The pattern templates were made out of tracing paper, carefully folded and each once sealed within a white paper packet. On the front of each packet was a drawing of what the pattern inside was for – a picture of a woman, blocked out in soft colours and wearing the dress or skirt or blouse the way it should look once all the pieces of the pattern are sewn together. The clothes in the pictures looked so old-fashioned they made Maud and me laugh. It was difficult to believe that anyone would ever have wanted to wear such things, let alone spend time in making them by hand. The faded women in the drawings all wore bright smiles, yet still they seemed sad. It was as if all they wanted was to be noticed, but they'd stopped believing inside that they ever would be.

Whenever I see Dodie now I think of those women, of those falling-apart sewing patterns in their faded envelopes, and I feel afraid for her. She's obsessed with Maclane, I can feel it. I think of Maclane's crisp linen shirts, the soft mound of his belly, the gold cufflinks – clink, clink – on the bedside table.

Can Dodie and Maclane really be lovers, or are they just friends?

I keep thinking something bad is going to happen. There's nothing I can do to stop it though, even if I'm right. It's none of my business.

Dodie's card parties in the saloon are now our main entertainment. In spite of what he said about being out of practice, Maclane turns out to have lost none of his talent. The game turns him from a considerate and courteous *gentilhomme* into a scheming Quest-demon. The Carola sisters, who play regularly at his table, are clearly enchanted with him. Dodie pleads with me to join their circle and although I am tempted because the game looks such fun I have to keep refusing. I know I am nowhere near good enough, and I don't want to put in the hours of study and practice it would take to be able to play against Maclane and the others. I watch the games sometimes though – I find them thrilling. There is another man who plays very well, Dagon Krefeld. Dodie says he is a professor of mathematics, travelling to Bonita to take up a post at the university there. His skin is dry and wrinkled as a prune's, but he has the gimlet eyes and wicked laugh of a TV vizier.

His main aim in life at the moment seems to be beating Alec Maclane at Quest. He hasn't managed it yet, though he is getting closer. I think Krefeld is sleeping with one of the saloon staff, a young and handsome able seaman named Vicente.

Not all of the passengers have succumbed to the Quest craze, and for some the tedium of the voyage has found other outlets. A married couple, Pierpoint and Mol Gillespie, are now sleeping in separate cabins. I don't know what's happened between them, only that Pierpoint will now be leaving the ship at Brock. Mol is sailing on to Bonita as originally planned.

For the first three nights or so after leaving Lilyat's waters people gather on the passenger deck after supper, to applaud as the search beams are switched on and to take part in what they call whale-watching parties. Whether these are meant as entertainment or surveillance I am not sure. No whales are spotted and the parties soon lose their novelty. Little by little the anxiety that marked the *Aurelia Claydon*'s passage into open ocean begins to disperse.

Even the idea of the whales is losing its fascination. It's much more fun to join in the gossip surrounding Dodie's card parties.

* * *

I am spending a lot of my time studying Thalian. Nestor Felipe has lent me a grammar book, and I am using it to try and make sense of *A Thalian Odyssey*. To begin with I go right through the text, checking each word in the original against the Crimondn translation on the opposite page. When I feel ready I cover up the translation and look only at the original. It's difficult at first, but the longer I persevere the easier it becomes, first to remember individual words and phrases, then to understand whole sentences. I have even begun to write out my own translations of my favourite passages, just for practice. At this stage I understand only about half of what I read, but every now and then I come across a line that stops me dead, that crushes the breath from my chest as if I've been punched. It's at these moments that I know I'm improving, that I am understanding the poem as it is meant to be read.

When Nestor Felipe gives me the grammar book I thank him in Thalian. These are the first words of the language I have spoken aloud to anyone, except myself. The syllables feel bulky in my mouth, and I am afraid I've garbled them, but when Nestor Felipe nods and smiles I know that these few simple sounds at least have been uttered correctly.

When you take the trouble to learn another language, you are giving yourself the chance to see the miracle of communication in close-up. For me, a Crimondn speaker since birth, a book is a book. That dumpy, single syllable is not just a word, it is in some sense the object itself, a sound-picture, the same as it would be for the smartdogs. For Saffron Valparaiso a book is a *livra*. We can grasp each other's meaning, but we can never erase or replace one another's sound-pictures. For me, *livra* can never *be* book, it can only *mean* book. It can only ever be a cipher, not the actual thing.

I once told Maud about a secret fear I had, that working with the smartdogs might eventually make me become unhooked from language, that words would not be words any more, they would just be sounds.

"Try it," I say to her. I print the word 'squirrel' on a piece of paper in heavy black capitals, then tell her to speak the word aloud and keep saying it, to repeat the word fifty times, a hundred, without stopping. "At the end you won't know what it means," I say. "It'll just be a sound. Even the letters on that piece of paper will stop making sense." Maud does what I say, repeating the word squirrel over and over again until she collapses on the bed. She's laughing so hard she's clutching her stomach. Her eyes are streaming with tears.

"What is it?" she says. "What the hell is a fucking *squirrel*?" Just speaking the word aloud sets her off again. She finds the whole thing hilarious, and I can understand why, but I still think it's terrifying.

A smartdog needs no words. It can live without words quite easily. Words do not help it to run and hunt, to love and mate and feed and find shelter. They do not further clarify the cool of the rain on its back on a warm spring day. It's not words that make a smartdog feel it could run forever.

Smartdogs sense the coming on of dawn or dusk hours before we can.

Words are for those who build cities, who build whirligigs and smartweapons and flame-throwers.

Words are for writing journals and counting the days, for understanding the purple-shaded, time-driven rhythms of *A Thalian Odyssey*.

Words are what humans are, even more than flesh.

If Nestor Felipe is not a good man, he hides it well, which is something I am not used to in ordinary people. Could Nestor Felipe be like Caine or like Sarah, like Margery Kim who Caine said was like a sister to him but who left for Thalia before I could get to know her?

Could he be like me? I don't think so, but if Felipe is a spy he has a funny way of going about it.

His tea-coloured eyes seem full of thoughtful amusement, at the world or at himself, I don't know which. His horn-rimmed glasses and slight pot belly make me think of Detective Selkirk, in Iris Mottram's *Selkirk* books. Which makes him more or less the opposite of Peter Crumb.

I spend time with Lin Hamada every day.

We eat our meals together in the saloon. Afterwards we will sometimes go up to the passenger deck for an hour or so, to look at the sea and exchange news, such that it is, of the things we've seen or done during the day. With all the days being the same it is surprising how much we find to talk about. Every so often we spend the whole day together. It's not something we plan – it's more like we forget to move apart.

"Lin seems like a nice girl," Dodie says to me. I don't see

so much of Dodie now – she's either with Alec Maclane or playing cards – but when I do she is the same as ever. She is a gossip, I know that, but not of the kind who enjoys hurting people. What Dodie enjoys is *information*, for its own sake, the possession of secrets.

When she says to me that Lin seems nice, I know that what she wants is for me to give up some piece of information about Lin in return, some piece of private knowledge. Most of all she wants to know exactly what it was that happened to Lin's face.

She still thinks that Lin's face is the most important thing about her. If I were to deny that, she would find it astounding.

"She is, very nice," I say. "I like her a lot."

She nods, conceding defeat. "I'm glad you've found a friend, Maree. It's not good for you to be with old people all the time." Perhaps she's bored with the subject already. Most likely she simply accepts that as Lin's friend I'm reluctant to gossip about her. Either way she doesn't press me any further.

A little later I see her walking arm in arm along the deck with Alec Maclane.

When I was fourteen I thought I was in love with Maud. By the time I reached the age of sixteen I was beginning to realise that I was just passing the time with her, that in spite of all the sex we were having we were more like sisters than lovers. That our closeness was to do with chance, with our constant and inescapable physical nearness to one another. There was no deeper connection, not really.

I could never let Maud learn this, or guess that the only thing that kept me from breaking up with her was knowing that I would be leaving soon in any case, that we were destined to be parted anyway.

Leaving her was still awful, though. Those emotions were real.

I have not written her a single word since we set out from Faslane.

My love for Caine was something different, an infatuation that could never have lasted, I see that now. We're worlds apart – he is as distant from me as I was from Maud.

The question now is: am I falling in love with Lin Hamada?

It's a question I don't want an answer to. Loving Lin can bring only pain, and I want the time that remains to us to pass without any feeling other than the contentment that comes from being in one another's company. It should be enough just to be near her, day by day, to let the future feel as distant as the shores of Thalia.

"Are you really going to do it?" Lin says to me. "Do you really mean to sign your life over to these people, no questions asked? You don't even know who they are."

She means the people who run the compound in Kontessa, who are in charge of the programme. It's true that I don't know, that I have put my trust in them only because Kay and Peter Crumb have trained me to do so. But then Kay also encouraged me to put my trust in her story about the tramway crash that killed my parents, and so far as I've been able to discover that never happened. I tell Lin I don't know what I am going to do, that I need time to decide, words that sound reasonable enough when I say them but that afterwards – when I'm alone in my cabin – seem shaky and unreal, even cowardly. I cannot imagine not going to Kontessa, because I cannot imagine what will happen to me if I don't. Perhaps I am afraid to. The word freedom sounds exciting when you say it, but it has implications. When I tell Lin what Kay said about the tramway crash she doesn't say much of anything. But three days later she tells me she's been looking online and she can't find any record of it, either.

"There's a satellite connection in the radio room," she explains. "Juuli let me use it. I didn't tell her why I needed to and she didn't ask."

For a moment I can't think who she's talking about, then I realise she means Juuli Moyse, the woman with the short grey hair who works in the engine room.

"I'm not trying to be nosy or anything," Lin says. "I'm worried about you, that's all. I don't like what's going on."

"I don't think you're being nosy," I say, and I don't, although to be honest I don't feel comfortable with what she's doing. She is trying to nurture my own small seedlings of doubt, trying to give me the idea that if I've been lied to about one thing there's a good chance I've been lied to about everything else.

That what I've been told is not the truth about myself, but a convenient story for the benefit of others.

Lin is trying to help me prove that I don't exist.

* * *

There was no Internet at the Croft, because Peter Crumb forbade it. I don't know if he knew you could go online for free at Asterwych library. Maud liked to sneak off there and surf the net sometimes, though I think it was more to prove that she could than because she wanted to.

"It's boring, isn't it, staring into a screen all day?" She said that after a while everything she read online began to sound invented; even the most ordinary facts started to take on the appearance of elaborate fantasies. Peter Crumb always said that the main reason he wouldn't allow an online connection at the Croft was because the Internet had stopped being independent decades ago, during the war with Thalia. The restrictions were meant to have been lifted once the war was over, but according to Peter Crumb many of them were still secretly in place.

He said the Internet had become a vehicle for propaganda.

Caine thought he was probably right. Wolfe said that Peter Crumb was bullshitting us.

"He just wants to control what we know," he said. "That's all it is."

I don't know what to think, especially now. Everything I know about politicos is dismal and tiring.

If I refuse to comply with the programme, or ask questions about it, there is a chance that the protection I have always taken for granted will be withdrawn.

I have no idea how I might begin to live without it.

I know so little about the world, only that it is dangerous.

The word for freedom in Thalian is *liberta*.

* * *

Alec Maclane is gone, and our ship is saved. How much these two things are connected we may never know.

Not everyone watched. The Gillespies stayed below decks, and in the seconds before the whale dived I saw Nestor Felipe turn away and hide his face in both hands. Dodie lay crumpled against the deck like a broken doll. The Carola sisters were bending down to help her up. Their long grey dresses, drenched with seawater, clung about their legs like sodden newspaper.

The rest of us saw everything. I saw it all. Also I saw Lin Hamada, leaning against the guard rail and gazing down into the churning water like she was watching a movie.

Terror makes insects of us all, because it reminds us we can be nothing in less than a second.

There is no warning, no premonition of any kind. At this point in our voyage, we are six weeks out from Faslane and more than halfway across the Atlantic. The crossing has been much calmer than I expected. It is still rare for us to sight another ship, but the ocean is not entirely without traffic and we do sometimes see freight steamers like the *Aurelia Claydon*, and fishing factories, and on one occasion we pass close by an enormous grey vessel with an extended rear deck that Lin tells me is an aircraft carrier operated by the Thalian navy. The sight of the vast ship unnerves me, but it soon sails past. It flags up neutral codes, but other than that it's as if the carrier hasn't even noticed we are there.

There is no sign whatsoever of any whales.

I think of the file of statistics we made, Sarah and Maud and I, the macabre reports of sinkings and fatal collisions that we clipped from the newspapers. From what I can remember, most of the attacks happened in the eastern part of the Atlantic, on the routes processing out from Barane and Jonestown harbour. There have been sinkings to the west of Lilyat, just as there have been sinkings everywhere else in the Atlantic, just not as many.

There is a feeling, among the crew I think as well as the foot passengers, that we are out of the danger zone.

I am not saying that the search beams are not switched on every evening at seven-thirty as usual. Just that none of us are really expecting anything to happen.

When the siren finally sounds, there is a sense at first that this cannot be real, that it's some kind of drill. It is around nine o'clock, and not fully dark yet. Most of us are in the saloon, dawdling over coffee or playing cards. For thirty seconds no one moves – there is just the heavy drone of the siren: parp-parp-PARP.

Then we hear the sound of running footsteps outside in the companionway.

"Oh my God," says Mol Gillespie. She is sitting on the couch in the corner, doing a crossword out of one of her puzzle books. "It's a convoy. It's really happening."

Her words seem to break the spell. Everyone stops what they are doing and makes a run for the door.

* * *

The fore and aft search beams light up the water for a mile around. The name of the crew member on watch is Marianne Roach, a deck steward on her first tour of duty.

Her reason for sounding the siren is obvious. It's as if the passage of the *Aurelia Claydon* has suddenly become obstructed by a range of hills.

It is impossible to say how many whales there are in total. There have been convoys recorded that stretch for hundreds of miles. In a convoy of that size there might be three-dozen whales, perhaps more. From where we're standing on the passenger deck we can see three long, slipper-shaped mounds of blackness, thrusting up through the surface of the water like small dark islands. We have no idea what might be happening on the other side of the ship, but Lin is able to tell me afterwards that Juuli Moyse said we were surrounded on all sides.

"She spotted four to starboard, definitely," Lin says. "And it looked like three following. She saw them through the drive room periscope."

There is no sign, as yet, of the baer-whale. We stand together at the rail, staring out at the water and waiting to see what action will be taken. Some captains choose to kill their engines and angle up their search beams, to let their ships hang silently in the water. Their hope is that the whales will ignore them and glide harmlessly past. Once the convoy is ahead of them they alter their course slightly, allowing the route of the ship and route of the whales to safely diverge.

Others will open the engines full throttle and try to get ahead of the baer-whale. Of the number of ships sunk each year by whale convoys, the number that hold their position and the number that run are roughly equal.

The captain of the *Aurelia Claydon* opts to hold. There is a sound like a muffled cough and then the engines fall silent. It is only then that I realise how much I've come to take the sound they make for granted, the constant hum beneath my feet, the sensation of movement. Its sudden absence is unnerving. It's as if the ship has stopped breathing.

I can hear footsteps clanging on the upper decks, the shouted instructions of one crew member to another, the faint slap-slapping of the ocean against the ship's plump flanks. Normally the sound of the engines makes that inaudible. I keep expecting Djibril or one of the other stewards to appear, to give us instructions on what we should do, but no one comes. There is a breathless silence among the passengers, as if we're afraid to raise our voices, in case we are heard.

Then suddenly Dagon Krefeld raises his arm. "The baer!" Fear and excitement lend his normally melodious speaking voice an edge of coarseness. We all press forward against the guard rail, looking to where he is pointing. At first I can see nothing, just the foaming water. Then the baer-whale raises his tail like a gigantic flag.

The tail is vast, wide as a street maybe. Its upward movement, like an underwater earthquake, causes a miniature tidal wave. The *Aurelia Claydon* rocks under the force of its impact and for a second I am convinced we will capsize but it doesn't happen. All I can see now is that tail, impossible, ship-sized. Beyond the glare of the searchlights the night is dark, but that tail is blacker still. It's as if someone has torn a hole in the sky.

Then the baer-whale slams the tail down upon the sea's quaking surface and pulls it under. There are more and more violent shock waves, and then it is gone. I release my pent-up breath, thinking that the baer-whale has dived deep, away from the surface and away from our ship. Then I gasp again in horror at what Dagon Krefeld and Ana Carola and everyone else has already seen: the steady line of ripples, a hump-shaped displacement of water rushing towards us, crossing the distance so quickly and so near-invisibly it's as if we're about to be attacked by a ghost.

"It's coming alongside," yells Nestor Felipe. He points, and it's like something is tunnelling through the water to get to us, a giant rat beneath a giant black hearthrug. Everyone but Lin Hamada and the Carola sisters scrambles back from the rail.

"Where the hell's the damned crew?" says Nestor Felipe. I see that his teeth are chattering, and I realise from his voice that he's afraid, more afraid than I am even. A sense of unreality has descended upon me, like a dome of glass. I can see but I can't feel, not for the moment, and in this way I am protected from the worst of my terror.

I move quickly to his side and take his hand. His fingers tighten around mine, a panicky, reflexive grip that hurts my knuckles. When he looks down and sees who it is he seems reassured at once, and a little calmer.

"Do you know," he says, "I always dreamed of seeing one of these creatures for myself. Now I wish I'd never wished that. Do you think it might be all that wishing that helped them find us?"

I search his face for signs that he is joking and do not find them. His expression is blank and white as a frightened child's.

"I don't believe in such things," I say. "The old orthodoxies. The whales would still be here, whether we were or not."

I gaze down at the water. The baer-whale appears to be circling now, some two-hundred metres from our starboard flank perhaps, cutting steep runnels in the black water. From time to time it lifts the front of its head, a blunt, featureless mass that is like a vast brick wall. Its movements seem indecisive, ragged, almost a taunt. Suddenly I have a horrible realisation: the baer-whale is trying to make up its mind whether to ram us.

A sick, wet panic comes over me at the thought of that blunt head, like a thousand-ton mallet, striking the side of the ship and keeling us over. I imagine flying through the darkness, hard objects striking my head, the freezing, angled catch of the viscous water.

Is this the end? I realise I cannot imagine anything beyond the moment of hitting the sea's surface, just a sense of not being able to breathe, then a gut-churning, endless horror that I cannot dwell on.

Strangely, I think of Maud; her tangled hair and damp pubes, her schoolgirl laugh.

Tomorrow we'll be an item on the news and nothing more.

I fix my eyes on Lin, who is still at the rail. Something

about her stance – its straightness? – seems exultant, stern as the night sky and yet riotous as revolution, filled with sweat and smoking gunshots and ravishing song.

Lin Hamada does not seem frightened, not at all.

Further out to sea, beyond the pacing baer-whale, the dark shapes of its brothers and sisters lie in wait.

"Could you speak to them?" says Nestor Felipe. "Do you think you could try?"

He speaks so quietly I wonder if I've misheard him, if I've imagined the words inside my own head. And yet I grasp the sense of what he's saying almost at once.

He's asking me to make contact with the whales, to try and persuade them not to attack us, to assure them that we mean them no harm.

His knowledge of me explodes inside me like a thunderbolt. He knows what I am, then. But how?

As for his question, I don't know how to answer. I gape at him, wide-eyed.

"I don't know," I say. I have not, until this moment, even considered it. My mind is clamped tight with fear. It's said that fear sharpens the senses but it deadens them, too. When you're frightened nothing makes sense except the need to escape.

Is the baer-whale even aware of us as living creatures, or is the *Aurelia Claydon*, with her rasping engines and buzzing radio emissions, her infuriating light beams, as insignificant and maddening as a hornet?

Can I make the baer-whale perceive us as we really are?

The deck is slopping ankle-deep in water but I barely

notice. It takes a conscious effort to open my senses but somehow I do it, I make that leap, and suddenly it's as if I'm waking in another world.

Suddenly I'm in a splinter of nowhere. I gather the sound-pictures inside my head and fling them outwards:images of the sea in all her vastness, and of ourselves and the ship upon it, travelling westwards, like the whales. I grasp for an image of the baer-whale himself, a beast so vast and so powerful he is hard for us to comprehend.

I see you, I mind-speak. *And I am speaking to you – my name is Maree, maree, maree, like the call of the gulls.*

I try to welcome him into our world. What a fool I am.

For a short while there is nothing, just the gusting wind, the crash and crump of broken deckchairs sliding in a muddled heap across the soaking boards.

Then I hear him laughing inside my head. His great mind, like an open hand, flaps lazily at my song, perhaps to dispel it, then he turns his back on me and for a cold and endless moment I can sense the truth.

The baer-whale doesn't give a damn what I am thinking. The idea that I am thinking at all is an amusement to him. He cares as little for my song as the captain of the *Aurelia Claydon* might care for the thoughts of a tuna fish or a flounder.

From far away, as from another room, I hear him calling to the waiting members of his convoy. There is something in his calling to them that goes beyond tenderness. As the strain of quartz in a block of granite is part of its substance, so his vast concern for his brethren is an interwoven fibre of his being.

I do not know yet what they intend. It could be that they will leave us alone, it could be that they will destroy us. If my brief and pathetic attempt at contact will affect our fate in either direction I have no idea.

"What's happening?" says Nestor Felipe. He has grabbed my elbow, bracing himself against the deck to support my weight. Was I falling, or have I fallen? I can't remember.

"The whales are singing," I tell him. "They are singing each other stories about their world."

I have a moment to consider Lin's words from before, about the Atlantic whales being gateways to another universe, and then Alec Maclane is hurling himself at the guard rail and toppling over. Plummeting, like a plump, pale toad, into the sea.

He falls so fast, his limbs crooked out at odd angles, and there is something horrible about the whiteness of his body against the darkness. I see that he is naked apart from his underpants. Where has he been until now? I realise I have not laid eyes on him since the siren sounded, since the saloon, and in those moments of his falling I gain an image of him, going below to undress, then lumbering, fat belly jiggling, along the companionway. I can even see his discarded clothes, neatly folded across the pull-out chair in his cabin. For some reason it is this image that disturbs me most of all.

In his final flight towards the water he is beyond vulnerability, reduced to a thing. The loud smack of his flesh upon the ocean's surface is like the slap of raw meat upon a butcher's slab.

"Man overboard!" cries Dagon Krefeld. He is leaning so

far out over the guard rail that for a moment I am convinced he is going to fall in also. I stare at his feet, slipping and sliding on the wet boards. I clap my hand to my mouth in horror but I cannot move. It is Lin who rescues him, catching hold of him by his blazer and yanking him to safety.

"Keep back," she says. "You can't help him now – no one can." She barks the order angrily into his face. I feel someone tugging at my arm and when I look to see who it is I see it is Dodie Taborow.

"What's happening?" she says. I cannot answer her. She sits down hard on the deck – it's as if the mechanism that works her legs has given way. She is crying. I edge past her and look down over the guard rail.

Alec Maclane is swimming away from the ship and towards the whales.

He makes rapid progress through the water and I realise something I would never have suspected, that he is a strong swimmer. Perhaps his fatness makes him more buoyant. The skin of his back gleams smooth and pale, like the skin of a dolphin.

"My God," says Nestor Felipe. "Look what he's doing."

Somewhere behind us the Carola sisters are trying to lift the sobbing Dodie to her feet.

"We have to help him," Dodie is weeping. "We have to launch the lifeboats."

No one answers her, and for a moment it's as if the people gathered around her on the deck have become a single entity with but one thought in mind.

You go, if you want to. We're staying here.

Alec Maclane is growing more distant with every second. More distant from the ship, closer to the whales.

"What the devil," says Dagon Krefeld. He leaves the sentence hanging. I do not believe in the devil, but I have to believe in the baer-whale because he's there before me. As Maclane comes swimming towards him he ceases his pacing and lets his body drop downwards through the water until it's almost submerged.

Then he raises himself once more and begins to charge.

His jaws creak open like the gates of a monstrous castle. Water pours from his sides in glistening arcs. I recall the horrific death of Kollen Jonniter in the film by Duvall, but in the glare of the searchlights I am able to see that what happens to Maclane is actually worse.

At one moment he is still in the water. In the next the whale imbibes him, drawing him inside its mouth like a floundering seal. The baer-whale shakes its head from side to side, clearly irritated by the obstruction, and I remember that Atlantic whales are unable to process solid food. The beast expels Maclane from its mouth like a child spitting out a pumpkin seed, then dips its vast head beneath the water and sucks him in again.

The baer-whale rears up like a monstrous stallion and then he dives. The ship shivers beneath my feet, and when I glance upward I see the crew are lining the guard rail of the deck above.

We wait, breathless, for the whale to resurface, but it never does.

After some moments spent in silence, Krefeld slowly

raises his hand and points out to sea.

"They're swimming away."

We all look to where he is pointing and see it is true. The whale convoy is departing. For a long while we stay where we are. Whether we're standing in vigil or waiting for sunrise I'm not sure.

At some point I become aware that the ship's engines have been switched on again, and we are on the move.

Early the following morning Dodie comes to my cabin. She taps softly on the door, as if she is afraid she might wake me. She need not have worried. I have lain awake most of the night, how could I do otherwise? I could not imagine being able to sleep, or even trying to. One of the after-effects of what has happened has been to make the idea of night and day as separate states lose most of its meaning. Darkness and light seem incidental. There is just the passing of hours.

Dodie is crying, very quietly, her tears falling softly and rapidly, like April rain. She is in her dressing gown, a silk kimono, printed all over with a pretty design of tiny red birds. Her face is bare of makeup, and she appears both older and younger than before, as if the shock of Maclane's death has thrown her mind back to girlhood, while propelling her aging body ten years into the future.

It is now that she finally tells me Maclane was suffering from a degenerative disease of the spine, a condition that would eventually have left him paralysed. The doctors had given him two years, three at the most.

"He was depressed about it of course," Dodie says. "But three years is still a long time. And doctors can be wrong, everyone knows that. I told him he should carry on with his life as usual and keep hoping. Hope is always the best medicine, don't you agree?"

I agree that it is. She gazes at me, red-eyed. There are new tears already threatening to spill over. I see one of them fall into her lap, making a small transparent blotch on the silk kimono.

"I know he cared for you, very much," I say to her. "Anyone could see that." I remember Maclane's oddly lopsided walk, that curiously limping gait he had. I realise it wasn't arthritis after all, but the first grim indication of the disease.

"He seemed so happy last night," Dodie says. "We were having such a wonderful party." As she begins to cry again, this time in earnest, I find myself thinking of the last moments of normality before the siren went off and we all rushed on deck. They were playing Quest, of course – Dodie and Luisa Carola, Dagon Krefeld in his purple blazer, Maclane's face a little puffy from too much wine. Dodie seemed very excited. She was wearing a pair of showy teardrop earrings, set with rhinestones. They flashed daggers of bright blue light every time she moved.

I try to imagine how Maclane must have felt in those seconds when he first hit the water. Did he have time to regret what he had done? Did he think of the lighted saloon, the card game, Dodie's breath, warm on his cheek, as she leaned in close to tell him a joke? Will we all, in our final moments, see the whole of our lives as that lighted saloon?

Later on that same day, Lin tells me something Juuli Moyse has told her, that one night of the previous week Alec Maclane went to Juuli's cabin and offered her a thousand shillings if she would let him fuck her.

"Juuli went crazy. Asked Maclane if he was calling her a hooker. They ended up doing it anyway. Maclane shoved the thousand shillings under her cabin door when she was asleep, apparently."

"Did Juuli keep it?" I ask.

Lin shrugs. "She was thinking about it. I mean, it's half a year's wages. I bet she's glad now that she hung on to it." She raises her one puckered eyebrow and we both burst out laughing. I am appalled at myself but at the same time I feel much better.

"He was a brave man," I say to Dodie. "He acted to save us."

"You don't believe those old stories, surely?" Dodie stares at me as if she thinks I've gone deranged. I can see weariness in her eyes now as well as grief. It's the first time she's seemed normal since it happened.

"I don't know," I say. "There are still people who do believe them, though. Perhaps Alec was one of them."

"People will say I was after his money," Dodie says. "But that's not true."

We sit side by side on the bed and for a while neither of us says anything. In the end I ask Dodie if there's anything I can do for her. She sighs and shakes her head. Her tears are all gone now. She looks pale and very tired but utterly calm.

"I'm too old for this kind of thing," she says at last. "I

know I've acted like a fool. I'll be glad when we get to Brock."

She leaves my cabin shortly afterwards. For the rest of her time on board there are no more card games.

After Dodie has gone I lie down on my bed and fall asleep. I wake about three hours later and realise that I am hungry, but the thought of going to the saloon feels somehow impossible.

I go to Lin's cabin instead. I cannot imagine she is asleep and she is not.

"Hey," she says. "I was wondering where you'd got to. Are you okay?"

"I'm okay." I realise we have not actually spoken to one another since the siren sounded, and for a little while I sense an awkwardness between us, almost a shyness. It's as if the events of the night before have cancelled out our certainties, not just about each other but about ourselves. As if we're having to start our friendship again from scratch.

"You saved Dagon Krefeld's life last night," I say to her. It's a start, at least.

"Not really. I grabbed his jacket, that's all. The idiot nearly gave me a heart attack, leaning over like that."

She smiles at me cautiously and I smile back. She has some food in her cabin: bread rolls and some cold cuts of salami she must have filched from the saloon – or perhaps Juuli Moyse in the engine room keeps her supplied with provisions. We divide the food between us. I eat my share greedily. I tell Lin what Dodie has told me about Maclane's illness. It's a relief to share the knowledge, to reach towards a way of talking about what happened.

"I suppose that explains it," Lin says. "He knew he was dying, and thought he might as well go out a hero. You get people in the military like that sometimes. They're real loose cannons."

"He wasn't a happy man," I say, and in the instant I speak the words I know they are true. "Do you believe any of it?"

"Any of what?"

"What the old Hools say about the whales – that they're sacred beings?"

"They're big motherfuckers, that's all I know." Lin laughs. "It's not just the Hools that have a thing for them, anyway. I read an article about Atlantic whales once in a science journal. It said that according to the natural laws of biology they shouldn't exist. In theory there's no way an animal as large as an Atlantic whale can exist in our gravity without collapsing under its own weight, or suffocating. And yet there they are. So you could argue that what the orthodox Hools believe isn't really any more ludicrous than the existence of the whales themselves. Leave a gap in the floorboards, that's what I say."

"What?"

She smiles. "My mum always used to say that every room in the house should have a gap between the floorboards, so that certainty, boredom and hubris could find their way out. The more of the world I see the more I tend to agree with her."

"What's hubris?" I ask.

"Calling out the gods. Being stupid enough to insist that

miracles don't exist just because you've never witnessed one."

I like what she says. I can feel the truth in it.

"We never actually saw him die," I say.

"No, we didn't."

"Were you scared?"

"Too right I was fucking scared. I've been scared before though. Fear is like any emotion. You don't exactly get used to it, but at least you learn a little of what to expect."

Shortly after this we go to bed together. It is hot and rather stuffy in the cabin. We take off our clothes and lie facing each other. I press my face, my lips, my tongue first to the flesh of her stomach and then to her cunt. It should feel strange to be doing this, but it does not. I close my eyes, and I find Lin is my lover, sister, comrade, everything. I slide my mouth over her face, from soft warmth to coruscated hardness and then back again. The different parts of her no longer surprise or repel me. They are simply parts of Lin, the way she is.

"Does your face still hurt?" I say afterwards.

"No," Lin replies. "The burned parts are dead, just scar tissue. It feels like a lump of dry mud."

We cover ourselves with the sheet and sleep for a while.

In three days Lin will disembark at Brock Island, and I will go on.

Brock Island is humped and dark, shrouded in mist. A dingy rain is falling. The *Aurelia Claydon* would normally remain berthed here for a week – a number of the ship's crew have family on Brock – but this time for some reason it's been decided there will be an hour's stopover only for the unloading of cargo, then the ship will sail on to Bonita without further delay.

"There'll be a longer stopover on the way back, though," Lin tells me. "So keep that in mind."

She doesn't have a personal address yet, but she has given me the contact details of the mail company she will be working for. She has told me that if I change my mind about going to Kontessa I should come and find her. She has even given me some money, so I'll have no problem returning to Brock, should I decide to do so.

Our paths are taking us in different directions and it is painful. There's a part of me – a large part – that wants to disembark at Brock with Lin Hamada, to share her lodgings and her new life on this cold, stark island, so much more like the place I am used to than the place I am going.

I could do that, I feel, and be happy.

But I have to go on, or I'll never find out.

Perhaps Caine and Sarah are waiting for me, who knows?

"You've been a godsend," says Dodie Taborow. "I don't think I'd have survived this trip without you."

She kisses me once on each cheek and then we embrace. She has given me a pair of her earrings as a parting gift. She smells of well-cut clothes and expensive perfume.

"That's nonsense," I say to her. "You're the real captain of this ship, and everyone knows it." We smile, and hug again, this time more naturally. When finally she steps on to the gangway she doesn't look back. I watch her as she crosses the rough, concrete paving of the quayside, treading smartly in her shiny brown leather boots and red woollen cape. She comes to a standstill suddenly, and for a moment I think she's left something behind in her cabin, then I see there's someone coming forward to greet her, a short, rather stocky man in a long overcoat and grey felt hat.

I realise this must be Duncan, her son. He's older than I expected. She places both hands upon his shoulders and then they too are hugging fiercely.

I feel the weight of past years slipping away from them and heading out across the choppy sea.

Once the disembarking passengers and their luggage are all ashore, the large hatchway that grants access to the lower cargo decks is unbolted and a sturdy iron gangway is fixed into place. A man emerges from one of the buildings on the harbour side and goes to stand at the foot of the gangway. He is carrying a clipboard and some kind of LED swipe counter.

Moments later and they begin to come out – two, five, twelve, two dozen of them, their felted ears laid flat to their heads, their skewbald and dappled coats grown dull and woolly from the lack of sunshine. Their ribs show in their sides, and they blink nervously in the unaccustomed daylight, but other than that they seem to be fine. They have survived their journey, at any rate. Their feet clatter on the metal walkway – rat-tat-tat – like a soldier's tin drum. The man with the clipboard swipes each one across the neck with the LED as they file past.

Their emergence into the grey, damp light of Brock Island is like an image from a dream. They have crossed three time zones to be here. They are like a good omen.

Dodie was right. The ship was carrying horses after all.

In a little under a week we will dock at Bonita. The crew of the *Aurelia Claydon* will enjoy three days of shore leave before beginning the return journey to Brock, and from there to Faslane. For the remainder of its journey the ship follows the rugged line of the Thalian coast. After so long upon the open ocean, the sight of land is a constant novelty. We are still too far out to sea to spot landmarks or villages, but in spite of that I spend hours up on the passenger deck, unable to tear my eyes away from the grey-green smudge on the horizon that is the first sight of the country that will be my new home.

I don't know what to make of it, of anything. My grasp of the Thalian language is improving, so much so that I feel confident enough to exchange greetings and simple pleasantries with the Carola sisters whenever I see them on deck or in the saloon. They seem delighted by my efforts to learn their language, and often try to draw me into longer conversations, but although I can understand a fair amount of what they're saying I don't yet have the skills to talk to them as I would like to.

I feel embarrassed by my incompetence, but they don't seem to mind. They seem such generous-hearted women, and kind.

I thought I would dread the end of the voyage but I'm looking forward to it. I have become so used to the conditions and routines of shipboard life that in some ways it's difficult to remember the person I was before I came on board. I feel sorrow at the thought of saying goodbye to the *Aurelia Claydon*, but now that Dodie and Lin are gone everything is different in any case – there's nothing to stay for. It's like the heart has gone out of things, and I think all of us who remain feel the same. We try to carry on as normal but all we're waiting for now is the moment when we will go our separate ways.

Nestor Felipe is teaching me to play chess. We sit on deck together on the rigid wooden chairs that are so much less popular than the canvas sunloungers, either side of a folding table that Nestor has commandeered from the saloon. He shows me the various moves, explaining the laws that govern each piece and the problems they encounter. I'm not paying as much attention as I should, and in the end the only way I can keep myself in the game is by catching the sense of what Nestor is thinking as he plans his next move.

I am sure he knows that I am cheating. Luckily for me he seems to find it more amusing than annoying.

More than the game itself I am interested in Nestor's chess set. The pieces are made of scrimshaw – carved from whalebone – and are very beautiful.

"Where did you get it?" I ask him.

"I was given it, as a present," he says.

"A present from a woman or from a man?"

"A man. Does it matter?"

"Not at all. I'm curious, that's all."

We have fallen into a strange kind of intimacy, a jokey camaraderie that is not quite flirting but almost. It's like a dance where two people keep coming together but never touch. I want to know about him. He wants to know about me. We both tell each other less than we would like to hear.

I feel safe with him, though. I know, as I knew from the moment I first laid eyes on him, that he is hiding something, but I now trust I'll find out what this is in due course, that Nestor means me no harm, whatever his secret.

The final days of our voyage are hot, and languid, and full of hours that I know will never come again. I am beginning to count them down. In less than forty-eight of them we will be there. Someone will be waiting for me at the harbour side. They will come forward to meet me, perhaps take my arm. My small suitcase will be taken away somewhere, for safe keeping. The part of my life that I am living now will be over for good.

These things I can imagine, but not what comes afterwards.

Will I be allowed to have contact with people from outside the compound?

Will I be allowed to continue with my study of the Thalian language?

Will I even be allowed to ask these questions?

How much of myself do I rightfully own?

Before, when I was still at the Croft and getting nervous about the journey, I used to think that the worst thing that could happen would be to arrive on the quayside at Bonita and find no one there waiting for me – that great unknown city, sweltering in the heat, its streets filled with thieves and tricksters and me not having a clue where to go or who to turn to.

Now I secretly feel that if I had the choice, I would rather choose uncertainty than meekly follow the path I am expected to take.

On the last morning but one I am sitting in the saloon having breakfast with the Carola sisters. Ana Carola is asking me if I will come and visit them in their house in the city. She is writing down the address on a paper napkin.

I imagine tall white rooms with wooden shutters, a fan ticking overhead, the scent of bougainvillea and strong coffee.

Nestor Felipe is approaching our table. He exchanges greetings with the sisters in Thalian and then asks me if I'll come with him to his cabin.

"I have a book I'd like to give you," he says.

I sense he is lying, or rather that his story about the book is not the whole truth. What does he want, then? To attack me? The idea is unworthy, and I understand that this is the moment I have waited for. That if I go with him now, he will tell me everything. Why he's here and what he knows, the whole story.

Now, with the truth so close, I feel doubts envelop me.

I know my life is about to change forever and the thought is frightening.

I think of Lin, asking me what I'm going to do, and I smile at Nestor Felipe and follow him out of the saloon and along the companionway.

* * *

He hands me a book.

It is wrapped in newspaper, a double page of the *Brock Island Messenger*.

"It's nothing much," Nestor says. "Just something I thought you might find interesting. You can open it later." When I do, I discover that the parcel contains a novel by Saffron Valparaiso called *The Sea is Long*. It's in Thalian, and this time there's no Crimondn translation to help me understand it. A short paragraph on the back jacket tells me it's Valparaiso's first novel, written while she was still at college.

I perch on the edge of Nestor's bunk while he busies himself with the paraphernalia for making coffee. In spite of the many hours we've spent together in recent days, now that I'm here in his cabin I am embarrassed to find I cannot think of anything to say to him.

The silence seems to spread itself out between us, becoming denser and more uncomfortable with every second.

"What was it like when you tried to talk with the whales?" Nestor says at last. He hands me coffee in a small glass cup. It is hot and very bitter.

"It was – not pleasant. It's still hard to think about, although my actual memories of what it was like are becoming blurred.

"Didn't they understand you?"

"Yes, they understood perfectly. They just didn't care."

"About you?"

"About any of us. The world they live in – the world they

357

perceive – is different from ours. We're like scavengers to them, bottom-feeders. They find us repellent." I take another sip of the horrible coffee. "So far as the whales are concerned we might as well not exist. Trying to talk with them was like watching myself drown."

I do not tell him the rest of what I feel – that I failed, and that I am ashamed because of it. That I have come to doubt my idea of my own specialness. That I no longer know who I am, and what I am for.

"How did you know?" I ask him instead. "That I could talk with them, I mean?" The question is easy to ask now, and why not? It's why he's brought me here.

Nestor Felipe smiles a smile, deep in his beard. He has been waiting for my question. It is our fate.

"I know because I know you. I know everything about you, Maree."

"Then you are a spy, after all?" My heart is thumping in my chest.

"No, not a spy, a detective. I was paid to find you. I'm someone who is good at finding things, that's all."

I rest my cup on the wooden floor, to the right of my feet. It's still half full and I don't want to kick it over by accident. What a mess that would make.

Imagine being told that the man you always thought of as your father is not your father after all, that your real father is in prison for rape and murder. Or that you aren't even a proper person, but a clone of your brother. Or that the memories you carry are false, that you've actually been in a coma since you were ten.

What you have to decide, there and then, is how much you are going to allow this new knowledge to affect you. Are you the feelings you feel inside, or the facts you know?

Suppose someone tells you your parents are dead, and they turn out not to be?

"Who paid you?" I ask Nestor Felipe. I can feel his thoughts in my mind, the tension in his shoulders, the nervousness he feels because he is not certain he is doing the right thing, even now, in telling me the truth.

"I was paid by your father," he says. "Or not by your father directly, but by the person he hired. Your father has been paying people to try and find you for fifteen years."

Later he shows me a photograph. Two people stand before a house, a man and a woman. The house is built from breeze blocks, and has a metal roof. The woman is small and dark-haired; she's wearing jeans. Nestor Felipe tells me her name is Christy, and that she's my aunt.

The man is tall and skinny, and has a scowling expression. He's wearing a loose black T-shirt with an oversized white handprint on the front.

His hair bushes out from his head, the same way mine does whenever I go too long without having it cut. It's the same colour, too – the sun-dried, raucous yellow of summer gorse.

This man's name is Derek Hoolman and he is my father.

* * *

My name was Luz Maree, but everyone called me Lumey. I was born in the town of Hastings, on the south-eastern coast of Crimond and not far from the resort town of Boster. The contamination of the Rovensay Marshes sent the town into decline, although the popularity of smartdog racing has since helped to revive its fortunes. My father works as a yard manager in the racing industry. He once owned and trained the four-time league champion smartdog Morpho-Limlasker. My mother's name is Claudia. I have a younger brother named Jem who is now fifteen.

I was taken away from my family at the age of four.

"Your father was involved in criminal activity – drug running – and the people who were hired to snatch you used that to trap him. It was never about the drugs, though – it was about you."

"But why?" The question bursts from me like a cry. "I don't understand." I have become used to guarding my emotions, to protecting myself, but this time I can't. I feel like I'm falling. I want to reach out, to catch on to something, but nothing feels solid.

"Because you're valuable," says Nestor Felipe. "It's as simple as that."

Nestor tells me that I started out as just another missing person case, someone he'd been paid to find, no different from any one of the many other similar cases he'd tackled over the years. After a while though, that changed.

"I suppose I became intrigued," he says. "Not just in

where you'd disappeared to, but why. Most times the two
things are linked, so if you really want to find someone you
have to get interested, a little bit, anyway. But with you there
were so many dead ends. It always felt as if there was some
bigger reason behind it all. I couldn't leave it alone."

I ask him when exactly he learned of my whereabouts,
why it's taken him so long to make himself known to me.

"A while," he says, then hesitates, and I sense that some of
the facts of my story still make him uncomfortable. "It took
a long time to track you down – the people who took you
are experts in concealment. And then once we'd found you it
was difficult to know how to proceed. We knew we couldn't
involve the police because there was still a chance your
father might have ended up in prison. You could have been
taken into state custody, anything. In the end we decided it
would be better to wait until you were legally an adult, and
so could make up your own mind. Anything more drastic
seemed too risky."

"Who found me?"

"One of our contacts. He's a lecturer at the university in
Inverness."

"I went to Inverness once, Kay took us." I am remembering
the castle, the steel-blue loch the man in the gift shop joked
was bottomless, the upswell of mountains behind. All my
life I have loved those northern high-lands: the heather and
the gorse, the freeze-blood winters and dewy summers, the
scents of first snows and wild honey. Being in the high-lands
is like glimpsing the country the orthodox Hools still call
the Otherside.

My own Otherside, it seems, lies not in the northern high-lands but in the south, in a faded coastal resort at the edge of a polluted wasteland. They exchanged one of my names for another. What I own of myself, it turns out, is fifty percent.

"Did they really buy Sarah?" I ask him. I don't know why this question seems important suddenly, but it does.

Nestor nods. "Sarah's mother's parents were both politicals. She had no money and it was difficult for her to find work. She knew Sarah would be well cared for, that her talent would be nurtured in the way it should be. She did the only thing she could have done in the circumstances."

"Do my family know? That you've found me, I mean?"

"No one knows yet, only you. You're an adult now, Maree. Your father has no more right to you than the people who stole you. I think you should make up your own mind – whether you wish to continue your journey to Kontessa, or go home to Crimond. If you choose to go home I'll help you. But the decision must be yours now, yours alone."

"Isn't this against the rules of your contract?"

"Yes it is – but I think your human rights are more important than a business deal."

I have a fifteen-year-old brother. This, more than anything else, feels like the most important thing I have ever been told.

If my brother is safe and okay, then so am I.

"Tell me what you know about the programme," I say to Nestor. "Don't leave anything out."

My coffee has gone cold. Nestor rinses the cup in the

sink then offers me a fresh one. It is as disgusting as the first, but I take it anyway. I might even get to like it in time.

It turns out that Lin was right about the space facility. Nestor tells me it's been running for fifty years or more. About twenty years ago the scientists in Kontessa started picking up a series of radio transmissions of unknown origin. Teams of linguists and military code breakers and forensic physicists went to work, trying to discover what the transmissions meant and where they were coming from. At some point someone suggested bringing in the children and young people who'd been engineered and trained to work with smartdogs.

Nestor Felipe referred to these children as natural empaths, or naturals, but to the people who ran the programme they were known as the bomb kids. The most talented was a boy named Idris Chowdouray, a nine-year-old street child who'd been bought and sold so many times that no one could remember where he originally came from. At the time the programme bought him, he was being used by one of the corporate militias to run smartdogs, both in routine terrorist bombings and in some of the big international sweepstakes, for very high stakes indeed. Idris Chowdouray never saw a single shea of that money himself, of course, which is probably why he didn't seem too bothered about being sold and bought again and shipped to Kontessa.

The task he was given was simple: decode the transmissions.

In his first year at the facility, Idris Chowdouray was able to pick up eight different languages just from chatting to the scientists on the programme and the house staff who came in from outside to do the cooking and cleaning. When it came to understanding patterns of language, there was no doubt in anyone's mind that Chowdouray was a prodigy.

The radio transmissions, though, were beyond him.

He said the broadcasts were recognisable as organised language, but that he couldn't make sense of them.

He claimed it was too far away – not in terms of distance, but in terms of meaning.

"They're different from us," he kept saying. "They think different things." He seemed unable or unwilling to elaborate.

The programme's instigators refused to give up. They brought in more dog kids, both those who were fitted with implants and those who were naturals. But the longer the experiments continued without success, the more the rumours and gossip started to circulate.

"Different factions began to develop," says Nestor Felipe. "There was one group of scientists who claimed the transmissions were a hoax, a cover-up for a new smartweapons programme. They began calling for the facility to be shut down, the dog kids to be deprogrammed, all sorts of things. Nothing came of it, though – the scientists who were causing the problem were all given a raise in their salaries and that was the end of it."

"So what's the truth?"

He makes a gesture with his hands, the open-palmed shrug that usually means: *I give up*.

"I don't know. No one seems willing to say and I have

to admit I've stopped asking. I feel worried about what they might be hiding, but not enough to get myself killed over it, not yet anyway. The one thing I do know is that the children – the bomb kids – do appear to be treated very well. Natural empaths are still rare and that makes them valuable, a protected species. If you decide to work for the programme you would be safe, and you would have a good life. I've told you everything I know. I couldn't have lived with myself otherwise." He pauses. "It's what my wife would have wanted me to do. We could never have children of our own."

His revelation about his wife comes as no surprise to me. I have sensed her in his mind now for many days. "Is there a chance," I say to him, "that the radio transmissions are genuine?"

"Oh yes, most certainly. There were people I talked to who believed the hoax story was put about deliberately, to avoid a mass panic. Just imagine what it might do to our world if we were to discover we weren't masters of the universe after all."

I do as he says and try to imagine it, and once I have started I find I cannot stop. I see my father's house burning, my brother prevented from having the future he might have chosen. I see riots in the streets of Lis and Lilyat, in the streets of towns and cities that are still unknown to me.

I see all these things, and none of them. How can we know?

I think that if these transmissions truly exist they must be like the song of the Atlantic whales: terrifying because we cannot grasp them, because they don't include us.

Nestor is insistent that I can decide not to go to Kontessa, that I should be free to make a life of my own choosing. But what if I am needed? If I can make a difference to the future as it now lies before us?

How do I work out the difference between what is right and what I want?

I remember that Caine and Sarah and I would sometimes sneak off together and do things without including Maud. None of the things we did were particularly secret – we'd go up to the back field and just talk, mostly. It was just that, well, Maud wasn't really one of us, and for Sarah especially those times when we could be exclusively together as empaths were very important.

Sarah was always insecure around Maud, mainly because Maud knew more about her and about her mother than Sarah felt comfortable with.

The thing was, Maud always knew what we were up to, anyway. She could not mind-speak, or read us as we read each other, but she found other ways of reaching a similar understanding. A blind man's hearing is always keener than a sighted man's. A woman with no sense of smell can distinguish colours in a way that others might abhor as witchcraft.

It's always wrong to assume that just because a problem is complex, people won't be able to get to grips with it. To suppress knowledge is always tyranny, even in wartime.

Caine never felt happy about shutting Maud out, but Caine was the best of us.

In the early months after they left, I kept hoping for a letter or even a postcard from Sarah or Caine. When none came, I said nothing.

I told myself they were too busy.

I told myself things would be different once we were together again.

I told myself anything that would let me believe they were safe.

It was strange, how quickly people stopped mentioning them at all.

It is the last night on board. The Gillespies are hosting a party in the saloon. Pierpoint Gillespie didn't leave the ship at Brock, after all. He and Mol have rarely been apart since the night of the whales.

I join the party for an hour or so and then slip away. There's no sign of Nestor Felipe, and when I go to his cabin he's not there, either. I go up on the passenger deck and stand at the rail, gazing towards the coast of Thalia, gliding past in the darkness. From time to time I glimpse lights, the shining spoor of coastal villages and small towns.

Our fore and aft beams have not been switched on since Brock. The shallower water should mean we have no need of them.

I now have less than a day to make up my mind.

* * *

We steam into Bonita harbour at around five o'clock in the afternoon. It's the port's busiest time of day, a fact that Nestor tells me will work to our advantage.

"We'll have no problem getting lost," he says. "So that's what we'll do."

The quayside is swarming with people – traders and tram drivers, navvies and fishermen, relatives and friends of the arriving passengers. I see at once that Nestor is right – it would be easy to lose track of someone here and never find them again.

Nestor Felipe has offered to help me get away from the harbour and find somewhere to stay.

The *Aurelia Claydon* is berthed beside a steamship of a similar size called the *Gravitas*. Nestor tells me she's from Cortez. As I stare down at the upturned faces on the crowded quayside I have the feeling that I am walking along a knife edge. The sheer size of this place turns out to be as daunting as I had imagined, and it is hot here, hotter even, I think, than it was in Lilyat. The air is sticky and pungent with the reek of fish.

And there is so much noise. After all the weeks at sea the noise is overwhelming. The sand-blown flagstones of the harbour teem with donkey carts and rickshaws and black marketeers. There is a smell of human beings and horse dung, smashed fruit, fresh tar. Everywhere luggage is being loaded on to barrows. I see a tall woman, hauling a handcart loaded with suitcases. The underarms of her T-shirt are stained darkly with sweat. Dogs run everywhere, yellow-bellied, brindled creatures with skinny legs and tails and sticking-up ears. They seem wild but they are not starving – it's clear to see they are practised scavengers.

My heart is beating hard and my palms are sweating. The cacophony of thoughts and voices and scents is like nothing I've experienced. In spite of my fear I find I'm eager to be in amongst it.

We are ready to go ashore. "Try not to stare at things too much," Nestor says. "It makes you seem like a tourist. Or as if you're looking for someone. Keep your eyes on me instead. Try and make it look as if none of what you see here is new to you, as if we're interested only in each other." He stands close beside me, speaking quietly and reassuringly into my ear. "Talk to me. Say anything you like, any nonsense, it doesn't matter what."

We are pretending we are father and daughter. I am wearing a wide-brimmed sunhat – it's Mol Gillespie's – to hide the colour of my hair, which also has the advantage of shading my face. Nestor Felipe takes my arm and we smile at one another as we walk down the gangway. I hear my sandals slapping noisily against the sunwarmed metal.

Nestor will return to fetch my luggage later on. The only thing that matters for now is for me not to be seen.

I feel like a moving target, utterly vulnerable. As we step from the iron walkway on to the sharply grooved concrete that makes up the hardstanding of the docking area I feel my body go rigid with tension, yet at the same time here I am, chattering away to Nestor about the overpowering heat and the stink of fish. I keep expecting someone's hand to grab my shoulder, for a voice to shout my name, for – and I know how foolish this sounds – a shot to ring out. We pass through throngs of traders and tourists, seamen and women, porters. I am drenched in sweat.

"Do you think you could get a message to my brother?" I say to Nestor. All at once it seems crushingly important that I should say this, that I should make sure – if something goes wrong – that my brother is at least told that I know he exists.

Jem, I say to myself. His name is Jem.

"You'll be able to do that yourself, as soon as you like," Nestor says. He smiles. His hand is steady on my arm. "We're almost there."

He helps me into one of the donkey carts then gets in himself. He speaks some words to the driver – an address? – and then we're moving away from the harbour and through the streets of the city. I catch glimpses of tall houses and sun-dappled courtyards. There is a constant stream of people, many on bicycles. I keep wondering what would be happening to me now if I'd waited on the quayside as I was supposed to. Is the person sent to fetch me still waiting, or have they already raised the alarm?

I feel confused, as if another, alternate version of my life is still going on somewhere. Perhaps that is the real life after all, and this the illusion.

We come to a standstill on a wide street, full of potholes and strewn with litter. We are in front of a large, pink-painted house, the topmost layer of paint peeling away to reveal the dirty yellow colour of the layer beneath. Two rickety-looking tables stand side by side on the front veranda.

The metal signboard above the door reads HOTEL CHARLOTTE.

"You can stay here for a while," Nestor says. "Just for a couple of days, until I can find you something more permanent. It's a bit rough, but it's safe, and the rooms are clean."

"I don't have much money," I say, and it's true, I don't, just the money Lin gave me. This is a problem I haven't thought of up until now.

"Don't worry about that," Nestor says. "Your father paid me well. There's plenty to spare."

He takes me inside the hotel. There is a tiled foyer, a wide, balustraded staircase. A woman is seated behind a Perspex-covered counter, reading a magazine. Nestor speaks to the woman in Thalian, but I'm too overwhelmed by the strangeness of everything to make the effort to catch what he says.

I see money change hands. The woman writes something into a ledger and then hands me a key.

"I can't go up to the room with you," Nestor says. "A man can't go to a room with a woman here, not unless he is also staying at the hotel. Will you be all right here until the morning? There's a *cantina* just across the road – you can buy a cheap meal there."

I nod. I do not trust myself to speak in case I burst into tears. "Your room's on the third floor," Nestor says. "Just follow the staircase around to the right. I'll return in the morning. Wait for me here in the lobby, at around ten o'clock? I'll bring your luggage. We can work things out then. For now, just get some rest. You'll feel better tomorrow."

He nods to the woman behind the counter and then he leaves. It is only once he's gone that I realise I don't have his address or his telephone number, or any way of contacting him at all, should he not reappear, as he promised, the following morning.

It comes to me that I am more alone than I have ever been in my life.

I hear the pht-pht-pht of the overhead ceiling fan. I glance quickly at the woman behind the counter, but she's gone back to reading her magazine.

My head is humming. I feel dog tired suddenly, tired as death. I feel as if my life has become unhooked from the rim of the world, as if it could spin off in any direction and no one would notice.

I climb slowly upstairs to my room.

The room is high up, under the eaves. The window is wide open, but the build-up of heat from the day still makes the confined space stifling. There is an electric fan in one corner and I switch it on.

The bed sheets are faded, but clean. The floor of the room is covered with green linoleum.

I sit down on the edge of the bed. From the open window I can hear the evening sounds of dogs and children, fighting and playing and shouting in the street below. It's as if I can feel the city breathing, yawning in the dusty heat, accepting me inside.

Big cities, I am coming to realise, are more complex than mazes. Keep their secrets, and they will do their best to keep you safe.

I know now that even if they find me, the person they are looking for is already no more.

What is happening now is happening to me, Lumey Maree.

Who I become from here is for me to decide.

appendix

BROCK ISLAND

'Brock Island' by Christy Peller. (This story originally appeared as part of the collection *At the Cedars Hotel*, Eltham House Press 2004.)

Maree came to Brock by ship, as she had done the first time. She remembered the island as a dour, grey place, but as the shore loomed closer she was surprised by how bright its colours seemed: the fierce blaze of gorse, the white buildings along the harbour front, the polished-looking surface of the surrounding sea. Duncan Taborow was waiting for her on the quayside. Maree recognised him at once. The dark grey overcoat he had on was so similar to the coat he had been wearing when she last saw him that Maree found herself wondering if it was the same one, although of course it couldn't be, not after twenty years. As she stepped forward to shake Duncan's hand she couldn't help but think of Dodie, Dodie Taborow in her handmade leather boots and diamond earrings, the tap of her heels on the worn concrete of the landing stage, and for those seconds it was like creeping inside Dodie's skin, being Dodie, just for a moment. Like reinhabiting her own recollection, but as the other person.

"You should have taken the hopper," Duncan said. "You could have been here two days ago." Duncan Taborow had made his fortune in the civil aviation business. When Maree last came to Brock aboard the *Aurelia Claydon*, there had been no commercial airport, just the single landing strip that had been used by military aircraft during the war. Since then, Niño Quaglia's life-size sculpture of the baer-whale had made the island famous, had given it a tourist industry. Now there were scheduled hopper flights from Bonita three times a week, more during the holiday season. But Maree had wanted to see the island as she remembered it: from the water.

"The ship was very comfortable," she said. "More relaxing than flying." She smiled. The emails she'd exchanged with Duncan the week before had prepared her for this. Like many successful businessmen, Duncan preferred to be the one making the decisions, even when the decision in question did not affect him personally. *Duncan's so like his father*, Dodie had written to her on more than one occasion. *But he's a generous man, and kind, at least he is to me.* Maree had been planning to stay overnight in a pension in Brock Town before heading inland, but Duncan had insisted she spend the weekend at the villa and it was difficult to think of a reason to refuse.

It would save on expenses, she consoled herself. And it would make her feel better about refusing the free hopper flight. There were things she wanted to see in Brock Town: the Fort Museum, the castle, Quaglia's sculpture.

She was curious about the villa, in any case, so in the end she said yes. Observing Duncan trying and failing to tamp down his delight in what he perceived as his victory was worth this minor capitulation on its own.

Duncan had driven to the harbour to collect her himself. Maree was surprised, a little charmed even, although she realised it was possible, probable even, that he simply enjoyed driving, that he enjoyed motor vehicles in general. It was impossible to believe a man who owned an airport wouldn't have a private chauffeur squirreled away somewhere.

The car was black with silver trim and tinted windows. The paintwork gleamed. The other vehicles in the visitor parking area, their flanks and windshields spattered with mud and dulled by dust, made it clear that it was someone's full-time job to keep this conveyance clean.

"I can put on the air conditioning, if you're uncomfortable," Duncan said.

"I prefer the fresh air," Maree said. "I like the smell of the ocean. It reminds me of the place where I grew up."

"Which was in Crimond, yes?"

"Scotland, actually. A town called Asterwych."

"I remember hating England. But then I barely remember it." He sighed heavily. "Do you still have family there?"

"My whole family is there. I've never been back, though." Maree expected him to ask her why not, but Duncan seemed to lose interest in the subject almost immediately. He pointed instead to an anomaly in the landscape, a deep fissure in the ground that appeared to be working its way inland from the cliff face, bisecting the main road into town, as if someone had cleaved the macadam across its width with a monstrous axe.

"It's called the Devil's Grin, if you can believe it," Duncan said. "It runs inland for over ten miles. There are locals who say it's bottomless."

"And is it?"

Duncan laughed. "Well, you can't see the bottom from the top, if that's what you mean. All I know is that every year some fool gets themselves killed trying to abseil down it." There was a slight bump as Duncan took the car over the road bridge that linked the two sides of the abyss. Maree felt a brief sensation of weightlessness, followed by a moment of anxiety, as if she'd narrowly escaped a danger she hadn't been aware of, although she supposed it was entirely possible she wouldn't even have noticed the crack, had Duncan not drawn her attention to it.

"The bedrock here is solid granite," Duncan said, as if reading her thoughts. "It's been stable for millions of years. There's nothing to worry about."

"I didn't think there was," Maree said. It crossed her mind that Duncan had shown her the crack deliberately, that he wanted her to feel uncertain and in his power.

That's ridiculous, she thought. He thought I'd be interested, that's all.

It was not yet midday. The sky was overcast, the pale clouds fraying in patches to expose the blue beneath. Maree felt surprised by the amount of traffic on the road. When Dodie first came to the island twenty years ago private cars were in a tiny minority. Dodie's dead, Maree reminded herself. The idea that she would never write to her friend again, that Dodie's visit to the mainland, long-proposed but never actualised, would now never take place, was like a message in a foreign language, only roughly translated.

The villa lay about five miles inland, within walking distance of the town centre and yet still somehow removed from it, a house that attracted attention, even if that attention was not directly sought. The place was more modest than Maree had expected, less ostentatious, anyway, the only concession to grandeur consisting in the massively imposing gateposts: granite, topped with globes of green-veined marble. There was no name plate, but then, Maree supposed, there wouldn't need to be. Beyond the gateposts and at the end of a gravelled driveway the house itself was a two-storey dwelling, excluding the attics, elegant in its proportions and with a stone facade.

"It's three centuries old," Duncan said. He brought the car to a standstill to the left of the entranceway. "It was Monsignor Calhoun's house. Calhoun the gunsmith," he added, sounding as if he expected the name to mean something to her, although it did not. Maree knew only that Brock Town was one of the oldest settlements in the whole of Thalia, that it had enjoyed a millennium of stable prosperity before Crimondn forces razed it to the ground during the first months of the war.

If what Duncan said was true, that would make the house of Calhoun the gunsmith one of the oldest properties of the island's renaissance.

"I bought it for next to nothing and refurbished it from scratch. There are three acres of virgin forest out the back," he said – as if trying to compensate for the mansion's plainness, Maree thought, although he loved the place, that much was obvious; he was *in* love with it. "Don't worry about your bag, I'll have it brought up." Maree opened her mouth to say there was no need, she could manage, there was just the one small holdall, and then thought better of it. If Duncan wanted to show her he had staff, people he paid to keep things tidy, to fetch and carry, to bring up her luggage, then let him. She was his guest after all, not his guilty conscience. Still, she could stop him opening the door for her, at least. Maree stepped quickly from the car. As she did so she heard the sound of rapid footfalls on the gravel, a loud bark. A large dog bounded into view: tan, with black hindquarters, a Weihund.

"Kiril!" Duncan called. He hunkered down in the driveway, reached out his arms. The dog rushed forward to greet him, its vast paws plumping down on his shoulders, its tail wagging frenetically. Maree caught the scent of its emotions, the backwash of wellbeing and relief that coursed through its being at the return of the loved one, the true companion, the alpha, their scents pooling and weaving together like coloured smoke. In the presence of the Weihund, the man's thoughts also became clearer to her, more aromatic, less cloaked in ambiguity and reserve.

The dog's devotion makes his master less afraid, Maree thought. Of growing old, of losing his power, of seeing the things he has worked for slip away. There was a joyful eagerness in his movements as he caressed the beast, an ease of being she would never have guessed at, had the dog not been there to reveal it to her. The dog was beautiful – expensive too, Maree guessed. She wondered if Duncan allowed it to compete in the show ring. It would win prizes if he did, definitely, the creature was championship material. The dog glanced at her, sensing her closeness, and then looked away again. Maree felt the jolt, the burst of acute sensitivity she recognised as anguish as the Weihund shifted its attention away from her and back towards its primary node, its central axis. Her empathic abilities were declining with age, she knew that, leaching back into the atmosphere like radioactive energy from a mass of palladium; a diminishing that was to be expected, she knew, as something most empaths seemed to suffer, all but a very few anyway, a kind of lessening, a levelling-out, a dying-off.

Some felt the loss so keenly they self-destructed. Maree found she was able to accept it, as she had come to accept other equally unwelcome yet equally natural aspects of aging. And in other ways she had been lucky. Her abilities in language theory and linguistic cryptography had increased rather than decreased with age and experience. This was compensation at least, if not full recompense. But it was not like that for everyone.

"What a beautiful dog," she said to Duncan.

"Eight years old," Duncan said. "He's still a youngster,

really." He grabbed the dog by the scruff of its neck, play-wrestling. "Weihunds can live for twenty years now, did you know that?"

Only if they've been enhanced, Maree thought, although she knew it would be naive of her to suppose that any dog of Duncan's would be anything else. She wondered if Duncan used a chip, then decided not. He didn't seem the type, and besides, she would know: she could still detect a chip a mile off, even now.

"I didn't know that," she said. She stroked the dog's side. Its coat was soft and plushy in the way that was characteristic of Weihunds. She could feel the creature's heartbeat in the tips of her fingers, the steady tick-tock of a balanced pendulum.

"I'm surprised." Duncan glanced up at her, meeting her eyes, his arms still loosely clasped about the dog's neck. "You were part of the original smartdog programme, weren't you? Mother told me. I would have thought you would be the first to know about improvements in enhancement techniques."

"I didn't realise your dog was enhanced, that's all." Maree smiled, still petting the dog, and after a moment Duncan smiled also. They moved towards the house, the dog following. Maree could tell that the Weihund was concerned by what it sensed in its alpha as a mild dissonance, but it was a small upset, a wisp of apprehension that dissipated as soon as Duncan's mood had reverted to what the dog recognised as normal.

In Maree's mind the disquiet lingered, bluish, like a plume of cigar smoke, coiling and unwinding in the air directly in front of her. So what if Dodie had mentioned to Duncan that she'd worked with smartdogs? The programme was hardly a secret, not any more. Still, there was something odd about it, something she couldn't put her finger on until she realised she couldn't imagine Dodie discussing her with Duncan at all.

He's a good son, but we don't really talk, not about personal things, Dodie had written. *He's like his father in this way. He'd sooner do something than waste time discussing it. He hates talking about his feelings.*

Duncan had contacted Maree directly when Dodie died, first to send a formal message card and then a more personal email. *She left me a list, would you believe*, he had written. *A list of people I should contact. She even made her own funeral arrangements. She should have been in the army. She'd have conquered worlds.*

His humour concealed real grief, Maree could see that at once, and it was this – her realisation that he had needed Dodie, that he had been glad when she came to live with him on Brock – that had led her to reply more freely than she otherwise would have done.

Dodie was my friend for twenty years, she wrote. *I feel devastated to have lost her. I had no idea she was so ill.*

Mother may have been eighty-two years old but she was still as stubborn as a fool, Duncan responded. *She said nothing to me, either. I didn't know there was anything wrong with her until two weeks ago.*

Maree had found comfort in his letters, mainly, she supposed, because it was a relief to be able to speak to someone who had actually known Dodie. Now that she was here she was beginning to wonder if she'd been too open. The idea that Duncan might want something from her, that he had an ulterior motive in inviting her to his home, had not occurred to her before now, but his veiled enquiries about the programme made her feel as if she'd been stupid to trust him. To trust him so readily, anyway. All that talk about Dodie would have come as second nature to someone so used to manipulating words to get what they wanted, and she had been ripe for manipulation. She wondered if he'd been through Dodie's things, if he'd read her correspondence even, all the messages they'd exchanged throughout the years. It was not that the letters contained anything important, or secret, but the thought of Duncan eavesdropping on them in this way was deeply unsettling.

He's reeled me in like a fish, Maree thought. She did not know where this thought came from, exactly, only that it was there, and that it meant something. Her training had emphasised the role of logic in decision making, especially for empaths, who tended, or so their mentors insisted, towards an overreliance on intuition. Maree could see the reasoning behind such thinking, just as she understood that logic could be so irrelevant that it sometimes had to be disregarded entirely.

Her instincts were telling her that Duncan Taborow had an agenda. Even if she turned out to be wrong, she should keep this in mind.

* * *

The ground floor hallway was cool and bright: white-painted walls, marble floor tiles, an elegantly curving staircase.

"Mother lived in the downstairs flat," Duncan was saying. "It's being cleaned at the moment, so I've put you upstairs. I hope that's all right?"

Maree nodded. His words seemed to suggest he thought she might have preferred being in Dodie's old room, which was strange, to say the least. She felt eager to get away from him, to be alone for a while. She looked pointedly towards the stairs, and found herself staring at a large artwork that formed the focal point of the extensive half-landing. It was a picture of the villa, she saw, painted in oils but so realistically it could easily be mistaken for a photograph. Looking at it gave Maree a feeling of unreality, as if she were still outside the house, looking in. The effect was uncanny.

"That's one of my wife's," Duncan said. He turned away abruptly. Maree was surprised. Dodie had mentioned Duncan's wife from time to time but Maree had gained the impression that the two were separated. Maree realised she didn't even know the woman's name, which seemed odd, now she came to think of it. Dodie had never been one for holding back, not where gossip was concerned.

"Is your wife here, in this house?" Maree asked. "I'd like to meet her."

"No," Duncan said. Maree waited for him to say more, to clarify – did he mean no, his wife wasn't in the house, or no, they weren't to meet? – but he had already started to move away from her and up the stairs. "I'll show you your room," he said. "You must be tired."

"I am, a little," Maree said. The silence of the house unnerved her. She had expected bustle, she supposed. A sense of urgency. Staff. Yet the place hung in stasis, and if there were staff, which she knew there must be, then they were either used to keeping out of the way or else Duncan had told them specifically that they should not appear.

She did not like the idea of Duncan accompanying her to the threshold of her room. It seemed too close, somehow, too intimate. They had barely met. She began following him up the staircase. There was another painting on the top landing, a large canvas depicting a black woman and a white greyhound and obviously by the same artist. The woman was wearing gants, was clearly a runner. Maree felt moved by the picture, almost to tears, although she couldn't have said why. It was just a beautiful image, the woman with her dog, she supposed, simply that.

"Moonrise Kingdom," Duncan said. "He was famous on the mainland. He was a fine animal."

"Who's his runner?" Maree asked. "Do you know her name, I mean?"

"I don't recall." He looked down at his feet. "Laura had to travel to the mainland to paint her, some ranch to the north of Bonita. She was away for weeks. The painting was a commission, but the patron died, would you believe, just before she came home. I made sure she got paid, though."

I bet you did, Maree thought. "Your wife's name was Laura?" she said. She felt a shiver go through her, a sensation that was like déjà vu. Someone just walked over my grave, as Sarah would say. She found herself wishing she'd asked

Sarah to come to Brock with her, as she'd thought of doing, or that she'd never come at all.

Duncan either didn't hear her, or chose to ignore her. "This is your room," he said. He indicated one of the three wood-panelled doors that opened directly off the nearer end of the first-floor landing. "Dinner will be served at seven, but there's plenty of food in the larder if you feel hungry. Just help yourself. I'll be out for most of the afternoon but you'll find David or Agathe in the back office if you need anything."

"I'll be fine," Maree said. "Thank you."

"Well, if you're sure." Duncan stood there awkwardly for a moment or two and then retreated. Maree watched him as far as the half landing, then opened the door. Bright sunlight flooded out across the parquet. She stepped into the room, closing the door firmly behind her. The sense of relief was immediate, and enormous. The first thing she noticed was her holdall, standing by itself at the foot of the bed. She did not understand how it could be here already. There was another set of stairs, she decided, a back entrance the staff used. It was the only explanation. Someone went to the car and brought the bag up. No mystery.

And yet the house still felt empty to her, a place of ghosts. With Lin dead, and now Dodie, wasn't that exactly what the island was, at least for her?

She had requested leave to attend Dodie's funeral, and yet Maree knew there was more to it than that. So, apparently, did Loanna Nicolaides, the programme co-ordinator.

"Take a week. Two," Loanna had said. "We all get tired,

you know, Maree. We are all human beings."

One of Loanna's favourite sayings, which was ironic, Maree thought, given that Loanna had more enhancements and augmentations than anyone she knew. There were even rumours that she'd had certain brain pathways amplified at enormous risk to herself, in order to complement her already extraordinary ability in mathematics, but Maree didn't know whether to believe them or not. She used to wonder whether Loanna was at all affected by the way people saw her but had given up thinking about it years ago. Loanna was simply Loanna: vain, domineering, fractious, blisteringly intelligent, impulsive to the point of recklessness, inconsistent, sympathetic and generous. So human it was almost a joke.

Loanna would never lie to you but that didn't mean she would always tell you the truth. She was ruthless in the pursuit of her goals but if she liked you or considered you valuable she would go out of her way to help you, especially if helping you would also help her in getting what she wanted.

"You're overestimating my abilities," Maree had said to her when Loanna asked her to reconsider her decision to retire.

"I really don't think so," Loanna had said. "You love the work, you live for the work. You persevere. Staying power is more important than raw talent, in the long run. It is in all our best interests that you stay. Do you think we'd be having this conversation if I believed otherwise?"

I don't suppose we would, Maree had thought, but didn't say. She told Loanna she would think things over, then Dodie had died, and Maree had come to Brock instead. She knew that Loanna expected her to use her time on the island to come to a decision, which was not unreasonable, although Maree found herself resenting it anyway.

Maree couldn't remember the last time she had felt this restless.

She crossed to the window, which turned out to overlook the back of the house. There was a sea of trees down there, blue fir and sassafras, the bright glint of lake water. In one of her letters, Dodie had said she loved Duncan's gardens, they reminded her of Crimond. Maree had been surprised how easily Dodie, who liked expensive clothes and elaborate suppers, had seemed to adjust to life on Brock, which was a bleak place, without much in the way of entertainment, or at least it was then.

She'd had her bridge games, of course, her famous card parties. Maree wondered why she had never come to the island while her friend was alive.

She'd gone back to the programme because of Sarah, but it had been Loanna who made the contact, Loanna who came to Bonita to persuade her. They had met in a cafe in the city centre, not far from portside, where Maree had first arrived in Thalia on board the *Aurelia Claydon*. The place was crowded when Maree first got there, but identifying Loanna Nicolaides had not been difficult. Loanna made no attempt to conceal her augmentations, even though they were unusual enough at the time to make people stare. Maree found herself admiring her, even though they had not yet spoken a word to each other. Loanna ordered coffee, then handed her an envelope with Sarah's writing on it.

"I can anticipate your objections before you voice them," Loanna said. "So can we skip that part?"

She told Maree that the programme's work with empathic language systems had always been a cover for its real purpose, which was to decode a sizeable quantity of data whose origins lay, it was now generally accepted, beyond the solar system. The hope was – the hope of the programme's chief executives and their commercial sponsors, anyway – that proper analysis of the data transmissions would eventually provide substantive information on the whereabouts of a viable solar system within a reasonable distance of Earth's own.

"For viable, read commercially exploitable," Loanna added. "For reasonable, read broadly conceivable in finite numbers. The commercial exploitation of extraterrestrial resources is low down the list of priorities, scientifically speaking, but we had to get the money from somewhere, and business is, as they say, business."

"You don't need me for this," Maree said. "You can have your pick of anyone." It was the bomb kids she was thinking of, prodigies like Idris Chowdouray and Emma Cisco, though she didn't say so. She didn't trust Loanna yet, not completely. She wasn't sure how much she was supposed to know.

"Your empathic communications skills are adequate, but secondary," Loanna said. Our records suggest your innate logic scores have been exceptional, which when combined with your intuitive abilities makes you a remarkably astute lateral thinker.

So far as the programme is concerned, you are a valuable resource. A resource that is being wasted. Uneconomic for us, unsatisfying for you. In addition to that," Loanna sipped at her coffee, "your colleagues from Scotland have made it apparent that they would welcome your return as a priority."

Maree glanced at the envelope, which lay beside her on the table. "I haven't read it, if that's what you're thinking," Loanna said, and when she read it later Maree thought there was at least a chance she really hadn't. *Loanna's OK*, Sarah had written. *She can be a bitch sometimes but not in a bad way. You can trust what she says. Some of the management here are complete idiots but our team's fine. I think you'd love working here. Caine is predictably obsessed, so I need you to keep me sane! I miss you. Please come.*

"My life is here now, in the city," Maree said.

"I'm sure it is," Loanna said. "Shall we order some lunch?"

"I want to speak to Sarah," Maree said, when they had finished eating.

"Fine." Loanna took out her mobile and drew down the menu. "Call her. The number's right there."

Why am I not surprised, Maree thought. The promise of seeing Sarah again, of hearing her voice, filled her with a gladness that surprised her. She'd been lonely in the city by herself, she realised, although until that moment she had never found the courage to call the emotion by its proper name.

The whale had beached on Brock ten years ago, twelve. Maree had watched the news reports, awed and horrified that a creature that appeared invincible had come to grief, against all reason and so publicly. It was a young beast, still relatively small, and for the first hours there was hope that it would swim free on the next high tide. In fact it was dead by then. Marine biologists speculated that the whale's vast lungs had collapsed, suffocating the creature, although later on they were forced to admit they still knew too little about Atlantic whales to say for certain.

Large numbers of people came out to gape at the carcass. An enterprising shipping company arranged two-day excursions from the mainland. Fears about local water contamination and air pollution receded as hosts of sea birds and marine predators cleansed the corpse of its meat in less than a month. The skeleton remained, a cathedral in bone. Picture postcards were printed. A lengthy essay by the naturalist Paolo Suarez, together with a collection of photographs by students and schoolchildren, were published as a souvenir booklet. A line of kiosks, selling T-shirts and commemorative plates and other mementoes, sprang up along the beach head. This was the moment when Brock's formerly non-existent tourist industry began to boom. When Niño Quaglia got the go-ahead to cast the whale's skeleton in bronze and titanium steel, in order, as the project's steering committee put it, to preserve this unique natural artefact for posterity and to provide the island's economy with a signature artwork of world-class importance, Brock's new identity as a 'destination' seemed assured. A boardwalk was constructed, together with a pier and a viewing platform, so the sculpture could be observed at high tide. Maree had seen a documentary about Quaglia, and the hundred-strong team he assembled to bring his vision to life, but seeing the sculpture in reality was a different experience, not like seeing a living whale exactly, but a reminder, a kind of emotional aftershock.

"Would you like to go down to the beach?" Maree said. She and Duncan were up on the viewing platform. Quaglia's sculpture lay off to one side like a wrecked cruise liner, its fifty-foot ribcage towering above the sand. More than a dozen different metals had been used in the work's construction. These had been left to weather naturally, to tarnish and rust as the elements dictated, resulting in a variegated, multi-textured surface that in places gave the impression of being a natural object, something that had grown from the sand, or put down roots there.

Tourists milled about among the uprights, craning their necks to take in the spectacle, standing back to snap photographs. Children ran about excitedly. Maree wondered how many of them realised that the whale whose metal ghost they were dancing around in had been less than half grown.

"Not really," Duncan said.

"I suppose you've seen it hundreds of times." Maree imagined the people on the beach struggling in the water, like Kollen Jonniter in that old horror movie, like Alec Maclane. Once the picture was in her head it was hard to dislodge.

"I've seen it from the air, but not close to." He cleared his throat. "I'm terrified of those things. They give me nightmares."

"The whales, you mean?"

Duncan nodded. Maree felt surprised that he was able to be so open about it, to reveal himself to her that way.

Fear was such a personal thing. She wondered if Dodie had ever told him about Alec Maclane.

"Mother said you tried to speak to one," Duncan said suddenly. "Is that even possible?"

"It's not talking," Maree said. "What we do, I mean. It's more like feeling, or sensing. Touching minds. It's like the way you feel yourself, when you speak to your dog, only more intense."

She fell silent, gazing out towards the sculpture. It's like a temple, she thought. One of those Turkman temples on the shores of Aegea. The ruins of a civilisation. We believe we can understand it – through research, through study – but we really can't. All we can do is paint pictures, and dance in the sand.

"The whales can't be understood," she said to Duncan. "They don't care about us. They don't even notice us, really." She frowned. She still found herself occasionally mystified by the way people needed everything spelled out, articulated. And yet words were such clumsy things, blunt instruments. Speaking to dogs was so much easier, or at least it had been.

"Are they dangerous? I mean really?"

Maree laughed. "To a steamship in the middle of the ocean they're unstoppable. Set against humanity as a whole though, they're defenceless. They have no weapons, they can't threaten or bargain with us to keep us from fouling up the sea. All they can do is keep out of our way, and hope we destroy ourselves before we destroy them."

"You sound like you feel sorry for them."

"I do."

"Even after what they did to your friend?"

"Alec Maclane wasn't my friend, he was Dodie's. And you might as well blame a typhoon for what happened to him."

"A typhoon isn't a monster, though. A typhoon is mindless."

Being mindless is what makes it a monster, Maree thought. She felt surprised and disconcerted that Dodie had told Duncan so much about her. Again she had that feeling of being caught up in someone else's agenda, of being reeled in, although when she turned to look at Duncan he seemed calmly preoccupied, gazing at the tourists on the beach and fiddling with something he had rooted out of his pocket; a keyring, it looked like. He seemed to have almost forgotten she was there.

"When I first came to Brock it was a lonely place," he said. "I think that's why I came here, really, as an escape from everything I hated about England. It's changed a lot."

"You wouldn't leave, though?"

"Brock is my home." He hesitated. "I still dream about it."

"Dream about it?"

"The way it was, I mean. Before the airport, and the conference centre. I built them both, I know." He sighed. "People think I'm ruthless, but they don't understand. If I've been successful it's because I'm patient."

"I'm not sure I understand."

"What do you think all this has been for, the long hours, the risky investments, the lack of sleep? I'm not saying I don't enjoy what I do – if I didn't enjoy it I wouldn't be good at it – but if you think it's about money you'd be mistaken. It's what you do with your money that's important, the legacy you leave behind." He slipped the keyring back in his pocket and turned to face her. "I know about the scout mission."

Maree laughed. So he was one of the space nuts. Alien obsessives, like Caine. "You know more than I do, then."

"I don't think so. Everyone knows the source of the alien transmissions has been located."

"You're wrong about that."

"Is that what you believe, or what you've been told to say?"

"I haven't been told to say anything. All I know is that we're still years from any real answers, decades, probably. I'll be dead by then. You will be, too." She drew in her breath. "These rumours about a scout mission – they're just that, rumours. Even if we knew where we were going, we don't have the technology for that kind of long-distance exploration. You should know that better than I do."

"What, because of my extensive experience in the civil aviation industry?" He laughed. "Have you heard of SCIMITAR?"

"SCIMITAR?"

"They're a sponsorship organisation for the ET intelligence programme. They fund you, basically."

He was disappointed, Maree could sense it. So disappointed that he would rather believe she was lying than that she didn't have the information that would vindicate his beliefs.

If I worked for him, he would be thinking about firing me, she thought. "I'm a linguistic analyst, not a physicist," she said. She wondered why he cared, why this mythical journey into space was so important to him.

Everyone has something, she supposed. A private madness. Most of the time it stays hidden but it's the engine that drives us. She felt her customary urge to apologise, but resisted. If Duncan had invited her to his home under false pretences, it was he who should be sorry.

"Let's go back," Duncan said. He seemed less tense, almost chagrined. Perhaps he felt foolish. As they reached the beach head car park, a plane flew over. Maree looked up, startled.

"That's low," she said.

"The mail plane," Duncan said. He shaded his eyes with his hand. "It takes off not far from here, from the old airfield. Rickety old thing. Does the job though, I suppose. The islanders call it the pony express."

"I heard it crashed a couple of years ago," Maree said quietly. The smell of salt seemed to intensify suddenly. The tide's coming in, she thought. They need to bring those children off the beach. "I heard the pilot was killed."

"That was most unfortunate." Duncan kept staring out to sea, though the aeroplane had disappeared into the clouds. "She was an ex-fighter pilot, too. But then it's often the brilliant ones who take unnecessary risks."

"Did you ever meet her? The pilot?"

He shook his head. "She'd been badly disfigured, I heard. It might have been better if she'd given up flying altogether. Better for her, I mean. I imagine it's difficult to fully recover from something like that."

It was five years since Lin's death, and Maree had not

397

been in contact with her for some years before that. She had learned the news from Dodie, who had declared herself horrified, although she was mostly just dying to tell someone. Dodie had never been able to eradicate her love of passing on scandal. *She was a friend of yours, wasn't she?* Dodie had added, as if she had forgotten, which perhaps she had.

The programme's findings had been leaked and counter-leaked so many times that aside from a small and dedicated cabal of conspiracy theorists, the general public had more or less lost interest.

"Unless you can show them pictures of actual aliens, most people get bored," Sarah had said once. "Five thousand gigabytes of encoded gibberish doesn't have quite the same appeal."

Maree had told Loanna she would return to the programme on a trial basis, but that she should be free to return to Bonita to live if she wanted to, at any time. Loanna seemed unconcerned by these stipulations, agreeing to them without preamble, and as the months and then the years slipped by Maree began to understand why. For some months after coming to live at the compound, Maree travelled to the city frequently – she had friends there, she insisted; she enjoyed the bookstores, the bustle of portside, the free life of the capital. After a while though her visits grew farther apart and in the end she stopped going. The effort seemed not to be worth it, somehow. She realised she would rather spend her free time writing her journal, or walking the private tract of wilderness that she along with the rest of the programme's employees called the backyard. For Maree, the work of the program had become all-consuming. The problem of the data transmissions – not just what they meant but where they came from, whether they had been purposely directed towards the Earth or picked up by chance – was engrossing on a scale that made most of what had been her old life seem mundane.

Among those who worked at the compound, there was a sense of being involved in something that would one day change the world. How that change would manifest itself, and when, remained unquantifiable, but Maree had not let such questions disturb her on a daily basis. You had to draw a line somewhere or you couldn't continue. People like Caine, who did not draw a line, found themselves going under.

"Caine believes he can save the world," Sarah said. Maree knew what she meant – it wasn't delusions of grandeur that undermined Caine's sanity, but a sense of responsibility so acute it was impossible to live with.

Maree had told him, more than once, that he should take a break, but he had refused. "The work I'm doing here – that's my life," Caine said. Like the rest of them, he was addicted to it. His breakdown wasn't serious, or so the doctors said anyway, but the impact on his health in the long term remained to be seen.

The codes were truly alien, in the sense that nothing like them had ever been recorded or utilized on Earth; a combination of a mathematical system that remained partially obscure even after five decades of research, and a series of coded symbols that appeared to be a form of musical notation, or something like it, no one was certain. The encryption was further complicated by the fact that as many as twenty separate languages seemed to be involved, each with their own grammar and sentence structure and semantic emphasis.

Given that the majority of 'words' employed seemed to have no terrestrial equivalent, progress was often tortuously slow. But for Maree, the involvement with something never before seen, never before imagined, was rewarding to a degree she could scarcely articulate.

She sometimes wondered if there might be a word for what she felt, hidden in the alien transmissions. No one seriously questioned that the transmissions were in fact alien. There was a theory someone had put forward soon after the programme was initiated, that the transmissions were actually a scrambled feedback loop from one of Earth's own defunct communications satellites, data sent into space more than a century ago and then bounced back, partially decayed and no longer decipherable.

'Are We Talking to Ourselves?' was the title of a lengthy paper supporting this theory written by one of the programme's early detractors, now deceased. The theory had been comprehensively discredited since then. Lengthy papers had been written about that, too, though Maree had never bothered getting up to speed with them. She had never doubted the authenticity of the transmissions, whose eccentric, discordant rhythms had worked their way inside her, imprinted themselves on her brain like alien music – if there was such a thing, which she doubted; this was something else.

The feeling was similar to what she had experienced during her miserable failure to communicate with the baer-whale, and yet also different. The baer-whale had been indifferent to her, if not actively hostile, whereas in the alien transmissions Maree thought – believed – she detected the desire, the purpose of speaking to be heard. She had nothing to back up her theory, not yet, it was just a feeling. A feeling she trusted. In time she believed she could give it more cogent expression.

Proof, if that was the word they insisted upon. She would give them that.

Five years before she came to Kontessa, one of the programme's most gifted cryptographers, a brilliant, fragile mathematician from Venezuela, had produced the linguistics section's most significant achievement to date: a rough six-line translation from the part of the transmissions nicknamed the Bel Canto, because of the peculiar chromatic melody some said they could detect when the data stream was amplified through loud speakers.

> *My sisters we are coming*
> *We sing bat's wing night clock war ring*
> *We are divided*
> *Divided comes the landslide then united*
> *Sister rose sister blanchflower*
> *Maelstrom life song lifelong glow glow glow*

The obscure beauty of the six lines held Maree captive. She dreamed of perfecting a similar accomplishment but in spite of her efforts success still eluded her. From the data she was working on, she had managed to isolate a small lexicon of terms, but these remained unproven, intermediate status only, and although Loanna commended her work on a regular basis, Maree had begun to wonder if she was capable of achieving the goals she'd laid out for herself.

It was this mounting sense of her own failure that had made her start thinking about retirement, although she didn't tell Loanna that. She said she was upset about Caine's breakdown, which was also true, although not the main reason.

The truth was, she was scared. She could still remember how it had been when she was younger. Her empathic rapport with the smartdogs had been so acute she had stopped verbalising entirely for a while. This worried the adults who were in charge of her, but for Maree, who excelled in sub-audible communication, the medium of the spoken word seemed ugly and clumsy by comparison.

With time, her natural abilities as an empath had become blurred, overwritten by learned responses and applied logic.

So far as the alien data was concerned, Maree knew that logic alone could not help her.

The bus she transferred to at Paloma was much smaller, a scratched and dented single-decker with uncomfortable metal seats and noisy gears. It was still pretty full. At

Paloma, Maree bought extra food from a cafe on the square and browsed the souvenir shops. One of the shops sold nothing but cow bells, beautiful objects made from silver and copper and engraved with a variety of attractive designs. She decided to buy one as a gift for Belen, then wondered afterwards if she'd been foolish, buying someone a souvenir of their own region. Belen would hate it, probably. She also bought some postcards of the waterfall, which was famous on Brock, a furious, narrow cataract, pouring two hundred feet down a granite cleft before collecting in a pool of blue-black water just below the town.

Maree had glimpsed the waterfall from the first bus as they approached. Three youths stood on the ironwork footbridge that traversed the pool while a man in a leather jacket photographed them from below. The youths were dressed in long grey tunics, and their heads were shaved. They looked like monks, but why would monks be having their photograph taken? Maree had wondered. The journey inland from Brock Town had been strenuous – three hours along a narrow road over rough terrain – but full of similarly interesting sights, and Maree had barely glanced at the book she had brought, a translation of Meriot's essays on the origins of computing.

The green-grey valleys and granite villages made her think of Asterwych. She remembered Maud, the coach trip to Inverness, the way Maud had lost her temper when Maree had decided to sit next to Sarah on the journey home.

These memories hurt, but faintly, like a bruise that had mostly healed but that was still sometimes visible in cold weather. It was all so long ago.

The road from Paloma to where Belen lived in Juan Lacruz was even narrower, the landscape of moorland and pine forests still more remote. Maree dozed for a while, cushioning her head with her pullover and resting it against the window frame. By the time she woke up they were pulling into the square at Juan Lacruz. Besides herself, there were only two other people getting off: an elderly woman wearing a padded anorak and a black headscarf and a man with a goatee beard and long grey hair. The man seemed oddly familiar, and after a moment's thought Maree realised she'd seen him in Paloma, photographing the monks beside the waterfall.

"I'm looking for this place," Maree said to him. "Do you know where it is?"

She handed him her notebook with Belen's address in it, then glanced briefly at the old woman, who was already shuffling away across the cobbles. Juan Lacruz was tiny, smaller even than Maree had anticipated, a sparse assortment of buildings clustered around a crossroads on a windy hillside. She wondered if it was the cross formation that had given Lacruz its name, then decided not. There were towns with the same name, or variations of it, scattered all over Thalia.

"That's on the same street as the hotel," said the man with the goatee. "That one." He pointed across the square, then handed back the notebook. "I think you'll find it's impossible to get lost in this town, actually."

Maree thought he was probably right. "Do you live here?" she said.

"Most of the time. Why, does it look like I shouldn't?"

"I thought I saw you in Paloma, that's all."

"I was photographing the novices. One of them is the son of a friend of mine, from Brock Town. I visit him quite often. My friend, I mean." He raised his eyebrows and grinned. "Do I pass muster?"

"I was curious, that's all. I'm sorry." Maree laughed a little.

"Well, if you feel like being curious again, I usually eat supper at Dino's." He gestured towards one of the buildings facing the square, a yellowish, slab-like house with all its shutters closed. "Breakfast too, when he can be bothered to open. Drop by any time."

"Perhaps I will," Maree said. She smiled again briefly then hurried away. She found herself wishing she hadn't shown the goatee man Belen's address, then chastised herself for being paranoid. At least she knew which way she was supposed to be going. She passed the hotel, a crumbling antique of a building with wrought-iron balconies and a rash of yellow roses scrawled, like irate graffiti, across its facade. Belen's house was fifty yards further on, past a telephone kiosk and tobacconist's shop, a square, barn-like building set back from the road and surrounded by a low stone wall. Maree recognised it easily from the description in Belen's email, but seeing it in reality was still a surprise, like catching sight of someone she knew in a place a hundred miles from where they lived.

Belen looked older than Maree had expected, a short, muscular woman with a silver ornament in her left eyebrow and closely cropped grey hair.

"The bus is late," she said. "I was beginning to think you weren't coming." Her manner was brusque, not unwelcoming exactly but cool enough to make Maree wonder if she would have been better to reserve a room at the hotel. Perhaps it had been a mistake to come here at all. When Belen asked her if she'd like tea, Maree said yes at once, hoping it would lighten the atmosphere between them. Belen lit the stove in silence. The inside of the house was cool and rather dark. Maree thought about asking where she was to sleep, then settled for setting down her holdall on the floor instead.

"Oh, sorry," Belen said. "You can put that in here. I hope it's all right." She crossed to the far corner of the kitchen and moved aside a curtain to reveal a sleeping alcove. There was a single pull-down bed, a blanket chest, a small, high window. Like a monk's cell, Maree thought. It's all about monks today. She wished she could close the curtain and lie down on the bed, shut out the world for a while. She placed the holdall next to the bed then returned to the main kitchen area. She could always leave early, she reminded herself. It wouldn't be too difficult to think up an excuse. Belen moved silently about, filling the kettle, fetching mugs. Maree noticed that her feet were bare. She found it difficult to tell if the woman resented her presence or if she was normally this taciturn. She tried to imagine Lin in this place, and failed to do so, although of course Lin had never lived here anyway. Belen had moved to Lacruz after Lin's death. Before that they had lived closer to Brock Town, in the peculiar old army building Lin had insisted on calling the Post Office.

Lin had loved it there. She had never used those exact

words, but Maree had known, from the careful way she described everything, how she felt about the place.

It was the aircraft, Maree supposed, most of all, but it was not just that. In the windswept uplands and cloistered settlements of Brock Island, Lin had finally found a place where she felt at home.

Would she have been happy in this strange little town, this smattering of buildings so far from everything, even the sea?

Their time together had been so short, after all. What she knew of Lin amounted to no more than isolated memories, like a handful of old holiday snaps you take out of an envelope now and again and then put back again. She had never known her properly, not in the way Belen had.

These thoughts were unwelcome, painful even, but she could not help recognising the truth in them.

"I hope you'll excuse me," Belen said suddenly. "I do want you here. I'm glad you came. It's just a bit strange, that's all. I'm not used to visitors."

"That's all right," Maree said. Her relief was palpable. "It's strange for me, too."

Belen smiled. "Here's your tea," she said. She placed a mug on the table in front of her. The mug was dark brown and heavy-looking. Its upper portion had been coated with a yellowish glaze, glinting with darker specks. The kind of object you immediately wanted to touch.

"Is this one of yours?" Maree asked.

Belen nodded. "I have to check on the kiln, actually.

That's part of why I'm anxious. Come with me, if you like? It won't take long. You can bring your tea."

They went outside. Immediately to the rear of the house there was a wide veranda, with plant pots and an outside tap, but the land beyond was untended, a wilderness of overgrown grass and untidy shrubs, a couple of weedy-looking trees Maree thought might be mountain ash. Belen's pottery kiln stood on a patch of bare earth, a brick-built, conical structure with smoke rising gently from a hole in the top. Maree watched with interest as Belen peered through a spyhole that had been bored through the brickwork about halfway up the cone. There was a smell of woodsmoke, and the heat was intense, even from a distance.

"It's finished," Belen said. She straightened up and replaced the bung. "Let's go back inside. You must be starving."

"What happens next? With the kiln, I mean?"

"We leave it to cool. That takes twelve hours, maybe fourteen. Then you take out the wares."

"How long does it burn for?"

"Most of a day. I put in the last fuel about an hour ago. You have to keep the temperature constant or the glaze won't mature. Are you interested in ceramics?"

"I don't know much about them. But I like this mug." She turned the vessel in her hand. The idea that Belen had made it, that it had not been produced in a factory along with thousands of identical others, seemed to grant it extra significance, as if it were not simply a mug, but part of Belen as well.

Lin would have liked this, too, she thought. She felt a stab of regret.

"It's kind of you to say so. You can help me unpack the kiln tomorrow, if you like."

"I'd enjoy that. Thank you."

They returned to the house. Belen had supper already prepared, a bean stew, which she heated on top of the stove. The food was tasty, and as the talk between them began to flow more freely, Maree could feel herself start to relax.

"I don't miss being in Brock Town at all," Belen said, describing her move to Lacruz five years before. "It can be tricky getting hold of materials, but it's a small inconvenience."

Belen sold a lot of her pottery locally, she said, although there were galleries in Brock Town and Paloma that also stocked her work.

"Have you always worked by yourself?" Maree asked.

"Not always," Belen replied, but did not elaborate. Maree sensed that the older woman was still holding herself aloof from her, at least a little. Was it because of Lin? Maree did not think so, not exactly, but there was still something. As she fell asleep that night in the small cubby hole of a room Belen had prepared for her, Maree found herself wondering for the first time what Lin had told her. That they had been lovers, certainly. But about her work with the programme, her life at the Croft before that? Maree had no idea.

In a place as small and isolated as Juan Lacruz, Maree soon discovered it was possible to spend whole days just walking and thinking. Belen made it clear to Maree that she was on hand to offer help or advice if it were needed, but otherwise she should feel free to do as she chose. Maree was grateful. It was what she had planned, after all, in as much as she had planned anything. She liked Lacruz much more than she had thought she would. She enjoyed the fact that within just a couple of days of arriving there the place felt familiar: its buildings, its backyards and street corners, the town square with its drinking fountain and war memorial – she knew each of these things intimately, and by heart.

By the time she encountered the man with the goatee beard again, he seemed to belong to a different time.

"You haven't absconded yet, then?" He was sitting outside the restaurant – Dino's, he had called it, although there was no name board. The shutters were open though, and there were tables set out under the awning. Goatee man was drinking coffee, a basket of rolls beside him on the table.

"Did somebody actually serve you those," Maree asked, "or are they just stage dressing?"

He laughed. "If you sit down you might find out," he said, and after a moment's hesitation Maree did so. She could see no harm in it, and it made a change, after all, to talk to someone.

"I don't even know your name," she said.

"Essat Kadris." He put out his hand. "I'm a photographer."

"Maree Hoolman." She grasped his fingers quickly and then let go.

"You're not from Brock, then?"

He said it as if it were a foregone conclusion, as if he already knew the answer she would give. And yet he was curious about her, she could tell. So he's inquisitive, what can it matter, aren't we all? she thought. The truth was, she found him easy to talk to. She liked his sense of humour.

"This is my first visit. I came over for a funeral, actually."

"A funeral? Not in Lacruz?"

"Oh, no. I'm here visiting a friend. The funeral's in Brock Town, next weekend."

"Whose funeral are you going to, if you don't mind my asking?"

"Her name was Dodie. Dodie Taborow. I travelled over with her on the steamer. She was good to me and I was glad she was my friend. I miss her already."

"Taborow? As in the aeroplane guy?"

Maree found herself blushing. She knew Duncan was rich, of course, but the idea that this might make him an object of public scrutiny had never really occurred to her and it made her feel uncomfortable.

"Dodie was his mother. Why, do you know him? Duncan, I mean?"

"Never so much as laid eyes on the man. Well, on television, obviously, but I think you'd be safe to assume that Monsignor Taborow and I move in different circles." He was still smiling, but Maree found it difficult to read his expression. "I have no interest in tycoons. I only mention him because of Laura."

"Laura Taborow?"

"You speak the name as if it means something to you."

"You mean Duncan's wife – the artist."

"He's spoken to you about her? I'm surprised."

"No, he hasn't."

"How did you hear about her, then? From your friend Dodie?"

"Dodie barely mentioned her. Duncan doesn't talk about her either, but he still has her paintings. I know, because I've seen them."

"I see, Essat said. He glanced away briefly, as if he'd caught sight of someone he recognised, but when Maree turned to look there was no one there. "Well, it's all common knowledge. I've not seen Laura to speak to for years, not since she married the aeroplane guy. She was Laura Christy when I knew her. I was still in college then myself. Laura came here from abroad on some sort of student exchange programme, fell in love with the island and never left. She was an immensely talented artist. I think it was her talent that stopped any of us from seeing how out of her depth she was. You see a gift like that, you assume things. Then she got involved with that philistine and suddenly she wasn't around any more – she dropped us, or we dropped her, it's hard to say which now, really. If I were the kind of person who was into self-pity I'd say I blame myself for what happened, but I'm not, so I won't. If she had asked for help, I would have tried to help her. She didn't, though."

The door to the restaurant opened and someone came out, a young woman in faded jeans and a black cotton T-shirt.

"What would you like?" she said to Maree.

"Ask her for one of those special pastry things they do," said Essat. "They're delicious."

* * *

"Were you in love with Laura, then?" said Maree.

"Good God no. I was too busy making a fool of myself over one of the drama students. Paolo Julich, his name was. He's on the mainland now, of course." Essat made a face. "There was a good friend of mine – a poet named Simeon Castile – who was keen on her for a while, but so far as I know it never came to much. Laura Christy was one of those people. Everyone knew who she was, but no one knew her. She didn't go to clubs, she wasn't interested in being part of the scene. Folk like that tend to put people's backs up, especially when they're as gifted as Laura was. People said she was standoffish but really it was just shyness. She didn't like being in crowds."

"Why would she get together with someone like Duncan, though? I can't imagine them having anything in common."

Essat shrugged. "Lord alone knows. Perhaps it was the money – that's what most people think. I'm not so sure. She never seemed to give a damn about money, not when she was at college. All I know is that after she married him she became even more reclusive. Then she vanished completely."

"What do you mean?"

"What I say. Laura disappeared. No one seems any the wiser about what happened to her. Of course there were some charitable souls who insisted Taborow must have murdered her, or had her murdered, more likely, but the police didn't think so and where's the motive? People say he's been moping around that mansion of his like a lost soul ever since she went. Hardly Bluebeard."

"What did you mean when you said she was out of her depth?"

Essat stretched in his seat. He took a roll from the basket and tore it in two. "It's an interesting phrase, isn't it? Makes you think of water, and drowning. Drowning wasn't what I had in mind, though, or not literally. I mean I think she was struggling, psychologically. She had some strange ideas."

"What kind of strange ideas?"

"Laura believed she had a twin. Or not a twin, exactly, but a woman who was identical to her in every way, except she lived inside a parallel universe. Laura claimed to have seen this parallel universe, to have experienced it first-hand. She even painted pictures of it. She talked about our own world being in danger from invaders, all kinds of odd things." He paused. "I never spoke to her about any of this myself. As I say, I didn't know her that well. But I heard she was depressed because of the twin thing. Separation anxiety, apparently. That's what I meant by out of her depth."

"You don't think she committed suicide?"

"I hope not."

"You don't have a theory?"

"What would be the point, when there are already so many? It's all hearsay, anyway. The police gave up looking for Laura a long time ago. She's a responsible adult, after all – perhaps she meant to disappear. She was married to Duncan Taborow, after all."

"You don't like Duncan, do you?"

"I know nothing about him. I don't trust his motives,

that's all. He's trying to take over the island." He sighed. "Don't take any notice. I just wish you'd seen Brock before the airport was built, that's all."

"I don't know. Nothing seems to have changed much here." Maree glanced around at the empty square, the poppies blooming on a patch of waste ground beside the hotel, a skinny lurcher drinking from the granite trough in front of the water fountain.

"You're right, of course." Essat swirled the remains of his coffee around in the bottom of his cup. "Artists like to pretend they're the gods of change, the vanguard, the harbingers. Whereas what most artists want to do is plaster 'I was here' across the walls of the establishment in six-foot-high letters. Metaphorically, I mean. Although you'll find some are doing it literally, I'm sure. Most art isn't about enacting change, it's about the preservation of memory. If change happens as a by-product, then fine. But that's not the impulse behind it."

"Do you think Laura was trying to preserve her memories?"

"Yes, of course. She more than many, I'd say. Look her up online if you don't believe me. There's plenty of information about her. She was a regular cause célebrè for a while."

"I'll do that," Maree said. She thought of the painting in Duncan's hallway, the one of the villa. She remembered the way it looked to her – as if she were seeing through Laura's eyes, remembering the scene even though it wasn't hers to remember.

The painting of the dog was different, though. That was her own memory, not Laura's, and yet how could that be?

She thought about trying to explain how she'd felt to Essat, then decided not to. He'll think it's catching, she thought. She smiled.

"What's so funny?" Essat said.

"Nothing. I was just thinking you remind me of a friend of mine."

"Someone fabulous, I trust."

"Oh, yes." She liked Essat because he said what he thought, without caring much about the consequences. He was intelligent, and a little arrogant, and she liked that, too. In a strange way he did indeed remind her of Caine.

Tash. The thought came to her suddenly. The name of the woman in the painting of the dog, of Moonrise Kingdom – her name was Tash.

The fragment of memory pierced her consciousness like a sliver of glass.

"I thought you wanted not to be working while you were here," Belen said. They were sitting on the back veranda, eating cheese crackers and drinking the locally brewed cider that seemed to be Lacruz's single convenience store's most profitable commodity. Kicks like a donkey, Belen said. But it keeps out the cold. Belen's wrists and forearms were stippled with dried clay. She had been in the studio all day, creating a series of loosely thrown, deep-sided bowls on her potter's wheel. Maree had wanted to stay and watch, but she sensed that Belen was used to working alone and wished she would leave. With her day's work behind her she seemed more relaxed, eager to talk, even. The sky was covered with clouds. Will it rain, do you think? Maree had asked. Belen shook her head. Not until tomorrow, she said. The evening was pleasantly warm. Warm enough to sit outside, anyway.

"I haven't been working," Maree replied.

"Frida told me you were in the library most of the day."

"Who's Frida?"

"The librarian."

"That wasn't work. I was looking something up, that's all."

"Oh?"

Belen sounded genuinely curious, and so Maree told her she'd been searching for information about a local artist. "The wife of a friend, actually," she said.

"And did you find what you were looking for?" said Belen.

"I'm not sure. Sort of." Maree fell silent, gazing out at the garden. She didn't feel like discussing Laura Christy with Belen. She didn't like the idea that the librarian had been spying on her, either. Library was, in any case, a somewhat fanciful term for the haphazard assortment of books and out-of-date periodicals that had been collected together in an upper room of one of the tottering converted tenements overlooking the square: novels both incongruously new and hopelessly old, medical textbooks and wildlife identification manuals and tourist guides to Brock Island that looked as if they had been printed before Maree first came to Thalia and certainly before the construction of the airport. There was something charming in the very randomness of the selection, it was true, the possibility of finding something of interest in such an unlikely setting. The library also seemed to be just about the only place in Lacruz with a reliable Internet connection.

"Why didn't you come over for Lin's funeral?" Belen said suddenly. "You do know you were invited?"

"I couldn't," Maree said. She felt surprised by the abrupt change of subject, disconcerted that she hadn't seen it coming. She glanced across at Belen, but Belen looked away. "There wasn't time. There was no airport on Brock then, not for commercial flights. Anyway," she added. "I didn't think you wanted me here."

Belen laughed. "You could have brought your partner." She took another swig of her cider.

"I'm not sure what you're getting at."

"Just that I don't think you realise how upset Lin was when you stopped writing to her. People thought she was indestructible. They didn't know how easily she could be hurt."

Maree couldn't think what to say. She felt uncomfortable with the turn the conversation had taken, with the resentment she could hear in Belen's voice. Why Belen would want to bring this up now she had no idea. "It was a long time ago," she replied in the end. "I think the main reason I stopped writing was because of you. Because of you and Lin, I mean. I didn't want to interfere. It didn't seem right."

"You know that isn't true," Belen said. "There was no reason you and Lin couldn't stay friends. Why we couldn't all have been friends. You'd met someone else by then anyway. I know because Lin showed me your letters."

"I don't remember why we stopped."

"Yes, you do." She paused. "I have a daughter with Lin, did you know that?"

Maree stared at her, amazed. It was as if the world as she understood it had been pushed sideways.

"Don't look so surprised. Her life didn't stop because you weren't in it, you know."

"Where is she now?" Maree said finally. "Your daughter?"

"She's in school. On the mainland. We argued about it, Lin and I. Lin wanted her close by, on Brock. I said if she won a scholarship she should take it. How many children get this chance? I said. In the end we let Nelly decide and she said it sounded like an adventure, so off she went. She's doing very well, or so her teachers say. You can imagine how much I miss her, or maybe you can't. Still, she comes home for the holidays."

Belen's anger seemed to have passed. Now she just sounded sad, forlorn in a way that Maree found it difficult to contemplate. She had felt that way herself, she supposed, when she finally realised Caine did not love her, when she'd said goodbye to Lin on the morning the *Aurelia Claydon* docked at Brock harbour, when she first found out she had a brother she would never meet.

Not like dying, exactly, but as if dying would be acceptable in the circumstances, just to stop the pain.

A lifetime ago. Had Maree been the same person, even?

"Do you have a picture of her?" Maree said. "Of Nelly, I mean?"

"Of course." Belen got to her feet and went inside. A

moment later she returned, holding a leather-covered photo album, the kind with plastic wallets to contain the prints. "We took hundreds. But these were some of our favourites."

Maree turned the leaves of the album, the photographs inside documenting the life of a child she had never met or seen or even heard about until ten minutes ago, a child she nonetheless recognised, because she looked so like Lin. Lin sleeping, Lin playing with wooden bricks, Lin making a model aeroplane, Lin in a bright orange Parka halfway up a mountain. Lin in a grey school cardigan glowering. Lin holding tight to the string of a silver helium balloon, her mouth wide open, caught in mid-laugh.

Lin as she must have been before the accident.

"Nelly's twelve now," Belen said. She smiled. She seemed much calmer suddenly, as if the sight of the child had restored her equilibrium.

"Thank you for showing me these," Maree said. "I can't believe how alike they look."

"Nelly has her determination too, I can tell you," said Belen. "I'm sorry for what I said. It was wrong of me. I think it's because you knew her, you know? None of my friends here did. And that can be hard. Not being able to talk about her, I mean."

"I understand," Maree said. "Really." She remembered she'd had the same feeling, or a version of it anyway, about being able to talk to Duncan about Dodie. Grief was strange that way. It could trick you into feeling closeness where no closeness existed.

"It's getting late," Belen said. She turned to face her in

the dusk, and there was a moment when they might have kissed, but the moment passed and later, as she lay by herself in the dark on the narrow bed, Maree felt relieved. The thought of Belen's tight, muscular body and work-hardened hands aroused her, and yet where could it lead? Maree did not want to be tied to this island, she realised. Or at least if she did, then it should be on her own terms. The letters, the partings, the guilt – these were not what she wanted. There were times when she missed the electricity of sex, the culmination and satisfaction of desire, but she did not miss the sense of another's expectation, of being owned.

She lay on her back and gazed up at the ceiling. She could not stop thinking about what Belen had said, about there being no reason why she and Lin could not have remained friends. If they had stayed in touch, as Lin had wanted, Maree would now have a share in the island, in Belen, in Nelly's childhood. She would have the photographs on her shelf to prove it, back in Kontessa. Why had she resisted?

Growing up at the Croft, they had been warned against trying to form friendships with the young people who lived in the town. There was an unspoken understanding that such friendships could not last, that the differences that divided them would in the end prove insurmountable. She and Sarah and Caine had always been scornful of such ideas, such *propaganda*, as Caine had labelled it, but had they been wrong?

She thought of Jutta, the mathematician whom she'd lived with at the compound, for a time, until Jutta got sick of the programme and went to work for a tech company in

Bonita. ("This place," she had said. "It's like a fucking zoo.") Maree had stopped writing to Lin because of Jutta, who had obsessed her thoughts for more than a year before they finally slept together, and yet when Jutta had asked her to move back to the city with her, Maree had said no.

"My work is here," she'd said. Part of her had been pleased to see her go.

The world called them empaths, and yet the one thing Maree had never experienced was true intimacy, the loss of herself in feelings for another. She understood so much of how people felt, what it felt like to feel – and yet the knowledge had remained at least partly theoretical.

Her brand of empathy was a closed thing, a private thing, as clear as leaded crystal and as cold to the touch.

Maree slept without knowing that she did. She woke early and packed her holdall. The bus to Paloma would be leaving at midday. She treated Belen to breakfast at Dino's, hoping she might see Essat, but he wasn't there. "You will come again?" Belen said. "You could meet Nelly." Maree said yes, of course, not knowing if she meant it or not. She tried to imagine herself sitting at one of the tables under the awning, eating sweet rolls and writing her journal. The picture did not displease her, but it didn't feel like the future, either.

"I almost forgot this," she said to Belen. She handed her the silver cowbell, still in its shop wrapping paper. Belen shook the package to make it ring, then smiled. She kissed Maree once on the forehead, and then again on the lips.

[From the *Brock Island Messenger*: **Disappearance of Troubled Artist Laura Christy]**

Police continue to make enquiries into the disappearance last week of Laura Christy, an artist whose controversial solo exhibition *Portraits of My Sister* made her a finalist for the lucrative Diego Martinez Prize. Christy, who painted and exhibited under her maiden name, had recently become the wife of multi-millionaire property developer and airport magnate Duncan Taborow.

When asked at a press conference if his wife had changed her behaviour or shown any signs of distress in recent weeks, Taborow replied absolutely not. 'Laura is a very private person but her disappearance is completely out of character. I feel certain that she would not have abandoned her home or her family unless she had been coerced in some way. I am extremely worried for her safety and wellbeing and will do everything in my power to assist the police with their enquiries.' According to an anonymous source, Duncan Taborow was detained briefly for police questioning but released without charge.

['Portraits of My Sister: an Introduction', by Karolina Klaas. Excerpt from the catalogue essay, *Portraits of My Sister*, **paintings by Laura Christy, The Ramona Vult Gallery, Brock Fort July–August 21—.]**

Though the twenty-four canvases that make up Laura Christy's most recent series have been executed using a broad palette of colours, it could be argued that their most striking feature is their lightness, their luminosity. These paintings are immediately, indeed forcefully reminiscent of the iconic stills routinely excerpted from films of the black-and-white movie era. It would be easy and obvious to attribute this quality to clarity of line and depth of field, to Christy's pinpoint-accurate skill at representation. In all probability though it is something less tangible, the sense of apprehension and portentousness that emanates from these images, the sense of having borne witness to something important.

The mystery inherent in this exhibit of twenty-four exceptionally candid and emotionally exacting self-portraits is further compounded by its title: *Portraits of My Sister*. Laura Christy is clearly fascinated by issues of siblinghood, as evidenced in the titles and subject matters of earlier series, *Objects from My Sister's Dressing Table* and *Our Sister World*, a personal preoccupation that would appear to stem, ironically, from the artist's family status as an only child. This new set of works takes the obsession one stage further, as the artist grapples with problems of identity and alienation in the digital age.

Laura Christy paints solely in oils, and rarely makes preparatory sketches. As part of a characteristically cryptic essay to accompany this exhibition, Christy insisted that the paintings should be taken literally as portraits of her sister and not, as some had wrongly surmised, self-portraits.

['My Sister Sidonie: a personal insight' by Laura Christy, published as part of the exhibition catalogue for the 21— Diego Martinez Prize.]

I didn't realise I had a sister until my early teens. Because of my upbringing in a state-run care home it was difficult for me to get accurate information about my background. It is still illegal for foster carers or employees of local authority care facilities to give out the personal details of birth parents, natural siblings or even place of birth until a child turns eighteen, and even then the amount of information that can be released is severely restricted. My care counsellor told me on numerous occasions that it would be better for me to concentrate on my school work than to waste time fantasising over aspects of my life that were already in the past. The reality – that I didn't have a past, that the system that purported to care for me had stripped my past from me – never seemed to occur to her. At the time, I believed my dreams about my sister were proof that I had a twin, that we had been separated at birth or soon after. I read a lot of case studies of twins who had grown up apart, and yet seemed to retain a knowledge of one another in spite of outside attempts to eradicate it. Everything seemed to fit. I made a promise to myself and to my sister: that I would discover her whereabouts and travel to be with her, as soon as I could.

The years leading up to my eighteenth birthday seemed interminably long. Throughout the whole of this time I thought about my sister constantly: did she have a family who loved her? Was she safe from harm? Was she aware of my existence, as I was of hers? The idea that time was passing, that we were losing memories of one another, the shared childhood we were being denied simply because the law insisted we had no right to it, was a constant source of anxiety and depression.

On the day I turned eighteen, I put in an application to the board of my care home for the release of any and all documentation in their possession relating to the identities and background of my birth parents. My counsellor warned me the process might take a while, but even so I was unprepared for how daunting it eventually turned out to be; not just the endless paperwork but the repeated bouts of questioning and so-called psychological counselling. I made no complaints, hoping that my cooperation might speed things up, but inwardly I felt angry that the doctors, social workers and teachers who advised the board – many of them complete strangers to me – felt they had more right to the facts of my life than I did myself.

It is still difficult to describe the shock I felt when I was finally allowed to see my case file and discovered I didn't have a sister after all. I had been so certain of what I would find that at first I refused to accept what the file was telling me: that I was an only child, that I had been placed in care at the age of two when my mother, Ann Allerton, was killed in a road traffic accident and my father, Derek Christy, had been unable to continue caring for me on his own. 'Depression following the death of the spouse, together with the lack of any meaningful or practical family support network make Derek Christy an inconsistent caregiver as well as a potential suicide risk, read the file. Heavy financial pressures would seem to indicate that an imminent return to his previous employment in waste management is inevitable, which would in its turn further aggravate the immediate crisis as well as contributing to Mr Christy's more general and ongoing mental health issues. In the opinion of this department and in the absence of any viable alternative the removal of the child to the care of the local authority presents the only workable resolution of this unfortunate situation.'

The other items in the case file – a photostatted copy of my birth certificate, some preliminary reports by the social worker assigned to my case after a neighbour reported her suspicions that I had been left in the house alone for more than four hours while my father worked an emergency shift to cover for a sick colleague, a photograph of my mother, three handwritten witness statements by friends of my mother, a preliminary medical report – seemed to annihilate even the possibility of a missing sister. The words 'sister' or 'twin' or even 'sibling' were never even mentioned. My initial instinct was to blame the local authority. Judging by their reluctance to release the information in the first place, it was easy for me to accuse them of some sort of cover-up. Why they would want to deny my sister's existence was less clear to me. All I knew was that she existed, and so there had to be a reason. The reason mattered less to me in any case than uncovering my sister's present whereabouts.

I knew I wouldn't get anywhere with the local authority – they would simply deny everything – and so I began carrying out my own investigation. At least now I had some facts to go on: my place of birth, the name of my father, the names *of people who had known my mother, even. I felt nervous about approaching my father directly. I was afraid he might reject me I suppose, or that he somehow held me to blame for the death of my mother. I concentrated instead on tracking down those friends of my mother who had provided witness statements to the family court. I found two out of the three in the end: one who had lived in the same street as my parents when they were first married, and another who had been a friend of my mother when they were both at college. I wrote letters to both of them, saying I had only recently discovered my parents' identities and that I was trying to trace my sister.*

The college friend never replied. The neighbour wrote me a long letter, saying she was glad to hear I was well, and enclosed a snapshot of me as an infant, sprawling on a blanket on the grass with her own young son who, she wrote, was now training to be an electrician. I'm so sorry about your dad, *she wrote.* He was never the same man after your ma died. There are people who will bounce back from a thing like that, and there are those who won't, no matter what you try and do for them. I know that losing you, on top of everything, hit him hard, but he was sinking already.

She signed her name, Malory White, and then added a PS:

You never had a sister, love. Whoever told you that's got it wrong. I don't think your ma wanted more kids, to be honest. She missed London a lot. I wouldn't be saying this if your dad was still alive, but Ann would sometimes talk about going back there, to London I mean. She wanted to take you and start again, get back into teaching. She loved your dad, don't get me wrong, but she never really fitted in here. That's what she thought, anyway. She was a special woman, different from the other people I knew back then. You'd have liked her, I'm sure.

Malory White's letter changed my life. The way she spoke about my father and mother made them feel real to me in a way that the social worker's reports and witness statements in my case file could never have done. They had been people with hopes and problems, fears and secrets. And I had been a part of their world, a world that was now lost to me, irrevocably. The counsellors and house-parents who had cared for me throughout my childhood and adolescence had encouraged me to think of my past as irrelevant to my future, of my mother and father as people who had forfeited their right to be involved in my life, even as ghosts. Malory White was telling me that my parents had loved me and neither of them was to blame for what happened. If my mother hadn't been killed things would have been different.

I think it was because of her honesty in speaking about my parents that I was able to believe what she revealed to me about my sister. I believed that she believed it, anyway. That she was telling me the truth as she perceived it.

At the same time, I knew she was wrong. I also realised I'd been looking in the wrong place. If Malory White insisted I had no sister, all that meant was that my sister had never existed in this world. She had been communicating with me in my dreams, because this was her only way of reaching me from where she was. Only they were not dreams, not in the normal sense, they were transmissions, like radio waves maybe, or some kind of 4G. A tension in the air, the feeling you get when it's about to thunder, or pour with rain.

I started seeing Sidonie more and more after that. It was as if she had been waiting for me to catch on to the situation before revealing herself. I would often catch glimpses of her as I entered a room: a kind of mist, the outline of a shadow, a fog that disappeared the moment I caught sight of it. Like radio waves again. Radio waves you could see.

The place I could see Sidonie most clearly was in the mirror. We would stand like that for hours sometimes, on either side of the glass, just gazing at one another and not exactly talking but not exactly staying silent, either. Finally I was able to tell her how much I missed her. She told me she was one of another race of beings, creatures who had evolved separately from humans and yet who were as close to being human as to make no difference. 'We each have a sister, or a brother, where you are,' she said. We have been trying to make contact with you for many centuries, but our messages have become corrupted, as information on a computer hard drive may become corrupted. That makes the messages difficult to read, but they will be read. We will be together again, I promise. I have missed you, too.'

I reach out my hand and place it next to Sidonie's against the mirror glass. When I close my eyes, I can feel her warmth. Although I know she is on the other side of the universe, we are yet closer than you and I are standing now.

[Extract from the radio play *Sisters* by Tomas Murtry]

DAMON — I don't have a clue about her work. I didn't even know she was an artist, not until the cops started sniffing around. She used to come into the restaurant, that's all. I remember her because I remember all my regular customers. It's part of my job.

CLEM — You're sure it's the same woman?

DAMON — I never forget a face. Like I say, it's part of my job. They're saying the husband might have something to do with it. The airport guy. You know, Tarkovsky.

CLEM — Is that what you think?

DAMON — Haven't got a clue. But it stands to reason the cops would think that, doesn't it? Don't they say ninety percent of people who get murdered are killed by someone they know? Especially if there's another bloke involved.

CLEM — Are you telling me that Catherine Tarkovsky went to your restaurant to meet men?

DAMON — Not that I noticed. She usually ate by herself, actually. You journos are making out she was some kind of nutcase but she never seemed that way to me, she was just quiet.

CLEM — Quiet?

DAMON — Yeah.

CLEM — But you did see her with another man?

DAMON — I never said that, so don't you go printing it in that rag of yours. Actually the only time I ever saw her with anyone it was a woman.

CLEM — When was this, exactly?

DAMON — Dunno. Last month maybe.

CLEM — Can you describe her? The woman, I mean?

DAMON — That was the strange part. I know there's a theory about everyone in the world having a double, but these two were so alike it was ridiculous. Even though they dressed differently you could see right off that they were sisters. It made me feel weird just to look at them.

CLEM — Can you explain what you mean by that?

DAMON — I suppose it was like that feeling you get with twins. There's something odd about people who look so alike, I reckon. You find yourself wondering which of them is real and which is the fake.

[From a notebook found in Laura Christy's dressing table following her disappearance]

Ashburnham Road, Baldslow Road, Elphinstone Road, Laton Road, Queens Road, Rock-a-Nore Parade, Victoria Park, Bohemia Road, The Stade, St Mary's Terrace, The Croft, Tackleway, Old London Road, The Bourne, East Hill, West Hill, High Wickham, Priory Road, Milward Crescent, Bembrook Road, Egremont Place, Rotherfield Avenue, Salter's Lane, Foul Ness, Emanuel Road, Castle Hill

Just a list of place names, thought Maree. Place names in Crimond, they looked like. She tried searching online for the less common-sounding ones – Rock-a-Nore Parade, for example, and Tackleway – but came up blank. It didn't help that she kept losing her Internet connection. She printed out the newspaper articles and Laura Christy's essay about her missing sister. Maree couldn't decide if the essay was meant to be taken literally, or if it was a piece of performance, as much a part of the exhibition as the paintings themselves.

Was Christy's account of her mother's death and being brought up in a council home even true? There was some evidence that appeared to support it, at least in part – a brief online biography of the artist stated that her mother had died when she was a child – but Maree could find no mention of her place of birth or anything else about her life prior to her nomination for the Martinez Prize.

On the night before Dodie's funeral, Maree lay awake for a long time, wondering what her life would have been like if she had refused to meet with Loanna all those years ago, if she had come to Brock instead, lived with Lin in the Post Office and forgotten everything she ever knew about the programme.

Like forgetting a language, she supposed, only to lose a language was to lose a fraction of the self. Most people tended to think of languages as if they were analogues of each other, lists of words and phrases and grammatical caveats that could be translated like for like, one for another. Yet a language was so much more than simply words for things. Language was like the soft clay used by naturalists to record the tracks left by elusive creatures in out-of-the-way places. It captured everything, reflected everything. You could say that language was a recording device for history.

The history of the programme was a narrative of failure, of grappling with a language that resisted every effort to translate it.

Was it possible that Laura Christy had somehow achieved what the programme, in its fifty-plus years of existence, had failed to achieve? Maree's logic was screaming at her to refute the idea, yet her instinct was telling her otherwise.

Her ancestors, the Hools, had believed there were conduits, secret gateways to another world, a world that might one day begin to seep through, enveloping our own world in chaos or destruction or nirvana as the legend demanded.

Maree thought of the twin cities of Rigan and Seneca, infamously destroyed by fire during the first week of the last war. The evening before the bombing, the cities' citizens had strolled through the streets and jostled in bars and put food on tables the same as any other evening, blissfully or damnably ignorant of what was to come.

It was all nonsense of course, there were no alien invaders. Aliens were just a game they played. A game for a summer's night, when the moon is full and the question of tomorrow arriving is never in doubt.

As throughout most of Thalia, it was the custom on Brock to cremate the bodies of the dead before the funeral, with no guests or family present. Maree had always believed the custom was sound. The farewell to the body was such a private, such an intimate matter. The thought of other, still living people bearing witness to it had always left her feeling a little queasy.

Dodie's funeral wake was being held in one of the round turrets of Brock Castle. The room was filled with candles, the long tables with their starched tablecloths loaded with assorted savouries, regional delicacies and gourmet patisserie. The large number of people in attendance – close to three hundred, Maree estimated – left her feeling unexpectedly at ease. She would scarcely be noticed in such a crowd; her absence would not be remarked upon if she chose to leave. She moved slowly around the room, a glass of sweet champagne in one hand and a plate of salmon canapés in the other, amused by the ostentatiousness of some of the outfits and hoping that no one would feel obliged to engage her in conversation. She kept catching sight of Duncan, circling the room, leaning in to catch an anecdote or to accept condolences. She had barely seen him to speak to since her return from Lacruz. He had been at the crematorium first thing, to sign the release for Dodie's ashes, going on to the castle immediately afterwards to oversee the final preparations for the guests' arrival. Once again, Maree had been surprised, that Duncan had insisted on organising his mother's wake himself. She found the sight of him replenishing glasses and handing out finger food strangely touching.

She was due to leave the island the day after tomorrow. I came to attend a funeral, she thought. And it's almost over. She would miss the sea, though. Since moving to the compound, she had come to love the arid, mountainous hinterland of Kontessa. Brock was grey by comparison, but still beautiful; she was glad to have seen it.

"It's a lovely party," she said to Duncan, when he appeared beside her. She was surprised he had sought her out. She had not expected him to find time for her, there were so many more pressing calls on his attention.

"I'm glad you think so," Duncan said. He hesitated. "I've been meaning to tell you. My mother left you something in her will, a sum of money. You'll receive a letter from her solicitor in due course."

"That's very generous," Maree said. She wasn't sure how she should react, how Duncan was expecting her to react. She felt surprised, but not astonished. Dodie had always been kind to her, and the bequest was simply a final expression of that kindness. She wondered why Duncan hadn't told her when she first arrived. Was this what had been behind his invitation all along, him sounding her out, checking her over to make sure she was worthy of his mother's munificence?

Men who have money are always suspicious, Maree thought. That's how they have money.

What she would do with this piece of good fortune she had no idea. She began to imagine herself buying one of the old *fincas* in the valley, outside the compound but still close to it. Scrubbed floorboards and rush matting, a bedroom in the eaves. Sarah and Tobias could have the cottage to themselves then, and she would be free.

Stop, she told herself. It's probably nothing, a token. Best not to think about it. Not until the letter comes, anyway.

"I wanted you to know," Duncan was saying. For a moment Maree assumed he was still talking about Dodie's bequest to her. Then she realised he meant his own part of it, the bulk of Dodie's fortune, the money Dodie herself had inherited from Duncan's father. "I'm donating it to SCIMITAR," he said. "All of it."

Maree stared at him, amazed. "There's no such thing as SCIMITAR, I told you. It's a rumour, a conspiracy theory."

"You're wrong. I know SCIMITAR is real because I'm a

member of the board. This is just the beginning. We're going to find those planets, and Mother's money is going to help us to do that. All I've ever wanted is to be a part of it. You of all people must understand that, surely?"

"I'm not sure I do."

"I hated Crimond, you know," he said. "I hated the smallness of everything, the greyness. I couldn't wait to leave. There was a film I used to love, called *Voyage to the Sun*. I watched it a hundred times, probably. It was about Donal Fairlie's first crossing to Thalia and it had me spellbound. I used to feel sad, knowing that nothing like that could happen in my lifetime, that all the great discoveries had already been made. SCIMITAR has given me the chance to change that, to make a difference. At least I'll die knowing I was a part of something great."

Maree had never heard him speak so many words together. She remembered her first sight of him, waiting for Dodie on the quayside, two decades before. He had seemed lonely to her then, a disappointed man. Being proved right brought her no pleasure. She thought it was sad.

"What about Laura?" she found herself saying. She wasn't sure what she meant, exactly – that Dodie's money might be better spent in trying to find her, maybe.

"This is what Laura wanted," Duncan said. "I'm doing this for her as much as for myself."

In an odd way that made sense, Maree supposed. It was the only thing that did. She thought she might even have seen *Voyage to the Sun*. She and Sarah had watched a lot of films like that at the Croft on the old kitchen portable, rubbishy adventure stories and horror movies, the kind of late night trash that was mostly forgotten by the following morning.

She felt almost certain that one of them had been a film about Donal Fairlie. Harmless enough, she supposed, although there would be those who insisted you could draw a straight line from Fairlie's landing at Las Juanitas to the bombing of Rigan and Seneca six hundred years later.

History and language, cause and effect. She wondered if she should say as much to Duncan, then decided not to. He would still donate the money, whatever she said. She wondered what they had promised him, whoever they were.

There were five of Laura Christy's paintings in the Fort Museum. The curator there had a reputation for acquiring rising talent, and even without her nomination for the prestigious Martinez Prize, the scandal of her disappearance and consequent flurry of news stories surrounding her marriage had lent Christy's work a measure of notoriety.

Three of the paintings were from the *Portraits of My Sister* series. The other two were earlier works: a still life of a porcelain piggy bank and three silvered pine cones, and a portrait of Duncan. Laura had painted her husband standing, looking out across the uncultivated land at the rear of his property. His back was to the viewer, his head half-turned in profile. He was wearing chinos, and a checked cotton shirt. He looked different, somehow, Maree thought. Happier.

I really know nothing about them, Maree realised. Nor does anyone.

Although the exhibition catalogue for the Martinez Prize had originally listed the three portraits as *Portrait of Sidonie 3*, *Portrait of Sidonie 8* and *Portrait of Sidonie 9*, the museum had chosen to display them simply as *Portrait 3*, *Portrait 8* and *Portrait 9*. Maree felt angrier about this than she would have expected. Changing the paintings' titles did not lessen their impact, exactly, but it stripped them of the meaning Christy had intended for them.

She stood in front of the portraits for a long time, moving back and forth between the three. If anything, their photographic quality was even more intense than in the paintings at the villa. Although Maree tried hard to think of the images as portraits of a woman who was not the artist, it was difficult to forget that whatever the titles Laura Christy had chosen for them, they were the closest likeness of their creator Maree was likely to see. Certainly they showed more than any photograph ever would – not just because every enlarged pore, every skin blemish was clearly visible, but because they retained a nervous vitality that no photograph ever could. Photography was an art of surfaces. In the portraits Christy had painted, it was almost as if the subject had become the image, as if the oils and pigments that covered the canvas had become imprinted with the painter's DNA.

With a painting, what you saw was only a part of what existed.

Sidonie was depicted as a dark-haired, sharp-featured woman with greenish-grey eyes. You might pass this woman by on the street without noticing her, Maree thought, yet there was something about her expression – the intensity of it – that made you notice her anyway, that made you think you'd maybe met her somewhere before.

In one of the paintings – *Portrait 8* – she was wearing round, wire-rimmed spectacles. On the table in front of her was an abacus, with a polished mahogany frame and glazed china beads. A beautiful object, Maree thought, and perfectly chosen to showcase the talents of an artist like Christy, who clearly revelled in the challenges of representation. The painted surface was immaculate, Maree saw, like a mirror, or like a window even. Looking at the painting was like gazing into a room you could never enter but that is always there.

The woman in the room, endlessly calculating her options, weighing her future.

Many people would think of an abacus as a primitive device, Maree supposed, and yet in reality it was a versatile coding system, a computer in embryo.

She drew a notebook from her backpack and copied down what she saw, sketching the abacus as a series of lines and circles, taking care to note the number and position of each bead exactly. I see you, Sidonie, she thought. She slipped the notebook back into her rucksack and left the gallery.

The tide was in, Niño Quaglia's sculpture of the baer-whale half-submerged. Small waves frothed and bounded around the steel uprights, playing with the idea of imprisonment before casually rejecting it. Maree could hear the water laughing, almost. The sea didn't give a damn for steel whales or the idea of containment or anything else. It simply bounded for the horizon and called it good.

Maree took out the sketch she'd made of the abacus and compared it with the pattern of binary she'd been working on in the weeks immediately before her journey to Brock. She had resolved to leave her databook back at the compound but had changed her mind at the last minute. She wanted her notes, at least. In a way they completed her.

You were born to this work, Maree. Loanna's voice.

Maree had always longed to deny it, but every decision she'd made in her life up until this moment seemed to prove otherwise.

If you know it, own it. Another voice this time, one she didn't recognise.

"Sidonie," she said. "Is that you?" There was no one in the room to hear her, after all.

The pattern of beads on the abacus matched the pattern of binary exactly. The language encoded within it – Maree had classified it as Rontana, which was the name of the author of the book on advanced linguistics she'd been reading at the time she first began making headway with the decryption – remained mostly opaque to her. She had not, as yet, managed to tap into the feel of the language, what Eleni Rontana referred to as its emotional atmosphere. Maree knew she wouldn't progress much further until she did so.

* * *

You now ours far far far horse stride coming read the words on the abacus. Maree copied the translation into the space below the diagram in her notebook. One day a billion years from now, she had no doubt of it, another woman in another star system would be working on a translation of the *Song of Achilles*, or *Invisible Cities*, or *A Thalian Odyssey*, Saffron Valparaiso's clashing cadences worn away by time into ancient hieroglyphs. As this woman far in the future parsed her words, Valparaiso would rise again from the ashes of this world, and another people would glimpse the wild horses of Patagonia, the scrubland and the dust and the sunsets, steeped in red fire.

They would glimpse these things, and feel the call of poetry. The wonder of written language never got old.

I never went home because I didn't want to, Maree thought. I didn't want to become someone else's version of myself, part of their story. Laura Christy might have wanted her past back, but I didn't. Secretly, I was glad to let it go.

She opened the shutters and leaned out into the darkness. The scents of a garden at night wafted up to envelop her: black earth and bracken and chervil and the brittle taste of brine. She wished her love of the Earth could keep it safe, but she knew it could not.

* * *

The ship set sail from Brock Harbour just after ten. It was a bright morning. The sea was choppy but the wind was decreasing and they made good time. Maree stood at the rail, keeping the island in sight for as long as she could. When it was gone she closed her eyes, wondering how it might have felt to have lived in a time when people still believed in sea monsters.

And if those times are come again, she thought, is that really so bad?

acknowledgements

With special thanks to Cath Trechman at Titan Books for her enthusiasm and support, to Ian Whates at NewCon Press for taking the initial leap of faith, and to Julia Lloyd for her spectacular cover art. Thanks also to the friends and colleagues who came along for the ride as *The Race* progressed: Andy Cox, Mike Harrison, Matt Hill, Simon Ings, Carole Johnstone, Joanna Kavenna, Joel Lane, Helen Marshall, Cleaver Paterson, Alastair Reynolds, Rob Shearman, Tricia Sullivan, Emma Swift, Peter Tennant, Douglas Thompson, Sam Thompson and Maureen Weller among many others. Thanks and love to my mother, Monica Allan, for her unstinting support and confidence in me, and to Chris, as always, for being there and being everything.

Nina Allan's stories have appeared in numerous magazines and anthologies, including *Best Horror of the Year #6*, *The Year's Best Science Fiction and Fantasy 2013*, and *The Mammoth Book of Ghost Stories by Women*. Her novella *Spin*, a science fictional re-imagining of the Arachne myth, won the British Science Fiction Association Award in 2014, and her story-cycle *The Silver Wind* was awarded the Grand Prix de l'Imaginaire in the same year. *The Race* was a finalist for the 2015 BSFA Award, the Kitschies Red Tentacle and the John W. Campbell Memorial Award. Nina Allan lives and works in North Devon with her partner, the science fiction writer Christopher Priest. Find Nina's blog, The Spider's House, at www.ninaallan.co.uk

For more fantastic fiction, author events, competitions,
limited editions and more

VISIT OUR WEBSITE
titanbooks.com

LIKE US ON FACEBOOK
facebook.com/titanbooks

FOLLOW US ON TWITTER
@TitanBooks

EMAIL US
readerfeedback@titanemail.com